William Targ was born and raised in Chicago. A bibliophile and editor, largely self-educated, he entered pu[illegible]g and became Editor-in-Chief at World Pub[illegible] and later at G. P. Putnam's. H[illegible] private press in New Yor[illegible] literary works of fine [illegible] *Pleasures* was publish[illegible] novel.

By the same author

Indecent Pleasures

For Roslyn
with love

'Let us not try and reconcile the fiction of facts with the facts of fiction . . .'

Vladimir Nabokov

'Most of the dates (names) and hard facts, confidently given in encyclopedias, soften and dissolve on examination . . . the story is just something to read; in fact a legend.'

Evelyn Waugh
Helena, A Novel

Prologue

When Adrian Breakstone was eight years old, he had his first authentic, traumatic experience.

He was gazing out of his bedroom window early one Saturday morning, watching the passers-by. His brothers slept in another room. He was alone, in a small, so-called maid's room. There was little activity in the street. Suddenly, a large black automobile pulled up directly below his window, and he saw a pretty young woman, pale-faced and frightened in manner, stepping out of it. She was followed by a man Adrian recognised, having seen him on several occasions in the presence of his parents and having once been introduced to him. The man's name, he remembered, was Hacha. Adrian knew that he was a man of some importance, active in politics; and that he was a goy, a Bohemian.

Adrian watched the two come up the stone stairs and heard the doorbell ring, then went back to his bed. His mother, Sarah, would be calling him. It was still early.

Twenty minutes or so later, Dr Breakstone, the physician and surgeon, found himself engaged in aborting the young woman who had been accompanied by Mr Hacha. The procedure was taking place in his private surgery, a well-polished and hygienic room on the upper floor of the Breakstones' two-storey brownstone on Chicago's West Side. Assisting him was a middle-aged nurse, whose services and confidence the doctor had enjoyed for many years. It was a very quiet Saturday morning.

The boy remembered then how desperately he was in need of some money – two dollars and fifty cents to be

precise – to buy a catcher's mitt. A ball game had been arranged for that noon by his friends, and Adrian had been chosen catcher, a great honour. He must wait until his father's visitors were gone, then approach him for the money. He wondered how long they would be.

Then a door slammed, an engine started. He jumped out of bed, and was at the window in time to see the car pull away.

Adrian climbed the stairs in his pyjamas, approached the surgery door and opened it slowly, quietly, a few inches. Peering through the door, he caught a whiff of strong medicine.

He stopped in shock. The young woman from the automobile, naked to the waist, knees up high, was strapped down to the metal table with her feet in stirrups. His father was leaning forward, brow furrowed, peering into the recesses of her groin; and he was holding outward with one hand a dripping steel instrument. Clasped in it was a shapeless red blob. The nurse was reaching for it; in one of her hands she held a sponge or cloth from which red drops were falling on the sheet. Adrian stared at the woman's white and bloodied thighs, at the dark and bleeding crotch – at his father's intent expression.

He hurried back to his room and climbed into bed; he lay there, traumatised. What had his father been doing to that woman? Why did Mr Hacha leave so quickly and why had he been there to begin with? Adrian had to know. And who was she – that pretty, frightened woman? Why was she not in Daddy's hospital where he usually performed operations? Adrian lay there, puzzled, his heart pounding. Finally he fell asleep.

An hour later he awakened to find his father sitting beside him on his bed.

'Adrian, sorry to wake you up. I want to talk to you.'

'Yes, Daddy.'

WILLIAM TARG

Secret Lives

PANTHER
Granada Publishing

Panther Books
Granada Publishing Ltd
8 Grafton Street, London W1X 3LA

Published by Panther Books 1984

First published in Great Britain by
Granada Publishing 1983

ISBN 0-586-05469-3

Printed and bound in Great Britain by
Collins, Glasgow

Set in Times

'You were at the door of my surgery. You saw something?'

'Yes.'

'Then I want to explain what you saw, so that you won't misunderstand, so that you won't wonder what I did and what it was all about. Are you interested?' He gave his son a swift smile.

'Yes.'

'Okay. What I tell you is for your ears alone. You must not repeat it to anyone, including your own mother or your brothers. Is that understood?'

'Yes.'

'I'm telling you this because you are my son and I love you and I will never tell you a lie. Okay?'

'Yes, Daddy.'

'You saw a young woman on the operating table. I was performing what is called an abortion. She is not married but she was pregnant, which means she was going to have a baby. It would have been a disgrace for her, since she has no husband. She has no money and her parents would have given her a lot of trouble. The man who made her pregnant just wanted to have some fun. He is a politician with many powerful friends. He doesn't want to marry that girl. He has too many other interests. He brought her to me to stop her from having a baby. That is what I did. I did my duty as a doctor. It is something one must never talk about – to anybody. I'm talking to you about it because I want you always to have the truth from me. What you saw and now know is part of every man's education. I hope you understand what I am saying. And since you must consider me as your best friend – I would do anything for you – you must keep what I told you to yourself. Some day you'll understand more about this. Enough for now. By the way, did you see the man who came with her?' He studied his son's face carefully.

'Yes, Daddy. It was Mr Hacha.'

The doctor stroked his son's black curls and sighed. 'Yes. And that is a very confidential matter. You must never mention his name to anybody in connection with the girl. You did not see him here with her. You understand, son? And – enough for now. By the way, I suppose you wanted to see me about something. What was it?'

'It's not important, Daddy.'

'Yes, it must be. Tell me.'

'I wanted some money to buy a catcher's mitt. We have a game today and they made me catcher.'

'Catcher! That's great. It is important, Adrian. How much do you need?'

The transaction was simple and quick. His father left and Adrian lay back, pondering, somehow elated. His father had treated him with trust – like a man. My old man doesn't talk to me like a kid, he thought. None of the kids has an old man like mine. He trusts me. But still he had some questions.

Miami, 14 February 1933

The doctor's attention was focused on the Mayor, about twenty yards away. The portly physician and his son were standing bareheaded under the hot noon sun watching the crowd assemble. The Mayor was in a gleaming white Shantung suit, his white waistcoat embellished with a gold watch-chain, and he was gesticulating and obviously arguing with someone.

Dr Breakstone turned to his son, Adrian. 'Doesn't Hacha look like a knight in shining armour?' As he spoke, he motioned with his bearded chin in the direction of the Mayor who was now surrounded by a dozen of his retinue.

'Sort of, Dad,' said Adrian, 'but not quite. Those

rimless glasses give him a new, shrewd air, a bit of glitter. And that suit – well, it makes him look like a band leader. But at least it doesn't have the potato-sack look. He's really got style today. A presence. And doesn't he know it!'

Adrian studied Hacha, felt an acute discomfort, a sudden pressure in his chest. He recalled that childhood glimpse through the half-opened door of his father's surgery: the blood-streaked blob, the dripping steel instrument in his father's hand. *Had it been an extraction or an expulsion?* He always remembered it whenever he encountered Hacha . . .

'Are you all right?' asked Breakstone, studying his son's ashen face, his withdrawn expression. 'Is the heat too much for you, Adrian?'

The doctor wondered whether he had made a mistake inviting his son to Miami, exposing him to the crowd in this heat.

'I'm okay, Dad.'

'Anyway, aren't you glad you came along?'

'Yes and no,' said Adrian. 'I have a few reservations. Let's face it, Dad. Miami is the asshole of America.'

'What do you mean?' Disgust showed plainly on the doctor's face.

'It's an American Calcutta. Even Capone's Cicero isn't this bad.'

'Let's keep our perspective,' said his father. Suddenly smiling, he greeted Ed McGrary, head of the city's housing agency, as he passed by. Then he continued, addressing Adrian with a tight-lipped expression: 'You're over-dramatising. You know you were anxious to come here, where, as you put it, history is being made.'

Father and son were standing in the midst of the loud and thickening crowd, behind the sea of grass-green benches, facing the great convention hall and platform.

'Just look at those men, the women,' said Adrian, hand outstretched. 'Look how they behave, how they dress, how they gorge themselves. It's a zoo.'

'Not much different from what we'd see in Chicago, eh?'

'Well, when I look around me I must admit that all men are not brothers. Look over there,' he said, pointing towards the police commissioner, 'an ugly carnivore!'

'That carnivore, as you put it, can be immensely useful to you if you are ever in trouble,' said Dr Breakstone. 'And I must remind you that his wife is a patient of mine . . .'

Dr Breakstone was a registered Democrat, a member of the Party in the best possible standing, and personal physician to the Mayor, not to mention several important judges and the United States Attorney for northern Illinois. As he stood there, a stocky, impressive figure of a man with a Vandyke beard and pince-nez glasses, he knew that he was observed, respected, favoured.

Adrian pulled out a large blue silk pocket handkerchief from his breast pocket and mopped his brow and cheeks. He felt acid rising in his craw. People eating and drinking in public always filled him with queasiness. Brueghel-like scenes had never really appealed to him. What he saw here, however, was not a group of happy, sturdy peasants – but a lumpen, noisome crowd. There was, in addition, a childlike quality in their behaviour; and some displayed fear in their eyes.

Standing in the scrub grass and gravel at the edge of the park, they watched the crowd assemble. Adrian and his father were on the fringe of an official-looking private group, Mayor Tony Hacha's party. They were self-conscious, keyed up, watchful and waiting for the arrival of The Man, the President-Elect, already overdue by half an hour.

Adrian and the doctor glanced ahead at the bare, makeshift grandstand in front of the hall near the ocean beach adjoining the boat basin. Perhaps a thousand men, women and children were standing there, a gelatinous mass, squinting and squirming under the hot sun. On the grandstand a giant black and white blow-up photo of the President-Elect dominated the scene. It set the tone for the event. The famous smile with the laughing eyes could be seen from every point of the park.

One man in a rumpled seersucker suit remarked, pointing to the poster, 'The man is dynamite. Dyn-a- mite. Yessirree.'

'That sums it up,' said Adrian to his father. 'Dynamite – but in steel braces.'

'Let's move forward,' said the doctor, taking him by the elbow. He smiled his public smile; smiled at his handsome, tall, tousle-haired collegiate son. He said, 'Political gatherings attract many people. They aren't fun, but it's good business, son, if I may be vulgar. I know how you feel about crowds, noise, heat – and politicians. Pretty much as I do.' He paused, turned and studied his son for a moment. 'But you're getting snobbish. And you're overlooking the historical aspects of this scene. Despite the ninety-degree heat (which they're also having in Chicago, by the way) this is an event with a capital E; an event I wouldn't want to miss. Nor should you.'

A moment later he added, voice lowered, 'Hacha's within hearing distance. Just remember, he's our host. Also, I've got a stake in his future.'

Dr Breakstone's pince-nez glittered an instant in the sunlight: beads of sweat were visible on his forehead, on his Vandyke. He seemed to be stretching his neck, studying the crowd, searching for familiar faces. Dust from the hot, brittle gravel and dry grass brought a sudden parched ache to his mouth and throat.

'Can you get me a Coca-Cola, Adrian?' he asked. 'This dust and heat are getting to me.'

Adrian moved off to a drinks vendor, kicking with his two-toned suede shoes at the trash underfoot, the orange rinds and cigarette packets and candy wrappers strewn on the path.

Dr Breakstone heard someone say, 'Ain't it a sizzler?' which only encouraged the thirst he was building up. He studied the burning hot blue of the Florida sky.

As Adrian returned with the drinks, the band struck up. The first sounds were the pure bell-like fairyland tones of the *glockenspiel*; then came the accompanying resonating tubes of a vibraphone. Next, the oompah sounds of a marching band – audible hot air, political rally sounds, Adrian thought. Appropriate. Likewise the familiar carnival smells and smoke. One could smell the fried-onion stench at twenty yards, and the *knishes* (Delicious Knishes) – the words were spelled out in great wide stencilled yellow letters on a foodstand's green umbrella; sauerkraut and hot dogs; and *shashlik* – charred kebabs of dubious lamb. And there were red and green balloons with the legend, 'Happy Days Are Here Again', a legend that was repeated on the hatbands – the hundreds of yellow skimmers worn everywhere by women and children as well as men. Bags of popcorn and peanuts, and shells in the grass, crushed boxes of Cracker Jack; soda and beer bottles. Carnival trash . . .

'Dad,' said Adrian, 'I think the food processors are behind all political rallies and meetings – they're the only winners at election-time.'

'You're getting pretty profound, my son; a bit cynical too.'

Adrian grinned.

'Well, I'll be darned,' Dr Breakstone said. 'There's Belcastro, a few steps behind Hacha. Heavy security. You

probably heard about Hacha's little war back home; a few unhappy citizens are out for his scalp, I hear.'

'Belcastro?' said Adrian. 'Do I know him?'

'I don't think so. But that's him, with the black fedora and the dark suit. Hacha's probably got half a dozen guards around the place. But don't look in that direction. Belcastro is someone you don't stare at, especially in public.'

'Seems to me a security man should look prosaic. This Belcastro is like something out of a gangster film.'

'Can't disagree with you, Adrian. Belcastro should be less obvious. But he's a dangerous man.'

Everyone seemed to be staring ahead at the great Shriner hall and the grandstand. Who was the benighted lunatic architect responsible for the design of this incredible building with the mammoth Turkish sword implanted on its rooftop? Adrian looked beyond the park, towards the sparkling blue-green ocean, and the sky. A great, unforgettable day, a red-letter day. This was the phrase Adrian kept hearing over and over from his father's friends, from Mayor Hacha's cohorts. It would mark the beginning of the end of the Great Depression. The speech would tell them not to worry about the money for the rent, the rats and roaches in the walls of their tenements. Yessirree. And the banks would be open and safe again, soon. Savings accounts insured. (Insured! Imagine.)

Hacha had some assurances to get. A huge RFC loan; a civil-service commissionship for one of his friends, and other favours – patronage in short. Surrounded by his pals, he took a seat in the front row, several yards from where the President-Elect would be speaking. Dr Breakstone and Adrian were close behind now.

'What about the rumour, Dad, that Hacha – a troglodyte, let's face it – will be offered a Cabinet post? Is that

possible? – Hacha, a presidential advisor? Socially, he'd be a monkey on the President's back . . .'

'I don't like your language, Adrian – troglodyte indeed! I thought you admired the man. Anyway, I wouldn't bet on it. He's come a long way from his saloon days, the young roughneck days, and I guess he can dream. But the time isn't right. He's a political force, no doubt about it, but he's still a diamond in the rough. He needs shaping and polishing before he starts mingling with the men in the Oval Office.' He chuckled. 'No, I can't see our Tony there yet. He'd ruffle too many feathers; he plays rough.'

Dr Breakstone paused, then turned to Adrian, looked at him searchingly and added, 'But we could do worse.'

Adrian would not deny that Hacha had muscle and push and the pragmatic approach to problems. He had the built-in qualities and instincts of a Machiavelli – American-style, often working by indirection, never losing sight of the goal. But there was still too much of the underworld aura attached to him to allow much dreaming of Washington. And his grammar was frequently a problem; quite apart from those rumours about his bordello connections, his real-estate coups . . .

Now the Dixieland band came alive, tuba and trombone, a jazzy razz-matazzy banjo, indescribably delightful American sounds that put everyone into a jig-time mood. Then – amidst wildest cheers, screams and whistles and mounting hysteria – there appeared, almost ghost- like, a light-blue open-topped Buick, a great sleek de- luxe six-seater with white-walled tyres and a uniformed chauffeur.

A roar swept through the crowd. The clamour made conversation impossible. There were explosions of applause, and cheers, but it was hard to see anything from up front. Adrian watched the car moving majestically now on the gravel path, surrounded by walking security guards

with sunglasses, proceeding in a great slow curve towards the grandstand. One could almost measure the growing vocal energy of the crowd – the mixture of joy and energy.

'That was him in the back of the car,' said Adrian to his father above the clamour. 'With the long cigarette-holder and all . . .'

'Yes, yes, that's his favourite car. Since he can't walk, or stand very well, he'll probably make his speech from his seat. That man has spirit, by God: he's a winner. Unconquerable.' He put his hand on Adrian's shoulder.

Adrian had expected better of his father than these catchwords, this mindless approval and worshipful devotion. He was too pompous, too addicted to comfortable assurances. He was also, one had to remember, the medical Grey Eminence to the Mayor and to numerous political and gangland figures.

Breakstone had not wanted to miss this event, this reminder of solidarity, political triumph, power. There was a rumour that Hacha was manoeuvring for him to become Commissioner of Health; it behooved him to be here. Besides, Miami was not quite the Calcutta his son called it. The doctor and his wife had wintered in Florida numerous times. Some of his friends – politicians, industrialists, meat packers and, yes, underworld figures – would invite him for weekends to their Biscayne Bay 'hideaways', as they liked to call them. Of course, Miami and Miami Beach were two quite separate worlds. Why his son disliked the place he could not say. His two other sons and their wives and friends enjoyed the little holidays they took here. But Adrian was the family sophisticate, preferred exotic places, Mexico in particular. One day he must take Adrian along to Paris – there he would show him what sophisticated living was all about . . .

His attention returned to the business at hand. He was part of the big-time show that was about to take place – part of it in a very small way to be sure, but nevertheless a member of the enterprise. Adrian should try to share the excitement of the event with him, its historical significance. It was something he'd be looking back on in his old age.

'It will be like seeing and hearing Abraham Lincoln – almost. Besides,' he added, 'I know you have a great respect for Hacha – you've talked about his leadership, the force of the man. Wasn't he a childhood hero of yours, Adrian? In some way or other?'

'Yes, in several ways. And I'm a Democrat by choice as well as by birth, you know.' Adrian paused. 'I don't want to seem a wise guy. Hacha appeals to me in a special way – and the Lord knows I'm aware of many elements in his life and career that speak of quote, feet of clay, unquote. As for a comparison with Lincoln, I'm glad you added the qualifying "almost".' They both laughed.

Then they heard another round of applause and cheers, and the band struck up again. A large group of men appeared theatrically in a line on the long platform. No women were present, Adrian noted. The City Fathers from Miami, Washington, New York and the Midwest were evenly represented. They were now standing at the very edge of the platform, leaning forward at the rim, their hands thrust forward and applauding. And The Man in the rear seat of the Buick raised both his arms and clasped his hands high in the air in the symbolic declaration of The Winner – of his personal victory. His teeth and glasses flashed in the sun. His long cigarette-holder held a lighted cigarette tilted upward – a familiar element in the portrait, known to everyone through the press, cinema, cartoons and in person. Everyone knew the face, knew who he was, and a great deal about his family,

friends and supporters. An aristocrat, fuelled with incredible energy and ambition, endowed with a personality usually associated with a Man of Destiny, possessing a resonant golden baritone, an instantly-recognisable voice; a man for all the people – yes, like Lincoln. Almost! Nothing adipose about this man's mind. And his diction and vocabulary were enjoyed and understood by people of every social level and idiom. One could almost hear a background chorus swell as he rose.

But there were those who reviled him, wished him dead. Republicans, of course. And others, including the anti-Semites, who called him vile names. The Man was ready and at ease, prepared to espouse every man's good cause. He had come here to greet his friends and Floridian supporters, to give them a few words of cheer and hope – and a view of his suntanned face. The polio-stricken man was indomitable, just as Breakstone had indicated to his son. Unconquerable. After two weeks of sunning and fishing and rest on Vincent Astor's yacht, he was bronzed, in excellent spirits, and triumphant in bearing. He would let the world savour a bit of his personal magic. He would set this audience afire. The *March of Time* cameras were there, he noted, and would capture the essence of it on film for everyone to see, everywhere . . .

The contingent from the Midwest watched and waited. Mayor Hacha had a fixed smile and watchful expression: he was a picture of calm and patience. He had made the trip after much political conferring, much weighing and measuring on political and psychological scales. History was in the making. He calibrated the situation like a skilled machinist. With him came certain friends, including the man to whom he had promised an important judgeship: his partner in real estate and his attorney, Angelo Minelli, a sinister-looking young man with glisten-

ing black eyes and vaselined black hair. No one mentioned involvement in the underworld; it did not bear discussion in the presence of strangers or the press.

Also among Hacha's guests (at the city's expense) was his personal physician-surgeon, a man of class and quality, together with his handsome young son, Adrian. These two – Jews, needless to say – added a facet to his entourage, ethnic and cultural, which his vote-getting mind did not underrate. The boy was a brilliant student at the University of Chicago, something of an intellectual celebrity there, and Hacha was pleased to sense that the young man admired him.

Tony Hacha beamed for the cameras and waited. Tall, thickset, muscular, he would never go unnoticed. His sparkling, rimless glasses gave him a look of competence. He had a natural if primitive gift for speaking. Voluble, addicted to short, pungent sentences, he was the reporters' favourite interviewee. He spurted miniature speeches, ready-made for the press – clichés coloured with Slavic swagger and a uniquely Czechoslovakian quality. His sense of showmanship and timing was well-established. He could play 'Boss Hacha' convincingly: he had made it emphatically clear long ago that he *was* boss, and the label was cherished by him, encouraged for general usage. Now, having supported the President-Elect he would expect some *quid pro quo*. Yes, he knew the Latin term well. It was part of his religion. His city needed heavy fundings from the government; there were jobs to dispense. The Party and The Man knew why he was here in Miami – and it was not for the sunshine. Okay. Fuck the Cabinet appointment rumours. Primarily, this was to be a great celebration, a show of friendship and political fellowship. Seekers of patronage, contracts, judgeships –they were all right here, quietly salivating. They had left behind, briefly, the stultifying stink of the Big City.

The excitement and tension of The Man's presence was almost more than many could bear.

Hacha stood with head erect, spectacles and white suit shining in the sun. His entourage, occupying almost two full roped-off rows of benches, watched him with pride. Adrian studied him, seeing him as a man with some style, balls, brains, dignity and vision – a fighter. His admiration grudgingly embraced Hacha's street-fighter background, but he was fascinated by the information he had about Hacha's great holdings in the prostitution syndicate. Through a friend of the Mayor, Adrian had once been given the red-carpet treatment in one of Hacha's more discreet bordellos, where an engaging blonde whore named Viola had indoctrinated him at the age of sixteen. The event, engraved imperishably on his brain, took place in a West Side apartment in the Slavic section of the city. Adrian's father, who had arranged the 'session', was given some of the details by Adrian one day shortly after the heady encounter, and Dr Breakstone had smiled, shaken Adrian's hand and said, 'Today you are a man – again.'

The President-Elect was now being helped to his feet in the rear of the car. He spotted Hacha, waved to him, motioning clearly for him to come to the Buick. They were about thirty feet apart. But Hacha smiled, waved in return and did not move. He would wait a bit longer. *Timing*. He was being busy at the moment – with his own people. To his immediate right was the Governor of his state, and he was giving him close and polite attention, radiating total and earnest goodwill. He had personally picked and helped elect this Governor; in public, he paid him every deference.

Pushing and shoving, the crowd jockeyed for position, to see the magical Man with Class who had applied the shine of his personality to the Party's image.

Now, he was about to speak. Once again the band struck up 'Happy Days Are Here Again'. There was a delicious, thrilling, keyed-up expectancy. Soon there would be heard The Man's ringing avowal of faith in his countrymen, in the future . . .

The band stopped, a hush fell upon the crowd. The President-Elect was speaking into his microphone. At which point Mayor Hacha pushed forward, followed by several of his group.

The President-Elect paused, reached out for him. The press photographers began snapping their cameras as the two men shook hands, exchanged amenities, both smiling broadly. *The Mayor had interrupted the speech* – an unthinkable breach, an unexpected piece of business – and the press was having a field day. (No weasel, no political supplicant, this bohunk!) Then Hacha backed away and The Man, with great aplomb, raised his head, studied the sky for a moment, proceeded to speak, and the opening words, 'My fellow Americans,' dissolved the audience, liquified their hearts and eyes, and enflamed their minds.

Essentially, it was an informal speech, brief, human, to the point, containing some modest humour. He made an amusing, mock-boastful reference to a giant fish he had almost caught – the 'one that got away' – and he described it in all its glory. The crowd loved the anecdote, and roared. The Man was human. They interrupted with repeated applause and whistles and shouts. But at the end, before the thunder of approbation diminished, another sound was heard, a sharp whipcrack of a sound which was repeated, and then again. And again. A look of consternation was on The Man's face. A woman screamed. Cries of fear rose in the park. There were five explosions, five pistol shots in fact; five separate bullets fired. It was all immediately clear to the hundreds of people in the park: *someone was trying to kill The Man*!

Their man. Five bullets from a nickel-plated revolver: death in the hot Miami sun.

Panic instantly washed over the crowd and a frightened animal roar wiped out the previous sense of elation. Hysteria moved like a small hurricane, focused near the big open-topped Buick. Several people had been hit, someone said; the shots had been fired by a stocky little man standing on a chair – a crazy anarchist foreigner, a lunatic assassin. He was grabbed, pulled down, pummelled and torn at, kicked . . .

The police prevented an attempted instant lynching of the gunman by piling on top of him. He was short, barely five foot tall, dishevelled; his thick hair was close-cropped and brushed erect; his face almost a double for the film actor, Stan Laurel – but an angry, square-jawed, wild-eyed Laurel. Who was hurt? Did any of the bullets hit The Man? Who was the intended target? Rumours and confusion. No one seemed to know.

Dr Breakstone, followed by Adrian, reached the Buick at a run, and there they saw Hacha, staggering, holding his chest, his glasses hanging at the edge of his nose, blood on his white waistcoat. He had been hit twice: Breakstone reckoned one bullet was probably lodged in the lung, the other in his throat. Hacha was stoically showing intense concern for the President-Elect when suddenly he swayed, sagged and crumpled to the ground.

Hacha's health, Adrian knew, had been precarious for several years, and Dr Breakstone sensed now that the Mayor was mortally wounded. Adrian could see the blood seeping thick and red from the side of his throat; saw him clutching at his chest wound. The smudged, demeaned and tortured face was now turning grey-white. Their eyes met briefly, then Adrian looked away as Hacha began to groan. Police and security men were running in all directions, many with guns in hand.

The President-Elect was now bending solicitously over the edge of the car, towards Hacha; an historic frieze, thought Adrian.

The victim was lifted and carefully placed in the automobile beside The Man, who took his hand and spoke to him. 'Tony, you're going to be all right. Just don't try to talk, don't move. We'll be at the hospital in a few minutes.'

At that moment, a young, rotund man in a navy- blue suit with a press card in his hatband, leaned into the Buick and said, 'Mr President, do you have any comment to make for my paper, the *Chicago Daily News*? Do you think Mayor Haçha was the intended victim?'

A photographer flashed his camera several times. The President-Elect shouted, 'For heaven's sake, I can't make a comment; this is no time for an interview. Please . . .' The Buick lurched and gathered speed in the crowded driveway, with security men pushing aside the curious, then headed for The Sisters of Mercy Hospital, a mile away.

The plump young newspaper reporter turned to the doctor. 'We've met before, Dr Breakstone. I'm Mordecai Ericson of the *News*. Can you tell me how serious Mayor Hacha's wounds are? I recall that you're his personal physician.'

Breakstone turned aside. An automobile was about to leave, to follow the blue Buick. 'Sorry. Must get to the hospital. No comment now.'

But the reporter had already spotted Adrian.

'Hello, Adrian, remember me?'

'Certainly I remember you,' said Adrian. 'We met at Sis Goldstern's studio. What a situation. Can we meet later? We're staying at the Bougainville Vista Hotel. May have some details for you there.'

'Thanks. Fine,' said the reporter.

Adrian had recognised Ericson, a reporter at the *Daily News*, a colleague of Carl Sandburg and Ben Hecht. They had met recently at a South Shore artist's studio where the local literati and young painters gathered. Ericson, he remembered, was an uninhibited and bright young man, addicted to food orgies and four-letter words, and also outrageous opinions. He had liked him at once.

Ericson turned as he saw the police moving forward, holding a small, hysterical man, the would-be assassin. He hurried after them and soon learned that the gun was a .32, bought in a pawnshop in Miami. The gunman even mentioned the price, eight dollars, and boasted, 'It was legal. No steal gun – pay cash.'

Then he was heard to shout, 'I no shooting at *him* – the man in white suit – but I no sorry. No sorry I hit him.'

The police dragged and pushed the man into a police car, handcuffed, bleeding from the near-lynching and rough handling by the police. He looked, nevertheless, triumphant. He alone was the hero of the day – this he managed to convey. Ganzara!

The man who fired the bullets that February day in Miami, in 1933, was named Giuseppe Ganzara. He and Tony Hacha of Prague, Mayor of a great city, friend of senators and judges as well as whores and saloon keepers, were unacquainted. The Calabrian immigrant and the man who had built one of the most powerful political machines in any American city, were unconnected by any bonds of background or common interests – they were simply two fish in an oceanic drama for which there has never been a name.

Book One

Chapter One

A gale-force wind was howling across the city, an icy womb its birthplace, somewhere north in the Canadian wilds, beyond the Great Lakes. It drove thick, wet snow and a near-zero chill into the ice-bound states of Indiana, Michigan and Illinois.

On to the city's lakefront and into the dreary leaden streets of its great sprawling West Side came the heavy, unjoyous snow, the whining winds. Along a certain forlorn West Side street in the section known as Greendale, the white filth – neither soft nor white nor crystalline – lay in soot-covered piles. Poets would make little of this snow, nor children at play. The street was sleeping, corpse-like. The stink of bituminous yellow-flamed coal was everywhere: the sinus-eating fetid gas. A mother-of-pearl sheen glittered on the icy asphalt in the hard dawn. Silent and marrow-chilling cold, the street was uninviting to living things.

Czechs and Croats, Bohemians and other Slavs – bohunks – had settled here. A few Polish families, but more Czechs than Poles, by far. Hunky immigrants who not too long ago had caught their first view of the Statue of Liberty.

Sooty mounds of snow stood chin-high at the kerbs and crossings. The rows of two-storey houses on each side of the street had all been shaped out of the same, sad architectural mould; they differed slightly only in colour and in the lay and pattern of the brick. The bushes, gates

and walks before each house were virtually alike. The alleys were stark and clean. Each house had its basement – and most were finished basements, a mark of financial status and solidarity. For the finished basements served all social and business functions including weddings and birthday parties, family pow-wows; simple card games or informal rousing beer-drinking get-togethers. The windows in most houses were lace-curtained.

An ancient twelve-foot high iron lamppost, fuelled by gas and capped in snow, stood at the street corner, frosted and glimmering feebly in the greying morning sunrise. The thermometer now stood at zero.

Instead of attending his morning class at the neighbourhood school, the plump, red-cheeked boy stood in the recessed saloon doorway, his eyes narrowed watchfully and fixed on a small house across the street. The saloon, a shambling wooden structure, was closed and dark within. Strong sour odours – the stink of stale beer – reached Tony Hacha's nostrils. He thought of the fat barrel of *pivo* in his father's kitchen in Braidwood: the family's favourite brew for all seasons, in which they buried their sorrows, from which they drew new hope. The Hachas and their friends drank vast quantities of it, remembering the foaming malt and hops of Pilsen.

Here, in Greendale, far from the mines and smoke, away from his family and in the big city, living with an ancient aunt, Tony suddenly experienced a peculiar deprivation, felt alone and friendless. His aunt who spoke no English and had to take in laundry, provided little companionship. But everything considered, Tony naturally preferred living here, where big city life and its opportunities beckoned.

At fourteen, he had already become conscious of the fundamentals of existence, the meaning of the American dollar; of power. He could lick any kid in his school, or on

his block. He had achieved the street-fighter's peripheral vision. He was maturing fast, far beyond his age, and he was already too big for his tight knee-length pants and thin brown corduroy jacket-coat. Even his cap and ear-muffs were ill-fitting, and allowed stray tufts of tawny hair to hang out over one eye. Everything he wore seemed tight. A close look at his eyes would show an intelligence and cunning, a shrewdness not to be equated with his youth. They were Slavic eyes, with an intimation of the Mongol; his muscular, thick Eskimo-like body, and round glowing face, spoke of his East European origin. He was anything but nondescript. And he looked tough – tough enough to win a fight, run a race, perform duties not normally assigned to young boys. At school and in his neighbourhood Tony Hacha was certainly a special case, but no one knew quite what to make of him, except that his fists were always ready to back up his views and wishes, and a knee to the groin was his trademark in a fast encounter.

Tony already recognised the throb, the pulse and power of the big city; its vastness awed and excited him. His family had come to America for security and work – and American gold. The gold was legendary and allegedly 'to be found on the streets'. They were determined to have it. A year earlier, the Hachas had lived in Joliet, near Chicago, where Tony and his father had worked in the mines. It was a cheerless, grimy time in his life; no child labour laws existed then to protect him from a killing job. But luckily for Tony, it was only for a short time.

A small village near Prague had been their home, Tony's birthplace in fact; but once in America he had quickly erased the memory of his childhood, a scant few months after settling in the Midwest. Here Tony began to reach shadowy conclusions, sensing and understanding

aspects of life in America undreamed of before. There was a slow burn deep within him, a hunger he was determined to satisfy.

The school to which, as a foreigner, he was obliged to go, was, he knew, essential. Though impatient with classroom routines, he nevertheless understood their importance. English, the language of America, was not easily learned, but he was picking up important, pungent, useful words and certain magical phrases. He was also learning from friends the American equivalents of Slovakian obscenities: *snekym*, *soustat*, *mrdt*, *Jebati* and such. Words could force situations, produce results. Words could bring respect, attention. Yes, language *was* magic.

Equally important, Tony's teacher, a passionate union activist, managed to convey to him the status and excitement of politics. The young fourteen-year-old roughneck immigrant was an eager student of politics at the most fundamental level – and understood intuitively the facts of self-preservation and power. He was responsive to his teacher's ideas of political stratagems, a man to whom he gave his closest and most respectful attention.

Tony was always impatient, irritated, asking impertinent but practical questions about American heroes and history. He was precocious in his concern for *getting* power, using it. How did one go about becoming a judge? How did one get elected? How could a poorly-paid judge afford to live in a fine big house with two servants, when his salary was known to be inadequate? Questions, questions . . . He would get the answers to questions. Answers unrelated to classroom tasks. He had to master the language. And he needed some ready money – not just nickels and dimes – if for no other reason than to buy a beer or a bourbon for a friend.

Living in a Slavic enclave made the outer world a no-

man's-land. Life revolved around school, earning a living, eating and drinking, making friends and keeping an eye out for the future.

But Tony had eyes beyond Greendale: he had already, secretly, experienced the peripheral taste of forbidden fruit – some of the sweets of American life, including a few humid encounters with girls. With a few friends, he had explored the lakefront and the exciting Gold Coast, and also the notoriously wild West Side of the city's Twenty-Second Street . . . had seen some of the *poulicini*, the *holka*, the street girls in action, hustling. He had listened to the jokes, the furtive references to the gaudy underworld. He stirred, ears stiffening, at the talk of payoffs, easy cash, crooked judges, fortunes made overnight, the painted loose women, the cathouses. But what intrigued him most of all was the concept of power and politics. The big shots, the leaders, he noted, wore black fedoras and tuxedos at night, with black patent leather shoes, and they sported velvet collars on their coats. Some of them, he saw, carried guns.

And Tony thought often of the women: their breasts and buttocks, warm flesh and crevices, shining red lips. The *kurva* (the whores) excited him and haunted his nights. Simply to watch them, posturing and soliciting, gave him pleasure, as did the racy words, the forbidden epithets used by men in order to show their authority or contempt. It was important to make the girls laugh or blush, make them look at him with interest. He had overheard young men discussing an evening of 'cunt hopping'. He had overheard details of adventures with 'cunt dates' along the Drainage Canal at midnight. He knew he had to be one of them, had to talk and act like them, had to lead them!

The yellow two-storey house directly across the street from the saloon, with its windows shielded by heavy red

velour drapes and beige lace curtains, held Tony spellbound. There were, he was told, three whores and a madam living in that house. He knew vaguely what *went on* there but his imagination couldn't evoke for him the true physical reality of its interior or inhabitants. How did they behave? How did they come together and couple with men? What were the special sex acts he had heard vaguely about (sometimes with animals), wondered about, for which extra fees were charged? He knew that whisky and wine flowed, and that aldermen and other politicians – some very powerful – patronised the house; that one of the sons of a local department- store owner spent hundreds of dollars in that house – sometimes in one single night! He tried to visualise the sexual activity, the services rendered; to his mind came scenes of wrestling matches: naked men and women in some sort of happy sexual combat, rolling about, coupling and laughing – the women often clad only in black lace stockings. He had heard stories . . . but his personal, first-hand knowledge was non-existent.

Tony rubbed his cold gloveless hands for warmth, stamped his feet. A grey kitten appeared from nowhere, brushed against his ankles and miaowed softly. He picked it up and slipped it within his jacket, stroking its furry, trembling head.

Thought Tony: the men in the bars, the guys I know – they aren't going anywhere – nowhere. I'm going somewhere. That's for sure. How, was the question. A job, something with a future, offering special rewards. A friend had told him a job was open at the yellow house; that 'Big Olga', madam and hoor, needed a handy boy. What the duties were he couldn't imagine. But he found himself tantalised by the prospects; and he tried to calculate the financial possibilities, based on hearsay. The money was said to roll in. Great sums were to be made

from the business in that house – and others like it. Millions of dollars were apparently spent in the cribs on notorious Twenty-Second Street each year – and he believed it, having walked the street several times, observing the gay activity.

That small, quiet house across the street – a mere five blocks from where Tony and his aunt lived – could be the magic door to prosperity, not to mention any fringe benefits of sensual pleasure. The instincts of entrepreneur and physical man stirred within him and he felt a rush of excitement as he stared at each of the draped windows. Not a curtain was moving. It was an early morning in January and, *Jezu Maria*, it was cold. Only a *crazy* would be out on the street. Or an ambitious boy.

Then Tony saw a flicker of movement at one of the upstairs windows. A curtain was parted a few inches. His attention was riveted by that tiny aperture, in which appeared a young and beautiful woman. At least he saw an eye and a nose. A strand of long blonde hair hung over one eye. A young blonde *kurva*! He stood motionless, barely breathing. He waited, muttering *I want the job, I want the job*. Then the curtains closed. But a moment later they parted again, wider. A tall, heavy woman, red hair piled high above a mushroom-grey face, appeared at the window. She raised her hand majestically towards Tony, then made a quick beckoning gesture. She was summoning him – inviting him to cross the street! At that, the young blonde reappeared. Slowly she opened her robe to display her large pink breasts, shimmied them briefly, smiled, then closed the curtains.

Tony walked almost in a trance across the icy fluorescent-pink street. He was still holding the kitten to his chest.

Big Olga, austere and vermilion-cheeked, dominating the scene like an aged operatic queen in her overstuffed

chair in an overheated room no larger than the living-room in Tony's aunt's house, greeted him with a grunt and a frown. The furniture was plain: two sofas and five assorted chairs placed along the walls, with a large oak table in the centre, standing on a worn oriental rug. Behind Olga stood a tall *étagère* filled with dime-store bric-à-brac. An ecru lace cloth covered the table and on it stood a red Bohemian cut-glass decanter and six matching glasses.

Tony removed his cap and stood before her, wondering what he was expected to say or do. She was sipping something from a large china cup, coffee he presumed although he could smell whisky. She looked at him, yawned, and asked his name. Behind her on the wall was a large oil painting – he had never seen one before – of a semi-nude woman, lying on a yellow sofa, eyes closed, plump pink arms outstretched.

A powerful scent – a sweet incense odour – penetrated Tony's consciousness and he could not help comparing it to the American Family Soap odour that was ever present in his aunt's house. He thought of the harsh climate of the street, and almost dissolved in the warmth and the sensuality of this place.

Olga's flaming bouffant hair and heavily rouged face presented a vivid picture to Tony: she intrigued him, though her green and staring eyes frightened him.

'I know you're a tough bohunk punk,' she said, softly, slowly, taking a sip from her cup. 'But I think maybe you're smart enough to know how lucky you would be working for me here, and that you could make a future for yourself – and some money.' She paused to see that she was registering, and went on, 'I want you should be straight with me, no tricks, no bullshit, no crooked business; and if you can't be square with me, you're no good here. What do you say?'

Tony replied, eyes meeting hers bravely, 'I will do a good job for you. I'll work hard. No bullshit. No crooked.'

The exchange with Olga was brief. He was to come to the yellow house after school, and in the mornings on Saturdays. Errands, cleaning around, shopping, these were some of his duties. Handy boy. He was to tell none of his family where he worked. 'I'll cut your balls off,' she said, huskily, licking her lips with a small pink tongue, 'if you tell your teacher where you work. What you see here is our private business. Real private,' she added, sipping from her cup again.

'Yes ma'am,' Tony said softly.

'I won't repeat the warning.'

Tony said, 'I live with my aunt. She don't ask me no questions, nothing. I don't tell her nothing.'

She studied him for a moment. 'I want you now to have a little talk with Viola. She's one of your people from Greendale – a bohunk. Nice girl. She is the best.' She paused to study his reaction. He stood there stonily, prepared for anything. Then she continued:

'Do you like to do some extra special bizness?' She leaned heavily on the *z*. 'Ohkay, go see her, she'll give you some instructions.'

The maid appeared and led Tony up a short flight of thickly carpeted stairs. They walked down a hall and the maid knocked on the third door. They entered when they heard the 'come in' from Viola. Tony was introduced. It was the girl in the window. He stood, cap in hand, waiting, wondering.

The room reeked of the familiar incense; the bed was piled high with colourful pillows. Two extravagantly shaded floor-lamps – one bright red, one green – illuminated a cluttered dressing table, a small footstool, and a giant *armoire* with a lifesize naked female figure painted

on the door. A fire-engine-red shaggy rug on the floor dominated everything, and the total carnival effect was almost overwhelming.

Viola wore a purple chiffon dressing gown through which he could see her shimmering breasts, shadowy crotch and long legs. She came forward and shook Tony's hand.

'Leave us alone for a few minutes, Minnie,' she said to the maid. Then pointing to one of the chairs she said, 'Have a seat, Tony.'

Tony sat in a large red wicker chair with a high rounded back, and found his feet barely reached the floor. Viola circled him, studied him, pulled a footstool over with her toe and sat down before him, smiling.

'I've got a business proposition for you, Tony.' She thrust her hand forward, touching Tony's chest. 'What have you there, in your coat?' she asked, leaning towards him, her breasts almost touching his chest.

Tony pulled out the kitten and held it out to her. She laughed and stroked its head as the kitten miaowed, pawing the air.

'Tony, there's room for only one pussy here; take it away when you go, but put it down for now.'

Tony placed the kitten on the floor and it ran over to a tasselled cushion near the window.

'Tony,' Viola said, 'we can make some money together, you and me, if you'll help me. You do your part, I'll do mine. Okay?'

'Sure, ma'am, what do I have to do?'

'For Jesus' sake, don't call me ma'am,' she said. She began unbuttoning Tony's fly. 'Now be relaxed, don't get nervous – and take off your pants. Your shoes, too.'

His throat became tight and dry, and his hands began to tremble.

'Here, take this.' She handed him a glass. He realised it

was real whisky, saloon bottle whisky. He sipped from the glass. Strong and cutting, it helped to relax his throat. He removed his pants and stood there in his long underwear, waiting.

'Take off the rest of your stuff, all of it, and go to the bed,' she ordered, turning away to the bathroom door.

He undressed and sat on the bed gingerly, waiting, naked and fearful, yet somehow proud of his involvement, and curious about this exciting new situation. He found it hard to believe that it was happening to him. He would have liked another sip of whisky, but he hesitated to ask. The kitten was miaowing. He waited.

Viola returned from the bathroom, carrying an aromatic, damp towel. She sat down in a chair across from him and leaned back, opening her robe. She was naked. Paradise. A blonde angel with soft pink skin. As she slowly spread her knees he saw her entire genital area. She had obviously shaved; her crotch was a pale and powdered pinkish-blue, with the slit a reddish-pink. Tony's eyes were glued to her vagina.

'Have you ever seen a real pussy?' she asked.

'Yeah, a couple times. We call it *kunda* – that's Czech . . .'

'Yes, I know,' she said. 'I'm a bohunk like you.' Then she added, 'Did you ever suck a *kunda*?'

'No, ma'am.'

'My name is Viola, Tony – not ma'am, f'Christsakes.'

'Yes, Viola,' Tony said.

'Now, would you like to try my *kunda* – lick it, maybe, just a little?'

'I don't know . . .' said Tony, beginning to perspire. His throat was tight and dry again. He could barely speak.

'Okay, Tony, maybe later, suit yourself. Don't be so tense. Now relax.' She rose, approached the bed and

gently pushed him back. As she bent over him, releasing her hair so that his entire midsection was covered with the flowing blonde strands, he felt himself drowning in the warmth and odour of her body.

In a moment he realised that his penis was in her mouth and that he was experiencing the most exquisite feeling he had ever known. He had heard about this kind of sex. This blonde hoor was giving him the works. A few moments later he exploded in her and she drew back coughing and laughing, wiping her face with her hand. Then she dropped the robe, and pressed her bare pink thighs and powdered crotch against his face. 'In a moment,' she said, 'I'm going to make you come again, and you can suck me if you like. Try it. It's called sixty-nine.' Now she was finding him excitedly responsive, and surprisingly aware of his responsibilities.

A few minutes later she had accomplished her purpose. Seduction and corruption. She wiped him with the aromatic towel.

Very businesslike, she said, 'That was a sample, a free sample. And here's where you and Viola go into business. Now listen to me carefully, Tony.'

'I listen,' said Tony. '*Dekuji,*' he murmured, thanking her. Little did he suspect, then, what a role this charming fellatrice would play in the rest of his life.

'I usually charge three dollars,' she said. 'I'm supposed to be the best cocksucker in the city – ask Olga if you don't believe me. Maybe you believe me now that you got a free sample. Anyway, I want to have you send me a lot of customers – your friends, people you meet around town. The rules are: they pay me three dollars cash in advance. They must ask for me, Viola; and they must say Tony sent them. That's it. And for every customer you send me I will give you a half-dollar.'

Tony stared at her, then said, 'Sure, I can get you

customers. At the saloon, at school – I know lots of guys. Fifty cents a shot for me. Right?'

'Yeah, right.' She stood up, moved to the window and said, 'Okay, Tony, start right away. If they say you sent them, I'll write it down and pay you a half-buck apiece. I'll pay you every Monday. Okay? And you can tell your friends – if they got real money on them – that I've got some tricks you don't know nothing about. Yet. I know how to keep you from coming for a half-hour if you like. I have a Round-the-World special treatment that makes 'em see stars and stripes forever. That costs five bucks. I can do a lot of tricks with your cock – and your asshole too.' She winked at him. 'Now, get dressed and get to work.'

When Tony left the house his world had changed completely; he knew he would never be the same again.

As he walked home he began to calculate the number of prospects – boys and men – he knew and might approach; the money he would make.

Tony remembered the pay he had once received – $1.50 a day for grinding work in the Braidwood pits – a mule-driver. He would make more money from Viola than his father did! But it had to be a secret. He would organise and keep a careful record of his customers. And he would manage to have Viola's lips and tongue around his *curak* again.

He would approach, not only the bar-room pals he knew but even moneyed strangers in the bars; he realised that he could branch out into the world beyond his neighbourhood. He would solicit men driving expensive cars, hot shots in public places. Intuitively, he knew that word of mouth would work for him. He would block print slips of paper with Viola's name and address, and pass them out to likely candidates in front of restaurants, hotels and theatres in the Loop. He began to whistle as the prospect before him expanded.

'I will do big bizness,' he said aloud to himself. 'Today I am a man.' But what Tony was unaware of was that as of that morning he was a member of the world's second oldest profession: a professional pimp. And he would be reminded of this from time to time as he prospered and advanced in the world.

On this Saturday morning – more than two years later – Tony was lying spreadeagled on Viola's bed, fully clothed.

'I'm telling you,' said Tony, 'Bruno is crazy about you; he talks all the time about how he wants to marry you. I know he sees you three times a week; he's a real spender; he says he wants to be with you every night. Does he tell you?'

Viola shrugged. She was sitting across the room, painting her nails. 'I know what he's thinking,' she said. 'I got him on the ropes – I know what he likes and he goes crazy every time he comes here. You know what he likes too.' She stuck out her pink tongue at him. 'But I'm not marrying him – nobody! I'm a businesswoman and my business is good. That's how it's going to stay.'

'Good,' said Tony, pulling himself upright, resting on the brass uprights of the bed's headboard. 'That reminds me, Viola, I gotta proposition. I'm ready to go into bizness. Wanna hear it – my proposition?'

'Ah, so, I'm listening. So talk.' She sniffed the air, sensed what was coming and smiled, marvelling at his rapid maturing. Sixteen! Sweet sixteen.

'Don't let Olga in on this – she'd bust a gut.' He raised his forefinger. 'You and me are making good bizness, no? Well, we can make lots more, I figure. Real big bizness. I know you can handle ten, fifteen, twenty customers a day, no? Right, now' – he lowered his voice to a whisper – 'you gotta split fifty-fifty with Olga. That's crazy.' He paused. 'No more, Vi, no more.'

He got up and paced the floor. He was wearing his first pair of long pants and he struck her as a very young, almost ludicrously young businessman. Then he stopped in front of her and pulled over a chair and sat down.

'Now here's what I think,' he said, putting his hand in her lap. 'Let's go into our own business – our own, me and you. I'll take care of the business, the customers and the money – you do the job. You won't have to split with Olga – nobody. You can pay me twenty-five per cent commission on what you get. And I can promise you I'll bring you some real rich, high-class customers. Even a few big politicians, maybe a judge, too. I'm getting a few connections. And I know some guys at the Green Mill and the Chez Paree. Don't ask me how I got to them, but I did. These guys spend a hundred dollars a throw. I've been listening and watching. Why split with Olga? Huh?'

'Keep talking,' said Viola.

'So my proposition is this: you and me, we move to a flat on Division Street. I know a place. I leave my aunt's house. She's an old cunt – don't talk English, no write, no nothing. A greenhorn. I know a man who will rent me a flat for fifty dollars a month. No questions. We can fix it up nice. You know I got some good connections. Saloons where I go.' He stopped and chuckled. 'I'm politicking now, too.' He leaned towards her, smiling. 'Your friend and manager, Tony Hacha – me – I'm gonna be *assistant* precinct worker. How do you like that? That's where the big bizness is. I see, I listen, I learn.' He paused again.

'Keep talking, Tony, you got me kinda interested.'

'The trouble is,' he said, 'I'm not old enough to rent a flat, sign a lease. Not legal. They won't let a *boy* sign a lease. Not until I'm twenty-one. You come with me and we do it together. Today or tomorrow?' The eagerness was in his voice, his eyes.

She studied his bull neck, his broad shoulders, the

piercing determined eyes. She saw power in the making there. It would be a good move. Who needed Big Olga? The bitch would scream and threaten and blow her top. So what? Viola could take her clientele with her anywhere in town.

Three months after settling down with Viola in his Division Street flat, Tony drew up plans for the next phase in his career. He realised that he had some problems; some were obviously related to his character and personality. He did not make friends too easily, except with the roughneck types who drank and roistered with him. He drank heavily and was involved in brawls, fist fights of a near serious nature, ugly, drunken bouts. Most of all, he knew it was bad for his record to be arrested so often. He had been thrown in jail five times to date, mostly for beating up girls. Booze was the problem; frustration set the drinking off. He was known as a bully and while he enjoyed being tough – his rowdy reputation pleased him – he didn't enjoy being called a *bully*. He was shrewd enough to know that he was in a steady, responsible set-up, with Viola; this was where his future was and it had to be considered soberly.

As a precocious teenager Tony was maturing far beyond his age. Despite his drinking, pugnacity and money-making, he was getting a reputation as an achiever. He was a leading member of a 'tough babies Czech gang', a wild saloon-centred group. It didn't add up to a future, however. Toughness wasn't enough. Although inherent in his toughness was a potential for power.

A seasoned labour negotiator took him aside one day and gave him a dutch-uncle talk; it left an impression on Tony, made him realise that he was, as the man said, 'jerking off'. He needed to discipline and direct his energies and brain. His regular Saturday night skirmishes

at the Benevolent Society dances were bad for his reputation. If he was going to advance himself, he had to behave. 'Join the School,' he said. 'Become a businessman.'

Suddenly the light went on, the sky cleared. He saw the entire picture with a clarity that almost frightened him. He took a bird's-eye-view of himself, and it dawned on him how he could, and would, be Somebody.

He began to develop social contacts among the residents of the Greendale district, and in particular the men who patronised his Division Street 'parlour'. He heard himself referred to as a pimp and didn't relish the label, but he would change that.

First, he wanted to build up what he had already established. He let it be known that he was available for the most menial political jobs including leaflet distribution on street corners, doorbell ringing, vote hustling. His social and political life blossomed, not to mention his private business. He had (with Viola's help) persuaded another young whore from the Yellow House, Annie, to move in with Viola and himself – much to Big Olga's fury. His income almost doubled overnight. The two women made an irresistible pair, often serving as a twosome and earning up to $200.00 a night. Annie was as gifted as Viola; she had an amusing, childlike personality that delighted many men, and nothing offended her. It was all fun – at least she made it appear so.

'I like a straight man who is just a little bent,' she explained. 'Kinky is okay up to a point.'

Viola and Annie were money-makers and life was sweet for Tony, as he began to explore new avenues for revenue and power.

The local Democratic Party, in the person of a quiet, tough hawk-faced Czech Jew, Adolph S. Katz, a man of political and financial importance among Chicago Czechs,

with strong gambling connections not to mention underworld ties, took Tony aside in a Greendale saloon one day. He spoke to him about improving himself.

Tony informed Katz that he had been given a similar lecture recently by a labour negotiator, and Katz merely said, 'Then it's time you listened, young man.

'Tony, do you know the word, "*schmuck*"? It means prick, or jerk. Mainly, it means "fool".' He peered at Tony through his thick lenses and continued, 'Stop the fighting and boozing. Don't be a *schmuck.* You've got the brains to be a politician; you could go places. Are you interested?'

'I'm interested, Mr Katz,' said Tony. He had observed the man at a few political meetings, had heard of his power, his money. He was alleged to have many millions of dollars mulcted from numerous casinos, and to 'control' several race-tracks. A force, Mr Katz. And so quiet, so sober. 'The Jewish Connection', he was called.

'Take a job as assistant secretary, make some contacts,' he said, 'learn the ropes, get to know the party leaders, the whole caboodle. Lend a hand.'

As a result of the meeting with Katz he became an example of energy propelled in the right direction. In short order he became a precinct election official, then a captain. Two months after his meeting with Katz, he was appointed bailiff in a West-Side justice-of-the-peace court. A beginning. As precinct captain and bailiff his status was socially and politically exciting to his Greendale friends. Tony bought himself a double-breasted navy-blue suit, a broad-brimmed felt hat, and two pairs of the latest style shoes with pointed toes. He suddenly discovered that he was an eligible young bachelor; invitations to dinners began to come his way. He was barely twenty years old.

One day Mr Katz introduced a handsome young Italian

law student to him. 'Meet Angelo,' he said. 'You two should be good friends. You can help each other. Here, let me buy both of you a beer.'

The friendship between Angelo and Tony blossomed and bore fruit. Each found mutual involvements, socially and in business. Mr Katz was almost like a father to them and they swore they would do anything for him – all he would have to do was ask.

By now, Tony and Viola had taken a larger apartment on Division Street, with two bedrooms. And they added a fourth occupant named Dolores. She was black, fun-loving and capable of out-fucking any two whores, given the chance. Tony had taken her on as a gamble, and discovered that his clients had a distinct liking for dark meat. There was never a dull moment at Chez Viola. And it was a mere beginning.

As for Adolph Katz – whose comings and goings and whereabouts were always ambiguous, whose role in politics and the underworld was never clearly defined or understood by most of the people who obeyed and respected him – he found Viola's place of occasional interest, on a personal basis. Everyone felt power in his presence. Like Johnny Torino, he preferred anonymity. He was the example to his colleagues: one could survive in the big city jungle, enjoy the fruits of the underworld, and live to a ripe old age. Providing one learned the art – the rules of survival. Which of course involved unquestioned obedience.

One of his philosophic precepts was, 'Never blow the whistle on a friend – a friend is better than money.'

Once, at Viola's, he had taken Tony aside. 'If you ever get into real trouble, call me. If you need some muscle-help – you know – rough up somebody, look up a handy man I know, name of Jimmy Belcastro. He can be located at the Lucerna bar on Division Street. Mention my name.'

He studied the young man for a moment, then added, 'Belcastro. Don't write it down, just remember it.'

Adolph Katz left Tony bursting with a sense of newly acquired power.

Chapter Two

It was Angelo's fourth trip in eight months to New Orleans, a city he had come to love. He sniffed the cool and fragrant spring morning air as he stepped out of his Basin Street hotel. Dressed in his natty blue pinstriped suit and black homburg, he felt at the peak of his potential. Angelo Minelli was twenty-two, a student of law, and procurer extraordinary. He stood five feet eleven inches tall, had gleaming blue-black vaselined hair parted sharply in the centre, burning Sicilian eyes, full red lips, and a strong protruding nose. He gave an instant impression of Medician authority. He hailed a cab with a sharp whistle. He had several personal visits to make and arranged with the taxi driver that he wait for him at each stop.

This would be a mission that Johnny Torino, his boss and mentor, need know nothing about – yet.

Angelo had already accomplished his business purposes the day before: he had negotiated for and secured three new women ('fresh cunt') and had arranged for them to be transported to his home town. They were from the 'Countess' Pitzelli's stable (one of his prime sources) at one thousand dollars each. There was a vivacious, sharp-tongued French Creole, actually a native Louisianian, who handled language – obscenities and the patois – with charming unselfconsciousness; a genuine blonde Eurasian, an uncommonly sensual maverick beauty; and a girl barely a month from Dublin, vivaciously Irish, with the bounciest pair of tits in all Louisiana. The three were all in

their early twenties, fresh yet obviously well-disciplined. They would be leaving for the North the following night, by train, in a separate compartment, with Angelo riding in a car at the rear.

A protégé of Johnny Torino, of the same ethnic and moral heritage, Angelo was a bright, avid student of the flesh market and the underworld. Possessing a prismatic mind and being street smart, he knew the underworld's mores and strictures, the codes, and where he could bend the rules. He was also concerned with the multifarious loop-holes of the law. He was a student at University Law school, from which he hoped to depart in two years, to practise. He'd have his own office; and one major client: Torino. The financing had been Torino's all the way.

Angelo's father was a superintendent in Torino's apartment house. He had arranged for them to meet. He was a dutiful father, a quiet widower, unwell and ageing rapidly, happy to see his son well-launched in a noble profession, and sponsored by one of the 'kings' of our time. Which in a sense – by divine might – Torino was, considering his power and wealth.

Torino was a man who avoided the limelight. He had problems in abundance, as does any businessman with a variety of investments and financial pursuits, and he needed a trusted, bright young legal eye and brain. His vision of power and wealth encompassed a vast terrain. Aside from being Capone's mentor, he was probably the most feared man in the American underworld. And yet invisibility was part of his style. While undisputed ruler of Chicago's gangland, a man who could order a killing as coolly and softly as he did a plate of *linguine*, he was never seen in the night-clubs, saloons or casinos he controlled, nor with any of the women whose bodies he traded. Any night he could be found in his house-slippers, sheltered in

his favourite rocking chair at home, with his wife and daughter: a model of civic propriety. But prostitution, gambling and liquor were his main business interests, in addition to labour unions – and the police department. (He was said to have several hundred policemen on his personal payroll.) His army of workers knew him as a fox – and deadly. Formidable and rock-firm, he nevertheless treated Angelo as a son.

Torino's ruthlessness was recognised by everyone who worked for or about him. Associates knew that when one of his men became recalcitrant, loud, suspect, careless, he would suddenly disappear. And it was lese-majesty, against Torino's dignity, to refer to or inquire about that missing person. When Torino ordered his uncle, the flamboyant Jim Colosimo, killed, because he did not see eye to eye with Torino and did not share his vision or philosophy, the world came to understand him well. Torino invited the New York hood, Frankie Yale, an ex-partner of his, to come to the city; and on 11 May 1920, Colosimo met his death in his Wabash Avenue cabaret. Torino immediately took over his uncle's various business activities, including his houses, and the still menacing and functioning Black Hand. He also made Al Capone his chief lieutenant.

Angelo Minelli was deeply proud of his association with this quiet little man, and the complex Torino empire continued to fascinate him. While Angelo's services were concerned primarily with the brothel area of Torino's interests, he was appreciated and observed with satisfaction by Capone himself. He recognised Angelo's loyalty, his clear-headedness, his legal mind, and his precocity. Angelo Minelli, attorney-at-law-to-be, was moving up the ladder of power.

Angelo's path often crossed 'the Big Fellow', Capone, and he knew that the Capone organisation looked on him

with special favour because he was Torino's young man on the move, a smooth, iron-fisted hand in the prostitution department. Angelo knew intuitively how to handle the personnel, the records and payoffs, the cash flow. He knew what information to keep concealed; he was a dependable and promising gangland executive: to the world at large – a student of law.

Torino's espousal of Angelo – delegating delicate tasks to him, funding his personal and school expenses – added to the impressive image of this young, ambitious Siciliano. One day, Angelo felt, he would be in a position to repay and help Torino in major ways, through his legal expertise. He would also show that he knew how to buy and control police, judges, senators and other men in power. Doctors and hospitals, the medical world, were part of his envisioned terrain, his network. Also, having a few good and discreet pharmacists in his pocket, with access to drugs, was a priceless asset.

Angelo was probably the most promising and dedicated young man in Torino's 'family'; but one of his visits in New Orleans this morning was extra-curricular. Walking slowly down Royal Street his thoughts turned to a personal matter.

His interest was in the young octoroon, Cora. He had first glimpsed her in Eulalia Harris's house. One of the city's few black madams Eulalia was visibly ageing now, and worried about the rumoured state crackdown on all (including legalised) prostitution. She had begun to make plans for the future, and she had discussed the situation with Angelo on a previous trip. She had also introduced him to her 'daughter', Cora.

Cora, aged fourteen, was not on the staff of Eulalia's house. She was the crown jewel, a princess not to be fucked or defiled. While Angelo had grave doubts about Eulalia being her mother (Eulalia was about sixty-five

years old) he nevertheless listened attentively, and observed Cora with growing interest.

She was indeed a New Orleans flower, with large lustrous eyes; and her black glossy hair was of thigh-length, draping her youthful but already well developed figure. Her *café au lait* skin was rose-tinged and unblemished except for one tiny, perfectly round mole beneath her navel. Her silken and softly modulated voice helped to complete Angelo's enchantment.

'I've had some terrific offers for her,' Eulalia told him. 'But I want her to be with me as long as possible – I just can't stand to part with her. She's a darling. I don't want her in any New Orleans house. She deserves a fine man and a wedding ring. She's got some education and *ree*-finement.' She paused. 'She reads books, you know,' she added proudly, eyes widening for emphasis.

Angelo had heard about Cora in some of the District houses, where he drank coffee and gossiped in the kitchens. The impending closing down of Storyville threatened the future of many girls – the inmates of the numerous mansions, houses, cribs – and of course Angelo was interested in recruiting a few of the best of them to place in Torino's houses in Chicago, particularly in the Twenty-second Street and Cicero stations. Two madams, Lottie Fischer and the Inimitable Lulu Block, had mentioned Cora to Angelo, knowing of both his connoisseurship and personal penchant for young, exotic and flowerlike women.

'She ain't no cheap trick,' Lulu told him, 'and Eulalia ain't gonna pass her on to no up-north cunt house, no Four Deuces (you'll excuse the specific reference, Angelo), no Cicero crib. My god, Angelo, Cora's a virgin!'

Angelo smiled.

'Why the smile, Angelo?'

'I was thinking how nice a cold beer would be right now.'

She shouted the order for a beer and a double Wild Turkey for herself, sat back for the negotiation, lips pressed firmly together. She put a slender black Cuban cigar to her mouth, lighted it and inhaled.

Cora was obviously Angelo's passion and mission. He would, somehow, bring her north as his own personal and private property. His problem was twofold: how much to pay and how discreetly could the matter be handled and controlled. Should he actually marry the girl and guarantee his exclusivity with a legal document? Finally, there was the possibility of preparing a phoney marriage certificate – something that would keep him legally unattached if necessary. One thing he knew: he could never present Cora socially to his father, nor to his patron Torino, nor to his law school associates.

Marriage was definitely not in his immediate programme. He had to stay unencumbered. Torino would lose respect for him if he heard that his protégé, Angelo, was committed to a whorehouse madam's girl. It was contrary to Torino's 'house rules': *don't fuck with the hired help*.

And there was the law school: two more grinding, tough years, before he could practise and shift into high, and a real career. He must remain unhampered. So, he decided he would *adopt* Cora as his niece. He knew of similar instances that had worked out.

The drinks arrived and Angelo drank his beer with gusto. Eulalia tossed back a stiff slug of the bourbon and waited.

Angelo was silent. Yes, he would work out the *adoption* thing; the public would know it was pure bullshit, but the ruse would be, could be respected. As for the price . . . He had discussed Cora with Radie Young, a tough old

bird of a madam, a seasoned and worldly woman who knew the price of everything.

'It's gonna cost,' said Radie. 'Maybe for the rest of your life.' Then she smiled, adding, 'Lots of the beautiful green stuff.'

'What does that mean?' asked Angelo.

She had studied him, nodding slowly. 'I think a thousand down and a hundred a month for the rest of Eulalia's life.'

Angelo jumped as though his ass was scalded.

'You're joking. What does that mean?' he asked.

'That could mean maybe ten grand, more. Eulalia isn't a spring chicken, but she may have another ten or fifteen years left . . .' He pulled out a thin cigar from his jacket pocket, bit off the end and put a match to its tip. 'You must think I'm real hard up for tail, Radie.'

'For that quality tail, yes,' said Radie, smiling. 'I ain't too sure you appreciate quality. Real sweet, virgin tail –that comes high, Angelo – that kind of ass.'

Angelo got up. 'Bears thinking about,' he said, 'and I thank you for the advice. I'm too young to get hitched, and that kind of money – out of my own personal private pocket – is kinda rough. But we'll see.'

The taxi took him to Eulalia's house. He knocked at her great red door with the gleaming brass knocker, and was met by Eulalia herself. She took him directly to her office. 'Gotta talk to you in private,' she said.'Glad you came at this time.' She poured two large brandies in snifters and handed him one.

Eulalia was in black, a lacy black silk dress, and she was wearing her pearls – at least half a dozen strands, some of them reaching down to her groin. Her face was heavily rouged; her black wig too obvious, and askew. The clown quality of her face, the heavy worry lines, saddened Angelo; he had always liked and respected Eulalia. She was obviously crumbling.

'Angelo, I've got real trouble; they're coming down on me real hard. The cocksuckers are asking me to close up shop right away. They want me out of business by the end of this month. This month! They're not foolin'.' She paused, sipped her brandy, then continued. 'A minister – I guess he was a Catholic priest – and a cop suddenly came here this morning. They were asking about Cora. They've got a bug up their asses about her. Can't figure why, after all these years. They were asking about birth certificates and stuff. Legal stuff. I told them she was my natural daughter and the miserable pricks laughed at me. Imagine, laughed at me, Eulalia! I told them to come back next week: I gotta talk to my lawyer. Tell me, Angelo, what do I do? You're a lawyer, aren't you?'

'No, Eulalia, I'm going to be a lawyer, in two years, but I've learned enough already to know you have a problem.'

'What do I do?' asked Eulalia, moaning.

Angelo studied his fingernails; then he looked up and directly into her eyes. 'Eulalia, I can help you. Listen. Relax. I'll take care of Cora. I'll adopt her as my niece. All legal. With your written approval, of course.'

She peered at him, clutching her pearls.

'How much, Angelo, how much? In dollars?'

Angelo pulled a sheet of paper from his inside jacket pocket and said, 'I'll give you a legal document, a simple agreement, right now. Just give me your approval, Eulalia, and you'll have no problems. And by the way, Eulalia, I'm a religious man, Catholic. I'm going to have to have Cora converted. Okay with you?'

He handed her the document and a fountain pen, and proceeded to count out ten one-hundred-dollar bills, saying, 'On account, you understand.'

What an eccentric, thought Eulalia as she signed and

nodded. She could imagine the ceremonies, the kneeling, the praying. She smiled.

The following night, Cora was serenely asleep in a private compartment on the train to Chicago. The three young women Angelo had recruited were each in separate bedrooms. Earlier they had been playing poker and drinking from a quart of bourbon which Angelo had supplied. He sat in his own private bedroom at the rear of the train. They had been given strict orders not to speak to him or even to appear to know him. Not until they touched foot in Chicago, *outside* the station.

He had lectured them about one James Robert Mann, author of the Mann Act, the White Slave Act, to which they only half listened. Mann, he had explained, was an Illinoisian and had been responsible for a law imposing heavy penalties on men who transported women from one state to another for immoral acts. Angelo told them he had no wish to risk his neck, and when he explained the law and the hazards to them, they all laughed.

'What dat – immoral acts?' asked the Creole, giggling.

'Fucking without pay,' said Angelo. 'That's immoral.'

Angelo and Cora arrived at the La Salle Street Station on a hot steamy Saturday morning. Following his instructions, she left the train first, carrying her new pigskin bag and alligator purse. He followed, a few dozen steps behind, with his own smaller valise. He exuded lilac aftershave and talcum; she radiated happiness and excitement. She had never been away from New Orleans, and her excitement delighted Angelo; he was observing a fourteen-year-old's response to a first view of a great city. He approached her finally, took her arm and held it closely for a moment, then freed her of the large bag and said, 'Stand right over there next to that pillar, and I'll be back in two minutes. Don't move from that spot.'

Cora leaned against the pillar indicated and surveyed the scene. She noted a sleek limousine, with a uniformed chauffeur beside it, and wondered . . . will I have one of those for myself?

Angelo waved to Scotty, the chauffeur-handyman employed by the Four Deuces, who came forward, saluting and smiling broadly.

'I got three heads for you, Scotty. Stick around a minute.' At that very moment he saw his three recruits step down from the train. He quickly pointed them out and left as Scotty approached them. He turned to make sure all was in order, and watched Scotty take their bags and proceed to shepherd them towards the exit gate. Then he returned to Cora, who was standing motionless, a wistful smile on her face, waiting for the city to envelop her.

Angelo hailed a cab, while out of the corner of his eye he saw Scotty leading the three New Orleans damsels to a Packard limousine. He could hear the squeals of the girls as they saw the elegant car; and Scotty was all smiles and hospitality. They were now in the big-time. Here was the ultimate in automobiles waiting for them, the classiest of cars (except the Rolls, of course), waiting to take them to – where? What matter? The city was theirs.

Cora and Angelo entered their taxi and he directed the driver to his hotel on Diversey Boulevard. The three recruited girls were on their way to the Four Deuces at 2222 South State Street, their future home, where they would service truck drivers, ward heelers, stockyard workers and others; the Four Deuces where the great Torino himself had his private, heavily secured office.

As they began driving, Angelo changed his mind. 'Honey, I'm gonna give you a de luxe tour of the city before we go home, okay?'

He instructed the cabbie to take the outer drive, giving

Cora a sense of the city's beauty, its lakefront, the skyscrapers including the Tribune and Wrigley Towers on the Chicago River's edge. As they drove along the Gold Coast he pointed out the Potter Palmer and Edith Rockefeller mansions. The driver made a detour so that she could see the famous flower shop across from the cathedral on North State Street – the shop that had been operated by the infamous Dion O'Bannion.

'Deanie was bumped off in his shop a long time ago,' said the driver. 'He started out selling newspapers, then he became a singing waiter, and finally owned the 42nd and 43rd wards – tough and rich territory. Then Frankie Yale rubbed him out.'

'You sure know your Chicago history,' said Angelo, smiling.

Then they made another detour so that Cora could see the garage on North Clark Street where the famous St Valentine's massacre took place.

As they rode along the lakefront, Angelo took her hand and rubbed it affectionately. He felt good. All missions accomplished. He had delivered three choice broads and brought home for his own delectation a Louisiana flower whose beauty all of his friends would envy. His mood was relaxed, introspective. Cora's was eager with unanswered questions: while she loved her native city, Chicago seemed exciting, magical and promising beyond all her fantasies. Angelo would make her fantasies come true.

When they finally turned in to Diversey Boulevard she felt a slight disappointment. The terrain was commonplace, drab.

'I hope you'll like our hideaway,' said Angelo as they pulled up before his building. Cora would be ensconced in his small 'bachelor apartment'. It was modestly furnished with minimal kitchen equipment, but it had a good bathroom and a large living-room which also served as a

bedroom when the huge sofa was pulled out from the wall. It had a private bath, and elevator service.

They unpacked. He opened a bottle of scotch and poured two stiff shots as a toast to each other and their future. Angelo noted that she could drink scotch straight, without a chaser, and without blinking.

'Well, Cora, we gotta case the neighbourhood for you, first. So's you'll know where you are and what it's all about. And I'll show you some of the best places for shopping.'

Angelo sensed her disappointment.

'Well, honey, this ain't the Gold Coast, but you'll be comfortable.'

He did not tell her that two blocks from his hotel apartment he controlled, under Torino's auspices of course, a seven-girl, twenty-four-hour, day-and-night whorehouse. Diversey Boulevard was not a notorious street, but a great many local men and out-of-town visitors were acquainted with the private 'clubs' and gambling parlours hidden behind its façades of respectability.

They began strolling along Diversey and Cora spotted a pet shop at once. A black French poodle caught her eye and she was entranced. Angelo bought it for her; it was love at first sight. The dog was named Napoleon.

'It'll be great company for you, Cora, when I'm working or at school, nights.'

She cuddled it, put it down gently on the sidewalk and began strolling with it on its leash, bending down from time to time to stroke and fondle it. Angelo was enchanted with her affectionate behaviour. They stopped at a news-stand and he bought an armful of magazines, some of them devoted to movies, fashion and gossip – stuff to keep her busy or amused. Then they stopped in a util ities shop and he bought her a small phonograph. 'For

the tiny rosebud aperture. Cora let out a scream. He saw at once that she was bleeding, but did not, could not stop. Moaning with pain as he plunged; she tried to dislodge him, but he put one hand over her mouth as she struggled.

'You'll get to like it,' he said, gasping. 'Stay quiet. Wait and see,' and then he exploded in her rectum, collapsing over her body. She lay flat beneath him, weeping, shaking with anger, tears and pain.

'You sonofabitch, you,' she muttered over and over again. 'You hurt, hurt. You hurt me. It hurts. I'm bleeding.' She touched her bottom.

'It's nothing,' he said. 'It's like losing your cherry.'

'I don't believe you,' she said, tears flowing again.

'I didn't mean to hurt you, Cora,' he said, as they lay side by side. 'Didn't Eulalia explain these things to you? Didn't you ever see a man and woman fucking as we just did?'

She moved away, turned into a guarded foetal curl.

'Never! I don't want you ever do that to me again. Never,' she shouted, bursting into tears again. Then she rose and staggered to the bathroom where she remained for long minutes, quietly. Finally, after ages, he called to her. She didn't reply. He opened the door and saw her sitting on the seat of the toilet, head in hand, still weeping. Bits of bloodied paper were on the floor.

The next morning she was up before he was. She had bread in the toaster; the coffee-pot was bubbling.

'Morning, sweetheart,' he called from the bed. 'Feeling better?'

'Better,' she replied.

'Well, come here and give us a kiss.'

Cora bent over him, letting her long hair drape across his face, and kissed him quickly.

Soon, they were seated in the living-room, drinking

coffee, talking about Chicago, his friends, business associates, his law school and his plans for the future. He did not refer to one of his chief occupations, procuring women for Torino's whorehouses, but he assumed that she knew about this; there was nothing to discuss. The subject of last night's argument did not come up again – not for some time.

After breakfast he took her hand and led her back to bed. He kissed her, stroked her gently. 'Cora,' he said, 'I love you, and I won't hurt you again. I want you to be happy. You're beautiful and you are going to be my number-one sweetheart.'

She studied him for a moment. 'And who is the number-two sweetheart? How many are there?'

He laughed. 'There is no number-two sweetheart. You're the one and only. Everything else is business.'

'I know about your business,' she said. 'Mama told me. You're a procurer of women for this famous Al Capone and Johnny Torino. I know about all this. But Mama told me you will be a big lawyer some day, a big man in Chicago; very important and rich. Is that so?'

'That's my plan, Cora. I hope so. And when I graduate from law school, I'll show you and the whole world a thing or two. And I'm going to make a lot of money. Without money we are nothing – nothing. We're going to be rich, like Rockefeller!' He laughed. 'We're going to have a big car, a chauffeur, a maid for you, a big house in the South Shore and in Florida, like Capone. We will travel, to New York, Paris, Rome, Palm Beach. For fun. But – ' he paused, 'right now I must concentrate on work. I must do my job for my bosses. They pay me well.' He paused again, eyes narrowed. Then he added, slowly. 'Don't ever use that word, *procurer*, to me, ever. Understand?'

He watched her face, saw her parted lips, a glimpse of

her snowy teeth. The bitch was irresistible; he'd break her in yet.

'Okay,' she said. 'But I thought you were rich . . .'

'No, not rich, but I have enough to keep you happy. You'll need for nothing with me. All you've got to do is make me happy.' He looked at her young upright breasts, the glistening nipples; he thought of the previous evening's histrionic display. 'Concentrate on making me happy. And don't interfere with my business.'

'Interfere?' she asked.

'Yes, stay out of my business. Enjoy yourself. Make love with me. And don't ask questions. Don't talk about my business to anybody. Never! One day you will be mistress of a big house, servants. We will be big society people.' He paused. 'Do you know what my dream is, Cora?' She shook her head, waiting.

'I want to be a famous judge. Do you know how powerful a judge can be in this town? He can say yes or no, and that's that. And everyone comes to him – with money. He can take what he wants. No morality bullshit for him. There will be lots of cash for us. Meanwhile, I must work hard, keep my bosses satisfied – and I must graduate from law school. I must also keep Mr Torino satisfied. That's my number-one job. Mr Torino. One day you'll meet him. Not right away, though. You are beautiful – my beautiful secret, my secret princess.' Laughing, he grabbed her shoulder, pulled her towards him. 'Enough of this – let's make love.'

In Angelo's view of life, one must be master or slave. A colt, a woman, a servant – they must be broken in. Early! He tried twice again to achieve anal entry, and in both instances she resisted with force and tears.

'You stupid cunt,' he said. 'Most women beg men to give it to them in the ass. Don't you know anything? It's a compliment to a woman that a man can get it up – and

hard, hard – otherwise you can't make it in the asshole – too tight. It's gotta be rock hard.'

He began to seek out women, young and old, who would submit anally to him, and every time he would think of Cora and her beautiful haunches, her chocolate-and-rose ass, and its inaccessibility. And Cora discovered later that she preferred sex with other men – even brutal men – and was capable of acts with others she would not condone with Angelo. Oral sex became one of her passions; only anal penetration was taboo.

Cora's brief love for Angelo turned to an unspoken hate. And Angelo became more silent in the days ahead. An inner fury within him could have led to murder. But he contained himself and managed to accommodate his situation.

Gradually certain adjustments were made in their lives. Angelo was caught up in his work, his law studies. In time his life took on an altogether new style. He secured his law degree, began to practise. Church attendance became a regular habit. After a number of courtroom appearances in which he comported himself with a stiff but correct dignity, he acquired a widespread reputation for knowing his business, for winning difficult cases, for exercising an authority not usually encountered in young attorneys. He even spoke of *moral conduct*.

Cora, for her part, settled down to a comparatively quiet life. Her affairs were carefully managed and remained unsuspected.

One day Angelo acquired a windfall and he took her for a drive on the South Side. He drove up before a large house surrounded by trees and bushes, and said, 'How would you like to shack up in that twelve-room house, Cora?'

They studied it from front to rear, and after a slow walk

through the rooms with the agent, who had been waiting for them, they decided it was perfect.

'It costs plenty,' he said, 'and it will take fifty grand to furnish. But we can do it!' He put his arm around her shoulder.

'Cora, baby, we'll swank it up. I'll get a cook and a house man. You tell them what to do and they'll do it. We'll invite the right people. The residence of Judge Angelo Minelli.'

'Did you say Judge?' she asked, staring at him. 'And what about me?'

'Maybe in six months, baby, Judge Minelli and niece, but keep it to yourself. A few friends, including Papa Torino and Tony Hacha will be arranging it. Nice?'

'Wouldn't it be better if I was your wife?' she asked.

'I didn't say anything about wife, baby. You're my niece, remember?'

'Can't you marry me, Angelo? Nobody believes I'm your niece. I'm nigra.' She fumbled for her handkerchief. 'I ought to be married – your wife.'

'Let's drop the subject for now, Cora. Okay?'

They returned to the car, and Cora remained silent for the rest of the drive.

Within six months, after the house had been bought, decorated, furnished, and the gardens manicured and augmented with rosebushes and young fir trees, Angelo and Cora began to entertain some of Angelo's friends and clients. Paintings, heavily carpeted floors and gleaming furniture gave the visitor a sense of opulence.

The Torino family came to dinner one night, when Cora was away visiting in New Orleans, and were pleased to see the elegant atmosphere Torino's protégé had arranged for himself. Torino nodded with satisfaction as he ate pasta and veal, and drank his favourite chianti. The Torino daughter studied the contents of the house, but remained silent. Angelo smiled at her.

As Torino was cutting himself a wedge of apple, to accompany a small slice of provolone, he said, 'Angelo, all you need now is a nice wife, to manage your life, your house.' He smiled and munched his cheese.

'Oh Johnny, he's not ready for marriage yet,' exclaimed his wife. The daughter's eyes were downcast and the blood drained from her cheeks.

'One of these days,' said Angelo, 'I must give it serious thought. I'm so busy in the court – you know how it is.' Then he smiled, adding, 'Wait until I am a judge.' He looked meaningfully at Torino.

'One of these days,' repeated Torino, 'suddenly you're an old man.'

'One of these days,' said Angelo. 'Soon, I hope to give some serious thoughts to marriage. And I know exactly who the girl should be,' he added, smiling into Torino's eyes. 'I only hope I'll be the lucky one.'

Chapter Three

Adolph Katz approached Tony Hacha at the Greendale Democratic Club one day, invited him for a walk and a cup of coffee and surprised him with a highly personal proposal.

They were in Sam's Prague Restaurant, seated at the counter.

'I've been watching you, young man,' he said to Tony, as he sipped his coffee. 'You're doing fine. I like what I see and hear. But you could improve your position a lot by one little step.'

Katz paused and studied the young man's reaction.

Tony's expression was polite. 'You sure got me interested, Mr Katz.'

'Marriage.' The word was uttered and Katz sat back waiting for a reaction.

'Marriage? You mean for me to get married? I don't even have a steady girl,' said Tony, laughing. 'Mr Katz, don't you think I got a lot of time yet, before getting hooked up?' Shyly he said, 'I'm kinda young.'

'Yes and no,' said Katz. 'The future I see for you calls for having a family background. A wife, a coupla kids, a solid home. A real, dependable citizen. A lot of people respect a family man. They would rather vote for a married man with children, than a bachelor. Some people even think bachelors are fairies.' He laughed. Then he added, 'And I got a wonderful girl for you. Comes from a good family; the girl's clean. Pure. Know what I mean? Not a floozy. She'll make a good wife, a mother.'

'Who is she?' asked Tony. 'Do I know her?'

'Alex Havlecek's daughter. He owns a chain of meat markets. You've seen his name around? You heard of him? No?'

'Yes, I know his markets, Sure. A rich man, no? I see his trucks.'

'Very solid. Comfortable. And the girl – Lucy Havlecek is her name. I want you to meet her. A very sweet girl; plays the piano, sings nice. Meet her, Tony. Soon. Want to make it this Sunday? We can drop in for a drink, coffee, a beer. I know you'll like Lucy. A pretty girl – and I will guarantee it, Tony, a virgin. Her father is strict. They'll like you. Is it a date?'

Tony thought quickly. Something important was beginning to happen. His instincts told him to accept Adolph Katz' guidance – the man was powerful and was looking out for Tony's future. What could be wrong with getting himself a nice young wife, with a rich father-in-law? His brain began to whirl as the potentials started to fall into place.

'Do you think Havlecek would finance me in the real-estate business?' he asked. 'I've got some ideas and I have a lawyer – maybe a partner. But I'll need maybe an extra ten grand or so to start. I would want a nice office; something respectable. Know what I mean?'

Adolph Katz beamed. The boy was a fast learner, thinking in the right direction.

'You can count on it, and Tony, I like your thinking. Real estate is where you can be respectable: solid; a nice place to make money. You'll be a real somebody, yet. You'll see. So we have a date. I'll notify the Havleceks: Sunday, for a little visit. And Tony' – he smiled, putting his hand on Tony's shoulder – 'get that suit pressed. I want you to look like a proper businessman, a somebody. Okay?'

'Mr Katz, I'll buy a new suit. I need one anyway. Leave it to me. And a fresh shine on these shoes, you bet.' To be a somebody!

'Good boy.' Mr Katz was gone. Tony sat for a few moments, then ordered a beer. A golden sunrise was building in his brain.

Lucy Havlecek turned out to be a pleasant surprise. She was a jolly, plump girl, with mature breasts, a bright smile, and alert eyes. The eyes got to you at once, smiling eyes. She seemed to respond to Tony's style, traded wisecracks with him. He was at ease immediately and was informed, with a giggle, that a few of the special dishes to be served for dinner were hers: a great dumpling with apples and raisins of which he ate two large helpings; and a nut-bread served warm, baked in individual portions in miniature loaves.

Tony and Lucy's family took to each other with warmth and good spirits, and Lucy's mother whispered to her husband that a 'marriage made in heaven' was in the offing. At which he nodded gravely as he puffed on his Dutch Masters cigar with satisfaction. Yes, Tony was a good catch. He liked a man who could tell a joke, and this one seemed to be on his way up. Adolph Katz would never steer them wrong.

After two months of dating with Lucy – involving several evenings at the Golden Slipper where she proved to be a lively dancer – they made their decision to marry at once.

Tony's head was spinning. Despite all his experience with whores in his Division Street apartment, he was aching to take Lucy to bed. Seducing her before their marriage was, however, unthinkable: bad strategy.

Telling Viola and the girls of his impending marriage called for a special kind of tact, Hacha realised. The girls would have to be understanding, sympathetic to his needs

and purpose. He had a position to maintain, and he was moving up in the world. They would have to want the liaison, for his own good, which meant their own good, too. There was a mutuality of interest here.

It was almost midnight on a hot Saturday. The radio was filling the air with Sammy Kaye. Tony had ordered two very special bottles of champagne – the best label – and three four-ounce jars of Iranian caviar. (They had been lifted from the Stop and Shop stock-room refrigerator that noon, on his orders.) He didn't particularly care for caviar and champagne: beer, cheese and salami were his favourites in addition to bourbon. But he knew class, wanted his announcement to be dramatic, gala, snazzy. So he provided the fancy trimmings, and when the last john had left, he called the girls into the living-room. All the lights were blazing. There was an expectant look on the girls' faces.

Tony sat down heavily on the sofa, in its exact centre, with a great smile on his face. He was wearing his new 'executive' rimless glasses, and they gleamed brightly under the ceiling lights. (Adolph Katz had instructed him in the matter of the style of glasses.) The girls had been told that an important announcement was going to be made around midnight; they were to be prepared for happy news.

Viola came first; she had obviously repaired her make-up and looked reasonably fresh, her blonde hair brushed and shining, her lips freshly painted. A pair of red satin slacks and a white chiffon blouse comprised her costume. Her high, spike-heeled slippers gave her, Tony thought, an especially sexy look.

Annie and Dolores came in shortly after, also freshened up and sprightly despite a long hard day and night in their bedrooms. Annie sat on a hassock in the corner, hugging her knees, her naked crotch in full view.

Tony, noticing her, studying the exposure for a moment, said, 'Annie, go to the refrigerator and take out whatever you find there.'

The bottles of champagne were properly iced and the jars of caviar had their covers removed and stood in the centre of a platter with lemon slices and chopped eggs and onions, with small crackers all around. The little grey-black eggs glistened.

'Wow,' said Annie, setting out the feast. She repeated the 'wow' as she scooped out a cracker full of caviar. 'A birthday party, huh?' She grinned. 'Whyncha tell us and I'd a baked a cake,' and she wolfed down her caviar.

'Hey, what gives?' asked Viola, studying the bottles and tray. She waited for Tony to speak, then said, 'Gotta surprise for us, Tony? Somebody hit the jackpot? Somebody die and leave a million, huh?'

'Sure, sure,' he said, smiling, arms stretched out along the back of the sofa. 'But come on, get yourself some of that caviar and bubbly. Here, let me do it for you.'

Annie brought over the first bottle and he proceeded to open it. The wine came foaming out and he poured it into kitchen tumblers. At that moment, the doorbell rang.

Framed in the doorway was a young man, good-looking in the Hollywood style, tough, sleek but not cocky. Probably in his late twenties. Hair black and slicked down, shining like enamel; fashionable black patent leather shoes; a grey pinstripe double-breasted suit with a red silk handkerchief just visible in his breast pocket. A snappy dresser and sexy. George Raft's long lost brother! thought Viola, but more intense. His smile did nothing to improve the first impression on the girls. His eyes missed nothing, and he was secure.

Tony greeted him with great warmth, called him Counsellor, brought him into the room and introduced him elaborately.

'Meet my good friend, Angelo. He'll be a judge soon, confidentially. He and me gotta partnership plan set up. But first: a big piece of news. Are you ready? Wait! A glass of wine for Angelo.' It was poured and fetched, and as he sipped the wine Tony said, 'Ready?'

They all nodded, fear, apprehension well concealed. 'Yeah, Tony, spring it.'

'I'm getting hitched! Tomorrow is my wedding day.'

He waited, searching their faces. Viola responded first.

'Terrific news. You son of a gun. Who's the lucky broad – I mean lady?' she asked, her jealousy and growing anger concealed.

'You don't know her. But I can tell you, you'll like her. A real doll. Aside from liking her, you'll be crazy about her father. Guess who her old man is . . . Alex Havlecek! He owns a chain of meat markets – Havlecek's six markets all over town. From now on, we get the best steaks, the best cuts, wholesale.'

Angelo put his arm around Tony's shoulder and bear-hugged him. 'You sure know how to keep a secret. I'll bet she's a beaut and you're not trusting her with any of your friends. Right?'

'Yeah,' Tony grinned, 'I wouldn't trust her with you, my partner.' He laughed and they all joined in, although none thought it much of a laughing matter. Pimp was written all over Angelo's face.

Tony broke into a boxer's stance, made a grimace of ferocity, then dropped the pose. 'Let's fill 'em up. I've got more to report.'

The girls came over and each gave him a sisterly kiss on the cheek. Dolores brought him a glass of wine. He took it in one long gulp.

'So, you like the idea, huh? Me, a married man. Well, it will be good for my politics. But, I gotta tell you this. She's great, my wife-to-be, but she don't know nothin'

about my private business, neither her father. It gotta stay that way. I'll tell you something else. You all know who Adolph Katz is. Well, he's my friend. He introduced me to my wife-to-be. He got big plans for me, in politics. He's got big connections, you know. He got more power in his right thumb than the police commissioner in his whole body, maybe more than even the Mayor. Capone, Torino, Nitto – they all listen to him. The bankers too. And the bookies, hah!' For some reason he began to laugh, then he continued, pointing his finger at no one in particular.

'Well, he got big plans for me, like a father. One: for openers, I'm setting up a real-estate office, real legitimate. Two: I'm joining the Benefit Societies, the Building-and-Loan Associations, the Sokols – every organisation you can name; you name it and I'll be there! Three: I'm gonna be a big man in Greendale. I'm gonna organise Greendale and deliver the new Mayor's votes – one hundred per cent Democratic – we gotta win the next election. How do you like that?' He was sweating suddenly. He removed his glasses and polished them with his necktie. He seemed to be rethinking, reviewing what he had said. He examined the girls' faces for reactions. Viola studied him, remembering his beginnings, the tough kid of about ten years back. He had done his computations.

'We gotta look into the unions,' Tony continued; 'we gotta help the labouring man. Right, Angelo? I'll be busy, very busy. Angelo will be helping out. Right?'

'I'll be there, where and when you need me,' said Angelo, smiling.

Sweat was dripping down Tony's forehead and Tony pulled out a giant-sized red handkerchief and mopped his brow. His stomach was bubbling. He shoved the kerchief beneath his shirt, blotted his chest, wiped his armpits. 'We'll show the bumfucks downtown some muscle, eh,

Angelo?' said Tony. He grabbed the second bottle, twisted off the wire and fat cork and began to refill the glasses. The girls slapped him on the back, kissed him affectionately.

Angelo was smiling broadly now. 'Attaboy, Tony. You're going to be a big man in this town: and I'm here to help.'

'I know I can count on all of you. Did I mention that Angelo – he's gonna be a lawyer in three months, and then a judge, yeah, he's going to be my partner? When he talks to you, he's talking for me. He's my friend, my partner – and *your* friend.' Tony paused, narrowed his eyes, and the silence was suddenly ominous. He added slowly, 'And nobody fucks up our plans, see, nobody; and everybody gets a cut. Okay? Live and let live. And boy, have we got plans.'

'When do we meet the bride?' asked Viola.

Tony grinned. 'Ah. Soon, but you gotta excuse me for not inviting you to the wedding. It's kinda private. Family stuff, you understand. You'll meet Lucy by and by. That's her name: Lucy Havlecek. Havlecek's Meats. And Lucy ain't bad in the meat department. She got a nice pair.' He roared and everyone applauded.

If ever a *gemütlich* atmosphere prevailed, it was here and now. They all helped themselves to more caviar. They would not forget the name, nor the substance of Tony's announcement. Times were a-changing, Viola said to herself. No reason to feel insecure; but watchful, yeah. And she was mindful of the fact that, for the first time in their relationship, Tony had not confided in her in advance.

Tony left for the bathroom. Angelo said, 'I hear great things about you broads. I got a coupla places around town; Mr Torino is my boss. You all know Mr Torino. A great man. No bullshit with Mr Torino.'

Annie looked at him and said, 'I know Mr Torino. Nice man. Real quiet, a sport too.' Privately she thought, Man, you are a real operator. With class. Watch out.

Angelo looked at his watch as Tony emerged from the bathroom.

'Tony, girls, you gotta excuse me. Gotta get some shut-eye. It was a real pleasure. I'll be seeing you in a day or two, Viola. We got some business details to discuss.'

'A pleasure,' said Viola. 'I'll be here,' she said, smiling.

Tony saw him to the door, stepped outside for a few moments, then returned.

'Well, kids, let's knock off for tonight.'

Viola stared at Tony; he recognised the look. The sensual lips, the invitation in the eyes.

'How about one for the road, Tony,' she said. 'You're getting hitched tomorrow. You gonna be real faithful to Lucy, I hope – after tonight?'

They all laughed. It was good-natured fun; fooling around on delicate ground but nothing mean intended. Tony put one thumb under his left suspender and grinned broadly, proud of his success, his growing powers, proud of the sexual potency he felt, the friendship of the girls and the many colleagues he had working for him, with him. Producing cash regularly. He was getting to be a real somebody. He glanced proudly around the bright, garishly furnished room. He stood at the threshold of a great career, was already up in the world and climbing.

'Viola, you gotta big heart. Sure, why not,' and they both went into the bedroom. He had one hand on her ass and she gave it a wiggle as the door closed.

Later, when Tony had left, Viola climbed into bed with Dolores. She turned out the light and cuddled behind her, spoon-fashion.

'You know, I think I smell trouble ahead. I think Mr Angelo is a shit.'

'I can smell it too,' said Dolores. 'You and me, we got problems. And everything was going so good with us here. Sheeit!'

'Yeah, Angelo is trouble – 'cause he *is* Johnny Torino. Double sheeit!

'And Dolores,' said Viola, her voice trembling, 'don't ever trust a man, ever. No man. I taught Tony everything he knows, and I helped him become a man, a somebody. I gave him the best times of his life; and I don't get invited to his wedding. Remember this, Dolores, as long as you live; men are shit. The funny thing is, they think we are.' Then she added, 'And watch out for that Angelo guy – that big nose of his – it tells you a lot. A horned monster!'

She turned over and was soon asleep. But as she slipped into unconsciousness, her mind was on vengeance. Anger was in her blood; the thickness of it was in her throat.

The wedding service, performed in the Greendale Church of the Holy Name, by the priest whose friendship Tony Hacha had enjoyed – through favour and financial contribution over the years – gave him a satisfaction and mystical fervour he had never before experienced. He had, standing beside him, this young woman, Lucy, an innocent and eager girl, unspoiled and certainly unaware of the true character of the man she was marrying. He had an inspired, lofty overview of his life, past and future, rich in resolve and dedication. Certainly, neither she nor her mother or father knew of his background, his activities with whores, the bribery and skulduggery in real estate and political matters. But now that he had reached this new plateau of respectability, a man of substance with community position and city- , nay state-wide reputation, he was fulfilling a dream and about to realise the power and position that befitted him. This young and pure wife would be there to serve him and his needs, would help

him establish the image he was determined to achieve in the public forum. A pillar of society, a force!

Tony participated carefully in the elaborate ceremony of marriage. A smile was on his face as the words rolled over him. His rimless eyeglasses gleamed; his new, blue-black tuxedo had been cut to order by a Michigan Avenue tailor patronised by the fashionable men of the city. As the ceremony came to its climax, as the great organ and the choir built up sound and emotion, he felt that he was floating upwards, and he raised his eyes to the stained-glass window overhead. As the sun's rays suddenly refracted and intensified, pouring downward upon him and his bride, he felt sanctified, anointed and appointed.

How Lucy felt at that moment was another matter. Her thoughts were on her bridal night and the responsibilities involved. Her mother had given her oblique indications and warnings, hints of painful pleasure, and she could feel, standing beside this young bull of a man, intimations of a memorable night to come. Lucy was also mindful of the proud position fate had chosen for her – a man with a golden future before him. She would manage!

He made a resolve to contribute substantially to the church, to the local charities. He also thought, in passing, that the school system was about to benefit him personally. The six-acre plot of land on which the city would build a small athletics field for the high schools in the area, would be coming to him since he had, by curious coincidence just two weeks previously, purchased an option on the land. His father-in-law-to-be assisted him in this delicate matter. A profit of some eighty thousand dollars, give or take a few thousand, was to come his way. It was a good life and he would secure it well for himself and his family.

The Hacha-Havlecek wedding was one of the biggest,

gaudiest events in years in Greendale. The Havleceks arranged for a catered party on their lawn which was almost an acre in size, overflowing with flowers, fruit trees, potted plants. A five-piece band, ten barrels of beer, two bars running with wine and hard liquor; steaks, turkeys and hamburgers, cakes and cheeses and fruit – it was a dazzling display for the hungry, the celebrants. And a polished dance-floor had been set up. More than one hundred guests and numerous children made the wedding an unforgettable shindig. Some of Tony's top brass friends were there including well-known byline newspaper men, local and state-wide political figures, and the powerful Mr Katz together with his handsome blonde wife. Katz introduced Tony to his wife and she proved to be a gentle woman, elegantly dressed but modest. He learned later that she was an ex-manicurist and that Katz was mad about her – trusted her totally and took her to Palermo and Cuba and Vegas.

Angelo Minelli was there, and also present were construction contractors, a few lawyers, several judges. The physician Dr Breakstone and his wife were present as well as two of their sons and their wives. And surprising, Johnny Torino and his wife and daughter were on hand. Torino's presence was the most surprising since he almost never attended public or social affairs.

The wedding presents were piling up conspicuously. Tony and Lucy danced and cavorted happily. He joked, hugged the women, sparred with the men, drank and made sure that the newspapermen had the best cigars and plenty to drink. Lucy's parents beamed, proud of the distinguished guests brought to their house by their new son-in-law.

While whirling Lucy around, Tony spotted a familiar figure in the distance – a young woman in a yellow flowered silk dress and a wide-brimmed garden hat with a

narrow veil-edging that covered her eyes. He realised suddenly that it was Viola, and he suppressed a curse, a cry of anger, as he had told her – only yesterday – that he couldn't invite her to the reception. In bed with her just the night before, he had assured her of his warm feelings for her, his devotion, but pointed out the folly of her appearing and meeting his new family. The bitch, she couldn't resist coming.

Tony decided to ignore her, concealing his fury by kissing his bride conspicuously and taking her off the dance-floor and into the house. Once in the house he said, 'Let's ditch the party now, let's get lost – just you and me. We done our job as hosts.'

'Oh, so soon? Aren't we even going to look at the presents?' Lucy pleaded. But she sensed that something was wrong and decided to leave well enough alone. Tony was not a man to argue with – this she knew.

'We got a terrific double suite at the Seneca Hotel, just you and me, we'll have a private party, just you and me. Let's scram.' He ushered her out of the front door, ordered the specifically hired chauffeur to drive them off to their honeymoon hideaway.

As the chauffeur drove them away, Tony patted her thigh.

'This is the way real honeymooners do it,' he said.

Viola saw them leaving. Furious at the rebuff, she went into the dining-room where a mountain of wedding presents were on display. She knew that Tony hadn't seen her gift. She removed the gift card from it, borrowed a pencil from the security guard at the door, added a few words to the card and replaced it on the animal's cage. Her gift, a white Siamese kitten, with a huge pink silk bow, stood in the handsome wire cage, miaowing, waiting to be released. The security guard smiled as he saw the unique gift and she winked at him.

'I don't know about Mrs Hacha,' Viola said, 'but I know that Mr Hacha likes pussy.'

Angelo Minelli watched her leave the room and couldn't resist inspecting her gift. When he saw the message, he grinned, removed the card and put it in his pocket. The young couple never did learn who gave them the Siamese kitten and Viola was shrewd enough to know when to keep her mouth shut. It remained one of Minelli's secrets, and he often chuckled as he recalled the audacity of Viola's attempt at revenge.

Having left his wedding party early, Tony missed the surprise of the day – a blazing display of fireworks: bursting rockets and flaming wheels, star shells and exploding firecrackers (courtesy of the paving contractors, the Giancana Brothers) began to appear at early twilight.

The dancing and music continued into the evening, the beer continued to flow from the barrel-taps; fast duple and other dance rhythms had the crowd laughing, fevered, sweating. Red and emerald flares emblazoned the sky; a breeze suddenly began to blow up, causing the garden lanterns to swing almost in time with the music.

While the Giancana Brothers' firecrackers and rockets continued to explode, Tony, at the Seneca Hotel, was busily indoctrinating Lucy in the honeymoon arts: champagne and fellatio. She became gaily drunk and followed his orders in quick-study fashion. She even introduced a few of her own innovations.

So they missed the wedding party fireworks, but staged their own, memorable fleshly pyrotechnics. After consuming two quarts of champagne in their bridal suite, they passed out on the living-room floor, naked as the proverbial jays. A maid, attempting to prepare their beds for the night, studied them on the carpet, bodies entangled and bare, and she waved to her floor associate, a little Polish

maid, to come and look at the 'floor show'. They closed the door quietly, stifling their giggles outside.

'I must tell my old man about this tonight,' said the older maid.

Adolph Katz phoned Tony two days after the wedding. 'That was a fine wedding party,' he said, 'a real blowout.'

'Thanks very much, Mr Katz.' Tony was still on semi-formal terms with this so-called king-maker. 'My wife and I were proud to have you among our guests, and many thanks for the present – and everything else. The missus says thanks, too.'

'Don't mention it. A fine girl, Lucy; you'll have a fine family. Anyway, if you can spare the time, I'd like to see you in the next few days or so.'

Tony was flattered. 'Name the time and place. Maybe I can buy you a lunch?' Acting as luncheon host to Adolph Katz would be a new social rung on his dream-ladder.

'No, Tony, you be my guest. How about tomorrow, at Mike Fritzel's?'

'It's a date, Mr Katz. What time?'

'Twelve-thirty. I'll make the reservation.'

'A date, and thanks very much, Mr Katz. See you tomorrow.'

Tony hung up, beaming. He took off his glasses, sat back in his swivel-chair. What could be on Katz' mind? Mr Katz didn't waste time with pikers, small potatoes. Lunch at Fritzel's! All the newspaperboys would see them together.

'Sophie,' he shouted to his secretary.

'Yes, Mr Hacha.'

'Make a note: lunch with Adolph Katz at Fritzel's tomorrow, at twelve-thirty.' As though he might forget.

'Wow,' she said, softly, but loud enough for him to hear.

'It's confidential, Sophie. Got it?'

'Yes, sir,' she said, smiling.

'Come in with your book. But first, get me a double liverwurst on rye, with a slice of onion, and two Schlitz.'

'Coming up,' she said, ready to perform an over-familiar errand – for the man she suspected would soon be running for the Mayor's job. No less!

Adolph Katz was, in a sense, monitoring Tony Hacha's life. Six months after the wedding, he proposed that he expand his private operation, and he helped Tony rent a double apartment one block from his former Division Street address. Though never personally present, nor in any overt manner active in this phase of Hacha's business, Katz was aware of his activities. Two more girls were added to the establishment: a Chinese girl, aged eighteen, from Taiwan, and a Jewish girl from New York. A roulette wheel and several slot machines were introduced to 'add a little extra attaction to the joint'.

The Jewish girl Selma was, like Viola, a specialist in oral sex and loved to instruct the girls in exotic practices not commonly employed. Her clientele built up rapidly and her income (shared by Tony of course) became a major factor in the establishment's weekly take. Selma was volatile, insatiable. Short, plump, with curly red hair, a blazing red pubis, protruding breasts and wide hips, she was in every respect a red-hot asset, a 'live number'. She also loved telling sex stories and one-liners. The place hummed. New clients began asking for 'that Jewish broad'.

Tony had meanwhile moved upwards, politically, and become secretary of the United Societies for Local Self Government, spawned in the sawdust environment of saloons. Later, he became a leader in the Democratic House, representing Greendale. He began to sound off about the Republicans, and in particular, made crushing

and obscene remarks about Big Bill Thompson. One of the most corrupt mayors the city had ever had, Big Bill hated Hacha with a burning passion; but despite his vile remarks and his belligerence, Hacha's name began to be whispered about as a personage with a Great Future – unlimited potential. It was during this period that he amassed a personal fortune of two million dollars, his first two million.

The baroque lettering in gold and black on the store-front window declared boldly:

ANTHONY HACHA
REAL ESTATE

* * *

ANGELO MINELLI
ATTORNEY-AT-LAW

At the lower right corner of the window, in smaller, simple letters, was *Greendale A.C.*

The office was located in the heart of Greendale, on the city's West Side. Looking through the large plate-glass window one saw two giant rubber plants in huge wooden pots, one on each side of the window. Beyond were four desks, and behind them a frosted-glass partition. Two young women, both attractive, were busy at typewriters. A young man, a teenager, was busy at a large filing cabinet. A Siamese cat was sunning itself in the centre of the window. It was a warm, late spring morning and all seemed quiet and wholesome on the street: a typical peaceful big-city neighbourhood street.

There was a serenity about the office and the street itself. A few pedestrians were out strolling. Next to the Hacha-Minelli office were a barber's shop, a Chinese

laundry, a confectionery shop where tobacco was sold, and bets allegedly placed, in the rear. Dobrovsky's Saloon was at the corner of the street and it was already busy despite the early hour. There were the regulars, old-timers who required alcoholic eye-openers before noon; a few retired teamsters who made it their first stop of the day, taking a few modest beers for openers.

Many of his neighbours were Germans, Swedes, Poles, Bohemians, Irish and Italians – but the majority in the area were Slavs, Czechs. There were dozens of saloons within a space of five square miles, and also beer gardens and cafés, and reportedly, about a dozen 'houses', or brothels, ranging from two-girl flats to houses with as many as ten occupants. If the police or the housewives were aware of them, nothing was ever said. But each of these establishments was controlled by what came to be termed the Syndicate.

Tony Hacha was known to all of them, as was Angelo Minelli, newly established attorney-at-law; and notably, Johnny Torino, whose presence was felt everywhere although he was rarely seen except in his 'office' at the Four Deuces on State Street.

Tony patronised most of the saloons, beer gardens, cafés; he would drop in for a glass, a joke, a slap on the back and a reminder of political allegiance to the Party. Even though he had dinner at home, he would make impromptu visits to cafés late at night, 'for dessert and fellowship'.

At the back of his office, behind the frosted glass wall, he and Angelo had large oak desks. There were a few extra chairs, cigar boxes and huge ashtrays; there was also a small bar against the wall where bourbon and rye were always handy. Tony closed his deals there, but other business was handled as well, political matters, including simple jobs for relatives and friends – and relatives of relatives.

Tony was available to everyone. And his two attractive secretaries were trained to be extra courteous to all comers, particularly the poor, jobless, troubled. There were always candy balls in a jar on their desks, for the children.

Often, when complaints were made to him about crime or prostitution or gambling, Tony would quote an earlier political figure, Mayor Harrison, who said, 'You can't legislate morality.' And Tony would add, 'And who would want to?' with a laugh and an invitation to a drink.

Tony Hacha was the prototype of the go-getter. He was now more disciplined, more in control. After all, he was a family man and pretty prominent at that; married to a respectable woman from a well-respected family. He owned his own home now and had an infant daughter whom he treated like a princess. He was frequently seen pushing a perambulator on a Sunday morning, cigar in mouth, eyeglasses flashing in the sunshine.

A quasi-anonymous retainer and hanger-on was a young hood named Jimmy Belcastro. Hacha and Minelli employed him for serious, but tough assignments. He would drop in from time to time; take on tasks that called for roughing up. He was also an unofficial bouncer in the office when difficult situations arose. He was disliked by Hacha but he yielded to Minelli who favoured his all-utility usefulness. Belcastro was also feared since he was totally fearless. He and Minelli had an understanding that was never discussed with outsiders.

The incumbent Republican Mayor, Big Bill Thompson – a clown and blow-hard but nevertheless a third-time winner as Mayor, boasting twelve years of riotous, vaudevillian behaviour – was surely going to be stopped. The city's bankrupt treasury was an asset to the Democratic Party's campaign, and Hacha had developed a reputation for financial savvy as well as political cunning. He was

constantly espousing labour union causes and attended many of their meetings. He was popular where it counted and one of the few politicians welcome to Schlogels, the hangout for newspapermen and writers, including Carl Sandburg and Lloyd Lewis.

Angelo Minelli, who had now achieved his law degree, gave him a helping hand in legal matters. His advice was shrewd. He managed to get information, through pipelines and 'connections' unnamed, about the city's construction plans – playgrounds, schools, paving programmes, city properties – long before they were made known to the contractors. Hacha knew how to manipulate a contract, secure the bids. Several large parcels of land, including some rather remote farmland, came under the Hacha-Minelli axis – in the name of Hacha's father-in-law – and was then resold to the city. A large new school was built on Hacha-Minelli acreage, held and sold in the name of one of their relatives. Their dealings were legitimate. Everyone made a profit, and Tony's numerous bank accounts were growing spectacularly. He treated himself to a summer house near the lake, in Ann Arbor, Michigan, a house that became a special gathering place for 'pow wows'.

Tony knew how to handle dissension. He could read a political situation or a labour union problem like an accountant reads a balance sheet. And he would zero in on the problem, iron it out, end up with drinks all round, and a suggestion that they all take a drive with him to a certain hotel on Twenty-third Street, for further discussion of a more relaxed nature.

By 1931 Tony Hacha and his partner had more than two hundred whores working for them, in seven different districts of Chicago and its outskirts. And Tony was also about to become a father for the second time.

Tony knew the whole town. While he owned Greendale

(*owned* was his boastful word) he was recognised and respected in many other areas. Occasionally, in tough situations, with Jimmy Belcastro accompanying him – quietly as a shadow but menacing – he was able to create an atmosphere of awe.

Tony's intimates knew that it was from Viola that Tony had received his sexual initiation as a boy. Despite the many women available to him, Viola was the woman he loved. Subconsciously, he knew she had corrupted and enslaved him, sexually. And he loved the enslavement. He had offered to set her up in a private hotel apartment – as his private domain. But she laughed it off.

At thirty-three, Viola still thought of herself as a girl, as did Tony and everyone else. She seemed ageless in dress and manner; her eyes were clear, her skin unmarked, her teeth even and bright. And she spoke her mind.

Angelo often joked about Viola, said Tony was in a rut, needed a transfusion – younger blood.

'Sure,' said Tony, 'I'm game for some fresh cunt, but nobody takes Viola's place; she's got somethin' special for me.'

'Yeah, I know,' said Angelo, suppressing a smile, 'she copped your cherry.'

Tony often bragged that he didn't understand the word 'defeat'. When he became president of the County Board, and also Democratic political boss of the state, friends thought he had reached the summit. 'King of the Hill,' Angelo called him. But for Tony it was merely step one. He tried for the United States Senate and lost. But he refused to face it. 'Can't hit home runs every time at bat,' he said. 'Not even Babe Ruth. There'll be more chances – and I still got my health. There's ginger in these balls,' he said, patting his crotch.

But his health was not precisely all it might have been.

From time to time, abdominal pains distressed him. Dr Breakstone called it colitis, something about the 'blind gut' or intestine. Medication and special dieting helped ease the pain, but there seemed to be no permanent cure, short of surgery, a procedure he was unwilling to experience – yet.

He worked harder than ever. He was speaking out publicly now against crime and corruption, and against the new evil known as the Mafia. He insisted that it was an alien idea imported from New York and Detroit, but in fact he knew better.

The cash flow from the brothels continued to increase; his talent for real estate was impressive, and while he publicly showed a passion for civic duty and morality, his true interest lay in land and buildings, and his personal fortune grew at a staggering rate. When pressed for details he'd put on a show of modesty: 'Oh, I got a couple candy-store operations and I'm not missing any meals.' Actually, he had lost count of his growing assets.

Tony had stopped using his fists long ago. By organising his countrymen, the immigrants, the greenhorns, he was able to make his climb. His United Societies organisation – his own invention – was the rock on which he built. His membership list was in part a *Who's Who* of gangland. 'I use my brain-muscles, no more knuckles,' he would boast.

Tony was invited and tested by an exclusive millionaire's group, The Club. While he may not have been sure which fork to use at dinner, nor whether the finger-bowl was for drinking or dunking, he found a warm response in his hosts. They knew he wasn't always after the last top dollar. Adolph Katz had vouched for his integrity and creative imagination, financially and politcally. A realist.

While they were going to use him – as he himself used

others – he found them in turn the best possible means of climbing his own particular ladder – to the Mayor's office. No less.

At one of The Club's impromptu 'inner sanctum' dinners, held in Wilmette at the home of a member, Hacha was delighted to see his old friend and doctor, Jeremiah Breakstone. Said one of the members to Tony, 'Confidentially, even though he's a Jew, he's the only doctor in the city I'd trust in the case of an abortion or a stomach cancer operation.'

Hacha was already aware of the doctor's credentials, intimately aware, having employed his services in some private and trying situations, going back to his young manhood.

'By me,' said Hacha, frostily, to the silver-haired, oyster-eyed Wilmette blue blood, 'religion don't count. Breakstone is solid gold, and my friend.'

Dr Breakstone had a good part of his assets tied up in real estate. He complained constantly to Hacha about the excessive taxes he was obliged to pay. Several of the mail-order and department-store owners, not to mention a famous meat packer, asked if Tony could not work out a means, legal of course, to help them lessen their back-breaking tax burdens. It was suggested that Tony Hacha might be the man, the catalyst, to tackle this particular problem.

Tony's foot was now in the door. He did indeed have some suggestions, and after conferring with Adolph Katz and Minelli, he came up with a confidential proposal. It was not long before Hacha became in effect the city's one-man tax assessor.

As president of the County Board and Democratic boss of the state, Tony was ready to move up on to another plateau: he could name (with the covert assistance of certain Club members) the next Governor of the state.

First, of course, he had to be elected Mayor, no small enterprise. But that was now, it seemed, a foregone conclusion to Tony and his new-found supporters. Wheels were to be greased; highly respected members of the community were setting Tony up. Of course it was all legal; except that each member of the Tax Assessment Committee knew in his heart that he was perpetrating the grandest larceny in memory, a kind of miniature Tea Pot Dome rip-off, as one newspaper columnist later called it.

No one was ever prosecuted, nor any individual's name or reputation tarnished. Hacha was a co-operative man who could go far. Among his Club associates he was becoming a hero: a simple bohunk immigrant who, despite his lack of education, had worked out a vast tax loophole that would save his friends many millions of tax dollars.

It was in the course of setting up this operation that Tony learned more about his personal doctor's private interests and potential usefulness. Dr Breakstone's hospital affiliations (some new to Tony) were of the highest order; he also owned and operated an East Side private clinic where he and his staff performed delicate operations. His speciality was the gall-bladder, abortions, the prostatectomy, knife wounds and the unrecorded removal of bullets from gunshot wounds.

Tony could be seen often visiting, chatting with, union leaders. He would also stop and joke with street cleaners, cops, mailmen. He knew the gambling parlours and the pool halls. He always had two pockets filled with cigars – 'campaign bullets' he called them – of the best Havana quality. He would make unexpected appearances where Swedes, Bohemians, Lithuanians gathered, and at Sokol meetings. He was a frequenter of prize fights, ball games, the races. He was always ready with a joke, a witticism in the mother tongue, an amusing obscenity. Once, addres-

sing a South Side Negro club, he claimed to have some Negro blood. When challenged on racial intolerance, Tony claimed he had been breast-fed by a black mammy. A newspaper cartoonist once portrayed him in black face. H knew a dozen Yiddish expressions, too. Often said *'Shalom'* to Jewish friends.

Tony cultivated newspaper reporters, seeking them out in their favourite taverns in the Loop and elsewhere.

He was always good for a five- or ten-dollar touch, or a loan to take care of a medical bill, maternity expense.

Tony rarely got home until midnight. Frequently, he made a last stop to spend an hour with Viola. His relationship with her was deep, one of the most durable of his life, though it was virtually a secret from most of his friends. She was his touchstone, and he valued her frank, outspoken opinions. Hacha's wife had heard of her, but was shrewd enough to know that this was a subject best left alone – a closet secret she must respect.

The cultural and public relations development in Tony's life was a rapid one. He held two boxes at the opera – he was an early supporter of Samuel Insull's new opera house – and loved being seen there prominently even though he had trouble staying awake during most opera performances.

He wore white flannels and blue blazers frequently.

One of his greatest cultural triumphs was instigated by his most devoted secretary, Sophie.

One afternoon, thinking of new schemes to enhance his public image, he asked Sophie, the bookworm, as he called her, for her suggestions. He summoned her into his office.

'Sophie, I want some good personal and hoity-toity publicity. You're smart, you get around. You know about books and opera and stuff like that. How do I reach the white tie-and-tails Society muck-a-mucks without having

to join their horse clubs? Charity contributions aren't enough. Everybody gives. What I want is publicity; you know what I mean – publicity that pays off where it counts – on the Society pages. I'd like a few stories in the *Tribune*, for instance.'

She thought for a moment then said brightly, 'One of the greatest Czech composers is Smetana. Do you know of him?'

'Never heard of him. Czech, you say?'

'Yes, Bedrich Smetana. He died about fifty years ago. They are giving an all-Smetana concert at Orchestra Hall in about ten days. He was a big man in our cultural history. A lot of Society people will be there, and the press of course. It's a special affair – the very first all-Smetana concert in our city. Frederick Stock will be conducting. Why not buy some seats and give them away to the people you want to impress? Won't cost you more than four or five hundred dollars.'

He thought a moment, then struck the desk with the flat of his hand.

'You're a real smart girl, Sophie. Smart girl. When is the concert?'

'I'll look up the date – on my ticket.' She smiled. 'I already bought one for myself.' She delved into her purse. 'It's a week from Saturday.'

'Okay,' he said, 'order one hundred seats – fifty pairs. Prepare a list of guests: Society people, some brass from City Hall, some of the department-store execs, the Breakstones, Minelli, some of my cronies – you know what I mean. Get a coupla big-name writers too. Tell them the tickets are from me, free – they're my guests, see?'

He considered this for a moment, then added, 'Let's do it right. Set up a fifty-plate dinner at Henrici's after the concert; pick the top names for the dinner. I'll give a little

speech there. Eh?' He was smiling broadly now. 'And maybe you can fix a little background information for me, and a short speech. You know what I need.'

'Consider it done, boss,' she said. 'Now I got some work to do.'

She got to work at once; secured one hundred tickets and sent them, with an affecting note signed by Hacha, to fifty couples, letting them know how dear to Hacha's heart Czech music was and how proud he was to be their host at the concert – and at a supper later. Not a single ticket remained unused.

At Orchestra Hall that evening as he sat, looking about, waving to a few of the members of his Club, he felt he had reached the pinnacle of social position and power. He noted in the programme that selections from *The Bartered Bride* were to be performed as well as *From My Fatherland*. Colonel McCormick's mistress, a singer of sorts, was to perform in *The Bartered Bride* sequences. 'A terrific composer, Smetana,' Tony kept repeating; 'a Czech, you know, the great composer from my homeland.'

After the concert the Hachas were escorted backstage where they shook hands with Stock. On meeting him, Tony said, 'Some time you must have an evening for the music of another great Czech composer, Anton Dvořák, and play his great "New World Symphony".'

Friends overhearing the comment were astonished at Tony's unsuspected musical sophistication, not knowing of course that Sophie had coached him carefully in this conversation piece in case he met up with the famous conductor.

Frederick Stock shook his hand, smiled and said that he had conducted Dvořák's 'New World Symphony' many times, and that he hoped one day to have an all-Dvořák evening. Ah culture, thought Tony; he must do more of

this. So easy, so inexpensive, so effective. It was a cement he would use to hold all areas of Society together – for his personal gain. Impeccably dressed for the occasion, with his wife on his arm, Tony was *somebody*. He would give Sophie a little bonus; a present for being so smart.

Later at Henrici's, when coffee had been served he rose, pulled out a small sheaf of paper and begged the attention of his guests. He read his speech, glasses sparkling, his diction in careful control. He spoke of the fact that from its beginning, the city had sponsored and encouraged musicians. He mentioned that the great Adelina Patti had come to sing here at the age of ten; how operas and concerts were a city tradition going all the way back to the old Crosby Opera House; how the citizens would line up for tickets to hear German, French and Italian operas when the New Orleans and New York companies were in town. And the great Jenny Lind, she sang here, too, and what an ovation they gave her! Cheering young men had unhitched the horses and pulled her carriage through the streets to her hotel. As Tony related this tale one would have thought he had witnessed it himself. He also spoke of Theodore Thomas, who came from Germany in the early 1800s, played and conducted throughout the land, and eventually settled in Chicago to conduct in the city's new auditorium, heading the great Chicago Symphony Orchestra. The hall seated five thousand people and it was always sold out.

'Mediocrity is the curse of art!' Thomas once said, and Tony Hacha echoed the precept in loud clear tones, and added, 'It's also the curse of politics.' Everyone applauded.

The evening was a triumph for him, there was no doubt. And privately, for Sophie too.

Again, it was she who alerted Tony when Karel Capek's play, *The Makropoulos Secret* came to the city. Tony

secured two rows of seats for the opening night, and hosted a dinner party for the Czech playwright-novelist. His political colleagues and acquaintances throughout the town were impressed, and the event was reported in the Society and literary sections of the press. He was mindful of the cultural impact he was making on the community: a reputation as an exponent of Czech art, music and literature. And the votes would come!

Another of Sophie's suggestions was that (although tone-deaf) he should subsidise an all-Czech string quartet. It was to be called the Hacha Czechoslovakian String Group, devoted to performing music by Czech composers. The group played throughout the United States and even produced some recordings. It brought Hacha's name to the attention of a segment of the population he could never have reached otherwise. His accountant showed him how the entire expense was tax deductible, which added to his pleasure in the enterprise. The children of his business and political friends were frequently sent complimentary tickets to the group's concerts, adding to his reputation as a true benefactor to the community's cultural welfare.

Judge Angelo Minelli sat in his study at home, on Greenwood Avenue, expectant but deep in thought. The desk clock showed the hour as nine, and the messenger was due. The street lights were on, the fireplace alive with a freshly-laid log fire. He had had his dinner, alone, and was enjoying his cognac quietly. As he checked the time he heard the doorbell ring and his servant open the door to greet someone. He waited, and in less than half a minute, his servant knocked.

'Come in, Jacob,' said Angelo, and the man entered, bearing a thick three-by-six-inch package, wrapped with adhesive tape in heavy manila paper.

'Thanks, Jacob. Take all phone calls. I'm not going to be available to anyone – except Cora, of course – for the next hour; just take messages. Okay?'

Cora had gone to the theatre with some friends and she was not due back for at least another hour and a half.

As Jacob closed the door, Angelo rose and turned the key in the lock. He then went to the windows and pulled the drapes together, shutting out the street view and the world.

Back at his desk he removed a knife from the drawer, snapped out the long spring blade and began to cut open the package. He enjoyed removing the wrapping, then he lifted out the contents of the box, softly. There were five hundred slightly-used fifty-dollar bills snugly packed and waiting. He sat back in his deep swivel-chair, continuing to stare at the money, the price paid by one of the city's richest meat packers for his playboy son's freedom. Bob Lavore, one of the multi-millionaire Lavores, had killed a whore in the posh new brothel, Alexandria's. The Lavore lawyer had argued self-defence. An emissary of the family then let it be known that Bobby's life was worth $25,000.00 in cash. Angelo, still in his judicial robes in the chamber, had nodded to the emissary, an elderly, elegant relative of the Lavores.

'It is obviously a case of self-defence,' he had said sagely. 'The girl did have a reputation for violence. The money must come in fifty-dollar bills – used bills – in a plain wrapper. To my home, tomorrow night at nine. Now, please excuse me,' and he rose to enter his private walnut-panelled lavatory.

Within a period of three years, since his appointment to the Criminal Court Bench, Minelli had recorded most privately in code that he had been paid off on twenty-two occasions; and always in the designated, used fifty-dollar bills, and always bills in non-consecutive order. In his four

safety boxes in four different banks in the city, he had safely stashed away, according to his notation in a vest-pocket notebook he carried, over four hundred thousand dollars.

Judge Minelli found cash, in particular fifty-dollar bills, almost the equal of sex – the pleasure he derived from young women's bodies. The tactile pleasure he got from riffling the green bills – especially when they appeared in three-inch thick wads – was indescribable. He had set his heart on the fifty-dollar note – it was the safest denomination – because there was virtually no hesitation on anyone's part in cashing it, whereas a one-hundred-dollar bill was often subject to scrutiny.

He sat back in his chair, cast his eyes upwards and contemplated his good fortune, his gratifying way of life, his power, the heaven-sent blessings. Life could be good, abundant. A smile crossed his lips.

Chapter Four

A mean pisshole of a room, thought Belcastro, slouching in his chair, observing the grimy glaucous walls over his five-card hand. Then he started to laugh – an odd *sotto voce* undertone, as he looked at the three hoods seated around the yellow oilcloth-covered table. What prompted the laugh – if laugh it could be characterised – was the realisation that two of them were named Jesus and Angel. The third one was called Stan. It had never occurred to him that many Italians were so steeped in religion that every other child bore a religious or biblical name. Christ, how many Marys and Josephs he knew. The Jews, too, favoured Old Testament names: Rebecca, Abraham, Moses, David, Isaac . . . Why not?

The three hoods, sitting and playing listlessly, began to annoy Belcastro. A hate was building like a slow fire within him.

Through the cardboard-thin wall he could hear someone's phonograph playing Ben Pollack's recording of 'Deed I Do', faintly. Suddenly, the green-shaded lamp hanging over the table bothered him. What was he, Belcastro, doing with these fucks, so definitely out of his class? He had brought them up to his room for a quiet game. Stan was an okay guy who understood Belcastro's problems; the two others, the hoods, were mainly for company, the game.

The music from next door was irritating Belcastro; he was not in a lovable mood. A straw-basketed quart of chianti stood on the table, together with assorted dime-

store tumblers. Stan, the young dirty-blond with oversized ears, was shuffling the deck. He was humming nasally, while sucking on a foul-smelling black cigar. His shirt was collarless, his pants too large about the waist and ankles, his braces red and three inches wide, a rustic clownish pair of pants and braces that belied his true profession: he was a killer.

'Stan,' said Belcastro, softly, pleading, 'can't you cut the hummin'. We don't need no floor show. And Stan, that cigar – it smells like camelshit. What is it, a two-for-a-nickel stogie?' He studied Stan's face: a lump of stale cheese, he thought.

Stan examined his cards, his eyes narrowed, and he made no reply. He laid down his cigar elaborately, paused in his humming. 'I pass,' he said.

Jim Belcastro was lean and swarthy, baleful-eyed, five-ten, an ex-pugilist with a boxer's putty nose. Gunwise he was, and past his mid-thirties. He sat in his sweaty white shirt with a black sateen necktie, his black trousers narrow at the waist, unpressed and showing a shine at the knee. He was playing draw poker with his chums for a half-buck limit on a cold, damp Friday on the South Side – the maggoty side – in a fleabag called Men's Hotel. It was situated on the edge of noplaceville, a kind of hell, on the lower end of Prairie Avenue where teenage girls – black, brown, grey and white – peddled ass, or blow- and hand-jobs at twenty-five and fifty cents; the hardier ones took it up the ass for a dollar. It was 1933. Post-Depression, many light years before the inflationary era, the era that history was to enshrine as the Time of Confusion.

The room was unheated. Belcastro was physically at odds with his environment and the climate. Three months earlier he had been the guest of the Big Fellow at his Miami Beach home, following the liquidation of a certain

party. Swimming in the Big Fellow's pool, surrounded by palm trees, was as close to heaven as one could hope to get. Gilded pleasure. Belcastro thought of the swimming pool, the sun lounge and the bar service, those Miami babes on call. Tits and ass, suntanned and firm and accommodating. The smell of suntan oil! It was all a bare three months ago, in a place where the sun warmed one's bones and ravished the skin with an aura of health.

Here, now, owing two months' rent, stewing in a rancid room, in the dying throes of ostracism, he knew what it meant to be without clout. A professional hit-man, shiv-for-hire, he had been placed in the deep-freeze for almost three months. On the skids, expendable. The ignominy of his status was chewing at his gut by the hour. And he was enduring, with growing pain, the socially unwelcome companionship of these hoods who sat here, drinking pisswarm wine – hoods fully aware of his tapped-out condition, his hour of shame.

'Let the music play just a little longer' was the number drifting faintly through the flimsy wall; shit music – how he hated it, detested Dixieland, swing – all that *shit*.

Belcastro was dealt a new hand. He sorted out the cards sullenly. He looked up and around the table, as though searching for a friend. Then turned back to his hand. The pathos of his situation struck him forcibly; he felt the acid rising in his gullet. Disgust, anger, defeat, then pure pain filled him so that he could almost feel a bubble of anguish swelling in his throat. He stifled a cry.

'These fuckin' cards,' he shouted, striking the table with his fist.'Shit cards you deal.' In a fury he threw his hand across the table then reached for his cigarettes. Then he poured himself some of the wine. He took a deep draw from his cigarette, drank some of the wine then spat it out on the linoleum. 'Piss,' he said in disgust. 'Pig piss.'

There seemed to be no reaction from the others. Only Stan's voice saying, 'Nice cards.' He was smiling.

'Nice cards,' repeated Belcastro. He muttered something inaudible, lifting the bottle to his lips, forgetting that he had just condemned the wine. He swallowed, sucked deeply on the cigarette and stared at the dealer.

Then he got up and went to the bathroom where he rinsed his throat from the tap, urinated, and combed his hair.

'Bug up his ass,' said Stan, to no one in particular.

The dreary scene was not lost on Belcastro. He had known many happier days, including a two-room suite at the Ambassodor East (*East*, mind you) with room service, a bar and one of the 'lovelies' from the Chez Paree chorus-line. The pathos and degradation of his present lot assaulted his consciousness, and he punched the offending wall twice, shouting at the wall, 'Turn off that fucking Victrola – turn it off!'

A muffled reply came through the wall – a woman's voice – and the words, 'Up your asshole, asshole,' came through clearly.

The deadpan humour of the response from the other room intrigued Belcastro. For a woman it was audacious, or it meant she was smashed. He appreciated it. It was nicely terse. Spiky and nice. He'd like to meet the bitch. Maybe, on this grim night he was destined to fuck, to ease his pain.

'C'mon, let's play,' said Angel. 'My deal.' Angel was a six-foot-four hulk, a one-time football star, a natural double for Frankenstein's progeny. He began to mix the cards, shuffling and reshuffling; then he dealt.

'This hand better come through,' said Belcastro, 'or I gotta find me another goddamn dump.'

Belcastro had been, in the past, a prime mover in heavy action, under the auspices of Torino, and also via the Big

Fellow. He had personally been entrusted with jobs by Capone, had disposed of six men in the space of two years. In all instances he had accomplished his mission quickly and efficiently. Garrotte and torch were two of his tools. His fist could crush a face. With a well-placed bundle of dynamite he could turn an entire city block into rubble. But of late, unwanted, in a kind of limbo, he had begun to ponder the mystery of human relationships. He had been loyal, dependable. Maybe he was fucking too much, and it showed. Cunt and booze. He needed discipline and confirmation of his worth and talent. Action. He was galled by the news of that young tough recently imported from Minneapolis. (The Polish hood who came to town with a Japanese broad. Imagine! They all called her Nookyaki.) Anyway, when they knew Belcastro was available . . . His image was fading – at thirty-four! Somebody was badmouthing him . . . Whose broad was he laying that could be responsible for his banishment? He could think of only one, and he hadn't seen her in a month . . . and he trusted her. A staleness was setting in. Paranoia was building up in and around him.

He studied his new hand. A fistful of nothing. Angel was examining his cards close, whispering to himself.

'F'rchrissake can't you read the fucking numbers without moving your lips?' barked Belcastro.

They began to discard and order new cards. The bidding started. Aside from being a sucker for high stakes poker, and not forgetting his first love, the ponies, Belcastro was notoriously sentimental and susceptible when it came to pussy: blond, *café au lait* or black – in that order or in any combination. He was also partial to *zaftik* Jewish and Italian whores who were, he maintained, the most abandoned.

As he arranged his new hand, studying it languidly, his mind reverted to his last affair, the wife of a corporation

lawyer whose work took him to New York every few weeks. Sylvia Moroni was in her mid-forties, hot and tight, on the plumpish side; alive, eager, willing and able – and hungry; talented as a hundred-dollar whore but free of charge. Belcastro thought how he liked it when she whimpered as she came; it pleased him in some special way, to hear her cry like a child, vulnerable, as he stroked her engorged and welling clitoris. Sylvia needed no fancy dates, no night-clubs or dinners, no gifts – but lots of fucking. She also had her fits of ferocity, when she would go down on him like a female Dracula, eating him endlessly, balls and all, until he cried uncle. Then she would come up from submersion, teeth full of hair, saliva and strings of gism all over her face – the mouth of a smiling, sated tigress.

She would tell him stories about her husband. 'In and out, push and pull, in and out, then over and snore, snore, snore. That's my husband the great corporation lawyer. Always on Saturday night – once a week. A five-minute operation including, you should excuse the expression, foreplay.'

'Tell me about the foreplay,' said Belcastro, grinning. 'I might use a little education.'

'Do you really want to know?' she asked, searching his face.

'Yeah, does he go down on you, stick his tongue up your ass, what does he do?'

'Wrong, wrong. He pinches my nipples, then runs his finger up and down my pussy a couple times; also he squeezes my ass – he likes that.'

'And this is his foreplay?'

'The whole ball.'

They would howl together. She would recite the ritual and end with, 'But he makes good money, buys me everything: and a cook – a cook for the two of us, with a

little company once in a while, like his mother or brother. Dullsville.'

'You've got it made, baby,' Belcastro would tell her solemnly. 'It's every girl's dream. All the money you need and a good stud on the side.' He would examine her, eyes narrowed. 'Do you think of me as a good stud?'

'Oh more, Jimmy darling,' she would reply. 'I wish you and I could get married – you're everything I want, always dreamed about. If only you had a good steady job, a good profession.' She paused, hesitating to ask. 'I don't even know what you do for a living.'

'I told you,' he said smiling. 'I'm a prize-fighter, except that I haven't had any matches lately. I live off my savings.'

Sylvia laughed. 'You don't even let me know where you live. I never saw you fight – I'd love to see you in the ring, with those gorgeous muscles going; but I wouldn't enjoy seeing you bloodied up. No, Jimmy, I couldn't stand seeing you hurt.'

He would laugh, telling her it was much more tame than she imagined – a lot of fakery, phoney punches, a friendly give and take.

'Yeah,' she said. 'Well, I don't believe that. I've seen some fights, and movies, and I don't like it. I hope you don't have to fight any more, Jimmy. You're gorgeous. I'd hate to see you hurt.'

'What would your husband say if he heard you were fucking a boxer? Such a refined (hah!) Society lady. Going to the fights!' He shook his head. 'No, Sylvia, we gotta keep our arrangement private – a secret. Just between us. And by the way, I'm temporarily broke. I need an emergency loan. Sorry to bring it up but I think of you as my friend.'

'Sure, Jimmy.' She reached towards the chair where her handbag lay. 'How much?'

‘Can you make it two hundred?’ he asked, softly. ‘Until the first of the month?’

‘No problem.’ She handed him two crisp bills. Then she brought out another fifty. ‘Just in case.’

A broad with a heart. That was two months ago or so. He had moved out of his hotel room and had not given her his phone number. He was unable, unwilling to call her; and his cock had gone into a remission he had never known before . . . His pride had been struck below-the-belt.

As he sat there, playing his cards dejectedly, he continued to think of the sexual side of his life, how women rarely failed to respond to him, to his loving toughness in bed. He thought of the octoroon in Judge Minelli’s house; and his crotch swelled as he recalled his last visit with her – actually in the Minelli house, in their very own sacrosanct bedroom no less, a kind of miniature cathedral with portraits of Christ, a huge crucifix, a great Bible and the incense odour of the church everywhere. It had made him feel like an evil cardinal. He had enjoyed the desecration he brought to the bed in that oppressive, heavily furnished, ecclesiastically solemn room; and he remembered vividly Cora’s flesh, her pinkish, dusky skin against the satin sheets. He had been there just once, but they often met in hotel rooms when the judge had to leave the city on business. Belcastro had met Minelli several times and privately conceded that he would not care to have him as an adversary. The judge’s power in the city was well-known; the Big Fellow was his friend, as were Torino and Hacha. Cora feared the man. According to her, she had been bought in New Orleans. White slavery, thought Belcastro, of a very high order. Like a Turkish sultan, no less.

Well, Belcastro too could consume women as he chose. Yet he knew, somehow, that Judge Minelli was a voluptu-

ary of a special kind and that he, the stud, was not and could never be on his level. Besides, his profession and rumoured wealth made him a kind of fortress one did not readily approach, or encroach upon.

Suddenly, the phone broke through the atmosphere like an alarm in a funeral parlour. It wakened him from his reminiscing mood. The players froze, halted with the cards and turned to Belcastro. A fucking tableau.

A call at last. Mission? A job? His hard-muscled face tightened; then he pointed to Angel and said, 'Say it's the Belcastro *residence*. Ask who's calling. Keep it crisp.'

Angel rose and picked up the instrument.

'Mr Belcastro's residence.' Angel made it sound like *reddidenze*. Angel had cauliflower ears and didn't hear so good, either. As they waited, the intensity of the silence in the room became painful.

'Tell him it's a very close friend of his; he'll want to talk to me.' The voice was female, honeyed, southern-accented. Such women rarely spoke to Angel.

'Gotta tell me your name, lady,' Angel insisted.

A pause. 'Tell him it's Cora,' she said softly.

His hand over the mouthpiece, Angel said to Belcastro, 'A real cunt voice, nice. Cora she says.'

This is spooky, Belcastro thought. ESP at work.

He rose. 'Fuckhead,' he said in a whisper. He held up his finger and Angel said into the phone, 'Hold it a minute.'

He took the phone from Angel, holding the mouthpiece close to his lips. He studied the greasy top of Stan's head, eyes slitted; saw the prognathous grin on Angel's face. He heard Cora's breathing. She was obviously trying to control her agitation. The sound caused his crotch to expand. God was good; Cora cunt, you gorgeous cunt *calling me*; luck is still with me, on my side. Spread your legs, lady cunt, please, he was saying without speaking.

He pressed the receiver tightly to his ear, nerves taut and ready. This could be the turn of the cards, the great golden royal flush hand in the sky he'd been waiting for.

'Jimmy, I need your help,' she said finally.

'Sugar,' he said, trying to control his eagerness, 'it's great to hear from you, real nice.' The jovial, buoyant macho Jimmy, cocksman and bon vivant (not forgetting hood) being asked to help by the great judge's girl, a.k.a. niece! The jurist's private stock who two-timed him for reasons that eluded Belcastro – patently a dangerous game considering the judge's temperament, power and connections. He remembered the judge's warning eyes when Belcastro once appeared to greet Cora a bit too warmly at a reception. Luckily, Cora barely smiled at him in public, passing him quickly. A smart little octoroon who had made it in Society via a dynamite judge.

'Name it, honey.' A trickle of sweat was moving down Belcastro's loin.

'I can't take it any more, no more,' she moaned. 'He's killing me. He's crazy.' Then she added, crisply and clearly. 'There are fifty C-notes on my bedroom dressing-table, under the jewellery box. They're for you, waiting for you to pick up. All for you, Jimmy. Fifty C-notes.'

Incredulity. She was about to reaffirm the fact of life. But what sort of job did she have for him?

'Keep talking, sugar.'

What he wanted were those C-notes but also that honeyed octoroon tongue in his mouth, and his in hers. 'Keep talking . . .'

Then he heard her say the word, 'Iced.' He waited. The message was already clear. The juxtaposition of their needs was instantaneous, the purpose of the call understood, foreordained, a matter so urgent and desired, as though an electric current had produced and delivered this

message of intense mutuality and all he had to do was say yes.

'Not tomorrow, tonight, tonight. I want the sonofabitch iced, tonight.'

He said, slowly, his old professionalism at work, 'Where, when?' And he was already wondering about the means he would employ. 'Details. Give it to me slow. Play it out slow – I'm with you.' He would not pronounce her name – the hoods at the table were intent on the conversation.

'Okay, listen. I'm checking into the Sherman Hotel in an hour. The kitchen door here will be unlocked; the key will be in the lock, for you to take when you leave. Come right away. Go to my – our – master bedroom, the big one; wait for him, Jimmy, he'll be here in a half-hour or so. Close the back door when you leave. Come right away – to the Sherman. Got it?'

'What else? The hotel room number?'

'Room 1202. I have a reservation. Come as soon as you can. Don't fumble it; he's tricky, real smart, strong. You know what to do? Then hurry.' And she continued in another tone, 'Jimmy, I'll have a very special bonus ready for you; and the two quarts of Black Label. Also' – she paused – 'the perfect alibi. And listen, Jimmy – you are listening to me, honey? – pussy wants to say hello. I'm putting her on the mouthpiece now. Taste it, sweetie.' She added in a whisper, 'I just dusted her with Joy, Jimmy.'

She sounded like a New Orleans whore now. His kind of whore. She waited for his reply.

Finally he said, 'Done.'

Belcastro hung up, went directly to the bathroom and opened the tarnished mirror-window of the medicine chest; a quick snort of the white stuff was in order. But the Bromo Seltzer bottle in which he kept it was gone. Shit! Some sonofabitch had swiped it.

A swarm of roaches suddenly appeared and skittered away in all directions. He searched the shelves in vain, slammed the door in disgust, cursed. Aside from the almost empty bottle of chianti, there was no booze in the place. He needed a lift. Gin would help, he'd pick up a pint on his way. An amphetamine. An upper was what he needed, but his source was uptown, and there was no time. Shit. Shit!

'Some cocksucker took my Bromo Seltzer,' he said, to the room in general. No comment. 'I've gotta go uptown,' he said, stressing the 'uptown', indicating in unmistakable terms where he would say he had been in case questions were asked. Despite the missing coke, his performance was flawless. He'd pick up some coke after the job was done, do a number on that old, steel nerve on his way to the Sherman – and Cora.

He would indeed be going uptown, to the Sherman, but first, the rendezvous elsewhere. In his gut he felt a power building; and he saw a naked Cora sprawled across her bed, waiting. He sketched out the job to be done. Target: Judge Minelli. His pocket held the weapon; it would be quick, one shot below the ear. No games, no discussion, no questions. Quick. Bang, *finita*. And the C-notes were waiting for him: under the jewellery box. He hurried down the stairs, hailed a taxi. The sky was a glaucous smear with flashes of neon here and there. The stockyard smell was hanging suffocatingly in the air like dirty laundry. But the traffic was light and the driver silent. He was on his way. And as he rode, he thought, Tomorrow we go to Miami Beach, Cora and me. Two weeks of fucking, sucking, sunning: lobster and ribs and good booze and every fucking night-club in town, and a terrace of our own for sunbathing, and the biggest suite at the Fontainebleau. Fuck the cost. And now, operation Minelli.

There was one detail of which Belcastro and Cora were

unaware: their conversation had been automatically wire-tapped and recorded on a plastic spool in the locked tool-room of Minelli's backyard garage. Nor had Cora heard his car pull into the yard as she was hanging up. In less than ten minutes, after checking his recorded messages, including the conversation between Cora and Belcastro, Angelo Minelli was in the house, up the stairs and in their bedroom. She was almost dressed now. Before she could speak he was upon her. He was a raging, roaring bull. He ripped off her unzipped dress, her bra and panties. From behind, he caught and held her head with thumb and forefinger; then he pulled a penlike instrument from his inner pocket and pressed a button that released an awl-shaped needle which he held to her throat. As his lips moved close to her ear his eyes swept across the head-board of the vast bed and he saw, momentarily, the gleaming life-size crucifix, a sixteenth-century gilded wood-and-ivory carving he had purchased in Rome. It dominated the wall. He averted his eyes, uttered a few words in Italian, a language he barely remembered.

'Don't move. Bend down, forward,' he ordered. He held her with one hand while he unbuttoned his pants and attacked her ass with a fury she had never known; and when his cock entered her rectum in its second thrust she had no way of knowing anything as he slipped the needle into her ear. It penetrated two inches into the brain and she fell forward, flat, to the floor, with the judge upon her, panting.

After a short pause he rose, studied her face and buttoned his fly. He lifted her up, pulled the body to the door, a thin trickle of blood oozing from her ear and rectum. In death Cora looked wide-eyed, supplicating, extraordinarily seductive.

He was now breathing normally, his equilibrium restored. There must be no tell-tale evidence. He turned

and surveyed the room: noted first the purple and crimson altar cloth, embroidered with heavy strands of gold, on which stood a huge branched candelabrum with two thick white candles. Beside it lay a leather-bound folio Bible, edged in gleaming gold, on an ancient, elaborately carved Spanish table. In opposite corners of the room stood two dark mahogany and leather chairs; and there was a glowing, darkly varnished painting on the wall – a massively framed, splendid and certainly costly, copy in oils of El Greco's *St Veronica with the Sudarium* – with the face of Jesus to which Angelo Minelli prayed and crossed himself each day. The sense of Christ – his crown of thorns – the trickle of thick crimson blood – permeated the room. The air was heavy with incense, commingled with Cora's perfume and sexuality: the effluvium of cunt. Cunt, sperm, musk vapours. The naked woman on the floor near the door, the frozen and tragic figure of the man above her, the scene was pure opera, touched with the Grand Guignol. One could almost hear the cello-laden orchestral accompaniment, underscoring the tragic moment. Minelli stood there as though lost in prayer, lost in some kind of canonical hour; and then he pulled himself out of the reverie, searched the floor quickly for incriminatory signs. The anal and aural ruptures had produced tiny pools of blood, caught in the pale texture of a small Aubusson rug. There were no other signs of violence. He pulled the rug forward, wrapped Cora in the tapestry, mindful of the extravagance of his action. Carefully he surveyed the room, avoiding the religious objects, crossed himself, and muttered a prayer for forgiveness and understanding. The he dragged the body out of the room, carrying the calamitous burden down the back stairs and out to the yard and garage.

The Minelli house, a Tudor replica, tree-protected, on Greenwood Avenue a bare mile from the Black Belt, was

the former home of the city's leading mail-order merchant. It was located two miles from the Drainage Canal. Angelo Minelli, jurist and devout churchgoer, given to charitable acts and various forms of justice, had a job to do.

Belcastro had his taxi drop him off three blocks from the judge's house. He began a slow saunter down the street. It was clear of pedestrians, clear of the security patrol. He turned towards the Minelli mansion. Suddenly, he saw the lights turn off in the upstairs rooms. His instincts screamed 'Cul-de-sac! Trap!' He moved cautiously towards the driveway adjoining the house, and then he saw a man, unmistakably the judge himself, carrying a rug-wrapped body. No mistake. The rug seemed to glow in the dusk. In a shattering, heart-breaking flash he realised what had happened. He ducked. What had gone wrong? His knees turned to rubber, his heart began to race. A nausea was settling in. He took deep breaths, turned, walked quickly into the shadows, trying to continue the deep breathing, keeping it deep and even. Should he take a shot at the judge, and would he be able to get him? He hid behind a row of privet and azalea hedges; the scent of an unseen flower assaulted his senses. Could it be forsythia? Was he losing his marbles? What was happening to him, why his concern for odours, flowers? Crouching and waiting, he decided to stay put, regain his equilibrium before moving. Everything was going wrong. He was in a play but without direction, without lines. Then he heard the roar of a car – a high-powered Mercedes-Benz – from the Minelli driveway. He had not noticed the car in the dark shadowed drive; and now he saw it speed off, southwards.

The situation was dismally clear, ironic. Paralysis of will set in. Belcastro realised that he could not act, could not

enter the house. He moved like a somnambulist. He had lost his nerve. Anguish and impotence were dissolving him. For Belcastro the Mighty, it was no hit, no run, no cunt, no C-notes – and a narrow squeak. The mother-fucking, cocksucking, buggering judge had unmanned him, taken his big chance out of his hands. Belcastro was now up to his knees in shit and there was no place to go because a criminal court judge named Minelli had top-dogged him, killed his dream and his darling octoroon. Farewell self-love; hello loser, champ jerkoff . . . His vision turned kaleidoscopic. Palpitations set in. He vomited.

The next morning a female body, aged about twenty-four, blue and naked, sodomised, was found floating in the Drainage Canal amongst human waste and used condoms. The medical examiner found blood in the rectum and some bruises at the throat; he also found a delicate gold 'slave chain' on her right ankle with the letter C etched in its diamond-studded locket. (A rich man's slave.) She had an icepick puncture in the ear, though some other instrument might have caused the rupture, the examiner said. She was placed in a long metal drawer, awaiting identification. The examiner commented to his aide that this babe was the most beautiful specimen he had ever handled in all his years with stiffs in the county. 'Where was she when I needed her?' he asked rhetorically, proud of his elephantine joke. The aide responded with a mortuary look, he being, as it happened, both black and the father of a beautiful young daughter of Cora's age.

Belcastro saw his horizon reduced and bounded by defeat; his cool was gone, as were his funds. Being totally broke can drive one to quick self-destruction, as many a stockbroker learned in the winter of 1929. He was fuelled by desperation and anger, with bile in his gullet. That

morning, at the crack of nine-o'clock, he checked his .32, tried for a quick hold-up in a small neighbourhood branch of the National Trust and Savings Bank. While the teller was complying and putting packets of twenties and fifties into a canvas bag, as Belcastro had instructed him from the front of the counter, an old guard, a codger of sixty-four, seated and hidden behind the teller's position, pulled the trigger of his shotgun. The bullet went clear through Belcastro's right eye and resolved his fiscal, venereal and other worldly problems for evermore.

The elderly guard received a ten-dollar raise; and in accordance with the custom of the county, when no relatives appeared to claim or honour the remains, Jimmy was buried in an unmarked grave.

The event earned minimal space in the city's newspapers. 'Hood goes berserk in bank; killed by elderly guard,' was the essence of the story. One reporter, an expert on the city and state crime circuit, realised who the victim was and the story got a column and photo in the *Examiner*. Johnny Torino, who read the story at breakfast, nodded, poured himself another cup of coffee and asked his wife to fetch him his shoes. He also put through a call to Judge Minelli, whose interest in the news items, he concluded, would not be casual.

The matter of the murder of Minelli's alleged niece was never interpreted as scandalous in the press. Rather, it came under the heading of unresolved crimes. Angelo mourned her death publicly – even wearing a black silk band for a week – and offered a reward for the apprehension of her killer. In a few months, the incident was forgotten by most Chicagoans. Minelli sent a substantial cheque to his friend and priest, Father Anselmi, to cover the expense of a few masses for Cora and some repairs to the church's ailing boiler. Father Anselmi also had a few personal needs: new dentures and a set of tyres

for his Dodge sedan. The cheque would also help Judge Minelli bury the terrible secret of Cora's murder . . . not that there were necessarily any guilt feelings related to the incident. The doleful trajectory of this young life, prematurely punctuated, was as meaningless, as unheeded as a pebble tossed into a lake. After a few weeks, the matter, as a topic of discussion or conjecture, was erased from the minds and consciousness of the persons living and concerned. With one notable exception.

Approximately six weeks after Cora's death, Judge Minelli was brought up short by a letter from New Orleans. Eulalia Harris, ex-Storyville madam and alleged mother of Cora, wrote, 'I see by the papers that a young octoroon was found murdered in a canal and she was buggered and other terrible things and I can hardly believe it is about my dear Cora and if it is, the subject is too painful to discuss further. I wonder who she was???'

The three question marks indicated more than curiosity. Minelli stopped reading for a moment. Obviously, she had had someone write the letter for her; obviously someone was coaching her; obviously Eulalia was sharing some very private matters with an outsider.

He went on reading the letter.

> I got a letter from Cora about two months ago and I didn't bother to write you, but it disturbed me greatly. My dear, sweet Cora said you were mistreating her, and that you brought her great pain. You know what I'm talking about, Angelo. I want you to be nice to my girl if she is not the girl I read about which I am praying is the case. I will say no more on the matter. I don't want to make any trouble for anyone – you understand.
>
> PS Can you increase my monthly payments; the cost of living makes the hundred dollars a month look

mighty small. I'm an old woman and my medical bills are big. Tell Cora to write.

Sincerely, your friend,
Eulalia

Minelli knew an extortion letter when he saw one. Medical bills indeed! Drugs and booze. When he arranged for Cora's custody he had no firm proof that Cora and Eulalia were daughter and mother. She was fourteen years old, an alleged virgin and a delectable creature: granted. The monthly cheques over the past ten years amounted to a generous – almost extravagant – sum. Minelli was a man of action. He struck a match and put it to the edge of the letter, watching it turn to flame, then to ashes. He rose, began pacing his room. Then he rang for Jacob, his servant.

'Get me a drawing-room to New Orleans, for Friday night,' he said. 'If anyone calls, I'm in New York – got it?' He paused, then added, 'And I want a return ticket for Sunday afternoon.'

'Yes, your honour,' Jacob said.

Minelli sat down. There was cause for care – and action.

Of course Minelli's old friend, the distinguished surgeon Dr Breakstone, had few illusions and, for that matter, little outward curiosity about the Cora matter. They had met a number of times, in his home and at social affairs, but discretion was bred in their bones, and friendship, confidentiality and loyalty were the bricks and cement of their relationship. They had powerful mutual interests and involvements – many financial – that transcended public gossip. Dr Breakstone's hospital, for instance, was a beneficiary of Minelli's charitable contributions. Dr Breakstone, in turn, was often to be counted on for unofficial and emergency medical assistance. As for

Johnny Torino or the Big Fellow, they would never bring themselves to touch upon the subject of Cora. They understood where the boundaries of privacy and propriety ended. The standards of good behaviour were clearly indicated in this socio-political world.

Soon after Cora's death, Minelli chose another regular woman for his needs. But he did not espouse her publicly. She was a twenty-two-year-old mulatto from Atlanta who worked in his house as cook and housekeeper. She was a servant with extra privileges, which meant she could skim money off the household budget – in moderation, of course. She was available sexually, exclusively that is, at the judge's beckoning. She was both amiable and disciplined, serving his sexual requirements without allowing personal problems to enter into their relationship. She was a servant, he was the master. He loved to listen to her speech, often teased her, and encouraged her to speak low-down and bawdy. Her speech was heavily accented. 'Aw shit,' she would say, when their relationship was on a bedroom basis, 'Ahm jist a dawk skinned woikin' woman what loves cock.' Then she would add, grinning, 'Speshly yoh hono's cock.' To please her, His Honour would import for her drinking needs a southern brand called Raleigh Rye, a whisky she would sip from time to time, to enliven her performance, to help her forget certain grievances or bruises. Angelo would occasionally compliment her for tolerating some of his more exotic sexual needs. He would tease her, in her dialect, 'Lou Prouty, Mis Prouty, you is a spo't – a real good spo't,' and he would pat her on her plump rump, saying, 'A great ass, Lou, a real nice rump.'

One day he said to Lou, 'Do you like Jacob, Lou?' He had been pondering the possibility of his manservant, Jacob, playing ducks and drakes on the side, poaching on

his domain, a suspicion that prompted a new line of thinking.

'Yeah, I like Jacob,' she said, 'we're friends. But if you mean fuck, the answer is no. Yoh hono, like and fuck is two separate things. Ah knows the difference.' Then she added, 'He's a fine man, a good man – but not my style.'

Angelo looked into her eyes for a moment, then smiled. 'Right. Jacob and I are quite different. But he could make a good husband.'

'Mebee,' she replied, smiling. 'But not for me.'

Minelli left Lou. He now needed a few moments of undisturbed self-conspiracy. Whenever approaching a crossroads situation, a crisis, he would lock himself into his private place of worship, and hold communion, namely a monologue, in which he aired aloud the problem before him. He would address Jesus by name, once, then proceed to state his case. He usually emerged, clear-headed, back on the track. The room which Minelli formerly used as his master bedroom was now closed off, kept as a place for his personal needs, namely worship and inner searching. The religious artifacts were all there, intact. It was his personal cathedral; he shared it with no one. He used the second bedroom for sleep, and amatory pursuits.

He spent half an hour in his sanctum sanctorum, then came out, locking the door carefully. He went quickly to his office, closed the door behind him, sat back in his great leather lounge chair and picked up the phone.

Angelo Minelli dialled a number, reaching Johnny Torino in his usual Four Deuces office on State Street. The conversation was brief. Angelo asked Torino for permission to call on his only daughter, Mary. An unattractive, sullen-faced girl, she had for many years given Angelo the eye. This call represented one of the major steps in the carefully planned career of Angelo Minelli.

The entire world, or rather, the city's underworld, knew that Angelo was Torino's number one 'boy', that Angelo was his protégé and had been financed by him through school, his legal expenses paid by him; that Torino had given him important clients and taken, in return, some favours. Angelo had earned his years of 'keep' by one favour alone, getting one of Torino's killers acquitted, a hood who had shot down a state's attorney in cold blood. It had been a front-page story for many weeks, and Minelli's adjudication of the case created a furore in the city, and delight among the kingpins of the Torino-Capone Syndicate.

Now, Angelo, always a realist and a man of action, saw where his next step must be taken. Marriage. Respectability. Family. Torino's daughter was more than ready for marriage, and Angelo was the one suitable prospect at hand. Marrying Torino's daughter was a two-edged proposition. The girl was no beauty, the father was an immensely powerful, dangerous and rich man, and any man who married his Mary would be walking a tightrope for life. At any rate, during Torino's life. On the other hand, marrying a Torino daughter would offer, indeed ensure, advantages too obvious to calculate.

The phone call to Torino proved satisfactory. Angelo had a smile on his face when he hung up; Torino was delighted, it appeared, and invited Angelo to his home for 'a family supper' the following week.

Angelo arrived for supper with flowers and candy in the best tradition of the romantic suitor. Mary was, he realised, flattered by the attention of so distinguished a man. He pulled out all the stops in his repertory, joked, gossiped, handed out compliments. They made general talk at the table, and later, Angelo asked to take Mary to a late movie.

Johnny Torino and his wife, Anna, smiled approvingly,

and the couple went off. Two young romantics. Angelo was on his best behaviour and Mary quickly came to realise that he meant business: he held her arm, and in the movie-house took her hand and whispered, 'I hope you like me.' To which she replied, 'Yes, and I always have.'

After two more dates, a marriage was arranged, and, a month later, it was announced in all the papers. Minelli did some careful house-cleaning, including the disposal of Lou, who was housed at the Syndicate's Division Street whorehouse operated by the able and understanding Viola. Viola would look after her, teach her the ropes. It seemed to Angelo less than prudent to keep the woman in his house in a reduced status. Jacob was to remain.

Angelo had already made the trip to New Orleans where he visited Eulalia Harris to discuss the contents of her letter. The meeting was followed by a tragic event: Eulalia died of a heart attack, and it was so reported in the local papers. One of the last of the Storyville grand madams was gone. Her personal history, together with a rehashing of the legends of Storyville, was a one-day item for the pimps and whores and madams of New Orleans. Angelo Minelli was back in court the following Monday morning. His disposition, his courtroom deportment, his general demeanour had about them a controlled radiance.

The Minelli-Torino wedding party brought together several hundred members of the city's social élite, including the Governor, Mayor, state's attorney, prominent lawyers, businessmen, patrons of the arts, and even the city's leading poet, an overstylised Swede with theatrical mannerisms. The publisher of the city's leading newspaper, a colonel, was there with his mistress. Everyone agreed that young Judge Minelli had a great future, and privately confirmed it by virtue of his father-in-law's incredible powers. Absent from the joyous affair was the Big Fellow, who was having some difficulty with the

Federal Bureau of Internal Revenue over unpaid taxes on an alleged $105,000,000 volume of business. As Torino's chief lieutenant, the Big Fellow should have been the most visible of all the guests, but was instead most conspicuous by his absence, and the cause for much cautious speculation. As for Johnny Torino, for the first time in memory he was seen beaming, offering Cuban cigars, and circulating among his guests.

Up until the time he reached the Criminal Court Bench, Angelo mingled mostly with madams, whores, pimps, hotel managers, drug dealers, policemen, court bailiffs, bartenders. He had built up an awesome reputation for skilful handling of the brothel business. The logistics and finances of whorehouses were a speciality. The cost of towels and contraceptives, the problems of venereal disease, the responsibility of the brothel bouncer – such details were familiar to Minelli. He understood the art of handling policemen on the beat and their superiors – what the price was in each instance. And his knowledge of the psychology and physiology of women was legendary. There were no mysteries for Angelo, no illusions. He had learned the essentials of criminal law; he also understood real-estate law, and this category, in association with Tony Hacha, became privately his second speciality. Law and investments eventually made him a multi-millionaire.

Now, as a judge, he recognised the importance of style and status. His man, Jacob, performed many personal duties for him; but he had two young law clerk assistants who were to be trusted with more delicate or dirty missions. And they specialised in real-estate contracts, too. Angelo must now be seen mainly in the company of the city's leading citizens and socialites. Like his ex-partner, Tony, he began to cultivate a public image through appearances at the opera, theatre, concerts, and

cultural events reported in the press. His name appeared on many contributor's lists including the Art Institute and the Academy of Ballet, not forgetting a few hospitals and a Cancer Research Foundation. While his charitable contributions were literally pennies from his piggy-bank, his serious funds were carefully concealed. His profile, he knew, had to indicate a life style based on his salary and earnings from real-estate investment. He was far too shrewd, too much on guard, to overstep his position. In Judge Minelli's community, respect was now his due on every level.

Chapter Five

One winter morning Tony Hacha was given a telephone message. The Club was holding an unscheduled meeting that night and his presence was urgently requested. An important unnamed guest would be present, and vital issues were to be discussed.

When Tony arrived at the private dining-room of the Drake, several of the members were already there. He was introduced to the mystery guest, a man named Ed Webster. He recalled having seen pictures of him in the business section of the *Tribune*. This man, still in his mid-forties, was from Louisiana, a multi-millionaire and a power in politics and the real-estate business. Later, he learned that Webster was also a major paper- and lumber-mill operator, a sugar magnate, and a force in southern railroads. To top it all, he had married into a rich family – rich in the Rockefeller sense – and was considered a tough, thick-skinned, ruthless and roughneck character whose favourite toast was 'a plague on my enemies'.

After dinner they sat down, with cigars and bourbon amply available; and Ed Webster was introduced as an honorary member of The Club, bearing a message of importance to all present.

There was respectful applause. Each of the group studied the man, some with apparent scepticism. How could any stranger presume to come up north and tell a group of successful hard-headed businessmen and politicians how to suck eggs? They waited while the proverbial pin could be heard to drop.

Ed Webster did not rise to speak, he slouched in his chair, surveyed his audience, and spoke slowly, spitting out short sentences. He was here for personal gain; he liked a good fight, political or financial, and rarely lost one. Though a comparatively young man, he took on the aura of an elder statesman, and each of the group felt his power and assurance.

'Some newspaper fellers call me the leader of the Golden Rule Gang,' he said, thin-lipped but smiling. 'Well, whatever that Gang is – and I'm not going to make a speech about that – I want you to know we are interested in good government, lower taxes and the protection of our interests. Self-determination is my religion.

'By interests, I mean not letting the niggers move in; not letting outsiders take over our banks; by interests, I mean making damn sure the right man gets in the right public office – and that includes the judges – so that we can sleep better.'

He chuckled, took a swig from his glass and continued, 'I'm considered a tightwad. It's true. I know how to hang on to a buck. It's true that I hate the unions and left-wingers and I say, a plague on them.'

His talk continued in this vein. It was obvious that he would look out for his mills and railroads and banking interests – and fuck the opposition. He knew how to manipulate in all areas of society including politics. He underscored this particular talent.

'One newspaper hack called me a pathological self-centred tightwad,' he said, laughing. 'The cocksucker didn't mention that I administer fairly and squarely a charitable fund running into the millions – for sick kids, hospitals, the aged.' He paused. 'I mention this because there are two sides to every story, and I never pay attention to the other side even though I appear to listen carefully.'

Finally, he said he was going to come to the point and purpose of his visit to The Club.

'I was invited here because someone felt I could make a contribution to your welfare, individually and collectively. Well, I can. I know something about your city, about your state, and I know what your problems are. I've made a study of it all. Your taxes are ridiculous, your political leaders are weak. Nothing personal, please. This is one of the richest territories in America and you fellers aren't getting your just share. Now I have a simple plan, a blueprint. I took the liberty of preparing it when you invited me here. I'm going to let you read it and then we'll discuss it. I'm not going to let you take the paper with you – no copy must leave this room. It is for your eyes alone. When we leave this room the details of my proposal will be clear and fixed in your minds.'

He studied the group, smiled, took another sip of bourbon. 'Now, before we get into the nuts and bolts of my proposal, I want to answer a question that each of you must be dying to ask me, namely, "What is in it for me?"'

He paused, looked around the room.

'Am I right?' he barked. His eyes glittered. Tony watched his behaviour with admiration. A man with iron in his guts, dishing it out, straight from the shoulder, to a dozen of the most powerful men in the city.

'Okay, here's what I want in payment for the proposal I'm giving you, a proposal that will make you money and save you millions in taxes. It will also show you how to reorganise and how to get in and stay in the driver's seat, politically and financially.'

Again he paused. 'Now, as for my personal compensation: I want all of the city-controlled lumber business that will be coming out of the upcoming Fair – all the lumber to be used in the construction to take place here beginning next spring. I figure roughly three and a half million

dollars worth of lumber will be needed for your Fair buildings, and my lumber mills just happen to need that business. I've done considerable homework, you see. Say the word – and I'm willing to take your collective word – and we'll get on with the proposal sitting there,' and he pointed to a pigskin-zippered portfolio on the table before him.

'Mr Webster,' said Tony Hacha, 'can you give us some hint, some idea beforehand, as to the proposal you have for us? It's possible we are already working along the same lines. We have a new tax programme in the works, you know.' Tony searched the table and saw heads nodding in agreement.

'Fair enough,' said Webster. 'I think I can place the right man in the Governor's mansion, and with your help (and my guidance) you can put the right man in the Mayor's chair – and that man is sitting right here in this room. I can show you how to do it. And *that* Governor and *that* Mayor will work with this present group of citizens, and everyone concerned or involved will profit, heavily. I've worked out a plan of operation that has worked elsewhere: it's foolproof. I know how votes are gathered: it's like kid's play, building a house of blocks. Get the foundation set first – and I know a lot about foundations.'

He laughed at the word 'foundation', because he had been given some national publicity on his handling of a multi-million dollar foundation which was in his personal trust. They all laughed with him, savouring the humour of the allusion. He had won the famous case and scored heavily for his personal interests.

Ed Webster could talk lawyers' lingo, and the lingo of the street. He was acquainted with art and architecture; he had travelled widely, consorted with world celebrities, and while he was detested by many, he was also respected for his shrewdness, his man-to-man approach. If he was

going to be a son-of-a-bitch, he would be the first to proclaim himself such. He was a man one could trust – on his own terms.

One of the members of The Club, Greg Mitchell, rose and said, 'If you will excuse us for ten minutes, Mr Webster, we will give you our answer to your basic question.'

'Certainly, gentlemen,' said Ed Webster. 'I'll treat myself to a fresh bourbon while you have yourselves a pow-wow.'

The Club members filed out of the room. Ten minutes later they were back and had resumed their seats. Mitchell was their spokesman. 'Mr Webster, we accept your proposition. We will make sure that the lumber contracts for the Fair go to the Webster Company in exchange for your proposal, the Webster proposal if we may call it that as long as we accept it.'

Ed Webster smiled. 'You may not – repeat, *not* – call it the Webster proposal: I am to remain anonymous. And in accepting this arrangement, I want you to know this is the first time in my life I have entered into a business transaction on a purely verbal basis. Now we begin.'

He unzipped his leather bag and removed a dozen thin folders, each comprising ten sheets of paper, giving one folder to each member of the group.

'Please follow me as we read the proposal, gentlemen. When we are through, I will want each of you to return your copy to me and I'll destroy them. No newspaper, no outsider must ever see it, or know about it. And now, to the nitty-gritty.'

Tony Hacha, it appeared quickly, was to be one of the key beneficiaries of Ed Webster's proposals. He was astonished at the intimate knowledge Webster had of the city's political structure, and about Tony in particular. With minute attention to the basics he outlined his plan

for the upcoming election and for the workers in the Democratic Party. He pulled out a map of the city, and another one of the State, and pinpointed the course of action. His strategy electrified the group: here was a man who was showing them how they – this group in this oak-lined room – could literally take over the city. Webster was familiar with the entire underworld situation of the city and state – Torino, Capone, Nillo and the others. He showed the Club members how they would be obliged to work together, and how it would profit all of them.

In the course of the meeting it became clear that not only did Ed Webster want the lumber contracts but also substantial banking business; for he was a majority stockholder in one of the city's largest banks. He also owned a large tract of swampland adjacent to the area where the Fair was to be erected. When he mentioned this, several of the group burst out laughing. 'Well, I'll be a son of a bitch,' said one of the members. Webster pretended he had heard nothing. He neither smiled, nor paused. He had done his homework very well indeed, and he was giving these fat cats a lesson in power and money manipulation that was worth the price he was extracting from them many times over.

'I'm returning home tomorrow morning,' he said. 'If there are any points you want to discuss with me, I'll give you my private number. I get up at six in the morning so don't be afraid to wake me.' He laughed. 'My wife understands,' he added. 'That's why we have separate bedrooms.'

When Tony got home that night, he awakened his wife and said, 'They're going to make me the mayor of this town – and we're going to be rich.'

Drowsily, she said, 'I'm so proud of you, Tony, so proud.'

* * *

Tony Hacha had a phone message one day that disturbed him; it called for an extra-curricular appointment with Viola at a busy time when he was preparing a report for his Club associates: tax revisions and assessment reductions were on his mind, and three court appointees. But Viola, trusted and shrewd, said it was urgent.

He arrived at her Division Street apartment which had now expanded to occupy the entire floor, with six active 'heads' on the job. It was at noon, and he went directly to her office-bedroom where she had some sandwiches, a pitcher of beer and a bottle of bourbon ready for him.

Tony was hardly through the door when Viola burst out with, 'This cunt, Lou Prouty! She's pure poison – and more than I can handle!'

'You mean Angelo's nigger girl?'

'The same,' she said. 'I wish Minelli hadn't sent her here. She's going to make real trouble if she stays.' She began pacing the floor.

Tony studied her, picked up his sandwich and began munching it.

'I'm listening, Viola. And believe me, I've got my own problems, but Angelo's nigger girl – well, if she's trouble, let's get rid of her.'

'Not that simple. Looks like she's got a big, fat gripe – and some real bad mouth. The victim is his honour, Angelo! Believe me, Tony, Lou is bad news.'

'All right, out with it. I'm listening. So far, you haven't told me anything.' Hacha took a long pull of beer.

'I'm talking about a certain lady named Cora,' she said. 'Seems like Lou knows somethin' about Cora and Minelli that she's achin' to talk about. Real bad news. My guess is, Lou liked her set-up with Angelo real good; she liked working for him, fucking him, and she got good money from him too; a cosy set-up for her. When he dumped her, got married and sent her here, she decided this was too

much work. *Bee-neath* her too. Yeah. What I'm saying, Tony, we don't want that cunt working here. She's creating disharmony, that's what. Also, Angelo (and maybe Mr Torino) would not like to hear some of the things she's saying. Or hinting at. About Cora. Real trouble, Tony. Got the picture?'

'Got it, Viola. You're okay.'

'And Tony, this you won't believe: she thinks that Angelo's wife – Mr Torino's daughter – ain't nearly as good for him as she, Lou, was. Now what do you think of *that*?'

'Did she mention Mr Torino's name to you?'

'More than mention. That's what bothers me. She might just be ready to talk to somebody where it will do nobody any good.'

'You mean she might talk to the newspapers and the cops?'

'She's crazy enough to talk to – to – maybe Mrs Minelli.' She let him digest the idea, then added, 'She's uppity and real trouble. Let's not talk about it. Just do something, Tony. Fast.' She paused. 'Real serious.'

Tony sat there, chewing at his sandwich, thinking. Finally he said, 'Viola, thanks. Keep all of this to yourself. It'll be taken care of.' He was silent for a minute or so. Then he said, 'Listen: tonight! Make sure Lou is relaxed tonight. She will have a client around nine o'clock. Be sure she's free and ready to handle him. He'll cold-cock her and a car will be waiting. She'll be out and off the payroll. Put a little of this' – he paused, reached into his vest pocket and pulled out a small vial ' – in her coffee or soup or drink before the client comes. His name is Stan. He's blond, big ears. Looks stupid but he's far from it. I think he's the guy I'll hire for this job.'

'Okay, Tony. You know best. I worry when one of the girls gets out of line. Besides, I like Angelo – I like to see

things running smooth. By the way, we had a terrific week; a Texas hot-shot came and left his bankroll: almost two grand.'

Tony stood up. 'Great. Viola, you're the best. I gotta run, but I'll stop in tomorrow for a visit.' He placed his hands on her breasts. 'Still the best tits in town. I'll see you, kid.'

At nine that evening the bell rang and Viola answered. A young blond punk with big ears was leaning against the door, smiling. 'Stan,' he said. 'Tony said to come.'

'Yes,' she said. 'Come right in.'

Lou and Viola were obviously drinking; a bottle of bourbon and glasses stood on a coffee table.

'Lou, meet Stan,' Viola said. 'A friend. I guess he heard about you.'

'Nice to meet you all,' she said. 'Who did you say sent you?'

He smiled. 'Somebody who thinks you're great.'

'Good enough for me,' she said. 'Have a drink.'

'Yeah, thanks, a short one,' he said, and sat down.

She brought it to him and sat down beside him. 'Yo mighty handsome, blond boy,' she said, placing one red-nailed hand on his knee.

'You're not so bad on the eye,' he said, touching her breast lightly.

She dropped the shoulderstraps of her dress, exposing her entire firm, upright, heavy-nippled breasts. 'Sho is gettin' wa'm here.'

'Yeah, let's go some place where we can cool off.'

She laughed. 'You real anxious. Okay, follow me.'

They proceeded to a room. He entered first and she kicked it shut behind him, with her heel. She started to undress.

'Nah, keep it on,' he said. 'Keep the dress on, baby.'

'Oh,' she said, puzzled. 'Watcha pleasure, blond boy?'

He studied her, smiling. 'Take out my cock and play Yankee Doodle on it. Know what I mean?'

She grinned, teeth displayed fully and gleaming. He sat down in a large armchair and she approached him.

'On your knees, baby.'

She dropped to the floor and reached for his fly. As she slipped her fingers around his cock he reached forward, pulling her head towards him. When she had her lips where he wanted them he lowered his hands, tightened them around her throat. In one minute she was limp.

'Bye, bye, Lou Baby,' he said softly. 'No more blabber-mouth.' Then he added, 'Too bad – nice mouth.'

He rose from his seat, walked around the collapsed body and studied the room. He zipped up his fly, put on his jacket and removed a skein of wire from his pocket. He tied her ankles together, and her hands. He went to the window, opened it wide and looked down at the street. He was on the second floor of the building; his pick-up truck was directly below, in front of the house. The street was deserted. There was a small patch of grass with a few bushes beside the entrance. His watch said nine-thirty. He waited ten more minutes, inspected the street again, studying each window across the way. All appeared quiet, windows dark, no movement on the side-walk, no cars. He picked up Lou, carried her to the window's edge, took one more hard and careful scan of the street, then let her drop. She fell to the earth below, and made virtually no sound. A small plop, a crack. Nothing more. He saw that her neck was broken from the fall – the head was twisted. He wiped the arms of the chair, and the windowledge. The he opened the bedroom door and walked slowly down the stairs. He glanced up and down the street, saw it was still deserted. Picking Lou up under her arms, he lifted her on to the truck and threw some potato sacks across her body. He got in and started

the motor, then he turned to face the house a last time. Viola was looking down from a window on the second floor. Seconds later, the lights went out. A quiet night in the Toddlin' Town.

Hacha's phone rang. He picked it up and said, 'Yes', waiting. The voice said, 'Track clear,' and hung up. Hacha sat back, smiling. Nothing he appreciated quite as much as assignments accomplished without fuss.

Then Hacha phoned his partner and friend, Judge Minelli, and said, chuckling, 'Angelo, you owe me one – details later,' and hung up.

The next morning, a faceless and disfigured mulatto girl was found in a cement-mixer in the grounds of a schoolhouse that was being erected in Cicero. It cost the workers over an hour to remove the 'foreign body' from the machine so that they could proceed with the day's work. The coroner and police filed the body as beyond identification. No newspaper carried the story. Cicero was nowheresville. Two mulatto girls had been found dead in mysterious circumstances in the same season, one in the Drainage Canal, and now another in a cement-mixer. Two bodies committed to love: undone, unsung.

Tony Hacha understood the value of talent and character. While loyalty was a factor in his choice of subordinates, he always made sure that subordinates understood who was boss. Meaning, Boss Hacha. He controlled his part, he alone. He had begun building a machine and within its matrix had been born an organism that was impervious to all unfriendly influences; it was to be envied and imitated in varying degrees throughout the country. He espoused the big lie, as a public relations measure. His programme to clean out gangsterism in the city was, as good public relations go, inspired, and he had lost no respect in the underworld for it.

Hacha's personal fortune had increased, mainly through the flow of profits from the whorehouses, gambling parlours and from the upcoming Fair; and like his friend, Minelli, he could put his hands on large sums of cash at a moment's notice.

His power was formidable, his popularity enviable. There was a magical inner cohesion at work in his organisation; its power was rooted in the saloons and brothels, not to mention the store-front social clubs where men drank coffee and beer, smoked cigars and made deals – or simply played cards.

Crime and good government, civic duty and venality were curiously interrelated. If you professed enmity or strong public criticism of Tony Hacha and his machine, you were declared an asshole. There was no other word to describe such a misbegotten soul. The Hacha Friendship List was a veritable army and included a roster of big-name gangster followers who respected him and his system. The machine Hacha created, worked. In Washington they were especially aware of his unique organisation, and he received respect from the White House. He had become the best-known Mayor in America.

Then one spring morning in Miami a man from Calabria, afflicted with a strange, asocial disease, pulled a trigger, and destroyed a man whose cunning, strength and will to power seemed unstoppable. Hacha could have sat in the White House if he chose – so said millions of his followers. But an assassin killed him inadvertently, proving for the uncountable time that murder can be mindless, virtually without meaning.

Early in the year 1933, in January in fact, shortly before the new President was inaugurated, a bloody war started to build up in the city. It began with a single killing of a hood, an enforcer who was booby-trapped; then occurred

clusters of murders, which increased in number to a city-wide epidemic, with the city's leading politicians at war with the potentates of crime. Onlookers from outside the ranks were confused.

Enforcers were busier than ever, and within a few weeks, nine murders took place and almost fifty bombs were exploded in bars, hotels, laundries and various retail shops, underscoring for the business establishment, certainly, that extortion was good business and that protection payment was, if not legitimate, at least practical.

While the city was busily preparing for the great Fair, gangland was tightening its noose to make sure that the tribute money from the colossal new 'gusher' would be secure. The Fair could easily produce revenue in hundreds of millions. The dollars to be derived from concessions and payoffs, the commissions on beer (3.2 per cent alcoholic content) and soft drinks, food, entertainment, popcorn, not to mention parking, were immense. And last but not least were the sexual offerings, unadvertised but the major fringe-benefit operation, controlled by Torino.

The city's banks were involved; big business was involved; the city's financial and tax revenue policies were involved; the income of the pimps and whores was involved; exhibitors and entertainers were involved, including a blonde fan dancer who achieved fame and fortune by displaying from the springboard of the Fair frontal nudity of a sort under blue lights.

The Fair's midway grounds, from Twelfth Street to Twenty-third Street, bedazzled the city's visitors. But others besides the Fair's exhibitors and concessionaires profited: the countless saloons and brothels on West Madison Street, South State Street, Rush Street and other areas of the city made a killing. Trucks thundered

through the streets delivering 3.2 per cent beer and illegal whisky, and the chosen few oozed with the fat of the profits gained thereby.

One gangster was heard to say that 'if a wheel turns on the fairgrounds, we get a cut of the grease on the axle.'

The casinos and floating crap games were wide open (though illegal) and the city had more sex parlours than any city in America. The hotels in all areas of the city were filled with call-girls to which Torino's well-oiled organisation offered free limousines. In short, gangland, with the aid of Mr Nillo and his organisation, had done a first-class job.

One visitor to the Fairgrounds, Mr Ed Webster, native of Louisiana, surveyed the many buildings – some historical replicas – and his face, which most infrequently displayed a smile, broadened into a radiant expression of satisfaction. He moved like a well-fed shark through the crowds. The land on which he walked (and formerly owned), the lumber which was employed in the numerous structures throughout, had provided him with over two million dollars clear profit. A fine civic event, and mighty good for business. He stopped at a facsimile of an old Western saloon, entered the swinging doors and moved to the ornate bar. He put his right foot on the brass rail and ordered a double Wild Turkey, water on the side. He raised his glass and uttered a strange, mumbled toast as he smiled at his image in the mirror over the bar. The final words that the bartender heard were 'to my enemies'. The visitor left him a dollar tip.

In the course of the Fair's run – it would end in late 1934 – many crimes were reported, some brought to trial. Violence, theft, rape and other felonies and misdemeanours: these matters came before the courts, where judges, friends and beneficiaries profited in bending the law to accommodate 'vested interest'. Among those who

helped to lubricate the wheels of the Syndicate's machine was Judge Angelo Minelli, one of the youngest to occupy a bench in the Criminal Court, an alleged protégé of Johnny Torino, an alleged ex-whoremonger and an alleged multi-millionaire.

Book Two

Chapter Six

Adrian Breakstone was revving up his faculties; scrutinizing for the unnumbered time the gleaming gold point of his fourteen-carat (*bar mitzvah*) fountain-pen. He was getting ready to compose one of his 'ease of entry' letters.

The target of his summoned energies in this instance was a young brunette, Ruth Davidson, daughter of a pharmacist living in the – to him – wasteland of the city, the West Side. (His own family had lived there until a few years before and he knew the area well.)

Ruth was a prize. He knew it by her handshake, the delicate hands, the firm yet feminine pressure, the glint in her eye, the high cheek-bones (and tits), the personality: a cross between hauteur and low-down mischief which he sensed at once with delight.

He decided to pull out all the stops and display the intellectual thrust, *savoir-faire* and precocity so much admired by his father and friends. In writing this first letter to Ruth he had in mind her bright liquid eyes and delicate olive-complexioned face, and the mouth which was almost too wide, capable of both grimace and raucous gamin laugh.

Dear Ruth:

I'm indebted to you for preventing me from being bored the other night; you saved my evening. So thank you. I'm grateful. Also puzzled, as you must suspect, because I feel that we've met before, possibly in another incarnation when we were – perhaps lovers?

I enjoyed our little debate enormously, though it did leave me unrequited. Let's face it, without sex there is an unfilled vacuum. I believe I argued this point with you. Even vegetables enjoy a form of sex, I'm told. Can you not see an erect *zucchini* and cabbage conjoined?

He put down his pen, resting it on his rosewood desk top. The pause in his writing was caused by certain uncertainties, and by a sudden blast of cold air against the window. He stared out between the heavy bluc velvet drapes at the cold tossing waves of the lakefront, across the Drive. A bleak spring day. The sky and lake were grey and deepening on blue. The waters, whipped by the high winds, pounded at the tall concrete wall protecting the Drive; and tossing fountains of spray cascaded wildly over the rocky point of the shore.

The March winds were lashing and bending the young birches planted along the Drive's edge. The sound of the wind, familiar to most of the city's citizens in March, made him think of death. And he also remembered earlier days when he had sat like this at his bedroom window in their old house on the West Side, when the view from his window was a dreary one, the days before his father had achieved success and fortune and a place in Society – and this elegant condominium in the city's fashionable South Side . . .

Adrian found an almost sexual release in writing to his newly found female friend – his hoped-for confidante. The mental image of Ruth was pleasurable. She was the first female to engage in him a total interest. Her mystery, beauty, wit and feminine piquancy had aroused his playful, loving, yes, even sadistic, inclinations, and of course his intellectual muscularity. He was aware of how special she was: wanted and needed to know her intimately.

To his mind came, briefly, unpleasantly, the recent calls he had received from a young Italian girl he had met at a beach party a few months ago, a girl pressing him to help in an alleged pregnancy. Janice Gambelli – how offensive the very name was, how lacking she was in all the qualities possessed by Ruth. He had denied responsibility for the pregnancy, told off the Gambelli girl, asked her to cease to exist in effect . . .

His thoughts returned to Ruth. He looked down and out at the lake's shore and the thought came to him that if he didn't win Ruth, he would not survive – literally.

Songs of unrequited love, of the lovelorn, lovelost, lovestricken – banal words and word combinations – they kept forming, dissolving, recurring in his young and fevered brain.

A general letter would be more in order: composed, rational, friendly, non-fevered . . . he picked up his pen.

On a political note: you know of course that the King is dead. Our bohunk Mayor, Tony Hacha, has gone to his reward in some Slavic nirvana. Assassinated. (I always thought assassinated was a word reserved for the murder of men of great stature; and, pray tell, why are *women* never assassinated?) Or maybe he went straight to some heavenly whorehouse, owned and operated by his cohort, Johnny Torino. The death of Hacha this morning (you did read the papers today?) after nineteen days of hovering in the valley of the shadow, is an event of prime importance, although I doubt that history will give it an asterisk. By the way, I was a witness to the act in Miami . . . I was there as part of my father's 'retinue' – or Hacha's . . . saw Ganzara, saw Hacha plain and bleeding, and also, I saw the great FDR plain.

Ganzara's so-called assassin's bullet may seriously

affect our political way of life here. The Machine Hacha built may or may not persist. Illiterate, demagogue or political genius – whatever he was – Hacha will not be easily duplicated or replaced. The King is dead.

I'm troubled by Hacha's death, Adrian thought. Why? Remembering the man from his childhood, when he had visited his father on the West Side for highly personal business . . . did he carry that burden of memory for some purpose . . . was his murder related to some subconscious relationship? Fuck it all, he said aloud. I'm writing a persuasive letter (I hope) to this female who has all the attributes I've been searching for, yearn for, but it's Hacha on my mind and there must be a correlation between my romantic yearnings, my itch – and my preoccupation with assassination . . .

Adrian was in a dilemma. After months of concern about his health, daddy-doctor had given him the low-down on his problem – that splintered instrument, his heart. The ailment about which no one in his family cared to speak.

The fibrillation he had been experiencing in the past year, the sweat, the pain and sudden awakening in the middle of the night – he had to be cautious now, sober, like an invalid. He was to be coddled.

'I'm giving you the cold facts,' Dr Breakstone said, voice trembling. 'But, son, don't be alarmed. People live to be a hundred and twenty with this condition – providing they take care,' etc. Adrian had let the banal phrases of fatherly reassurance drift out of his mind. He would be protected. In a cotton cocoon.

'I don't think I want to live to be a hundred and twenty. Perhaps twenty or twenty-five is enough . . .'

Now there was the matter of Ruth. She could prove as

vital to his well-being as his doctor-father's medicine and advice. More. He was minded to fuck and suck her brains out. What matter the cost. What concerned him, curiously, was whether she was a virgin.

Never before had he felt such a painful need, such a hunger for contact, and he knew, clearly, that he was virtually on a one-lane course; helpless. But he must not chance losing her . . .

He had met her twice, he believed. The second time he had escorted her home – from that boozy bohemian affair in the Near North Side. Before – where was it again? At a concert? *Déjà vu* – illusion or reality? At Orchestra Hall? But the first time? He did remember the face, remembered seeing her before, in some special situation – but where? Did he remember talking with her? He had mentioned it to her as they drove home from the party. But he was not clear now, where and under what circumstances they had met – if ever. Was he losing his mind, his objectivity? How could he block out a previous meeting with this irresistible female?

Ruth was vague about it all, but felt too that they had indeed met.

Adrian at his desk, in his favourite Savonarola chair, studied the wet, white ceramic female figure on the grass below, a sad example of the city's kitschy park-art.

Gold pen in hand, he presented a Pre-Raphaelite study: at nineteen, he was sporting a fine, thin moustache; his eyes were large: 'dreamy', the female admirers called them; and a strand of glossy hair curled over his right brow. His dark hair, thick with coils and ringlets, challenged the fingers of every young woman who knew him or observed him. His snowy-white silk shirt was open to the third button, displaying an ivory smooth and hairless chest.

He resumed writing:

Ganzara: what a name for an assassin. Giuseppe Ganzara. A mouthful. A film actor's name, or an Italian opera composer or tenor, perhaps? And Ruth, have you looked at his photos in the papers? An Italian Stan Laurel. But you can almost see a conflagration in his eyes. The question is: who was the intended victim? The President or the Mayor? Many say Frank Nillo was ordered by the Big Fellow to shoot Tony Hacha (a friend of my daddy's by the way); others say his job was to kill the man who was going to revolutionisc thc banks.

Anyway, Ruth, let's talk about this assassination thing when we next meet – and I'm assuming there will be a next time.

By the way, will you come to my mother's birthday party if I decide to go myself? I'm sure my family would love meeting you (providing you don't smoke in the family's presence).

Adrian paused and smiled, prepared to finish his letter with an intellectual flourish.

You may be interested to know that I'm study ing feverishly with my French tutor, and he says I'm quote, brilliantly, unquote, ready – ripe! – for the Sorbonne – as an instructor! I can read, write, discourse and dispute as well as any Frenchman, he says. Would you like me to instruct you in French – in French syntax and other French matters? [Adrian drew a thick violet line under *French matters*.] Think about it, dear heart. (A graffito impulse moved me at this moment but I resisted it!)

He closed his letter with a bold flourish, with the single

word, Adrian (as might a Caesar) with a large rounded uncial *A* filched from the Book of Kells.

Now, let's get together next Wednesday. I'll pick you up at 7:30 and provide you with a Lucullan pasta dinner at Riccardo's, and then we'll take in the new Garbo (she talks!) film. I love Garbo – next to you. And I do love you, Ruth.

The postcript was initialled AB, elegantly encircled; the sphere might have been the planet earth itself. In minuscule letters beneath the circle he printed the words, 'Will you marry me?'

On the next Tuesday, Adrian received the following reply from Ruth:

Dear Adrian:

The pretentious bullshit in your letter notwithstanding, I'll be seeing you on Wednesday, at 7:30. I must admit I'm somewhat curious about this madman, Ganzara; background, motivation, etc. But it will keep. I look forward to our meeting, dinner, etc. Attribute it to my fine Judaeo-Christian tolerance – and my passion for pasta.

Dear Ruth:

Thanks for your letter, tolerance, understanding, etc. Now – I've done some research on Ganzara and here are a few bare facts. What they add up to remains to be seen. Offhand, I'd say Ganzara's anybody's guess: fuck-up, assassin or nonentity gone berserk. (The brief view I had of him in Miami when he shot Hacha remains with me – a 'crazy'.) Hacha was the unintended victim (in my opinion) even though Ganzara was said to be a crack shot. But – did

Ganzara's bullet kill Hacha? (Again I say no.) Many believe that Frank Nillo had ordered Hacha's assassination, and that Ganzara was his hired hand. No evidence that this is so exists to my knowledge. It even appears that Ganzara had never heard of Hacha until after the shooting – after his arrest . . . To be continued tomorrow. Hold everything!

Hope our family's get-together isn't a bore for you. I'll try to make it painless. AB

PS. Herewith is a copy of Harriet Monroe's *Poetry: A Magazine of Verse*, current issue. In case you're interested you'll find a poem of mine on page 24, entitled *Moon Over the Stockyards*. This is my *first published* poem and if you ever pass by 543 Cass Street, please throw a kiss at the building where dear old Harriet works and where I met her to discuss my poetic oeuvre. I am now (without regard for the merits of my poem) in the company of Ezra Pound, W. B. Yeats, et al. This publication appearance may never happen again! Think nothing of it.

PPS. Just to complete my credentials dossier, I've also appeared in a recent issue of the *Little Review* which is edited by Margaret Anderson and Jane Heap, and alas, I don't have a copy to send you. It was a plea for the abolition of punctuation in poetry. I wasn't paid for my piece but it will, somehow, assure my immortality. In case you haven't met the above-mentioned ladies, let's set up a special meeting, an agenda – to cover them. Well worthwhile! Two Sapphic worthies, and my regard for them certainly proves how sexually eclectic I am.

Dear Adrian:

Violets and violence! And poetry. Bravo. You are really the one. The pink, blue and white African

violets arrived with your Ganzara brief. You are a dear, and the violets are dear and gently thriving in their white pots on my bedroom windowsill – reassurance of beauty and the durability of life. Heine (yes, I do read a bit of German) called the violet 'the blue eyes of springtime'. Alas, our springtime comes later than normal springtime – sometimes never. I thank you for the gift, the thought and exquisite generosity. And I love your Stockyards poem. (So Brechtian.) And it isn't even my birthday.

Speaking of birthdays, that was quite a party your family gave your mama. Your mother – really a sweet woman – is hardly a match for your father in *presence*. I never expected your papa to be so over-stylised: pince-nez, and Vandyke beard! – not to mention the paunch and cutaway and watch-chain. He's right out of central casting. Chekhovian. And his friends: that Judge Minelli – is he a patient of your father, or a Capone connection? He has the swarthy look of power and, too, a touch of evil. (That Medician nose!) Even when he smiles. A monster! (Okay, I'm being a bitch – I'm out of order, but really, I overheard some heady exchanges, political, sexual and unclassifiable.) And your brother, Harvey, he's a butterball. But, just because he is a rabbi, must he be so pompous? Please tell Harvey that I'll never be a member of any temple he heads up, because I think he's less than spiritual or humble; rather more of the earth, let's say. In fact, first and foremost, he's an authentic lecher. Loathsome in some ways. Now I've said it. He told me – at our first meeting, mind you – that on his wedding night he approached the bridal bed with a flashlight, in order to inspect in close-up, his wife's 'vestal-virgin-vaginal region'. Do all the Breakstone males behave in this

fashion? Was he putting me on? I suspect so, because your older brother, Ralph, told me in confidence (a confidence which he probably shares with half of Chicago) that he'd divorce his wife at once for anyone (me!) with an ass that was more assertive than hers – and that he considered mine exactly that! (More *assertive*.) He added that he was the assman in the Breakstone family. I was delighted to learn of his knowledge of music; he seems to know all the great baroque and rococo composers.

I know you are the youngest in your family – by how many years for goshsakes? – but, at the risk of sounding patronising, you seem to me slightly more mature than either of your older brothers.

More about your family when we meet . . .

I wanted also, most of all, to tell you how much I enjoyed dinner at Riccardo's (so Bohemian!). The man, Riccardo, is adorable; I'll never forget his entrance with the two white afghans, the red scarf and twelve-inch cigarette holder. And when he came up with his 'Donkey Serenade' – with the aid of the pogo stick – I was ready to embrace him. Actually I fell in love with Ric. Sorry to learn he has lung problems. The pasta and wine and all the paintings (Bohrod's; and Albright's, especially that horrible nude with the yellow, striated buttocks) on the walls – it all added up. *Grazie*. We don't have anything like that in our dreary West Side – not anywhere near Papa's drugstore, you bet. Saloons. Polish bistros, yes. Chicago Avenue is no Rush Street. I love the Near North Side and would want to live there some day.

Am sending you a present – a marvellous record: the Joseph Haydn Concerto in C Major for cello and orchestra; on its verso is Boccherini's Concerto in B

Flat for cello and orchestra. I know you'll love the record as do I. Also sending you a jigsaw photo of myself; couldn't resist it – Woolworth's made it! Hope you can assemble it!!

Yours,
Ruth

PS. Re your idol (or obsession) Ganzara, I disliked his face and his phoney antisocial (anarchistic?) outbursts. I've been reading your comments as well as some of the press interviews (thanks to your promptings) and find him pitiful, pathological – a nut. I don't think he's much else than a malcontent, a frustrate. He committed a mindless crime, and as far as I'm concerned he deserves to be put away.

Ruth:

Your letter received; loved every bit of it. In reply:

I'm interested, also amused, by your reference to Judge Minelli. There's much more to this man – including his nose – than meets the eye; he's an object of prime interest to a lot of people, and a prime subject for your vivid imagination. (You are a sharp one.)

I'll tell you a bit about Minelli. He acquired and imported (purchased) some years ago a very young girl of about fourteen, from a New Orleans madam. This girl, formally or legally his niece, privately his mistress, lived in his house until recently. You may have read about her death – found floating in the Drainage Canal, etc. From a New Orleans *maison de joie* to the Drainage Canal – what a sad saga. Gasp? Pause'?

The above was followed by a pen sketch in violet ink, of a young woman – an Ophelia – floating face up, in a narrow body of water.

‘To continue,’ wrote Adrian, ‘this particular companion of the judge is a very light-skinned octoroon: tall, slender, elegant, sensual – and I’ll bet she fellated the judge before breakfast each morning. Very seductive!

Her name was Cora, and the judge claimed her to be his niece – the daughter of a deceased half-brother. Mother’s whereabouts unknown. That’s the official legend. She passed as white, was rarely seen in public. I did see her a few times: at Henrici’s Restaurant (a largish Hacha dinner-party); at a theatre opening; and once at an Orchestra Hall gala. And she once attended my mother’s birthday party. A young beauty, exotic, odoriferous! She must have consumed half a gallon of perfume per outing.

I hope these details aren’t boring you! part of your education.

Anyway, the judge brought her here from a New Orleans trip some years ago. What I know about her, frankly, I overheard from a conversation between Papa and a crony of Minelli’s. The judge is said to be in good standing with Capone and Company. Nuff said? He was a pal of Hacha, a former real-estate partner of his, and from stories I’ve heard, involved in many underworld deals. He’s considered one of the city’s most powerful (read *crooked*) men, and he loves money. I heard that he has one hobby (other than women): collecting cash in denominations of fifty-dollar bills. They are, it is averred, delivered to him in blank envelopes and with great frequency. All earned from observing his duties as a jurist . . . a sympathetic jurist, that is.

As for your comments on the others, especially my family, you have seen only the tip of the iceberg.

You'll know the worst after you marry me – you know too much already! As for our getting married, I gather from certain connotations that it might occur if I proved myself able to support a wife. Dear Ruth: supporting a wife is no problem – I'll find the way; but *coping* – ah, there's the rub. We must meet soon to discuss this and other related matters. Next Saturday at 7:00 please?

AB

PS. I loved your jigsaw photo; had fun putting you together: It reminded me of Hans Castorp, in Thomas Mann's *The Magic Mountain*. Remember, he's mooning over the Russian Venus, Claudia, and she finally gives him an X-ray photo of her body to satisfy his sexual yearnings. If you want the truth, I gave your photo some unsatisfying labial explorations . . .

On the following Saturday evening, Adrian drove to the West Side in his new fire-engine-red Chevrolet convertible, to pick up Ruth. They were to meet at her father's drugstore which was two blocks from her home, on West Chicago Avenue.

Harry Davidson was balding, bespectacled, moustached – and an assertive 'liberal' and music lover. He owned, he claimed, over three hundred recordings of Mozart, with emphasis on the quartets and quintets. He read all the Russians, and had a special taste for Gogol's tales and plays. As Adrian entered the drugstore he saw him wrapping a large package for a customer and listening to a monologue that must have been painful for the man behind the counter.

Obviously the customer was Polish (the store was of course in authentic Polish territory and the centre of a dense Polish-Slav area); and the man's speech was heavily

accented and eccentric, and clearly alcohol-tinged. The monologue invited eavesdropping, and the subject appeared to be a curious one. The man was explaining to Davidson why he was buying so many bottles of a certain laxative water.

'I betchyu tink I got big case conspshun,' he said bending over the counter and eyeballing Mr Davidson. 'Wrong. Wanna know the truth? I use the stuff to wash my dog. I guess you don't know that citrate magnesia is powerful, is best medicine you can wash your dog in, specially if he stinks. My dog, twelve-years-old fox-terrier, has terrible smell. Smells like shit. I can smell him outside the door when I come home from factory – a mile away I can smell him that dog. So, I put him in bathtub and my old lady and me, we pour bottles of citrate magnesia – plenty bottles on him, two cases every week – and scrub him good with the stuff. He don't stink no more, but I gotta keep pouring it on him. You know how it is with dog, no? They grow old. Like you, like me, we get old. They stink, hah? The missus, too.' He grinned, heavily moustached; large yellow horse-size teeth protruding.

Ruth's father was exhibiting Christian martyr patience, with a few 'that's showbiz' glances in Adrian's direction, to indicate that this was all part of the job. Forbearance was an essential element in a druggist's life on West Chicago Avenue – in darkest Polskaland.

'Thank you, Mr Kowalski,' said Harry Davidson as he finally helped his customer through the door with the large package. The dog-lover was grimacing and muttering as he left, and Adrian got up to greet Davidson, smiling his sympathy. They shook hands.

Davidson was obviously glad to have a chance to talk to Adrian. 'We get some weird characters here,' he explained. 'That man buys up almost my entire stock of that laxative water just to wash his dog. Ever hear of such a

thing? He's always three sheets in the wind; not difficult, just boring. A lot of exotic medical and other practices take place around West Chicago Avenue, you know. While I enjoy being involved in ethnic elements of every sort (well, almost every) I must say that the Polish are often hard to take. Then there's this latent (and not so latent) anti-Semitism. To some Poles a Jew is the lowest of the low. I have a Polish physician who sends me around twenty prescriptions a day – a very important medical business-connection. You understand? I know he's anti-Semitic; you know it especially after he's had a few drinks. His anti-Jewishness is posted right on his sleeve. We both know it. But we have an understanding. He patronises me, I patronise him. One day you'll meet him here; he's slightly on the lunatic side. Most of his prescriptions are harmless, and most of his clients are women. I think he has sex in one form or another with most of them; they all speak so glowingly of him – and they give the impression he's God's gift to women. He once told me that he always manages to give women a massage on the small of their back, and the rest is easy. But – I shouldn't be talking this way. Excuse me, Adrian.'

But he continued nevertheless. 'Then there's Saturday nights; that's when they get drunk, wild, beat up their wives, play cards, go to the dances; and mainly they get drunk – and abusive. The prostitutes hustle on Saturday nights, which happens to be when the week's pay is still fairly intact. You find the young Polish girls hustling in almost every doorway.

'Now, take that man with the dog problem; that's special and interesting. If I had writing talent, say like Gogol or Chekhov, I'd use him as a character in a story. Did you ever, in your life, meet up with anyone like Mr Kowalski?'

Adrian agreed that he was a pretty odd character.

A druggist's life was obviously rich in possibilities, from the standpoint of the writer. Suddenly, out of the corner of his eye, he saw Ruth in an opulent red fox jacket, coming through the door. He turned to greet her, as her father turned to his post behind the counter, beaming. And Adrian's heart raced at the sight of her.

Ruth exclaimed and wowed appropriately over the gleaming new Chevrolet. As they got in she patted the red leather upholstery and asked how he had managed to acquire such exciting and conspicuous loot. Just a few days earlier he had been driving an old Ford heap. 'Did goodness have anything to do with it?' she asked, doing a respectable imitation of Mae West.

'Simple,' said Adrian. 'I made a bet with my father and he lost. I bet that I could get an A grade on a certain philosophy paper.'

'Some bet!' said Ruth, admiringly. 'What was the subject of your paper? And was your professor Mortimer Adler?'

'How did you guess? Yes, Adler, the Olympian. I'm fairly sneaky, Ruth, and I happen to have a special interest . . . my subject was – are you ready? – Søren Kierkegaard and his Sexual Drive.'

'Come on now, Adrian, you're kidding,' said Ruth. 'Sexual drive in Kierkegaard? Might as well write about the sexual drive in Cardinal Mundelein.'

'I'm not kidding. And that shows what you know about that crazy Dane, Søren. I'll let you read my paper if you behave. You have no idea how very human Kierkegaard was, spiritually pure though he may have been. You obviously never read his *Diary of a Seducer*. In it he refers to the risk a young woman takes when riding in a carriage.'

'Is it your intention to seduce me in your carriage – I mean in your convertible?'

'Not unless you insist.'
'Then there's no foreseeable problem.'
'Meaning?'
'Meaning that you should keep your eye on the road – the street is full of potholes. And your hand on the wheel, please.' The she turned and asked, 'And where, sir, are we going tonight?'

Adrian replied, 'Well, I'd like to take a slow drive in and around Greendale. Hacha country. I'll bet the house he lived in as a kid is smothered with flowers and wreaths. The funeral yesterday was an incredible spectacle, a Roman holiday.'

Ruth's contentment was deep; she was happier than she had ever been. They drove in silence, happily. She felt protected and privileged. In love. The car was a snug warm womb for the two of them. The gleaming cherry-red chariot was the magical vehicle taking them – where? – to ugly Greendale.

She thought of her very youngest days in a sad little frame house in Greendale. What she remembered most were the difficult hours sitting before the second-hand upright piano her parents had bought for her, to start her musical career. She recalled with pride how her father would boast to relatives how well she could sight-read, how well she could play Mozart and Bach; and the concerts he would take her to, pointing out that with hard work she too would be sitting on that stage, performing for large audiences.

A light snow-dust was in the air; it had already coated the grey streets and sidewalks. It was a not uncommon near-zero March temperature for the city, not permitting the lowering of the convertible's top. Adrian drove, absorbed and silent, in his big yellowish-grey and black racoon coat; and Ruth was equally pensive in her fox jacket – a thick, bushy, sexy and perfume-redolent fur.

(She had sprayed the coat a week ago and it was still present – vibrant, sweet and gala.) Adrian suddenly lowered the window at his side, to breathe, so that he could extricate himself from the musky atmospheric mood that was beginning to paralyse his brain.

They were now driving through dreary Greendale. Ruth pulled herself erect, sensing his mood, removing her hand from his furry arm.

'Adrian,' she said softly, 'aren't you overreacting to something? The death of Hacha? The assassination seems to have obsessed you. Am I missing something, underestimating the event? Is it *that* significant in our lives – the country's? Why you must see and touch each base relating to Hacha puzzles me. You're not even political. This crummy Greendale is the depths. Almost. Look at those houses: three- and four-room shacks – and all alike. It's almost as bad as the slums. It's bohunk-Polish submediocrity, and I can smell the stink of anti-Semitism in the air here. You know this area is familiar to me; I used to run errands for Dad after school, and I got to know some of these people. I was "that Jew girl from the drugstore", delivering their medicines and laxatives – the stuff they shoved up and into themselves. The stink and slime of unwashed bodies, their lard and cabbage cooking, the unpleasant encounters, the drunks in their beerswill trying to get into my panties – a kid of fourteen!'

She turned to face Adrian. 'You've been preoccupied with the shooting of Hacha for almost two weeks. Why?'

Adrian turned and gave her a frozen look. 'I'm preoccupied with human mysteries,' he said, pompously, she thought.

'Ganzara is a mystery. Why did he go to Miami to gun down Hacha? Why not the President? The city's hoods didn't need to go to Miami to shoot Hacha. They could have done it right here, on this street, at his doorstep.

Everyone knows his address. And where his whores work. And where his real-estate office was. And the motive does interest me intensely.' He paused to collect his thoughts, then added, 'Both Hacha and the President exercised aggressive egocentricity; each was completely different, each had an entirely different voice and vocabulary and background. There's a mystery here involving American history, personalities – paranoia. It intrigues me *very much*. Do you mind?'

Angrily, he pulled over to the kerb and stopped the car.

'I don't really mind,' said Ruth. 'I'm expressing my puzzlement. What interests me is to see you galloping in many directions. It's your affair. You're involved with poetry; with Kierkegaard; your French. You seemed to me the least politically conscious person I know.' She paused and smiled. 'Or are you also writing a paper on Hacha's sex drive?'

He didn't reply and she saw his scowl in the mirror.

'Okay,' he bowed his head in her direction. 'I apologise. But I want you to know I don't care for the word over-reacting.'

'I haven't used it lately . . .'

'Yes, but you're thinking it.' Then, with a rush, hoping to persuade her once and for all to take his views seriously, he continued, 'I am definitely not obsessive – that's a sick word. Ruth, I'm not a psychopath. I'm an investigative and objective sociologist and, if you will, a moralist. There's a pattern here that interests me and it's more than crime and punishment. This Ganzara is a Dostoevskian character, however, and I want to know what makes him tick. Of course he's totally irreligious.' He stopped and studied her. 'And I want to know why everyone's so anxious to electrocute the pathetic bastard – so fast.' He turned towards her and framed her face in his hands. 'And that includes you, Ruth,' he said

excitedly. 'In your last letter you pulled the switch on the guy. Why? What do you really know about him? The headline writers you've been reading think in eighteen-point type. They'd electrocute their own mothers for a front-page story and photo. And I merely want to know why. Why?'

Gently she took his hands and pressed them to her lips.

'There's too much killing, that's why. We're surrounded by murderers; I read the papers. Instead of intellectualising we could try to stop the killing by law. Maybe we can't stop it ever, but surely we've got to try.'

She took a deep breath, studied the low grey-yellow sky, then added, 'I rest my case.'

Dear Ruth;

Ganzara died in the execution cell of the Florida State Prison at Railford, at 9:15 this morning. Slightly more than one month after the shooting. Note: I didn't say killing. This sets some kind of record, I'm sure, for alacrity in the halls of justice. It's really not a killing matter, merely the old 'eye for an eye' bit. There's got to be a price paid if you want to rub out a guy. And it had nothing to do with killing, not what the state did. Ganzara did the killing. We, the people, simply made him pay his dues.

I intend to pursue the Ganzara-Hącha thing further even it if interferes with my university work. From Mole to Mayor to Martyr and Why? – that's my extra-curricular self-assigned task for the near future. Bear with me.

Adrian

Adrian and Ruth were driving, approaching the quasi-gothic Bahai Temple in Wilmette, a few miles outside

Chicago's city limits. It was a warm, humid Saturday noon.

Adrian parked his red convertible (top down today), took Ruth by the hand and they walked to a bench near the Temple and sat there, surrounded by bushes, trees and flowers. They were instantly enraptured by the peace emanating from the sanctified building, the fragrance of freshly cut grass and the flowers – enraptured by their togetherness. Ruth was hoping ardently that he would choose to seduce her this very day.

'Okay, Ruth, I want to talk about Ganzara. Interested?'

'Very,' she said, adjusting her mind and tolerance for a continuation of his lecture on assassination and assassins. She did find Hacha-talk boring and Ganzara an oppressive subject. That Ganzara should weigh so heavily on Adrian's mind and spirits puzzled her.

'I'm no admirer of his, make no mistake,' said Adrian. 'I find him a miserable wretch; he came from a wretched environment, the asshole of Italy, a forsaken place in Calabria called Ferruzzano. At the very tip of the Italian boot-toe.'

'I know all that, and before you continue,' said Ruth, 'aren't you hungry? I'm starved,' and she bared her glistening white teeth to indicate her ravenousness.

He studied her, annoyed. She knew then that he wouldn't attempt to lay her – not today.

'Right,' he said, 'let's get a bite. There's a place a few blocks from here; let's walk. Okay?'

She looked at him, admired and envied his glowing brown-skinned face, his Yucatan suntan. He was unsmiling. She had turned him off for sure. But not for long, she was certain. Somehow, she had to dispose of that contemptible twerp, Ganzara.

At the restaurant, over hamburgers and cokes, they

pursued the Ganzara saga; and almost formally, Adrian was in charge.

'He was sick most of his life,' said Adrian. 'At least he imagined himself sick though no doctor was able to find a specific ailment. The diagnosis would involve the man's fantasy and misanthropy. By the way, I got a look at Ganzara's so-called autobiography. I got a photo-transcript of the partial notebook manuscript from Ann Marsters of the *Herald*. I know Ann through my father. She's one of the key crime reporters in town. How she got hold of the manuscript I'll never know.

'Anyway, he seems to blame his sickness – a continuous burning in the belly – on his mother: he says he had no mother; she died when he was two years old. Felt abandoned, betrayed. He hated her.'

'He seems to have had some genuine Freudian – classic Freudian – symptoms,' said Ruth.

'Exactly what I thought,' said Adrian. 'Add to that, his father was a bastard, sent him out to work when he was eight years old. So he says. His father's severity added to his sense of the injustice of the world – the oppression of the rich and ruling classes. He remarks bitterly, angrily, on what he felt when he was working in the streets of Ferruzzano, watching the well-dressed, well-fed rich kids going to school.'

'Is his autobiography going to be published?' asked Ruth.

'I don't know what will be done with the thing; it's a sort of mess – but it is a confession and a memoir and valuable as such. Really a madman's spoutings, sounding off and ready to put a torch to the world. He escaped the dreary job he had as a street worker and joined the Italian army; he was still in his teens. He served for five years. While in the army he had dreams of glory including the assassination of King Victor Emmanuel. He writes about this but I

can't find any reference to an actual murder attempt. Actually, he is not a multiple offender. One of his fantasies, I suppose, was to kill some VIP and get himself in the history books.

'When he was twenty-three years old he managed to put together enough money to emigrate to America; he got here in 1923. He went straight to Paterson, New Jersey, which was, I gather, a hotbed of so-called anarchism. He mentions a book or booklet called *Introduction to Bakunin and Collectivism*, but I can't imagine his reading the work since he was almost illiterate.'

Ruth asked, 'Didn't he have any girlfriend, any woman in his life?'

'No reference to sex at all; no women, no men, nothing,' said Adrian. 'There are neutrals, you know – men and women who are totally asexual and, on the surface, contented. Turned off. But he was misanthropic as hell, and needed some outlet.

'Which reminds me,' Adrian went on. 'My bookseller, Ben Adamson, said a man came to his shop and asked him for a book on how to stop his daughter – fifteen-year-old kid – from masturbating; he called it "finger-fucking". He was always catching her in the act. Do you know what Ben told him? "There's no such book. Why not leave your daughter alone? it's good for her."'

Ruth grinned and said, 'Getting back to Ganzara: he was a runt, a malcontent, asocial, needing an outlet, a physical release – a need to express himself, be somebody. Elementary, Dr Watson.'

She took a huge bite of her sandwich. Then she added, 'You know, I noted Ganzara's final remark, just before they pulled the switch. "*Adios* to the world." And I say, *adios*, chump! or – poor chump.'

'You're callous, that's what you are,' said Adrian.

'Well, maybe so. I guess with his mother dying at age

two, and his father shoving him into the streets to work, as a kid, that helped him to start hating, started the bellyaches. Why he detested presidents (even Coolidge) and men in power is understandable.'

'Another thing,' said Adrian. 'I gather that Ganzara hated noise. His neighbours, he says in his manuscript, drank and made noise. He hated it. He wanted life to be quiet, painless, serene. Also, he couldn't stand the cold, New Jersey climate. He speaks often about how cold it was in Paterson, and how it aggravated his belly pains.'

Adrian pulled a sheaf of papers from his inside jacket pocket.

'Here it is,' he said. 'He suddenly decides that he must go south, to a place where it is warm. "For my bellyache," he said. It was in 1928, he records. He became a naturalised citizen that year. And that event, somehow, gave him a sense of freedom, the right to roam and find peace and warmth. He went to Miami.'

'That was five years ago,' said Ruth. 'Did he stay there all these years, work there?'

'No,' said Adrian. 'It says here, in his account, that he ran out of money, and had to go back to Paterson. He took whatever jobs he could, but the belly pains and the cold continued. So he decided to visit Los Angeles. He was quickly disenchanted with California and returned to New Jersey and his uncle. Probably ran out of money. That was in 1931. The he went back to Miami. I guess the climate there got to him – and helped his bellyache.'

Ruth interrupted. 'What did he do for a living in Miami?'

'I don't know,' said Adrian. 'He writes about how he liked to fish; he also enjoyed gambling at the dog races. He seems to have read the newspapers, because he made some scatological comments on Hoover and Roosevelt and the Depression. He was furious over Roosevelt's

triumphant election – hated the man fiercely. But he hated Hoover too. He writes that he would have enjoyed killing both Hoover and Roosevelt. He said,' and Adrian read from his transcript, '"make no difference. Presidents just the same bunch – all same."'

Ruth interrupted. 'Does he write about his plans to kill Hacha at any point?'

Adrian looked at her with respect. 'He never refers to Hacha in his journals. He speaks of Roosevelt coming to Miami; that he was going to Bayfront Park with the gun he had bought at the Davis Pawn Shop in Miami, and that he would finish off Roosevelt. No mention of Hacha. Actually, he originally says that he bought the gun to kill President Hoover. Hoover, for goshsakes! It seems to me absolutely certain that he wasn't hired by the Syndicate to murder Hacha – or anybody. The *Examiner* says that he was sorry he didn't kill the President. He said, "I want to kill all presidents – all officers!" He also said, "I am sore at government – because as a kid I had to work instead of going to school, and I'm sick now because I had to work."'

Adrian added, 'What I found interesting, for an illiterate, was that the police found on him clippings relating to the McKinley assassination and descriptions of Lincoln's assassination.'

'So,' asked Ruth, 'what do you make of it all?'

'I'm not certain yet, but paranoia is a factor in this case, and perhaps Ganzara should have been institutionalised. Maybe Hacha should have been too, for his ungrammatical comment to the President, "I am glad it was me instead of you."' Adrian chuckled. 'Well, he's gone and Ganzara too.'

'So it's just another one of those acts of violence,' said Ruth.

'Well, half a million people lined up to watch the Hacha funeral parade,' said Adrian. 'In City Hall over 75,000

people came to see his body, and you should have seen the cross of flowers in the stadium. I nearly froze my ass in the near-zero weather at the cemetery; everyone was there, every Lodge member, all the VIPs including Farley and Governor Horner. Someone called Hacha a symbol of democracy. They referred to his "unselfish public service".' He laughed and said, 'Let's get going, Ruth.'

'What really gives me a charge is that half a million people lined up for the Hacha funeral procession,' said Ruth. 'Aren't you concerned about the real reason, Adrian?'

'Which is?'

'Well, why bother? And why do so many people attend funerals – is it death that attracts them? Did they really love Hacha? Of course we all identify with death – it's our final commitment . . . it's what makes all life a tragedy . . . if you want to think about it.'

'Well, sure. Murder and death interest us all more than anything else. A man pointing a gun is probably the most dramatic, arresting image of all. In every act of anger or violence, we are killing. Even in sex there's death – and that's my cliché for the day.'

They got up, left the icy, air-conditioned Howard Johnson and found sunny warmth, an almost sensual delight in the scent of freshly cut grass and the flowers in the area. Adrian took her hand and she felt glad that they had finished with Ganzara – at least for the present. His cheek touched hers.

'You smell so good,' he said.

Adrian was reclining on his bed, in his cardinal-red bathrobe, a large thick pillow beneath his head. His crotch was uncovered, his cock shrivelled. In his hand was a slender volume bound in cinnamon-coloured cloth and white parchment: *The Ballad of Reading Gaol*.

Beside him, one of her hands on his chest, the other under her head, reposed his lately vanquished friend, Ruth.

Wearing only a pair of white panties which held in place a small Turkish hand-towel to staunch her bleeding, she was contemplating her new non-virginal status. In her gleaming black hair she wore a blue ribbon. She listened to Adrian as he read. 'The poor dead woman whom he loved, and murdered in her bed,' he repeated. And then, out of context, spoke the words, 'For each man kills the thing he loves.' The words were now gone trite. Every young wet-behind-the-ears intellectual had been reciting them since the turn of the century.

'Aren't we fortunate,' said Adrian. 'I love you and have no murder in my heart whatsoever.'

'No cause,' said Ruth. 'I've been faithful in the best possible fashion.' She lifted a single, oval, firm-fleshed grape from a cluster in a white bowl at the bedside, and placed it between her teeth. He moved his head, placed his lips on hers and sucked the grape out of her teeth.

'Of course,' said Adrian, 'you know what T. S. Eliot said on the subject of sex and love and murder: "Any man has to, needs to, wants to once in a lifetime, do a girl in."'

'I'm not familiar with that,' said Ruth. 'But it ties in with his sense of sex-guilt or sense of sin. Eliot was afraid of sex.'

'You are a smart broad, Ruth. I think I'll just feed you instead of intellectualising or whatever I've been doing . . .'

Ruth was thinking of her so-called deflowering and how she had assisted strenuously in its consummation. At the crucial moment the vital organ had failed to respond to the needs of the situation and Ruth was obliged to lend a hand, as it were. To have made the slightest reference to it would, Ruth knew, have provided Adrian with cause for

humiliation. A fact of life as well as a secret she must carry to her grave. Just one element of many in her secret life.

Adrian stroked her thigh; patted her towel-protected and lumpy crotch. He said, 'No man could be more grateful, more at peace with the cosmos, more happy. How fortunate we are.'

He was thinking of their good luck in having the house to themselves. His parents had gone off to Michigan for the weekend; the nosy housekeeper was taking time off. Adrian had managed at last to get Ruth into the sack and she had proved indeed to be a virgin. Also, a quick study. Both facts pleased him mightily. His father, he thought, would be proud of him and his conquest.

Adrian now turned, drew her to him and kissed her naked breasts. His lips became fused to her left nipple as he kneaded the other: and he found himself sucking like a child. Her breasts were larger, rounder, sturdier than he had suspected, and the nipples were wider, a delicate pinkish-brown. He moved his lips to the area between them, snuggling and nestling within the exquisite pneumatic pressure: pink aspic mounds moulded from the breasts of the Venus of Milo, he thought, smiling.

Finally, she drew up and away, murmuring. 'Enough, baby.'

He studied her breasts sadly. 'Carrara marble,' he muttered. Then he added, 'Marry me. Be my Carrara marble bride.'

She laughed and stroked his glossy hair. 'Adrian – I really love you and I must admit I love your love-making. But two fucks do not a marriage make, to paraphrase your favourite poet.'

Annoyance showed on his face. 'I'm being more serious than I've ever been. Why do you have to be so cynical?'

She turned and rolled off the bed. 'I'm going home.'

'No, you're not,' he shouted, anger in his voice. He grabbed at her arm and pulled her back.

'I won't be shouted at or bullied,' she replied, pulling away.

They began to wrestle. Finally Adrian was on top of her, holding her arms down, his face over hers.

'I'm going to fuck you again,' he said, eyeball to eyeball.

'If you can manage three fucks,' she said, 'I may reconsider your marriage proposal. But are you sure your heart can handle it? Also,' she added, 'we should let pussy rest; it's rather sore – and, I think, still bleeding.'

'What about my heart?' he asked, frozen above her.

'I dunno, something I read, somewhere, about male stamina, endurance in sex etcetera. How many times can a man really fuck within an hour, anyway?'

His body relaxed, and he lay down beside her.

'You've touched on something I should mention to you. I do in fact have a rheumatic heart.'

'I didn't know,' she said, softly, touching his hand. 'Is it serious?'

'Can't say,' he replied. 'My dad gave me a check-up a month ago. I take some medicine and I'm supposed to avoid tension and strain.'

'Then,' she said, moving away, 'enough for today.'

They lay there, silent, watching the cloud-filled Tintoretto sky through the wide window beyond their feet. The lake view was vast, grey-blue, turbulent, a scene that never failed to absorb Adrian.

After a few minutes' silence Ruth said, 'I can't get Cora out of my mind. Do you really think she was killed by some random lover or would-be rapist? Or did Minelli do her in?' Then she added, 'You know, I remember seeing

him at your mother's party, and thinking he looked evil. The essence of evil. I find it hard to give him the benefit of the doubt. He could have killed her – jealousy or something.'

'Well,' said Adrian, 'you know all about the niece bit and how he adopted her at age fourteen. The papers have covered it all – but there's more left unsaid. This man living alone in a house with a young octoroon girl – well, obviously she was his mistress. He claimed to have reported her missing a few days after she was gone; he said he thought she had gone off with some friend or lover. As her guardian, he said, he didn't want a public situation. He thought she might return. His story was too simple: he had returned from a business engagement. She was not there; money was missing, but nothing serious about that. He assumed she would phone or write him. He waited and then a few day later he reported her missing, to his friend the police commissioner. A search was set up and they finally checked the unidentified nude and found her to be his quote unquote niece.'

'Don't you agree that he could have murdered her?' asked Ruth.

'I'd hazard that guess,' said Adrian. 'Minelli was allegedly in love, madly in love with Cora, and I heard a few stories about their quarrels based on jealousy. Her affairs with other men, including some pretty ugly hoods, were common knowledge.'

'But Adrian, assuming Minelli loved Cora, and that whole niece thing was a sham, why kill her? Even if she was carrying on with a lover or lovers?'

'I know something about the mentality of the Minellis,' Adrian said. 'She was a valuable property and could have been placed in one of the Syndicate's whorehouses. But I think in the case of a super-pimp, murder's the appropriate style. Minelli's style.' He picked up the book of

poems and read, '"the coward does it with a kiss, the brave man with a sword!"'

'Oh bullshit,' said Ruth. 'Proving what?'

'Listen, Ruth. I'll be blunt – and I happen to be clear-headed about these things. I'd be willing to swear that the slimy bastard stuck a needle into her ear while he was sodomising her. Krafft-Ebing would understand this. The coroner's decision was vague. Phoney. Fudged! Ten years ago, Minelli was a pimp. Today he is still a pimp but now he wears a judge's robe.'

'Minelli is an old friend of your father's, isn't he?' asked Ruth, with a show of hesitation.

'Yes, they are old and close friends, but they don't get out together very often, socially that is.' Then he added, 'And don't forget, he's his physician.'

'So they're close friends but not socially – now that's odd.'

'Well, let me explain. Ruth, a man like Minelli is pride-motivated and also, he's a self-conspiring man. He's learned that the less he reveals about himself, the stronger he is. When in a social situation, he's uncomfortable, formal. Something obviously happened to him, personally, deeply, somewhere along the way. He's highly sensitive; if rejected I think he could kill, especially if his status, or a woman, were involved, a woman as sexy, as sensual as Cora, let us say. And Cora was something special, got under his skin. His property. Minelli is proud, cruel, terribly possessive. Don't ever let such a man come into your orbit.' Adrian hesitated, looked at her searchingly, then went on: 'Don't ever quote anything to anyone about this. Despite his judicial eminence, Minelli was and is a whoremaster, a pimp, a menace. In Chicago this is possible. He is, alas, a confidant of my father's. But I repeat, self-conspiring.'

Adrian paused, then hurriedly added, 'There must be

more pleasant subjects to discuss. For example you – or womankind.'

Ruth laughed. 'Womankind is a great subject; odd that you should bring it up. Right this minute, something I read in a book of Simone de Beauvoir's comes to mind, something about how a woman is essentially a creature who bleeds and leaks. What a dreadful summation of women: I'm a woman; ergo, I leak. Is that how I, Ruth Davidson, *femme fatale*, want to be described, summed up?'

Adrian laughed. 'That's refining it a bit too closely, but I'm curious to know how her chum, Sartre, manages to make love to such a woman. Imagine the discussions, the intellectualisation while genitally occupied.'

'I hear she's charming, feminine and of course sexually perceptive and responsive. But if she fell in love with that oddball, Nelson Algren, then she is naîve – to be pitied.'

'She's an existentialist, and as such, in revolt against the traditional approaches. It all started with Kierkegaard, you know . . .'

'I was never clear about existentialism,' Ruth said.

'Well, Sartre, who seems to be the foremost living exponent, says, I think, that there's no God and therefore there's no precise element in our nature that determines our behaviour. We're all free as birds, fully responsible for our actions, totally responsible for what we do with our lives.'

Adrian paused, then added: 'And that's precisely what Kierkegaard said was the basis for our fears – or something to that effect.'

'I doubt that anyone is free, in the purest sense, not even a bird. But be that as it may,' said Ruth, turning from him to lie on her side, 'I think de Beauvoir understands women better than anyone around, certainly better than any male philosopher.'

'I don't intend to explore the terrible secrets of women,' said Adrian. 'But I will certainly continue to worship them, in the person of one Ruth Davidson.' He studied her marble-smooth bottom, now fully exposed to his view. 'I think I'm going to eat you.'

'Don't, please,' she said. She turned round, sat up. 'Not that I don't like being eaten by you, but at this particular moment, you would not enjoy it.'

'You're the most considerate, the most sensitive cunt imaginable.'

'Fuck you, Adrian. You always manage to kill the thing you love – I hate you.'

Adrian smiled. 'I'm not a killer and you won't hate me for long, I hope. Let's get dressed and take a drive. There's a new pasta bistro on Rush Street that you'd love. The walls are covered with murals – all nudes, by a lesbian artist called Joy Mount. Isn't that a terrific name?'

Adrian arrived at the Davidsons' in the early evening; he was picking Ruth up at her parents' home, and he was bearing a gift.

Ruth kissed him, ushered him in, and he met Ruth's mother, for the first time, as she was emerging from the kitchen, aproned and smiling. She was almost a carbon copy of her daughter except for her greying hair and furrowed brow. What he noted at once, with delight, was the odour of freshly baked bread and Mrs Davidson's smile, her eyes.

Under his arm was a rare book – a gift for Ruth – a copy of Utamaro's *Insects*, published in the eighteenth century. He had secured it from his favourite antiquarian bookseller. 'Snagged it before some Philistine got it.'

Ruth opened the book with excitement; they both had recently visited the Art Institute and looked at the Utamaros and Hiroshiges from the museum's great collection;

they admired in particular Utamaros' sensuous prints – his women: geishas and prostitutes. Adrian had explained to her how Utamaro had spent most of his days and nights in Japanese brothels, painting, sketching the inmates. (Somewhat like Lautrec, Ruth reminded him.) While Utamaro was a gifted observer and recorder of nature, his vision of the erotic and his portrayal of beautiful women in particular gave him his immortality. Ruth was secretly pleased with his choice.

'This is a very expensive, priceless work of art,' she said. 'Too expensive, Adrian.'

'Yes,' he replied, 'but you are worthy of it. Besides,' he whispered in her ear, 'it will belong to me as well, as soon as we get married.'

'How very cunning,' she said. 'Meanwhile, I thank you. I love it.'

Harry Davidson came into the room bearing a bottle of scotch. He greeted Adrian warmly, and offered a drink which Adrian accepted.

The Davidsons' house was simply, almost sparsely furnished. But, prominent in the living-room was a grand piano, several large plants, and one entire wall devoted to phonograph records.

'My Mozart collection,' Davidson said, waving his arm proudly towards the wall. 'Care to hear something?'

'Some other time, thanks. We're going to be a bit late, I think.'

Ruth had been invited to the Breakstones for a 'family dinner'. Adrian had been pressing her for an official engagement, and wanted her to meet his family on an intimate basis. Thus the invitation. Was she to be on her best behaviour? While she had met them all previously, at his mother's birthday party, tonight she would be under scrutiny for certain. Examination day!

'Next time, then,' said Harry Davidson. 'I'll play you a

brand new recording of Mozart's *Requiem.* A Victor release, Toscanini conducting. Marvellous.'

'Yes, I know,' said Adrian. 'I have an older recording – Stock's conducting. Marvellous.'

'Ah, Stock's – I have that too, but it isn't nearly up to the new one. I know Stock, by the way. We attend his concerts especially when he conducts Mozart and Wagner. Orchestra Hall is my favourite home away from home.' He paused, then asked with a big smile, 'Did Ruth tell you she played with his orchestra, once?'

'Ruth, a concert pianist?' asked Adrian, turning to her, genuinely surprised.

'Oh, not quite a concert pianist, but I did play with his orchestra once, when I won a prize at the Conservatory; part of the award was playing a concerto with Stock at Orchestra Hall.'

'You never told me,' he said.

'You never asked,' she said laughing.

'Maybe you'll play for us tonight?'

'Well, I'm not sure; we'll see, Adrian. Getting back to Dad,' she went on,'he's a Mozart maniac, and don't get him started. He'll tell you how many quintets, quartets, etcetera etcetera he composed before he was eighteen years old – and then some.'

'Don't make fun of your father because he's a music lover,' he said.

She looked at him, went over and put her arm around her father. 'I wouldn't make fun of you, Dad. I love you very much.' She kissed him. 'Besides, I'm a Mozart maniac, too.

'Everyone has a secret life, Adrian, my father's is in Salzburg, Austria, where Mozart was born. Daddy's dream is for me to give a concert in Salzburg – at the Residenz and Mirabell palaces – where Mozart himself played and conducted. Daddy's secret life is in Mozart's

music. On Chicago Avenue he is known as a druggist – the Jew druggist. Sad, huh?'

Ruth's mother smiled. 'They're quite a pair, father and daughter. Actually, she has a good repertoire; I hope she plays for you tonight. Ask her nicely.'

Adrian looked searchingly at Ruth and asked, 'Do you have many more such secrets?'

'Wait and see,' she said, going for her coat.

The weather was fine, the late twilight sky a vibrant, clear blue, and the air fresh. Ruth and Adrian drove along the lake southward to the Breakstones' home. Adrian was feeling the effects of the scotch.

'He stocks very good whisky,' she said, when he commented on its warming effect. 'I think that what you got was from his very private collection; it's called Royal Salute. He keeps it for VIP guests and VIP occasions. Consider yourself honoured.'

'I do,' said Adrian. 'My father never served Royal Salute – not to my knowledge. As for me, I'm not sure I'm worthy.'

'Of course you are,' she said. 'For my part it's wasted on me – affects me quickly and badly.'

'What happens? Do you fall asleep, get garrulous – or uninhibited?'

'All of that. Also depressed. Mainly, though, I get sleepy. Depends on the amount. Sometimes I get plain dizzy.'

'You'll never be an alcoholic,' he said, 'not unless you really concentrate on your drinking. You've got to work at it.

'They think I'm too young,' Adrian continued, changing the subject, 'to think of anything but school and career. I have a year more to go at the U of C. I've got to work out my future, but it seems to me premature. Livelihood, money, marriage, they go together. Frankly, I

can't make up my mind about a career. Money. I should be giving it some thought although my father has plenty. And my uncle asked me to join his business when I leave school – he's got an old factory; he's a producer of small household objects made of wood – I don't think that's my cup. But the trouble is, I'd rather write or teach or translate. I like to play chess, and I get a charge out of mathematics. But getting married is what's really on my mind.'

'I get the picture,' she said. 'I had no idea you were interested in chess and mathematics though, I thought your first love was French literature. As for marriage, isn't that more than premature?'

'To some degree, yes. But it wouldn't preclude my other interests. I've a feeling for language and could easily spend the rest of my life reading, translating, teaching French. But I fancy doing a lot of travelling: all of France and Italy, Spain, too.' He stopped and searched her face. 'Do I strike you as a dilettante, Ruth?' The question was asked with a note of pleading. He added: 'I believe in marrying young – some day I'll give my rationale . . .'

'Adrian, one must live, survive – and work – in order to enjoy such gifts as books and music and life itself. Don't you agree?'

'Yes, work is part of living,' said Adrian. 'But the work should, ideally, be an occupation that gives one pleasure, too. I don't think I would enjoy working behind a drugstore counter, for instance. Forgive me if I sound rude. I wouldn't want to work behind *any* counter, nor any desk for that matter – unless it were the desk of a scholar or writer, in my own study. Not a nine-to-five desk is what I mean.'

'What is your vision of the ideal life for yourself?' asked Ruth, and a quality of earnestness entered her voice that touched him.

'First, I'd like to have a life with you. I'd like for us to marry. Then, to have enough funds to travel, to see everything that arouses my – our – imagination. I'd like to see all the great natural and man-made wonders of the world; all the unexplored tombs; all the museums. I'd like a 10,000 volume library. Be able to attend all the concerts and operas and plays that struck my fancy. I'd like to experience four-star, extravagant meals, also eat in the bistros. I'd like to wake up and go to bed with you beside me – also beneath and above me. I think that answers your question.'

Ruth laughed. 'I have the answer. Let's write to the Ford Foundation and have them subsidise the ideal life for Adrian and Ruth. The project to be called: Living the Good Life.'

'Now you understand. You're close to the solution of the problem – my problem. Write the letter at once! Or talk to my father.'

He paused, stroking his chin. 'But what about you? What do you want? As a certain Viennese psychiatrist asked of women, "What do you want? . . . what is your fantasy of the good life?"'

'On such questions,' Ruth replied, 'consider me unqualified.'

'Come on, Ruth. Everyone has a deep-down wish . . .'

'Well,' she said, 'I want to become a concert pianist; not only the best I can be, but *the* best. I want the chance to study, to work and perform everywhere in the world. I want to play and record beautiful music as often as I can. And be married to a man I can love – you.'

'Is that all?'

'Well,' she added, 'I'd like to concertise under the batons of such men as Stokowski, Toscanini, Monteux, Munch . . .'

'And become a legend in your time.'

'Right – more or less,' she added.

'Tell me about your secret life,' said Adrian.

'I'm not sure there is one,' she replied. 'Such as . . .?'

'The secret life is one not even one's best friend knows about, not even one's mother.'

'Well,' she said, laughing, 'if you promise not to tell anyone, I'm secretly in love – lesbian-like – with Christina Rossetti and Emily Dickinson. I love their poetry.'

'No kidding,' said Adrian. 'Having a secret passion for those two wonderful weirdos makes you very special for me.'

'Aren't you a bit patronising?' she asked. 'Why weirdos?'

'I'm really not patronising. I love you for opening doors of your secret life for me. Rossetti! I promise not to betray you. And Rossetti's "Bride Song" is one of my favourites – is it yours too?'

'Yes, very much a favourite.' She examined his face then said, 'But getting back to *your* aspirations, are you going on with your dissertation on assassination?'

'Definitely! It's not only Ganzara, but the whole bloody theme – killing. The value of human life. The need to kill.' He stopped and seemed to ponder his next comment. 'In some respects the subject of violence and murder and death are the most important of all matters to be investigated by modern man. When I read from Wilde about killing the thing one loves, I wasn't jesting. What is it that prompts us to violence, murder, war, torture? What makes us seek out death – for ourselves as well as for others? Is it for release, like sex; for specious gain as in Raskolnikov's murder of the old woman pawnbroker? He felt that murdering her was justifiable because she was a parasite. Poor Raskolnikov: as if most of us weren't parasites.' Adrian stopped for a moment, then resumed with, 'Perhaps all my answers can be found in Dos-

toevsky; *Crime and Punishment* may very well be the greatest study of crime and its motivation. Criminology may be the ultimate study of men; likewise victimology. I don't want to sound pontifical but all forms of life involve crime and punishment – criminal and victim.'

'And what about the spider who eats the fly? The ants that eat ants?' she asked.

'That's food,' said Adrian. 'Simply food.' He paused, then added the word, 'Protein.'

'Perhaps homicide is a form of psychological sustenance – a form of nourishment, a kind of food.'

Adrian looked at Ruth and did not reply.

They were pulling into the driveway of the high-rise condominium where he and his family lived, when he said, 'Yes, the fly and the spider – that is the question – and the answer. We'll have to go on with this. But now, my love, may I wish you a jolly evening, and don't let those brothers of mine give you a hard time.'

As they were going up in the elevator Adrian asked, 'By the way, Ruth, what composition did you play at Orchestra Hall, the concert your father mentioned, your debut. Was it something by Mozart? I have a feeling I might have been there.'

'You won't believe me, but I think – I'm not sure – I think I played Bach, from "The Well-Tempered Clavier". But I'm not sure. I was so numb and nervous, I've blocked it out. Honestly. Come around any Sunday morning and I'll serve you some Bach with our bagels. I play Bach often; sometimes we worry that we may be breaking our lease by playing on Sunday mornings. But who cares? The Davidsons are a mad family. Mozart and Bach. There are worse afflictions . . .'

There were vital questions she was eager to ask; but it seemed inappropriate just then. His health, for example – she was puzzled by his comments on his heart.

The rheumatic heart. She had recently read about it in a medical encyclopedia. She would ask questions about it next time she visited her family doctor, and her father could probably answer some of the elementary ones; but she was reluctant to bring up the matter yet. The whole cardiovascular world, the architecture, the chambers of the heart – it was like exploring a hidden cathedral. Intuitively, she knew that when she became familiar with it she might regret it. She had overheard too many discussions relating to coronaries and cardiac arrest. Sudden death. Heart failure striking like lightning. What the true nature of Adrian's condition was, she would have to learn later. Meanwhile, she was discovering that she could not live without him.

Chapter Seven

The Breakstones' apartment was extravagantly decorated with fresh flowers of every season: spring flowers, tulips, carnations and roses of every colour in profusion. Ruth felt a warm festive air, and in the background her ear quickly picked up a piano sonata coming from another room - certainly a recording. She saw that the *mishpocheh* had assembled early, and while they were casually standing about the large living-room, talking and laughing, she felt singularly on stage – spotlighted.

Adrian's mother, Sarah, was the first to greet her – a warm, *shmaltzik* woman, with a large bosom exuding waves of Shalimar; her head was adorned with a beehive hairstyle that looked more like the work of a topiarian than a hairdresser, giving her a deceptive height. She was small and dumpy, a woman who could be accepted with affection on sight. Ruth was given a warm hug and kisses on both cheeks and the lips.

Ruth removed her coat and saw it whisked away by a maid in uniform. She greeted Dr Breakstone next and he kissed her and embraced her with an elaborate, lilac-scented warmth. She felt instantly welcomed and relaxed.

She greeted Harvey the rabbi and his young flapperish wife, Marlene. Also, Adrian's older brother, Ralph, whom she remembered as the self-professed assman. Ralph's wife, Tania, a plump brunette, studied her (although they had met before) with cool, unsmiling eyes, and she wondered if this was friend or foe. She would be on guard.

'If there's any iced champagne,' announced Adrian, 'that's what Ruth and I will have, with some orange juice.'

'Are you kidding?' asked Ralph. 'That's a wake-me-up morning breakfast drink.'

'Exactly,' said Adrian. 'Anything wrong with drinking it in the evening?'

'It just isn't done, old chap,' said Ralph. He moved towards Ruth and said, 'May I suggest a nice Dubonnet on the rocks?'

'Perfect,' said Ruth. 'Exactly what I'd like before dinner.'

'See?' said Ralph. 'Drinking is an art; you've got to give it more study, more thought.'

'How lucky I am to have your advice,' said Adrian, turning away.

Unlike the previous visit when the apartment was crowded with relatives and assorted guests, the room seemed almost sparse; only the immediate family was present – a total of eight, not including the servants. Harvey brought Ruth her Dubonnet with ice, in a heavy crystal glass.

'L'Chaim,' he said, bowing formally.

'Thank you, Ralph; what a pleasure it is to be here.'

Adrian came towards her and took her arm, to show her, ostensibly, the rest of the apartment, as though she had never seen it.

'If this is a guided tour, Adrian,' she said, 'we can skip the bedroom down the hall. I vaguely recall seeing it before – under most interesting circumstances.'

Soon Adrian's mother began fluttering her hands, ushering them all into the dining-room, a spacious and formal room with vast framed mirrors on the walls, and more fresh flowers and exotic plants in Mexican bowls in each corner. A large floral centrepiece dominated the table. Ruth marvelled at the effort and expense involved.

Ruth's parents often bought flowers for their home, but a few vases of daisies or tulips or yellow roses was the extent of their need. The Breakstones obviously wallowed in flowers: there was a floral ostentation here, a smothering excess. It reflected Sarah Breakstone's effusive and opulent style.

Wine was poured and soon they were eating their first dish, chopped chicken livers with tissue-thin sliced onions and large black olives, surrounded by plump white radishes and celery stalks, all very pleasant and visually satisfying. Ruth sipped her wine and found herself chatting easily with Adrian's father at whose right she sat. The table glittered with gold plate and Ginori china.

Suddenly, Dr Breakstone tapped his wine goblet with his fork, and announced a toast. 'To the prettiest girl to sit at any table since my two beautiful daughters-in-law first sat here.' He raised his glass and they all said Hear hear.

Ruth was touched and said so. Adrian smiled and said nothing.

He had a plan and it seemed to him that the atmospheric conditions were right for him to move into top gear that very evening. Ruth knew something in a vague way of the scheme he was preparing to put forth to his father. Studying him from several chairs away she sensed that his mental wheels were whirling. She decided to savour the food, chat with the doctor, listen, observe and relax. She felt that she was genuinely approved of by the family, although she couldn't work out the precise reasons for what seemed their almost instantaneous acceptance of her.

'I understand you are a concert pianist,' said Dr Breakstone. 'Adrian tells me you are a genuine virtuoso, that you played with Frederick Stock at Orchestra Hall. I'm really impressed.'

'Thanks for being impressed, Dr Breakstone,' said

Ruth, 'but there's only one way to be properly impressed, one way to judge, and that is to hear a performance. I was a student when I performed under Stock; I was given the chance to play with Stock as a reward in the conservatory's annual contest. Really a modest achievement, and I was very young.'

'Would it be an imposition to ask you to play for us tonight?' Breakstone put his hand on hers and gave her his broadest smile, his pince-nez glittering.

'I'm flattered by your interest, but excuse me. Some other time. To be quite frank, I'm a bit nervous and doubt that this is the best occasion for me to show off. Please ask me again.'

'Of course,' said Breakstone. 'But I can't help admitting being disappointed. By the way, how long have you been studying the piano?'

'As long as I can remember,' she said. 'I'd swear that I began taking lessons at the age of four or five. A Russian with long blond-white hair first taught me – it was in a suite in Kimball Hall. A tall man named Bogorska, or something like that. He looked like Paderewski. He was a demon, used to strike my hands with a flat ruler when I made a mistake, or pull my ear. I think he enjoyed pulling my ear. His god was Beethoven. I went there twice a week – two hours per session. You must believe me – it was pure hell.' She smiled, sipped her wine. 'Later, I went to Madame Koussevitsky. What a woman she was. She died when I had been with her for two years. She made me understand music; made me love the piano, made me understand why it is such a beautiful instrument. I loved that woman. She restored my self-confidence. But that demon, Bogorska! He made my fingers turn to spaghetti!'

'Who are you with now?' The doctor seemed determined to get some of the basic facts about Ruth's musical education.

'I enrolled with a musical group where they provide concert contracts for the lucky few; but I'm not ready for that yet. Several concert pianists teach us; I've been concentrating on theory and harmony lately. They also give me an occasional accompanist job which I enjoy. I practise more than any student I know, and believe it or not, I don't mind; I don't find the scales a drudgery. I practise about five hours a day – Sundays, too.'

'Extraordinary. Then you will surely succeed,' said Breakstone, beaming. 'I respect discipline.'

'I agree,' she said, 'but there's much more to it than discipline.'

'But of course,' he nodded.

'Madame Koussevitsky,' said Ruth, 'insisted that to play great music one had to play fast and loud or soft and slow – but not in between.' Ruth laughed and continued. 'It may sound downright silly or simplistic, but to make good music, one must think of magic. Passion. Creating a spell. Not technique. Music disappears under excessive technique. Making music is a magical process – it's more than reading and memorising clusters of notes.'

'You fascinate me,' said Breakstone. 'I suspect you were a prodigy.'

'No, no prodigy, although I played well – quite well; so I'm told. At an early age. But I was no Mozart, no Mendelssohn. A great composer once said, "One learns what one already knows." And I think I know what he meant. Falling in love with a work helps. I've fallen in love many times, with works by Ravel, Chopin, Chabrier, Debussy . . . and when I fall in love with a given work, I think I do justice to it.' She stopped. 'I think I'm talking too much about myself.'

'No, not at all. And I predict, from the little you've told me, that you'll scale the heights – no pun, dear – and all sorts of successes and honours will be yours.'

'Well,' said Ruth, 'it's a matter of my life. I intend becoming a concert pianist and I know the work involved. It's an exciting life and the problems entailed don't frighten me.'

'Good. That's because you really, truly believe in yourself.' Breakstone patted her hand, refilled her glass. 'I would bet that you have a natural gift for more than the piano; meanwhile I would love to hear you play. But I promise to be patient.'

'Thank you,' she said. 'In due time.'

Then Breakstone asked the oldest question of all: 'Who are your favourite composers?'

'An easy question to answer,' she said. 'I love Vivaldi, Scarlatti, Monteverdi – but Bach is my first love, and then comes Mozart. I'm a baroque addict,' she added.

'So it's Bach as number one,' said the doctor. 'Any special reason other than your favouring baroque music?' His voice was deep, resonant, energetic. Suddenly, Ruth realised how overstylised he was.

'Well, there's the superior harmonic sense; there's his incredible technique, his marvellous exuberance. While I'm not religious, Bach wrote, he said, to the glory of God. Somehow that objective satisfies me.' Ruth paused for a moment then added, 'I have a dream – an ambition – to record, some day, the complete Goldberg Variations.'

Dr Breakstone smiled, patted her hand.

'Perhaps you know that Bach had twenty children,' he said. 'I wonder if that parental or sex drive had anything to do with his powers as a composer?'

Ruth smiled. 'I don't think so. Haydn was a prolific composer and I can't recall his having a large family. Same holds for Mozart. And for Beethoven. Actually, there are many mysteries surrounding Bach. He was a very successful man, financially as well as professionally, yet his

second wife was buried in a pauper's grave. That I could never understand.'

'I didn't know that,' said Breakstone. 'Perhaps,' and he grinned, 'she was not as prolific with babies as his first wife.'

'That I can't answer,' said Ruth. Then for some impish reason she said, 'Your son, Adrian, is a baroque person; don't you think?'

'I never thought of Adrian as baroque; is that a compliment, Ruth?'

'But of course – I mean it in the best sense. I haven't even told him that, of course, but I think of him in a sense as an embellished person, like an embellished melody as against a simple melody.'

Breakstone looked at her and said, 'You are a very interesting and rather surprising young lady. I must look up the word, baroque, and see if it really suits Adrian. Actually, I think, now the idea is laid out on the table before us, that his name, Adrian, could be called baroque. What do you think?'

She hesitated, awkwardly.

'Well, I don't know of anyone with that name. There was the pope, Hadrian, which is probably a variation of Adrian.'

'Yes,' said the doctor. 'And did you know that there was an English pope – the only one – whose last name was Breakspear? Now isn't that an interesting coincidence? Breakstone is probably derived from Breakspear, and probably the root of Shakespeare. Now there's something to explore. Wouldn't that be wonderful, to find we are descendants of Shakespeare?'

'We're having a pretty heady conversation now, Dr Breakstone, if I may say so,' she said. 'Educational and unconventional.'

He smiled and said, 'I like to explore all areas of human

life and history, human behaviour in particular. By the way,' he said, bending closely to her, lowering his voice, 'do you have a gynaecologist? Or is that too personal a question? Unconventional?'

Ruth distinctly heard Tania utter the word, shit, across the table. Obviously she had been overhearing their conversation. She was stopped cold by Breakstone's question. Was this how the Breakstones conducted themselves at dinner?

'Is that question relevant to anything in particular, Dr Breakstone?'

'Ruth, I wish you would call me Jeremiah instead of doctor. We are friends. As for the question, it helps me to become oriented with people, women in particular of course.'

'But why that question? Why not ask me about my dentist? Do you think I might need gynaecological help?'

'All women do at one time or another. But I see it's a sensitive subject and you needn't answer.'

'And why should I not be sensitive about the question – Jeremiah – no one ever asked me before? Isn't it reasonable to assume that one's family doctor serves his patients in that area unless serious problems arise?'

'Exactly,' he said, passing her a dish of huge and glistening black olives. 'Try some of these, Ruth.'

She took an olive and decided that the subject could, should, be dropped. But the impertinence stuck in her craw. Adrian's father was as personal in his conversation as brother Ralph.

The brisket of beef and horseradish, the steaming platter of potatoes, the carrots, pickles and French wine interrupted the conversation. Finally came the dessert, *lokschen kugel*, a great noodle pudding rich with raisins and almonds and orange rind. Followed by strong coffee in demitasse cups and a platter of chocolate cookies.

Mrs Breakstone surveyed the table, beaming. 'Anybody want anything else? Then everybody to the living-room, please. Take your coffee if you like.'

They all rose and moved away from the table. Immediately Ralph approached Ruth. 'You looked troubled. I hope my father didn't say anything to upset you.'

'Upset? Not at all, Ralph. We had a delightful conversation.'

Ruth saw Adrian leave the room with his father; they seemed to be heading for the library.

'Excuse me, Miss Davidson.' It was Tania. She turned to Ralph. 'Don't forget to make that phone call, Ralph. They're waiting for you to call, you know.'

'Ah yes, but it will keep, Tania.' He patted her behind which she seemed to resent, for she literally jumped at the touch of his hand.

'So what are you waiting for?'

'No hurry, Tania. I'll get to it. I'm having a nice chat with Ruth.'

Tania turned and walked over to the phonograph.

'Is it an important business matter?' Ruth asked. 'In which case, I'd hate to intrude.'

'Nothing is important except getting to know you better,' said Ralph. 'Let's sit over there and have a nice brandy.'

'No brandy, thanks,' said Ruth. They sat down. Then Ralph asked, 'Did you know that Adrian is a virgin?'

Good God, thought Ruth, sex is on everybody's mind around here.

'I must ask him,' said Ruth. 'The question never occurred to me.'

'Don't you think it's important?' he asked.

'Not really. Why should it be, may I ask? And isn't that an odd question – even embarrassing. Does one go up to a young man and ask him if he's a virgin?'

'You miss the point,' said Ralph, laughing. 'Okay, Ruth, let's talk about you. Are you a virgin?'

She burst out laughing. 'The Breakstones are really something. I was telling your father that I thought Adrian was baroque; I think that characterisation applies to him and you, too. Don't you think this conversation is baroque?' Suddenly she felt light-headed.

'I'm not sure that I do, ' replied Ralph. 'I understand what the word means in relation to music, to art, architecture. But how to a person?'

'Think about it,' she said. She paused, studying him closely, staring at the bridge of his nose. 'I think the male Breakstones are not only decadent or fantastically baroque, but verging on the surreal. This conversation seems to be taking place in a dream. There's a touch of lunacy to it, too. Forgive my bluntness.'

He ignored the comment but said, moving his chair beside hers, 'I think you have a terrific figure.'

'Thanks; what a nice compliment.'

'It's sincere. And I'm an authority on the subject; women's behinds in particular. Yours is shapely, seductive, irresistible.'

Ruth was studying him; feeling slightly sickish, but grinning.

'Flattery. What would Tania say if she were to eavesdrop on your comments? Do you say these things to all the women you meet?'

'First, Tania is not jealous, she is understanding. She knows I'm an open person who loves the female body. She knows how I respond to women's beauty. Answering your second question, I definitely do not throw around compliments indiscriminately. I am sincere.'

'Well, I must say, sincerely, I'm speechless,' said Ruth. 'But thanks, Ralph. And what I'm supposed to say next, beats me. By the way, your father asked me if I had a

gynaecologist. Don't you Breakstones talk about anything else?' She felt slightly ill again for a moment.

'What could be more important, Ruth? Tell me that.'

'What could be more intrusive and personal? My shape, my gynaecological needs, Adrian's virginity? Aren't you interested in, say, the death of Hacha? The election of Roosevelt? National affairs, and such matters? Or music, literature, art, the national economy?' Her voice, she realised, was getting high-pitched.

She stopped and looked at him. This crowd – the thought passed through her mind in a flash – belongs in an asylum . . .

'Sorry, Ruth, none of that stuff interests me. Although I must confess that music and art are important in my life. And I gather music is important in yours.' Sex hungry she thought, looking into his large liquid eyes.

'I'm interested in many things, and it's true, music is high on my list; and it occupies a good part of my time. I play the piano, I gather you've heard from Adrian. But there are many other things. As for sex – and I might as well use the simple blunt words – Ruth Davidson and her sex life are personal, private, non-discussable subjects. Period. Excuse me.' She was suddenly remote.

She stood up and walked towards the library just as she saw Adrian coming through the door with his father. Adrian was smiling.

'We're going to escape in about half an hour,' he said *sotto voce*, smiling, putting his arm around her. 'Are you enjoying yourself? You look tranced.'

'Having an incredible time. Fascinating conversation, great food. A ball, in fact.'

'You're angry about something. What is it?' he asked.

'Actually not angry, but eager for some clarification. It can keep until we leave. Okay?'

'As you please,' he said. 'How about a drink?'

'One small cognac if I may.'

'Me too,' he said and went towards the bar.

Ruth stared at Adrian's back. I love him, she thought, no matter what.

When Adrian returned with the drink, his mother had already approached Ruth, beaming, assuring her that it was a real joy to have her to dinner and hoping Ruth was having a good time. 'Only the family,' she said, 'my sons and their wives, my husband. Confidentially, they all like you,' and she patted Ruth on the arm.

'I'm so glad. I'm enjoying myself, and I must say the dinner was delicious; you are a wonderful cook, Mrs Breakstone.'

'Thanks, darling, but the cook is somebody else.' She laughed. 'But I taught her everything I know – which I learned from my mother. My cook is a diamond, a real jewel; she knows how to cook in the *tradition*. You know what I mean? She can cook Italian and French; but the Russian and Yiddish dishes – ah, there she's an artist. Her brisket, ah!'

'Mama, it was a great dinner; I noticed that Ruth ate everything. She must meet our cook some time and get a few of her recipes.'

Mrs Breakstone said, 'Yes, yes,' then excused herself. Adrian said, 'Let's scram in another ten minutes. Okay?'

'Okay,' said Ruth. 'You're in charge.'

Marlene and Tania came over and Tania said, 'What are you two lovebirds up to?'

'At the moment, to drinking cognac,' said Ruth, laughing.

'We've got an important date and we're going to leave soon,' said Adrian. 'Another party on the Near North Side. An artist friend of mine is having a few friends over and they insisted we come tonight. I promised.' He looked at his wristwatch. 'Heavens, we're late!'

They made their farewells and as they were leaving, Dr Breakstone saw them to the door. Mrs Breakstone kissed them both, eyes glistening.

'I hope you know you are always welcome here, Ruth,' the doctor said. Then he added, with a degree of solemnity, 'Adrian has an important message for you, and in advance, I give you my blessing.'

Nonplussed, she turned to him, then to Adrian; he clutched her arm and they were off.

'What's up, Adrian? I never felt so much unstated emotion, so much unsaid. I feel like a character in a play where everyone knows the plot, has lines to speak except me.'

'Wait until we get into the car,' he said, 'I hope you'll be pleased.'

When they were seated in the car, Ruth said, 'I felt like the day I was confirmed. My virginity – as well as yours, by the way – and my private medical and sexual life were examined, and I never felt so *violated*. I was turned upside down, feet to the sky, innards and privates exposed. I was humiliated. This sort of thing is done in certain Islamic countries, like, for example, checking on vaginal snugness; but surely not here, today!' She paused, trying hard to contain her fury. Then she added, 'Are they all sex mad?'

Adrian laughed. 'I think you're more than equal to their assaults.'

'Assaults! Is that the social behaviour the Breakstones cultivate?'

Adrian turned to her, saw Ruth's anger.

'I'm sorry, but I think I can explain – if you'll allow me.'

Her heart was racing. She tried to control her breathing, to listen as calmly as possible. Then she laughed. It was almost hysteria.

'That's better,' he said. He shaded his eyes, gazing at her. 'You do have a sense of humour – and you need it with my family. But they are harmless. And they really, truly, took to you. My mother and father love you. Did you know that?'

'On such short acquaintance?' She stared ahead, suddenly not listening. He was talking, explaining something and she was not on his wavelength.

'Ruth, you aren't listening to me. Did you hear what I said?'

She turned to him; his face suddenly came into focus. She had a sudden sense of fear. What had he said, and where was her mind, her attention? Did the inner fury she had been building block out his words? 'Forgive me, Adrian. My mind was out into space for a moment. I don't understand. I was trying to re-evaluate the evening. Please. Tell me what you said.'

He studied her, then said slowly, 'My father gave me permission to leave the university, to get married. He said he'd subsidise my marriage, my life, for two years.'

She listened, stunned. They had been discussing *her* marriage and she had not actually agreed to marry him, had not seriously discussed it.

'I'm absolutely astounded, Adrian. We haven't agreed to marry. How could you discuss it with your father? What a crazy thing to do.'

'Not crazy, Ruth dear. I had to know, first, if the practical aspects would be taken care of. I have no money, no job, no way to support a wife – yet. How could I propose to you until I was sure I could manage it all? So I talked to my father. I knew he'd understand. Are you really angry?'

'You might as well tell me the rest,' she said.

'Okay. Simply put, Dad will finance us for two years in Paris.'

Ruth made a full turn in her seat and stared at him.

'Have you lost your marbles, Adrian? What about school – my school? I've got a year to go at Roosevelt College. I have a musical career to think about. It's a very real thing to me. I'm not sure I'm ready for marriage. Nor you, for that matter.'

'Let me interrupt, please.'

'No, Adrian, let me finish. You're fantasising. Tell me what you and your father discussed, cooked up, decided for us. And, does he know how serious I am about my musical career?'

'I know I was impetuous. But I'm not mad, a fantasist, nor is there any question of losing my senses. Here's the scenario – ' He paused as if to sort out the details of his presentation, his plan – for plan it was and of a most unpredictable nature.

'To begin with, over a week ago, I told my father that I wanted to get married, now – to you. Realising I had no real funds, no job, no career and no college degree, it would be a tough piece of selling I had to do. But I had one ace up my sleeve – my rheumatic heart.'

'Your heart?' She stopped and burst out, 'What about your heart? Tell me the truth, all the facts. Everything. It's damned important.'

'Fact is, it would be difficult for me to take a job, difficult to work under any sort of pressure or strict regimen. As I see my life, it will be a happy one, a fulfilled one if I am able to direct my own destiny; in short, lead a productive, full life – but on my own terms, at my own pace. Essentially, I want to enjoy life – and that involves you, Ruth – and also, I want to study and write. I'd like to spend two years in Paris – in France, and a bit in Italy, and I know I can produce some publishable and useful books. I need you, Ruth, your companionship, your love – a sex life if you will – but it must be a life based

on a calm and undisturbed existence. My heart can improve, even heal to normality, Dad tells me, if I don't get careless. Equanimity is the operative word for my future.'

He took her hand, pressed it and continued. 'I know I was not fair to you – taking it for granted that you'd go along with my proposal. But I had to be sure Dad would accommodate my needs, my plan. I knew he was able to do it, financially. But I had to check out the heart thing first. He was marvellous, agreed to the whole programme. He'll pay for our trip and two years abroad.'

'What happens after two years, Adrian?' she asked. 'Forgive me for pressing you with boring bread-and-butter questions at this point. Very unromantic, I know. Shouldn't *I* plan for a career, and I mean a money-earning career? Shouldn't *I* work at my music, if we make this marriage and foreign life a reality?'

'I've thought of that, too, of course,' said Adrian. 'I want you to have a full life, and whatever you want and need to do with your life, professionally, is your right. Music would naturally be one answer to your question. Teaching another. But frankly, I don't want to look into the future beyond two years at this point. Let's enjoy the two years, live fully, happily together; the answer to our future will come. I know that if money becomes a problem, I can resolve it. Any idiot can make money. I can prove that; I see idiocy all around me, especially among the rich. I know that with my mathematical talent, I could teach, or write, or simply apply my mind to the matter of acquiring money. I'm not worried about money, and neither should you be.'

She said, 'I'd like for a brief moment to touch on what your father asked me. He wanted to know if I had a gynaecologist. Does he know that you and I have had sex together? Did you tell him that?'

Adrian frowned. 'I'm not going to lie to you, Ruth, now or ever. I did tell him. He's a mature person, a man of the world, my father. He knows that at our age we are almost at the peak of our sexual power. You know that, don't you? Men and women in their twenties and thirties are like rabbits, they can fuck day and night. And you know the saying: "It is better to marry than burn." It's that simple. I want to marry young – you should too – and enjoy what life has given us. Enjoy it freely, unhampered. No more secrecy. I think we are two of the luckiest people on earth, with this miraculous gift from my father. We can piss on the world; we'll never be lonely. We'll storm Paris and Italy. We'll have an early, simple, impromptu wedding, a beautiful ocean voyage, a nest in Montparnasse. The Left Bank, the Seine, the Louvre, the Tuileries – they'll be ours.'

Adrian went on, impassioned, sketching out their potential future. He explained that his heart condition would improve with care. He would work and study; he'd finish his long essay on assassination; he might write a study of the mathematical mind. The mysterious, rigorous laws of mathematics. Einstein had made up his mind about his future at sixteen, even though he was told that he would never amount to anything. Adrian was fortunate, he had a father who believed in him and was willing to subsidise his future and his happiness. Was that not beautiful? Golden luck? Yes, he could apply himself to higher mathematics and who knows, he might, like Einstein, emerge with a treatise as revolutionary as Einstein's theory of relativity. Adrian burst out, 'I'm hungry for life, learning, love; hungry for you, Ruth.'

Suddenly Ruth began to cry. Then she spoke in an uncommonly soft voice, slowly, letting the tears fall. 'This is the day of my life that I'll never forget.' She stopped, drifting into a kind of blissful silence which, in effect, was to allow him to continue with his exuberant vision. She had

expressed her deepest feeling and her love, in a few simple words.

Adrian's car had pulled up in front of the Davidsons' house. He turned off the motor, faced her and kissed her tenderly on each cheek, then on her lips. 'You agree, then?' he asked. 'You like my plan, my devious plan? And you forgive me for taking the liberty of getting my father's approval first? Say you do. Say you're happy that I acted for both of us. Say you think my scheme is good. Please.'

Ruth said, 'Adrian, I love you.'

'He who has objection to this marriage, speak up or else forever hold his lip,' said Adrian. 'No objection from the congregation,' he pronounced. 'We are now man and wife. Let's go and tell your folks and make them give us that Royal Salute.'

They raced hand in hand up the brownstone's steps. As Ruth placed the key in the door-lock he said, 'I feel like a nova – an exploding star!'

'We'll explode together,' she said, letting him enter first. Her husband to be.

'My folks are asleep,' whispered Ruth; 'let's go into the music room for a few minutes, and I'll get you a brandy.' Then she added, 'I have a present for you.'

She turned on a small lamp at the piano, went to a sideboard and poured a brandy for Adrian and one for herself.

'Come sit with me at the piano,' she said. 'Just for a minute.'

They sat down, Adrian looking puzzled. She ran her hand through his unruly hair, then said, 'I want to play something for you – something especially for you.'

She turned and stared into his eyes briefly. Then she bent slightly forward, towards the piano keys, as if to see them better. Then she began to play softly.

It was brief, obviously an excerpt and faintly familiar to Adrian, but not really recognisable.

'Lovely,' he said, softly. 'But such a small sampling. What's it from?'

Ruth smiled, stood up and whispered in his ear, her breath sending a trembling through his body.

'You've read your Proust,' she said in a whisper. 'You may remember Odette playing a Saint-Saëns Sonata – in D Minor – for Swann, and how one phrase haunted him forever after. You just heard the phrase.'

'You are a witch,' said Adrian. 'How did you manage to remember?'

'Be on guard, my love,' she said. 'And now, you must go home.'

Book Three

Chapter Eight

In their ship's cabin, Adrian and Ruth were lying side by side in a king-size Empire bed. The faint throb of the engines, the sound of the ocean provided for Ruth an almost musical experience: the beat and sense of motion, of engine and wave and occasional vibration of floor beneath her: she knew she would never fail to respond to the experience.

Adrian's father had given them first-class passage on the *Normandie,* the new super-liner; and the accommodations were breathtaking, with luxuries and comforts neither could have imagined.

They had come from an extraordinary first dinner – at the captain's table no less – a dinner at which they had eaten caviar and *pâté de foie gras* and Scotch salmon, and pheasant, and chocolate mousse. They were reliving the dinner, slightly affected by the several wines and the brandy and the general euphoria of their honeymoon. The after-dinner dancing contributed to their present mood of delicious exhaustion.

They had laughed between themselves at the captain's overstylised behaviour. They were amused by his meticulous, most detailed description of the might and magnitude of the vessel: four screw propellers, turbo-electric drive; 1,000 feet in length, speed 31.2 knots (whatever that meant), accommodating almost 2,200 passengers – the details were finally too much. Adrian leaned over to Ruth and said, 'If my mother were here, she'd say"*Gottinyoo!*" or "I wish he'd already stop *hocking* us a *chynick*."'

But the captain's elegance and his Gallic *savoir-faire* left a good impression; the man was cultivated, articulate, and handsome. As Ruth said, admiringly, 'A dream boat.'

Their decision to marry at once, at City Hall, had pleased neither Ruth's parents nor Adrian's mother. Somehow, Ruth felt that Dr Breakstone was aware of their plans and approved. A quick civil wedding at City Hall was hardly the romantic event Ruth had in mind, but she did not resist Adrian. The odour of carbolic acid in the ceremonial room, the speed and brevity of the ritual embarrassed Ruth and her two friends who were their witnesses. Adrian seemed indifferent and eager to have it over with. They quickly made their way to the Drake Hotel for a champagne luncheon. Then Ruth's friends were literally dismissed and the young couple headed for Ruth's parents' house – their first official stop.

The Davidsons were surprised and patently unhappy, but proved to be good sports. Harry Davidson wrote them a wedding-gift cheque for $5,000.00 and produced some scotch to bless the occasion.

Adrian's mother was stunned. 'How could you be so selfish?' she asked, bursting into tears. 'Depriving your parents of the pleasure – and I have so few pleasures left.'

But Dr Breakstone merely smiled. He said, 'Naturally I'm sorry we can't have a formal wedding, but that isn't of major importance. My pleasure is in having Ruth as a daughter-in-law – on any basis.'

Ruth embraced him for understanding their impetuosity.

'And,' said Breakstone *père*, imperiously expansive and with his broadest smile, 'it will give me great pleasure to send you off to Paris on the finest ship money can buy – the new *Normandie*. And my travel agent will do it at once!'

* * *

The *Normandie*'s dining salon, as it was called, overwhelmed them. Three decks high, it was larger, they were told, than the Hall of Mirrors at Versailles.

Adrian discovered that the ship had almost been named the Paul Doumer, after the President of the French Republic who had been assassinated by a lunatic in 1932. The protests over the contemplated use of a murdered man's name prevailed and the name Normandie was finally chosen. Adrian pondered long over the near-coincidence.

They were virtually always sexually engaged. Adrian proved insatiable, a passionate, a zealous lover, and Ruth, totally responsive. Now, on the Atlantic, in their cabin bed, Adrian turned to Ruth and said, 'I have a surprise for you. I know you're a woman of the world: you've shown yourself sexually alive thus far. Now I want to teach you a few arcane matters. Since we're going to Paris, you must begin to understand there is more to fucking than fucking.'

Ruth grinned. 'An epigram,' she said, amused by his pedantic tone, wondering if he was being serious, or putting her on. 'Consider me your obedient pupil, sir,' she said. But she found herself grinning, also wondering what he was really up to, knowing full well that he was not yet precisely a man of the world, sexually. She was prepared and eager for surprises, but wondered whether Adrian was going to produce them.

'I have a book with me,' said Adrian. 'Privately printed, very rare! It is not intended for unsophisticated eyes, only for serious students, only the most sensitive, the most worldly. Are you prepared?'

'I doubt it, master,' said Ruth, 'but try me; I'm willing to learn, to make the effort. But, if it's the *Kama Sutra* you're talking about, forget it; I've already read that book; I know all about the positions – *those* positions.'

'Oh, so you've read the *Kama Sutra*,' said Adrian.

'Well, then you're ready to move onward; for that's merely a kindergarten primer. What I have to show you, what I want to read to you, is an advanced manual of instruction by the world's foremost authority on the subject of organitalism.'

'What in God's name is that?' she asked, portraying fear and ignorance in the best Stanislavsky fashion.

'We are going to read it together,' said Adrian. And he presented her with a small volume, privately printed, illustrated: a book she noted, that concentrated on oral sex.

'Oh,' she said, 'it's all about sucking. What's new about that?'

'There's more to sucking than sucking, too,' said Adrian, smiling like a magician about to disclose some amazing new tricks. Then he added, 'I don't think I ever showed you some of my parodies of T. S. Eliot. One of them goes, "The women come and go/talking of fellatio . . ."'

Ruth laughed, slapped his arm playfully.

It was an exceptionally warm night; the art of air-conditioning had not yet reached that state of perfection where discomfort was turned into total unawareness of climate. Ruth and Adrian removed their remaining clothes.

She lay back, waiting. As master in charge, Adrian took the book from her and opened it. As he started to read, one of his hands began to stroke her silken vulva, and she, shyly, moved her slender fingers downward on his belly and began to caress his erect and throbbing cock.

He continued to read, but falteringly. Hopelessly in love, and now eager to devour each other, they were committed to discipline; Adrian would be the instructor of his wife, his mistress-cum-concubine, his lover.

At sea, Adrian and Ruth began to realise the full sexual

extent and potential of an ocean honeymoon. The roll of the ship, the gentle and continuous throb of the giant turbines all added to the excitation. While reading aloud, Adrian would try, between the punctuation marks (which he also spoke aloud), to demonstrate with hands and lips. Ruth tried to participate but could not control her laughter. Finally she succumbed to the sheer erotic pleasure that followed. He tossed the book across the room and embraced her, his tongue in her mouth, his fingers massaging her clitoris, her inner thighs, while she caressed his cock and testicles.

'Cataclysmic,' she murmured, turning over on her face.

'The divine slit – *merveilleux*,' he whispered.

'Slit!' she exclaimed. 'Is that what I am?'

'Time out for sleep.'

They rested.

An hour later, he picked up the erotic manual from the floor and continued to read aloud. The chapter dealt with detailed techniques employed in certain Asiatic countries, although, essentially, fellatio and cunnilingus were the same everywhere. Those were, he said, the keys to the outward limits of sexual pleasure. Only drugs could heighten what they had already experienced; and he was not in favour of drugs.

Adrian instructed her on the use of the pillow – a vital accessory in the game or art of love; showed her how to stuff it under her hips in order to relieve his shoulders of weight, and to give him freedom to perform. They spent hours sharing their sexual moistures, experiencing the innermost secrets of each other's anatomy. They dared to explore, pausing at times to pick out or spit out pubic hairs, followed by laughter and a call for towels, recess and a shower. As they resumed, they explored further. She ran her tongue into his anus and he almost fainted from the excitement and shock of pleasure. He repeated

the act on her and she responded differently, shyly. Orgasm after orgasm had them exhausted, lying spread-eagled, half-conscious, like wounded warriors on the field of battle.

Finally Ruth said, 'Adrian, I'm fucked out.' But he had already fallen into a deep sleep.

She picked up the book and began to read carefully. It opened up a wonderland of the senses for her, and she found herself thinking about the nature of the nervous system and sexual fantasy; of sexual taboos, sexual horizons. Did her parents indulge in these practices? Her grandparents? Finally, she too fell asleep, her hand resting on his groin, her mouth at his throat.

When they awoke from their siesta, in the late afternoon, Ruth arose, naked and still full of sleep. She saw a sheet of paper on the floor, near the door. Picking it up she read aloud the captain's invitation to a screening of *Berkeley Square* with Leslie Howard, following that evening's dinner. 'Oh, let's go,' she said. 'Don't you love Leslie Howard?'

Adrian yawned. 'Not my type.'

She moved to the cabin's porthole, and looked out, kneeling on a chair beneath it. 'There it is,' she said. 'Come, Adrian, you must come.' He joined her and they looked out at the heaving, dazzling afternoon water, the gigantic, staggering waves; a sky-view, with massings of clouds on the horizon, tinged with orange. They felt the movement of the ship, lunging forward like a monumental dolphin.

'It's all too marvellous – you, us, the water and the sky,' she exclaimed, putting her arm around his shoulder.

'The first thing I want to buy in Paris,' she said suddenly, 'is an African violet in a pot, like the ones you bought me, a reminder of your gift that first week we

knew each other.' She paused, then, 'And the next thing I want to buy – don't laugh – is a packet of Gauloises.'

'I'm not laughing,' said Adrian. 'But it so happens that you gave up smoking a week ago. Remember?'

'True,' she said, 'but now I've taken it up again. That is, when I can get those marvellous, fragrant cigarettes: they spell *Paris* to me.'

Adrian rose, went to the bathroom to shave. She suddenly remembered the sealed letter which Dr Breakstone had given her on their departure. Probably a personal cheque, a gift of her own to spend.

She took it out of her handbag, opened it, glanced at it, then folded it and returned it to the bag. A cheque was indeed enclosed. Also a letter.

The letter began on a highly personal note, asking for the utmost confidentiality. It was about Adrian's heart. She would read it later, tomorrow, when she was alone, when she could absorb it fully; it was a fairly short typewritten letter. The impact of the opening lines was enough to affect her breathing.

She sat down to calm herself, reached for a bottle of scotch on the sideboard and poured herself a drink. It helped somewhat, but she now felt a leaden weight. She thought: this cataclysmic heart thing, it will engulf our lives. Adrian on his poor tightrope-walk of a life. . . Could she play at self-deception? Pretend to herself that all was well? Tomorrow, when he took his 'constitutional' on the deck, she would beg off as being tired, and she would read the letter carefully. Again, she felt the weakness, the upsurge of concern.

Then Adrian came out of the bathroom, freshly shaven, combed, bright-eyed, handsome. He was wearing his light blue shorts. His legs, his chest, are those of a young god's, she thought. His face is radiant and those black shining curls; he is out of a Renaissance painting – a Botticelli

figure. Suddenly, there was one final burst of golden light as the sun began to sink. Adrian was bathed in gold for a moment and she thought: I now know his secret – he is the son of the Sun God. She experienced a private vision that would stay with her forever. She approached him, embraced and held him tight. The two stood in a rectangle of sunlight.

'No more *amour*,' he said, 'until after dinner and the movie.'

'I know,' she said. 'I also know something about you and your secret life. You are a Sun God!' As she spoke, a tear fell from her eyes and he smiled.

'Now you know all,' he said.

As she brushed her shining black hair, Adrian lay on the huge bed watching her. She pretended to ignore him as she combed and fixed her hair, allowing it to hang long and straight, parted in the middle. When she picked up a perfume bottle and sprayed her neck, the room was suddenly full of her.

She went to the extravagantly ornate *armoire* and selected a white, raw-silk waist-wrapped skirt. A long deep pleat in the centre of the snow-white skirt sent a shiver up his spine. Next, she put on a simple open-worked V-necked sweater, and over it a matching, softly yoked jacket. He watched all this with pleasure.

He thought: how lovingly and simply she assembles her clothes. How pure she is, how chaste in the soft white silk, her black silken hair framing her fine-boned face; how large, dark and liquid her eyes . . .

Her slippers were also white, with delicate straps at the ankles.

'Watching you dress,' he said, 'I can see why I fell in love with you. There is no artifice about you. You are purity itself.'

‘Ah, Adrian, I know,’ she said, ‘like Ivory soap.’ She laughed, came over to him and kissed him.

‘Get dressed, lazy. Maybe we can have a drink in the lounge before dinner.’

‘Ah, so,’ he said, employing a bad Japanese tonal expression. ‘In four minutes your humble servant will be attired and suited to accompany you to honourable dinner.’

‘You’re in the wrong cabin,’ she said. ‘Cho Cho San is in the next cabin. This is Mrs Davidson’s daughter, Ruthie: remember?’

He slipped into his clothes, sighing.

On their way to dinner Ruth and Adrian paused at the bronze doors leading to the dining-room. They sat down in the lounge near the doors, admiring the ten medallions that commemorated various French cities: Le Havre, Rouen and others. Suddenly, a couple stopped to greet them – the Merediths, friends of Adrian’s, South Shore ‘élites’.

The Merediths, so the gossip traders had it, decided to marry because his name was Jock and hers Jill. They fancied themselves well met and, as a team, the personification of Zelda and Scott Fitzgerald; believed themselves in fact, socially at least, assets to any occasion, in dress, style and sophistication. (Jock and Jill went up the hill to fetch a pail of water and came down bearing a bucket of champagne, was how they were often introduced or described.) They deemed themselves *the* avant-garde couple. And they seemed to have unlimited financial resources. They were welcome almost everywhere and especially where extravagant behaviour, the unconventional, was expected.

The Merediths lived less than two blocks from the Breakstones and Adrian often met them in the summer, at ‘The Point’, where the more daring would swim along the

rocks. Jill, everyone seemed to know, had once been arrested for swimming in the nude under a full moon, a stone's throw from the Drive, outdoing Zelda's New York Plaza Hotel escapade.

It would seem that the purpose of the Merediths' lives was to provide surprise, amusement, a fillip to social events. One of their caprices was to serve their guests the finest champagne in Lily cups. 'Let's all come back to our place for a nightcap,' they would say, and the knowledgeable ones would accept gaily, knowing that unlimited tins of fresh caviar and bottles of Dom Perignon were waiting for them, the chilled wine foaming – in paper cups. And who could fault them for so harmless a caprice?

The Merediths occupied a ten-room condominium on South Shore, similar to the Breakstones'. Adrian had been there once, and had also met them at a large country-club party in Wilmette. They had the services of a maid and butler, and could accommodate a dozen guests at any hour of the day or night, improvised parties being one of their delights. They also owned a flat in Paris, on the Left Bank, decorated in camp-cum-surreal, with a touch of Las Vegas – the obligatory and gaudy jukebox and slot machine. The Merediths usually spent their springs in Paris.

No one seemed to know where the funds came from. Jock understatedly postured as a La Salle Street man (broker), a specialist in commodities. To his credit he never solicited business from his friends or guests, nor discussed the market.

'But we're not going to talk shop now, f'heavens sakes,' he would say, reaching for a bottle. Jock wore braces with stars and stripes in vivid dayglo colours. He was seen more often than not in a blazer and white flannels; in the fall or winter it would be either a purple

corduroy suit or a black pinstripe suit. ('My tailor caters mainly to pimps,' he would say.)

Jill loved wearing oddities such as coolie hats. Of late she had been seen in shocking pink ('It's Scap's year' – pause – 'Schiaparelli, you know'). She constantly took up a model's stance, with a provocative pelvic thrust that ensured instant attention.

Jill looked fetching and youthful, Ruth thought, in her T-strap shoes and 'middy' leg-exposing shorts, ignoring all dress regulations of the dining-room.

Adrian knew a good deal about the Merediths, but Ruth would have to be filled in. On this voyage it was a foregone conclusion that the two couples would be crossing paths constantly. Adrian would see that Ruth was indoctrinated quickly, but there was no opportunity now, before dinner.

Jock took to Ruth instantly, boisterously and heavy-handedly. Ruth discovered at once that his frame of reference was poetry, art and some music. He was dogmatic in his views. He came on full force, ignoring his wife's presence, and had obviously been drinking. He proceeded to extol Ruth's beauty, comparing her face with the great classic faces, Dante's Beatrice in particular: the literal, the acknowledged portrait of Beatrice! And when Jock proclaimed her the 'embodiment of heavenly beauty', Ruth and Adrian froze in embarrassment. Jill showed irritation by opening her make-up compact and glazing her lips with a purplish-black lipstick.

'He's smashed, dear,' she said to Ruth, 'but you *are* beautiful.'

As they all moved towards the dining-room, Jock, who had had more than enough alcohol, seemed not to realise that Ruth and Adrian were on their honeymoon, were not to be imposed upon, and he proceeded to flirt in a loud, embarrassing fashion. Ruth, realising the condition he

was in, decided to nip the gibberish in the bud, and said, 'Dear Mr Meredith, that's a lot of bullshit. I'm from Chicago's West Side, Jewish, and there's no Florentine blood in my veins, no relationship with Dante, Beatrice, etcetera. Be nice and let's all have a good dinner.'

It had a sobering effect on Jock. Obviously Ruth had made an extraordinary conquest, a whopping impression on Jock; and Jill wasn't liking it at all.

She struck an insolent pose. Adrian looked searchingly at her, recognising that a contest was taking place, and she had turned mannequin to attract his attention. Adrian thought, 'She has good tits, a good mouth; she's okay.'

Ruth noted Jill's posturing, and made a decision to enjoy herself, no matter how preposterous the situation or the compliments became. Beatrice indeed. She turned to Adrian and whispered, 'He's too much. All that animal energy. What a pity.'

Adrian gave her a smile. He looked at her anew, studied her face, decided, yes, Dante would have been taken with her: her delicate Roman nose, the fine bones, the large and luminous eyes, the long black glossy hair, the marble-pure chin, the ivory throat . . . yes! Beatrice. And suddenly, he too decided to relax, play along, allow the Merediths to go whole hog in their fashion. Let Jock do his thing, entertain them with his clowning, his literary nonsense. The Casanova *manqué*. And at that moment Ruth saw Adrian's smile and thought, oh the joy of the trust in a lover's glance . . . Yes, the Merediths were potentially friends, would be fun to see in Paris and back home, despite the embarrassments.

There were a few Rabelaisian outbursts from Jock. Adrian responded. And they moved into the dining-room, found their table.

Near the end of the captain's table Adrian spotted the

ex-reporter and presently novelist, Mordecai Ericson. He led Ruth to Ericson's seat and introduced her.

'A fellow Chicagoan – a man of letters – an ex-*Daily News* star.

'Morty – Mr Ericson – covered the Hacha assassination in Miami – we were both there. I even contributed a bit to his fund of background detail. Fanny Butcher reviewed his novel – with faint surprise. I'm hoping to read it soon . . .'

'Don't hurry, Adrian,' said Ericson, laughing. 'By the way, Fanny Butcher didn't like Hemingway either.'

He turned to Ruth and said, 'Maybe we can all meet in Paris – I'll be staying there for a while. We Chicagoans must stick together. Right?'

'I hope we meet there,' said Ruth. 'We're planning for a long stay and our address will be the Pont Royal.'

They returned to their seats and rejoined the Merediths.

'That young man – I'd guess he's our age – ought to start dieting,' said Ruth. 'He's in his mid-twenties and he's already developed a double chin.'

'But I'll bet he's enjoying life,' said Adrian. 'Those chins and that paunch spell high living.'

Jock interjected, 'Ericson's book is one of the sexiest novels I've read in a long while. If it isn't banned in Boston I'll be surprised. I'll be surprised, too, if the movies don't buy it for Jean Harlow . . . '

Jock did not let up at the dinner table. He was obviously anxious to make an impression. He turned to Adrian who was eating oysters, and asked if he ever gave thought to the psychology of eating oysters.

'I'm not sure I understand the question,' said Adrian. 'Did you say psychology?' He exchanged a quizzical look with Ruth.

'Yes. Did you ever give thought to what the first man

who ate an oyster must have thought? Fears, questions, doubts . . . '

'I don't think any fears or doubts entered my mind with respect to oysters except their quality.'

'Well, Adrian, eating an oyster could be a strange, even a traumatic or erotic act, depending on one's imagination. Like what the first man who went down on a woman must have thought, wouldn't you say?' As he said this he lifted a large, succulent oyster – at least five inches in length – and placed it on his extended tongue.

Adrian bent over, unhinged with laughter. Jill put on her best patrician expression and turned her head. Ruth averted her eyes.

'I seldom eat oysters,' said Adrian. 'But when I do, I think of their texture and taste. But the whole subject does fascinate me. All the silent breeding and germinating – hermaphroditic animals; it really could get one to wondering.'

He raised his replenished goblet of wine and drank, as though to wash away the entire subject.

'No one has answered my question,' persisted Jock, his speech beginning to thicken, Adrian thought. 'The first man to eat an oyster . . .' continued Jock.

'Not much different, I'd say,' offered Ruth, 'from the first man or woman to eat a raw egg, or for that matter, fried brains or chopped liver.'

Jock appraised her for a moment, his vision blurred, it seemed: then he smiled sadly and said, 'You're a paragon of logic.' He picked up another oyster, saying, 'But getting back to the first man to eat a woman . . . '

Jill raised her arm and said, 'Please, for Godsake, Jock.'

He stopped, frowned, and began engorging another oyster. Then, putting down his napkin, he beckoned the waiter to remove the champagne bottle from its bucket and pour.

'The prudery of people,' he muttered. Then he continued, his voice raised slightly. 'Gastronomy and sex – they're related – why not discuss this relationship? Fish eat fish – nothing sinful or evil about that. It's nature's way.' He chuckled. 'People eat people, in different ways.' He turned to Jill and said, 'Forgive me, dear, but your lipstick is smeared.'

He took a sip of wine and added, 'If I could give myself head I'd probably never get out of bed.' A smirk followed this disclosure.

The reaction was stunning. Jill rose, tossed her napkin across the table, overturning Jock's glass, pushed her chair back and left.

Jock rose from his seat, simpered drunkenly, pretended to be puzzled, then followed her.

Adrian howled and Ruth asked, 'Did I miss something?'

'I'll bring you up-to-date later. That's Jock – he's a very funny man.' He studied Ruth absently for a moment, then added, 'By God, he reminds me of me.'

Of the dreams Adrian experienced during his voyage none disturbed him more than the one he had the night following the viewing of *Berkeley Square*, and the encounter with the Merediths.

A hag of a woman, wide-eyed, with lips blue-black and shining, was attempting to kiss him. It was a Lautrec character, a naked woman with flopping breasts, skin creased and powdered heavily; and she kept shrieking, 'You are a wounded bird.' She reappeared in his dreams three times, the third time, a terrifying, crazy sunset of black and orange behind her. She came to him, her lips parted for kissing, and a scum seemed to be flowing from the corners of her lips. Then there was a driving rain and he felt the need to escape, to seek dry shelter. He woke up confused, disoriented.

Should he relate this dream to Ruth? he wondered. He decided against it, for the present. He wondered about the dream: not so much in terms of its significance but of his health, since a cold sweat accompanied it, preceded by what he seemed to recall was a gusty, cold wind, and a driving rain.

The fibrillation he had been experiencing for the past several years was recurring, but this he decided not to report to Ruth for fear of alarming her. Did sex have anything to do with it? As a doctor's son he should have given more study to the matter. He might have asked his father for some advice, but had decided against it. Not that he was shy. But it was a matter of privacy, a matter too personal to discuss with anyone – yet. Perhaps he was being stupid. An ostrich. Unwilling to face reality. Well, it was his life. And thus far, Adrian was happy, ecstatic. Life at this juncture was a river of sunlight on which he was floating, and his companion, the most adorable female . . . A thought interrupted his euphoria: should he consult the ship's doctor? He would be ideal: an outsider, not invading his privacy. In the morning, Adrian would perhaps see him. A flip of the coin would determine his course of action.

He went back to sleep. In his dream he was lying on his back, facing the sky: immense, blue-black and emblazoned with stars beyond counting. In the morning he chose to erase it from his mind, but found that he could not. Well, better a sick heart than none. He had read that somewhere, he thought. Beckett? he wondered . . .

Another recurring and disquieting dream in Adrian's recent nights was based presumably on his preoccupation with Ganzara, and it brought a series of complex puzzles to Adrian's conscious hours: a short, angry man with fury in his eyes but melancholy in his stance, a little angry man, saying, 'I hate religion and presidents and capitalists and especially religion and priests and my non-mother.'

And then, of late, this Ganzara figure reappeared, quadrupled in mirrors, pointing his forefingers at him, saying, 'Sacrifice the Aztec princess. Kill her!' The situation, the voice, was clear, frightening, commanding. A recent dream had this man saying, 'Make a meal of her. Her hair will be an extra course, maybe dessert.' Then he would laugh and fade away.

These visions were frightening, and he would awaken, his heart beating wildly; unco-ordinated contractions of the heart muscle had him gasping. Maniacal visions, gaudy landscapes and sunsets, wild commands added to the rolling of the ship, leading to – what? A form of dementia?

And one night, a few days before he and Ruth embarked for France, he had a dream set in a courtroom: a governor (presumably of his state) and a judge (presumably Minelli) were sitting at a huge, ornate table which a group of men and women approached to purchase clemency and paroles. 'Ten thousand dollars,' he heard, or 'Twenty-five thousand dollars.' These two powerful, venal, men were selling freedom. The scene was barren except for the table and two chairs and the line of supplicants, together with the judge and governor. The central scene was laid in a theatrical spot of light – moonlight, white and cold, on a shining parquet floor. A Negro court attendant was saying, 'Youk'n hide de fier but wat you gwine do wid de smoke?' Everyone nodded soberly. And Minelli pointed to a witness and said, 'Remove that lying cunt.'

Adrian had been in a court of law only once in his life.

A shattering thought gave him pause: he must give up all concern with crime, murder, legal malpractice, for the sake of sanity and health and general self-preservation. For the sake of his pulsating heart. His pulsating subconscious.

The dream that caused Adrian the greatest pain – the dream he would surely never repeat to anyone, for inherent in it was evidence of a cowardice and weakness no human being would care to admit – was the one in which he found himself returning to their ship's cabin when he saw a huge masked man knocking on their door. His wife's face appeared in the opening and the man thrust a large revolver into her face and said, 'Come with me, woman.' In this dream Adrian shrank back, watching, observing his wife's fear-frozen face, watching her open the door wider and follow the man down the corridor as the gun was prodding her from behind. In this scene Adrian was silent, fearful that he would be observed, thinking, if that man knows I'm here he'll turn and kill me. If I run quickly, the man will simply rape or kill her and she will die and I'll be done with it and all. This dream had a reality to it so intense that when Adrian awakened, he lay drenched in sweat, shaken with fear and shame. Was he himself the masked man of his dream? Was it Ganzara come to assassinate his bride? Who and what was the demon and what prompted so evil a dream? 'What manner of bridegroom am I?' Adrian spoke in a whisper as he turned and saw Ruth sleeping quietly beside him.

Chapter Nine

Ruth and Adrian arrived in Paris at last. They had little difficulty in making connections, getting the right train, a good taxi, making their destination known: the Pont Royal on the Rue Montalembert on the Left Bank. Adjacent to *everything*! Including, he noted, the great publishing house of Gallimard.

Every block they had traversed was cause for exclamation: the chestnut trees, the shops, the ancient buildings, the intimate Utrillo streets, the out-of-central-casting-characters, the ancient houses, Sacré-Coeur, the drive, the Eiffel Tower – it was all a delight, including the traffic jams and taxi drivers' curses and shouting. And the almost sexual thrill of finally encountering the St-Germain-des-Prés quarter: Ruth was speechless.

The hotel sent a porter out to the street for their bags, giving them a cheery French greeting. His 'Bonjour, bonjour,' delighted them. Their 'rooms' – a one-bedroom and bath 'suite' – were on the top floor, with a view of Sacré-Coeur.

'Every inch of it is so French,' Ruth cried, as her eyes swept over the rooms – the flowered drapes, the sexy red velveteen bedspread, the window shutters, the bidet, the stingy little light bulbs, and the too few hangers in the too small French closet: 'I love it all,' she cried and performed a pirouette in the middle of the room.

'But let's unpack and get out of here *rapidement*,' she said in her best Chicago French. 'We must have our first

glass of French wine and some French bread right away: a first meal in Paris is a sacred affair. On to La Coupole!'

They tore open their suitcases, stacked and stuffed away everything in double time: luckily there were two tables and a bureau on which to pile books and packages. Soon everything was out and they freshened up in the bathroom.

They checked the desk for mail, found nothing there, then left, luckily getting a taxi that had just been vacated. The driver smiled, advised them to relax and that he knew perfectly well where the Coupole was. '*Très cher*,' the driver said, '*très cher*.'

'He's warning us that it's expensive,' said Adrian. 'As if we care.'

'I care,' she said, 'but not on our first day in Paris. Screw economy. Today is for pleasure and the carefree life. *Vive la France*!'

'Okay,' said Adrian, 'I'll let you buy lunch.'

'Well, sport, I'll just do that. You can't frighten me. I always suspected you wanted to be a kept man.'

On arrival they found the gigantic restaurant crowded, totally full, so they moved to the bar and at the maître d'hôtel's suggestion had two aperitifs apiece, toasting each other with each sip.

Soon, they were led to a table. Every face they saw interested, fascinated them. They were prepared to love everyone. There were Americans of course; also Germans, Italians, Algerians, British, Hindus, numerous Orientals.

'I intend having a gourmet meal here, starting with caviar,' said Ruth.

'Don't frighten me,' Adrian said. 'Besides you're buying the meal, you know.'

Just then they both spotted a famous face, Sinclair Lewis, sitting with a young woman – blonde and wearing mirroring sunglasses – and a fat man who was, sure

enough, their own Chicagoan, Mordecai Ericson. Lewis looked drunk. Ericson was peering into the woman's mirrored eyes and seemed to be in an animated conversation. Lewis's head was bobbing up and down, and he looked sullen, angry. There were heavy bags under his eyes. His long, lean face had a dog's look; it was an unhappy face.

'Should we intrude on Morty and his little party?' asked Adrian.

'I think not,' she said. 'Lewis looks surly, and I doubt that the young lady wants any intrusion; Mordecai looks intrigued with her.'

At that moment, Ericson, as though he had overheard them, recognised the couple and waved to them. They returned the wave. Five minutes later the waiter brought a bottle of champagne to their table.

'Compliments of Mr Ericson,' he said, opening the bottle.

Ruth caught Ericson's eye and blew a kiss towards him, and Adrian saluted with a broad smile.

'Now that was a friendly thing to do,' said Ruth. 'We've got to reciprocate, somehow.'

'Sure. Let's buy and read his book. I'm sure they have it at the Brentano shop.'

'Good idea. Also, let's ask Jill to invite him to their next party; I'm sure she knows where to locate him – probably knows him better than we suspect.'

'Well, I'm not exactly a stranger to him, either,' said Adrian. 'I wonder what he's doing with Sinclair Lewis. And who do you suppose that woman is? Probably an actress, a movie star. But who?'

They stopped a waiter and asked him to identify her but he shrugged and said he had never seen her before. 'Just another pretty face, monsieur,' he said, surprising them with this brand of levity.

Ruth proceeded to order without a glance at the menu. 'Caviar, smoked salmon with *beaucoup* minced onions and lemon and – hot toast; and a green salad with avocado.' She paused, sat back and smiled at Adrian.

'What about you, dear?' she asked. 'The wine Ericson sent will go nicely with my order.'

'You leave me breathless,' he said, then turned to the waiter. 'I'll have the same, but first, a very dry Beefeater martini with an olive.'

'Wow,' said Ruth. 'This is living. Let's have some of that crisp French bread and butter – at once!'

As they sipped the champagne they began looking around. There were some unattached and attractive women; also bearded, turtlenecked students, artists.

Adrian took out a pillbox, a tiny heart-shaped gold box she had given him, and removed a pill, swallowed it, holding his head back for a moment. She said, 'Adrian, you look so handsome in that white turtleneck. You must always wear white; or lemon-yellow; or blue.'

'Noted,' he said. 'Here's my martini – and, f'heaven's sake, just look at the caviar!'

It was 'mounted' for elegant display, on chopped ice, surrounded by quartered lemon and finely-chopped, diamond-like onions. They fell to.

After one large bite followed by a mini-spoonful of chopped onions, she paused and murmured through her teeth, 'Divine.'

When they left the restaurant Adrian insisted on going, first, to the Seine, to visit the bookstalls, to buy a dirty book: Frank Harris's *My Life and Loves*, in particular, which they found in three volumes. Copies of this bawdy work had been smuggled into America for some years and Adrian had read two of the volumes already. Now, he wanted Ruth to read the work.

'It's full of lies and boasts but it's great fun. Harris was

an Irish-born American citizen who simply couldn't resist bragging about his sexual powers. Every woman he met was a challenge to his masculinity and each of them toppled like a domino to his prodding.'

'Sounds repulsive,' said Ruth. 'Unless he has a sense of humour.'

'I promise you'll be entertained,' said Adrian, parting with his francs for the three paperbound volumes.

They walked to the Pont Neuf, the most ancient of Parisian bridges, watched some artists at work before their easels; the boats, the *bateaux-mouches*, the bookstalls with all the prints and multifarious books. They luxuriated in the late afternoon sun. Groups of students sat at sidewalk café tables, smoking, reading, drinking, ogling. After almost two hours of strolling, Ruth admitted defeat, calling for a nap. They taxied back to their hotel.

'Do you know what Jill told me?' asked Ruth. 'One must make love on the first day in Paris.'

'Well, if that's an order, so be it,' said Adrian, removing his clothes.

Several hours later, they awakened, refreshed and happy, ready to discuss their plans. And of course, they had their first social evening before them: dinner at the Merediths' house, at nine o'clock.

They agreed that, despite certain difficulties that Jock presented when drinking, his compulsive flirting, for example, it would be a great indoctrination opportunity for them; and they would probably meet some interesting people. They were promised a few dancers, writers, artists – and also a few boring but rich relatives.

Ruth stared at the ceiling, thinking about her present state, about Adrian. Her father had given her a generous cheque – what should she do with the five thousand dollars? She would open a bank account in Paris, and the

money would be used entirely for Adrian's pleasure, or medical needs. Perhaps a small portion for herself.

She remembered the half-read letter from Adrian's father, decided to give it a quick reading while Adrian slept.

My dear Ruth

This is a very difficult and painful task for me. Perhaps you should have known before, but I was afraid to tell you the truth. You and Adrian have been so marvellously happy together. I didn't want to intrude with the slightest doubt or worry. But now you must know the truth – completely.

When Adrian was five years old, during a very rainy summer, he contracted scarlet fever. (Warning: don't ever lie in wet grass or wet sand.) It seemed to be an unusually severe case and despite the use of a recently discovered sulphur drug, he took a long time to recover. I watched with dread for a most feared complication. Several months later, he developed a heart murmur and we knew then the valves of his heart had been damaged. Slowly, as he grew to manhood, his capacity for sports which he loved so well became diminished. Two years ago, he began to require the use of Digitalis every day. He remains mostly well with this drug, but still suffers from spells of palpitations when his heart races. There are also moments when he cannot seem to catch his breath at times of stress. These spells are brought on by physical demands, but even strong emotions can be responsible. He must be made calmer and allowed to rest immediately at these moments.

With care, you will have many happy years together, but you must be gentle with him, as he with you.

Adrian stirred and Ruth stopped reading, concealing the letter under her pillow for the time. She looked at his face, asleep, seemingly at peace . . .

Among the guests at the Meredith apartment on Rue de l'Université was a young ash-blonde English woman calling herself Lilith Kingsley. Never had Adrian encountered the name Lilith in any living person and his curiosity was aroused.

She wore black leotards under a transparent skirt, had an ivory-white powdered face and heavily kohled eyes. Her small, rounded breasts were unavoidable. As she shook hands with Adrian she palmed a miniature *carte de visite* surreptitiously to him, smiled and walked away. Other guests were a famous, middle-aged publisher of pornography who carried a tiny monkey in his arm; a painter named Voyex – a name unknown to the Breakstones but obviously a current celebrity; a lesbian pair named Jocelyn and Jacqueline who did not mix with anyone but sat together all evening, mooning at each other; a young male journalist from Algeria who spoke a charming brand of English; a famous feminist novelist and her young male escort; a few unattached young women, 'remittance girls' who had disgraced their families in England and been invited to stay 'the hell away from home'. They looked quite harmless and nondescript, but Ruth was told in confidence that drugs and promiscuity was the explanation. Why were they here? Simple: Jill and Jock liked them – they were good company.

An American jazz pianist was there, busy at the piano, with an endless repertoire of American music including Cole Porter and Gershwin. There was also an American novelist with two first names, a bearded and charming man who was alive and bristling with concern for Spain.

Adrian was taken with a young self-professed revolu-

tionary, a twenty-year-old French Sorbonne student called Marcel Solange. A Marxist, munching a caviar canapé and sipping champagne, he advocated the abolition of the American capitalist system.

'The most important single thing, the one thing worth fighting for, besides the love of a beautiful or loving woman,' he said, smiling, 'is pure socialism.'

'Well,' said Adrian, 'in America we have a modicum of socialism but as much freedom as an individual needs, providing he keeps his nose clean. We can call the President of our country a shit, and there will be no punishment. We have freedom of movement, of occupational choice, religion, of speech. We can write or print almost anything. We can attack church or state with complete impunity.'

'Yes, but what about the exploiters, the tyranny of the industrialists who grind the working man down to the dust?'

'That is a universal matter, a fact of life,' said Adrian. Then he added, 'Thoreau proved that it is possible to secure total freedom in America, showed us how to avoid industrial oppression; all one needs is character and self-discipline. I could become a beachcomber tomorrow if I chose. I could avoid all supervision and oppression. And I would probably not starve. There are always fish to catch . . .'

Said Marcel, 'America will never be free until it has a revolution.'

'That's bullshit,' said Adrian. 'I recall that we had a revolution. But frankly, I detest all revolutions, all holy wars, all fanatics. Most of them lead to self-destruction anyway.'

'We are getting away from the most important matter – Marxism – the answer to the human problem,' Marcel broke in. 'In another decade or so, by, say, 1950 at

the latest, Russia will be a paradise. Mark it down, my friend.' He paused, smiled condescendingly and continued, 'If you were versed in dialectical materialism, the language of the Communist world, you would understand what I'm talking about. Read Engels, Marx, Lenin; those men investigated and wrote about scientific and social problems.'

'Sorry,' said Adrian. 'I've read a good deal of the Marxists and I must admit that I find most of their political thinking and jargon out of reach. And when I think of the fate of the Russian poet – his name escapes me – I want no part of the Russian philosophies. When that poet's tragedy is justified, I'll listen to Communist talk. Until then, I pass. Please excuse me for the present.'

Adrian searched out Ruth and joined her as the room began to jump with the American jazz. The pianist, a man named Ernie Jackson, was still at the piano. He had once played in Chicago, at the Arsonia Café Adrian learned, and had known many of the Chicago-based musicians including Louis Armstrong and Manuel Manetta. He had a broad interest in 'loud and rough music', he said, laughing.

Jock approached him and whispered something in his ear. Jackson smiled and stopped playing. Then Jock got up on a chair, wine bottle in hand, and shouted, 'An announcement. Attention, please.'

He paused, then said, 'We have a beautiful and brilliant young American pianist in our midst. I suspect she knows some works that have outsold Irving Berlin's, like from a guy named Mozart. She and her husband arrived in Paris only today, and they don't know our Parisian custom. Which is, in brief, display all your talents at the earliest possible moment! Ruth Breakstone, will you kindly approach the piano,' he commanded.

Everyone applauded. Jackson vacated his seat and beckoned to Ruth.

She looked at Adrian, pleadingly. Should she refuse? He smiled and motioned towards the piano.

The Merediths' piano, a great Bechstein, awaited her. It was a formidable black instrument. She took her seat before it, looked at Adrian, Jock, Jill, the ceiling, the keys. Then she said, 'I can't compete with Mr Jackson and his marvellous jazz, which I love and envy. I'm a student, in love with Mozart. I will play for you some of *Eine Kleine Nachtmusik* with your permission. It is my own arrangement for the piano.' Jock beamed.

She played exquisitely and when she rose from the piano stool a young woman – a poet – approached her and kissed her on the lips. 'That was celestial,' she said. 'I look forward to hearing more, and to knowing you better. You are beautiful, and also an artist.'

Another woman, a visiting dancer from Vienna, put her hand on Ruth's shoulder and said, 'They would love you in Vienna, in Salzburg. You must come there and play for us; we will have much pleasure. In Grinzing, there is a special tavern with a piano, just for you and music lovers; you must come.'

Ruth thanked her, laughed and promised to visit Vienna and play and guzzle wine in Grinzing . . . some day. It was all very heady. But, on a double take, she thought, when I go to Austria I will not go to play in a tavern. It will be a concert hall for me, or nothing.

Proudly, Adrian approached Ruth and kissed her. 'That was perfection; beautiful. I love you.' Then he added, 'What a brilliant stroke, playing Mozart after all that Cole Porter. What a contrast!'

Jill Meredith also came hurrying to Ruth to thank her for her contribution to the 'evening's delights', as she phrased it.

'And I must say, Ruth, you remind me of another woman who played for us one night about three years ago.

She's much older of course – the legendary Magda Tagliaferro. She had the same elegance and taste and authority you show; have you ever heard her play?'

'Thanks,' said Ruth, 'and you're very flattering. I heard her play in Chicago about five years ago, and I have a number of her recordings. I think she's the finest pianist alive, a great romantic. I always remember one comment she made: "giving a concert means taking risks". I remember her face: she and Lotte Lenya are alike – and they both have red hair . . .'

In every way, the Merediths lived up to their reputation. Their apartment was decorated in both Art Deco and surreal styles, and the basic elements leaned to the permissive, with colour surprises and provocative objects at every turn. There were paintings and drawings on the walls that would have disturbed relatives and friends in Chicago: explicitly erotic art, photographically representational – a copulating elderly couple by George Grosz, for instance, a photo blow-up of a vagina by an American expatriate artist.

'A porno fun house,' remarked Adrian as he passed Ruth in the corridor. The vagina study was astonishing. No one could look at it without uttering some obvious or gauche remark. And yet, this photo, showing the full pudendum amply surrounded by hair, with its ultimate (magic) realism, could not be ignored. Was it art? An anatomy lesson? Was it justifiable in museum terms? Suited to a modern home? What was the point?

As Ruth stood before it, Jock came up to her, put his arm around her waist and said, '"The Mother of Us All". That is its title, that is what it is. You are looking at the ultimate artifact. But that's not the precise word. Actually, the accurate characterisation of this is Cunt. I asked my friend, Man Ray, to photograph the vagina. Forgive the vulgarity of my disclosure, but I paid him a

thousand dollars to photograph Jill's vagina. No one knows it's hers. I consider it the supreme subject for the artist or photographer. Isn't it beautiful? The Louvre, the Metropolitan Museum, the Art Institute – none of them would think of exhibiting it. And yet, to me it's more beautiful than Botticelli's *Birth of Venus*. This photograph is the epitome of pure sexual beauty and it surpasses anything by Ingres, Titian, Botticelli, et al. Do you agree? It also helps me to separate the Philistines from the rest of the world. Didn't Yeats say "Sex and death are the only things that can interest a serious mind"?'

Ruth, having passed through a kind of kinaesthesia at this point, was like the initiate running a gauntlet – an initiation that was painful and exhilarating, perhaps liberating.

'Jock,' she said, kissing him on the cheek, 'I love you and thank you for this evening. The people I've met here, the things I've heard, seen, sensed in your house tonight, and the pleasures I've experienced, thanks to you and Jill, I'll never forget. You can't imagine what it's like for me, an insulated Midwesterner, who always thought herself sophisticated, what I feel now, although I must say my head's a bit in a whirl, knowing you and Jill and your friends, and Paris, and, well, everything. As for this photograph of a vagina – and yes, I'll call it what it is, a cunt – it is one of the most exciting graphics – do we call a photograph a graphic? – I've ever seen . . . ' Then she added, 'I also think I'm drunk.'

At three o'clock in the morning Adrian and Ruth left the party, exhausted, surfeited, transported, incapable of further comment. They had been fortunate in their encounter with the Merediths; this was a certainty. It had been a landmark evening for them. They must now analyse the experience soberly. But who was sober? They

decided to walk back to the Pont Royal – a perfect night for walking, they decided. They agreed that Paris was the beginning of their true life, their maturity. Everything that mattered in their life would be calculated as from the day they arrived here. Ruth of course, in a moment of clarity as they walked back to their hotel, began to think of Adrian's heart, the letter Adrian's father had given to her, the disclosures made. There would be problems to face, medical issues, difficulties; and at once she was burdened with the custodianship of Adrian's welfare, his health.

She wondered whether Adrian knew as much about his condition as she did. Perhaps he did. But she could not discuss, nor share with him, his father's confidential communication.

Suddenly Ruth stopped, declared that her shoes were too tight. She proceeded to remove them, then continued walking in her stocking feet.

Her mind returned to the Man Ray photo, the vaginal Rayogram, wondered whether Jock was telling the truth, whether it was in fact Jill's vagina. But why not? She wondered whether she would have the courage to pose for such a photograph. She began to speculate on her own body. What would she dare show to the world through the eyes of a camera? She decided that her breasts were good. She smiled. She saw the photo, life-size: just her breasts. It would be framed, and a small plaque below the picture would carry the legend, *The Breasts of Ruth*. Or perhaps simply, *Breasts*.

'What are you laughing about?' asked Adrian.

'Was I laughing?' she asked, and she did indeed start giggling.

A private matter, she thought, a private matter.

He too was thinking of a private matter: he had escaped a most difficult situation in Chicago, thanks to his father's

generosity, and he hardly dared believe or imagine how happy he could be in this new environment.

One quiet early afternoon, a few days after their arrival in Paris, they were in their hotel room, Ruth reading a book by the window, Adrian opening the mail: three letters from the States. One was from a professor at the University of Calabria, forwarded to him by his father. Adrian had secured the professor's name, Giovanni Califona, from a friend in Chicago.

In response to his letter, the Calabrian, a sociologist, had given Adrian brief general answers to his queries relating to the Mafia situation in Calabria. No real specifics were provided, but Adrian did get confirmation of the criminal underworld's existence and power in Calabria.

He answered Adrian's particular questions about Ganzara.

> There are no public records of his life or family. To the best of my knowledge, he was an uneducated, ignorant man, a mentally disturbed trouble-maker, a malcontent. The assassination of your Mr Hacha was reported in the papers here, but there seems to be no existing family named Ganzara. His father, I learn, moved to America years ago; his mother died when he was a very small child. I don't know about brothers or sisters.
>
> I would surmise that Ganzara was an amateur anarchist who belonged to no organisation. There is no anarchist party here to my knowledge. No criminal would belong to such a party in any event. The Calabrian is an individualist. The Mafia consists of individualists. They are constituted like families, enclaves. Anarchists are, in my opinion, undisciplined madmen, misguided philosophers. Anarchism is a

political attitude. Ganzara may have been hired to fire the bullet, but I doubt it, and those with whom I have discussed the matter share my view. No one in Calabria would associate with such a man, never.

I would appreciate it [Professor Califona concluded his letter] if you would please destroy this letter after reading it. I'm responding to your query because of my deep friendship with our mutual friend at the University of Chicago, John Barrows. Please do not quote me or refer to this letter. My position at the university here is firm and I wish for no problems. You can understand my situation. Unlike Sicily, Calabria is little known outside, for criminal activity. I do not wish to be responsible for gossip of this sort spreading to other countries.

There was no signature, just the typed name, Giovanni Califano, at the bottom.

'*Requiescat in pace*, Tony Hacha,' murmured Adrian. 'You benighted bastard.'

Ruth, who was still reading, overheard Adrian's muttered comment. 'Who are you talking to and what did you say? Sounded like Latin to me.'

'Darling, I'm trying to sort out a few discrepancies. Pay no attention.'

'Is it the Ganzara business?' she asked.

'In part. By the way, what are you reading? That book looks unfamiliar.'

'I picked it up yesterday when I was out shopping, in the Boulevard St Michel. It's a play by Andreyev, *He Who Gets Slapped*. I'm fascinated by one of its key characters, a beautiful circus bareback rider named Consuelo. Love and death and identity are the themes.' Then she added, 'Much more interesting than anything related to that crazy nobody, Ganzara.'

'Maybe so,' said Adrian. 'Ganzara is turning into a fading footnote as far as I can see. But the subject of murder and violence is still my concern.'

'Well, in Andreyev's play there is murder and death, but also love and romantic action. And I love the circus life and melodrama the playwright is dealing with. You must read it, Adrian. Anyway, I think we ought to call a moratorium on violence today,' she said. 'Put Mr Ganzara on ice. Remember, you promised me a walk through the Tuileries, and this seems to me the day for it. Look at that sky; there's a real sun coming through. I'd love to take a long walk, then wind up at the Ritz for one of their famous American martinis. What say, chum?'

'You have a deal,' said Adrian. Gathering the torn bits of the letter from Califano, he flushed them down the toilet.

While shaving, Adrian shouted, 'And then we are going to do some browsing on the Rue de Seine where I'm told there's a marvellous little bookshop.'

Ruth took out her Paris map and studied it. 'Let's try to make the Louvre on our walk. Just a half-hour or so. I'm told that one should not spend more than an hour at a time in the place. A half-hour today, after the gardens. Okay. But first, that martini.'

'You're showing distinct signs of alcoholism,' said Adrian. 'That martini seems to weigh heavily on your mind.'

'It does my dear,' she said. 'I intend to indulge myself as often as I can. And how about making the Eiffel Tower today, too? All the way to the top. I hear it's a sensation, although some people, they say, lose their stomachs halfway up.'

'Be sure to take the camera,' said Adrian, coming out of the bathroom, freshly shaved, combed, smiling. As he stood there in his pale blue pants, barefooted, lean, Ruth felt a sudden ache in the centre of her being.

She embraced him briefly. 'And what will Michelangelo's David be wearing today?'

'White slacks, yellow turtleneck,' he said.

'Great,' she said. 'And I'll be your twin.'

In her white slacks and pink turtleneck sweater, with her long black shining hair down almost to her waist, she was an object of such beauty that Adrian sat down on the bed and looked up, jaws slack.

'Are you okay?' she asked.

'Merely stricken,' he said, 'by your beauty. You never looked so good, so beautiful as you do right now. So edible.' He studied her for a moment, then asked, 'How come?'

'Paree, Paree,' she sang out. She did a pirouette, moving towards the door. 'Fetch the camera, darling,' she cried, 'and let's taxi to the Eiffel first. *La Tour Eiffel* – the giant lady with the iron legs!'

'You're turning into an ugly American tourist.'

'Precisely what I am, and *intend* to be,' she replied, pushing the down button at the grille of the elevator door.

In the descending elevator, they looked into each other's eyes and saw the purest joy, the prospect of loving days and nights ahead. He must not forget, he thought, to write his father who had, after all, made this possible.

Halfway up the Eiffel Tower they did indeed almost lose their stomachs; the sudden awesome view of Paris produced a shock to their nerves and they backed into the rear of the lift and turned their backs on the city to recover.

'I didn't expect that kind of impact,' said Adrian. 'I hope the second half of the ascent doesn't cost me my breakfast.'

But when they reached the top, their vertigo passed and they stood at the edge of the wall, marvelling at the view. They could spot, instantly, the gleaming marble of

Sacré-Coeur, Notre Dame, the Louvre, the *bateaux-mouches* on the silvery, winding Seine.

They took snapshots of each other, and got a sailor to take the camera and photograph them together against the city. They bought ice-cream cones; another stranger snapped them licking away at their *glaces*.

Then they took their long walk through the Tuileries, and finally reached their martini destination, the Ritz. They toasted each other with their frosty, be-olived cocktails and decided to order two more. After which they were ready for high adventures. But suddenly Adrian felt chest tremors, difficulty with his breathing. A sweat drenched his body, and he urged that they return to the hotel. Ruth found a taxi quickly. As they got in she took his hand and expressed her guilt at overdoing, overdrinking, overreacting to the city, and tiring him. He was silent, withdrawn. Brow damp. When they reached their room, he pulled off his sneakers and threw himself face downward on the bed. She stood over him, fearful, helpless. Then she decided to administer Digitalis and a sedative. He did not resist, and shortly he was asleep. She lay down carefully beside him. Fear entered her body suddenly; she turned cold, then she wept, silently.

Adrian awakened but did not stir. Ruth was sleeping beside him and he began to backtrack on their day's adventures and his sudden malaise. He lay there mentally inventorying his state of health. The fibrillation and sweating he had experienced at the Ritz bar was gone. The drug had restored him. He listened to Ruth's gentle breathing. A slow anger began to grow within him; he could feel it, he could almost watch it build and he became tense. I must put a stop to this, he said almost aloud.

Adrian's view of his father's beneficence was mixed.

That he was the recipient of a generous gift no one could deny. Nor could he argue having in any way deserved or earned it. A two years' subsidy in Paris! Few if any of his colleagues at the university could have dreamed of such extravagant treatment. He had no job, no future career planned. His father was making no stipulations, no demands of him. Adrian and Ruth would work out their own futures in their own good time – at Papa's expense. Actually, Ruth's future was clear: she would become a concert pianist and/or teach. Two years' diligent work on her part, and she would be well on her way as a professional musician. As for himself, his various intellectual tangents, his self-admitted dilettantism, his forays into French translation; his concern with violence, assassination; his interest in philosophy, mathematics, chess – and what else! – what did it all add up to? Where in God's name was it taking him? An intellectual jack (jerk) of all trades – that would be an ironic ending for him, the intellectual *wunderkind* of the Breakstone family.

Obviously, Adrian's health, a matter no one seemed willing to discuss openly, was the factor, the key element in the decision to support the young couple abroad. Adrian's heart was obviously the basis for his father's charitable act, the honeymoon which he began to think of as his two-year French leave.

A resolve suddenly loomed before him. He thought of it as 'loomed' because the idea struck him forcibly, and visually. He would enjoy himself to the hilt, cease worrying about anything, and that included his heart. If he dropped dead tonight, so be it. He would not play invalid, nor allow his flawed heart to govern his actions. He would make the most of whatever was destined for him, whatever time was left. And he might – he grinned – fool them all, outlive many of his friends. 'Heart people' were

unpredictable, he had read. Everyone worried about them, and the invalids wound up septuagenarians or better.

He placed his hand on Ruth's ass, stroked the crevice with his forefinger, kept it there until she turned around, opening her eyes.

'Getting familiar?' she said, smiling. 'Groping? A pass, maybe?'

'No, just wondering if you were awake. I've just had a wonderful idea, an inspiration. Let's go to Place Pigalle tonight. I want to see the "Sin City" and its *filles de joie*. What do you say?'

'Well! And also, oh my!' she said. 'I'm up to it if you are. An erotic safari, what?'

'I'm curious to see if they have anything there like the Chicago night-clubs; the Four Deuces for example. Or the Hungarian Club, all of which, by the way, I've only read about.'

Ruth said, 'I was checking through a *Paris By Night* booklet and found what looks interesting, certainly unconventional.' She reached for a pamphlet at her bedside. 'Elle et Lui, 31 Rue Vavin. A bisexual dive, for dancing and drinking. Let's go there for champagne and watching, around midnight.'

'Just what I had in mind,' said Adrian. 'But there is another interesting place to go for a late dinner. The Crazy Horse Saloon, for *le strip*.'

Then Ruth said, 'I'm glad to see you're your usual self again, the American sex maniac in Paris. That Eiffel Tower reaction had me worried.'

'It was nothing,' he said. And he turned and kissed her on the cheek. 'I think I should avoid double martinis and high places. Anyway, it's gone and I feel fine and rested and – avid!'

At that point the phone rang, and it was Jill Meredith.

Could they all join up for dinner tonight, or were they tied up? Ruth asked her to hold on a second and turned to Adrian. He nodded and said 'Suggest the Crazy Horse and dinner.'

The Merediths seemed astonished at the suggestion, from two young lovebirds, but agreed. Jock would arrange the reservations since he knew the owner, not to mention a few of the lady entertainers and the green-haired hat-check girl.

'It could be great fun with these two,' said Ruth.

'Agreed.'

But when the hour approached for them to meet the Merediths, Adrian suddenly flopped back on the bed.

'I'm not going, I'm not in the mood.'

Ruth looked down at him in astonishment. 'You're not well?'

'No, I'm okay; just not in the mood for the frivolity. Besides, I want to do some writing tonight.'

'Please, Adrian. We can't cancel out at this hour. Are you sick? Please tell me the truth.'

'No, not sick. Not in the mood. But please go. You'll enjoy yourself. Take a cab and they'll see you home. I want you to have a good Parisian night out and I know the Merediths will be good hosts. Tell them I'd be a burden. I've got migraine or something.'

'I simply can't go alone and leave you here, Adrian; I don't get it. No, I won't. I'll phone them that we can't make it.' Ruth looked stern, then angry.

'No, you must go. I'll be okay. I'm just not up to the effort involved, can't make the scintillating conversation; not interested in the whole scene. Please, Ruth, you go and have some fun.'

'I really can't go. I hate to leave you,' she repeated.

She stood there, alternately angry and puzzled. Finally, being persuaded he would not change his mind, Ruth

kissed him, said she'd not stay out too late, and left: uneasy, perplexed.

Adrian lay spread-eagled on the bed. Why resist the impulse? he said to himself. This is what freedom is all about. Go!

He pulled out a small black notebook and found the miniature *carte de visite*, with the name, Lilith Kingsley.

He phoned and experienced a sexual tremor upon hearing her voice. He felt his heart pounding, then said, 'Is this the lady Adam befriended?'

'Yes,' she replied. 'And is this the naughty boy from Chicago who is in Paris on his honeymoon?'

Deadpanning his voice he said, 'Are you able to see me – alone and right away?' Then he added, 'On a most urgent matter.'

'You sound very serious,' she said. 'Is it really a serious matter, or are you playing naughty games?' The voice now of a cocotte.

'Who can tell? I have your address and my map tells me it is less than ten blocks from the Pont Royal. May I come over now?'

Lilith's card was actually pasted on the mailbox inside the door. He rang three times before she buzzed him back, and after climbing three flights of a murky staircase – one small bulb took care of the illumination of the entire climb – he reached a sickly, *chartreuse*-coloured door. It was open and he entered. She occupied a tiny two-room apartment, *intime* in every sense. There were soft pink lights, numerous pillows on the floor and a studio bed covered with a violet rug. A small print of a Chagall nude was on one wall. A desk and a chair stood near the window, and a small stand or bar leaned slightly awry at one corner of the room, cluttered with bottles and glasses.

She was standing in the doorway of the bathroom,

dressed in a long black linen kaftan; around her throat was a string of very large canary-yellow beads.

'Where does one sit?' Adrian asked, looking around.

'Since there are no chairs to speak of,' she said, 'I suppose the bed is probably the answer to your question, or one of the pillows on the floor. Unless you wish to sit by the desk near the wall? So far away.'

'The bed looks inviting,' he said. 'But do you mean it literally?'

'*Mais certainement*, monsieur,' she smiled.

Adrian sat down on the edge of the bed, his hands stroking the bluish-purple coverlet.

'So you did not throw my address card away,' she said.

'Hardly. It was an inspired idea. Otherwise I would have had trouble locating you.'

'Would you really have bothered?'

'Well, I'm here.'

'You are the first person I've ever known, ever met, from the city of Chicago. I always thought they were all gangsters, carried machineguns and wore black suits, pointed shoes and wide-brimmed hats.'

'Well,' said Adrian, 'I usually carry a machinegun, but this is a social visit.'

She laughed. 'Is there some special purpose in it?'

'Yes, an urgent matter to discuss with you.'

'If it's an intellectual matter, I may not be able to help you. I understand you're planning to study in Paris, perhaps at the Sorbonne, and that you come from the University of Chicago; an American intellectual, *oui*?'

'Not exactly. You speak excellent French for an English woman. But my question or concern is simply this.' He moved over to where she was standing. 'Is all of your hair so blonde-white – platinum blonde I think it's called – because Lilith's hair, I've heard, was red?'

She broke into another laugh, and he put his hands on

her shoulders, touching her hair. He was now almost certain that she wore a wig.

'Before answering that difficult, highly personal, question, may I offer you a drink?'

'Please. Whatever you're drinking would be fine . . .'

'Then it's champagne,' she said, 'which is all I drink other than gin.' She went to the bathroom where presumably she had her refrigerator; and returned with a magnum of Taittinger. 'Open, please.'

'Are we going to kill *this* bottle?' he asked. 'A half-gallon? . . .'

'Why not? The day is young, or rather, the night.'

'Now, about the red hair,' he said, removing the wire, foil, and giant cork from the bottle, catching the foaming wine in a goblet at hand.

His hand began to shake and he put down the bottle. She noted it, smiled, and took it up, pouring the second glass.

'You are nervous, my friend; let me do it; besides, we need a cloth for the bottle.'

She returned to the bathroom, and was back shortly with a vivid terracotta-coloured hand-towel.

'Now we're in business,' she said, sitting down beside him on the bed.

He poured more wine into a glass, touched it to hers.

'Coo-coo,' she said.

'Coo-coo – ' he repeated. 'That's a strange toast,' he said. 'Crazy, in fact.'

'So is *salut*.' She smiled defiantly. Then she put her nose close to his and said, 'Does your pretty bride know you are here?'

'No. Nor need she know, don't you agree?'

'I'm not sure,' she said, smiling. 'I find it hard keeping a secret. Is secrecy essential to our meeting? Or discussion?'

'Oh, yes,' he said. 'I'm working on a confidential

dissertation dealing with women's hair, for the Cosmetic Society of Cicero, and my findings must be kept confidential. Don't you think?'

'Yes, I think I understand. But first, let's be comfortable. Take off that tight blazer. Besides, I like that jolly red waistcoat you are wearing.'

He removed his jacket, tossed it across the room and leaned back on his elbows.

'Now,' he said, breathing slowly, deeply, staring into her eyes, 'I would like to see your cunt.'

For several moments there was a silence. She stood up and addressed the ceiling.

'You really are a pig,' she said, 'a Chicago pig. Or simply a very crude young man? Do you always behave so – so crudely?'

'No, not unless I'm provoked. You provoked me. Those black leotards, those eyes, that hair, your – your fucking breasts. I can see your vermilion bullet nipples clearly. And that perfume you're wearing: you are assaulting me. And that little calling card you gave me. How am I to interpret it all? Since I come from Chicago, and we usually call a spade a spade, I must call it now. Please – I want to see, to kiss, your cunt.' Pause. 'Please.'

'Ah,' she said. 'You did say please. Now you are behaving more properly. But frankly, you are just married; doesn't your bride meet your needs? Is there a problem between you? Is she indifferent to you? Frigid, as they say in the sex manuals? I'm curious.'

'My bride, my wife is neither frigid, nor indifferent. I met you. I responded to you. I want to know you intimately. Isn't it the most natural thing for a man? You're irresistible, you know.'

He studied her face, her eyes, wondering if he would be able to carry off his bold plan. He hoped he showed aplomb.

'You flatter me,' she said. She looked away, almost embarrassedly. Then, 'I would love to have you kiss my cunt. Are you qualified? Skilled at it? Do you know what a woman wants?'

Without waiting for a reply she sat down, lay back on the white fur spread and parted her legs slightly, affording him the pleasant task of raising her skirt, pulling down her panties and burying his head at the confluence of her thighs where he found, not platinum blonde hair but a dark, silky, perfumed bush that brought to his mind at once a young Chicago Jewish princess he had once dated – he was about seventeen then – and who tried to seduce him while drunk, a girl named Sally Rabinowitz whose father was the king of Chicago junkmen. Sally Rabinowitz owned her own Packard roadster and persuaded him to blow her while she was driving down South Shore Drive at eighty miles an hour and he remembered in that earliest instance, actually his first, how the line of poetry by Longfellow, 'This is the forest primeval', came to his mind as he burrowed among the hairy, mucous regions and when he finally emerged from the slippery depths he said, 'I'm going to call you Evangeline, Sally,' and she asked, 'How come?' and he told her about Longfellow's line of poetry and how it was like stepping back into a primordial incarnation, or at least his mother's womb. 'Evangeline' was the title of the poem from which the opening line came. They both howled, and she said, laughing, 'You mean my muff,' and they howled again, and she handed him her silver flask of scotch and they killed it between them and she dropped him off at his house and he never saw her again because he contracted a mouth infection which he attributed, privately, to his experience in the car.

He heard Lilith sigh and she moaned, 'More,' and he continued to apply himself to the enterprise of giving

tongue, and then, suddenly, she lifted his head by his hair and he rose as though rising from some frothy depths – a dream-dive – and as her fingers were locked in his dampened curls she drew his lips to hers and she captured his tongue and held it, miraculously, sucking it with a frenzy and possessiveness, as though she had a fear of losing it. And then her fingers, long pink-fingernailed tentacles, were at his zipper, then at his balls, gently clawing – clawing deliciously, without pain; stroking. And his fingers found her again and he continued the aquatic task, the primeval exploration with his fingers, while his lips were engaged, tongue with tongue, and he knew that if called upon, he would gladly relinquish his life in payment for the painful pleasure, the services to his senses now rendered. She was attacking his tongue as the vulva and vagina attacks the prick, the muscular structure of her mouth receiving and caressing with a kind of anatomical skill known to the hummingbird in its sexual courting, its hovering helicopter, vertical mating, beak to beak. How little, thought Adrian, man and science understand the magical organ at the floor of the mouth, the organ involved with taste and articulation and sexual cognisance, and the ecstatic utterance for which there are no words, only sounds. And, thought Adrian, this young woman's body – surely the name Lilith was not misapplied – has the potential of an army.

Then he began to fear that he was unequal to his hunger, his need, that he might wish to die in her arms, and he had not yet fucked her, having laboured in the byways where other delights were to be found. Lilith, he said (perhaps only to himself) you are, in truth, I suspect, an Egyptian courtesan, a daughter of Egyptian pharaohs, bald of head, bewigged in platinum, but actually bald, naked as a store-window mannikin: I want your eggshell bare head at my crotch, against my balls and cock; your

china-doll bald head is my desire, clown-white with scarlet lips to hold my mouth and tongue, your tongue entwined in mine, each searching out the other's honey. . . and then Adrian moved into darkness. Was she now at his cock, he wondered, as he found himself blanking out in sexual delight, a swoon that emanated from the solar plexus, then the genital regions; dreamless; weakened. He fainted.

He was awakened by Ruth around midnight.

Whatever pleasure or excitement she might have experienced with the Merediths at the Crazy Horse, she had put behind her.

'We missed you so much. The Merediths are genuinely concerned; did you get a good rest?'

He thought: there's something ominous behind her banal words.

He turned and faced her directly, eyes wide-open now. He suddenly knew, realised with a heavy sadness, that she was wiser than he, would outsmart him in the end. This beautiful Jewess bride would outsmart the world. He knew that despite his intellectual edge, he was, alongside this loving female, an asshole.

'Did you get a charge out of the Crazy Horse? Tell me all about it.'

'Well, the real show was off the floor; the tourists at their tables provided plenty of noise, vulgarity, crude talk and so forth. We saw *le strip* at its ultimate raw vulgarity. The Chez Paree at home is, by comparison, a Sunday School event. I saw some pretty elemental stuff, rough public sex. I don't think I want to go back, but it was essential as one of the attractions of Paris, to be seen once, no more. I must say, though, that the girls were striking, some beautiful, some right out of Lautrec. You know, the green make-up and the piled-up red hair sort of

thing. Some looked like they had not finished grammar school – real baby dolls, no pubic hair, in short white stockings, black patent-leather slippers, short organdie dresses revealing – well, everything. There was one young girl in a kind of Valentine Day outfit – red shoes, pink dress knee-high, with heavily made-up eyes and huge lashes. She put on an outrageous act of flirtation and I'm sure she had dates lined up after the show. *Très* sexy, Adrian . . . ' She thought a moment. 'Now I know the difference between our home town and Paris.'

'Perhaps as a student, I should have gone,' said Adrian. 'Would you come with me some night?'

'I doubt it,' she said. 'I can't imagine why I'd want to return to that place. There must be dozens like it all over town, especially in the Pigalle area. I notice that there's a Debussy concert tomorrow night – but let's talk about it in the morning. I'm so glad you're feeling okay. Now let's get some sleep.'

Ruth did not mention seeing scarlet lipstick on Adrian's shorts in the bathroom hamper. She chose to block the discovery out of her mind until the morning; there might be a satisfactory explanation. But intuitively, she felt that she had been, not so much deceived, betrayed, but rather, debased. Ruth looked at him as he lay there, eyes closed, perhaps asleep: she saw him as a handsome dissipated Adonis type, a debauchee. There was another word for it but it eluded her. She looked at the bedside clock and thought: 1:30 in the morning in a Paris hotel, I, Ruth Breakstone, learned on my honeymoon that I had married a depraved man. When I get up tomorrow I must either face the facts, face Adrian with my conviction, or wipe it out forever. The bullfighter's word, *veronica*, came to her mind: she would perform a veronica, sidestepping disaster.

She pulled her nightgown over her shoulders and slip-

ped into bed beside him but not touching him. You love him, she said, and this is the true beginning of your maturity – learning to live with certain grim facts of marriage. You've been screwed, figuratively. You must now sleep and pretend it never happened. This is the shape of things to come in your life. This is the beginning of your secret life.

The next morning she ordered shirred eggs for them both with their continental breakfast. She kissed him and ran off to her first class at the *Conservatoire*. Almost nothing was said of the previous evening. They shared the morning *Paris Herald Tribune* in silence.

When she was gone, Adrian made a call to Lilith Kingsley. A male voice, heavily accented, answered and said Lilith was not there. On being pressed, he was told that she had left for Morocco an hour ago, would be spending the next two months in the capital, Rabat. He, the speaker, was an old friend of hers and was subleasing the apartment. He did not have her address, he said.

A lie, of course.

Adrian hung up. He lay back on the pillow and thought about how he felt and decided it was what a cow must feel at the moment when felled by the slaughterer's hammer: a blow between the eyes. He lay there, then began to weep. 'Women's games,' he said quietly to the empty room.

His tears stopped suddenly; his mood turned from self-pity to pure burning anger; and a storm began building up in the chambers of his brain and heart. He felt pressure in his chest.

Stormy weather ahead, he said to himself. Playing women's games. Well, he had been wallowing in the low-pressure areas where lived a storm. He would remain calm even though he sensed a hurricane in the making; high velocity winds with which he couldn't deal. If that bitch, he thought, that white spider walked into this room right

now, his fantasy Egyptian princess, what would he do? He was a logical, thinking, sensitive man. A student of life and motivation. A poet! Ah. He would fall on his knees, he knew. He would ask her to come and live with him, somehow. He paused, thinking, then I am sick. Would I ask Ruth, my bride, my love, to tolerate Lilith?

Continuing pressure in his chest. Fear, pain and anger intermingled. He took his nitroglycerin tablet. His anger came and went with the cessation of pain. He knew he was not really up to this game, if indeed it was a game. He would phone Jill Meredith, a woman of the world, and tell her what had transpired, and ask for her advice. No! She would think him a shit. Women banded together. They detested the so-called philanderer. She would say, 'You don't give a shit.'

Women could be such bitches, acting out genital needs when in heat and calculating for an advantage. But they couldn't tolerate the male philanderer; the rogue dog, that would fuck any bitch in its path. Was he, Adrian, such a dog? In fact he was.

As for Lilith, he'd spurt and cream in his shorts if she smiled at him, stroked his prick, tongued his throat. Do I really give a fuck? he wondered to himself. Am I really, totally amoral?

In an hour, Adrian was up and sitting at his desk by the window in his jeans and velvet jacket, overlooking Paris, pen in hand, writing in his favourite violet ink, a mottled cement-grey sky overhead. Murky clouds were darkening the rooftops and streets before him. The automobile horns seemed to be noisier, amazing him more than ever.

He was writing now, almost aimlessly. The pen was taking over . . .

His subject: the meaning of violence: assassination and the myth called the brotherhood of man; the malpractice of Christianity. His love for Lilith was an unresolved

matter; he was at this moment a philosopher, an observer. Tomorrow he would curse her.

My beautiful bride (my sister – my bride) Ruth will be home soon and I will think up a surprise for her – a café where I will fête her, reaffirm my love for her. My true love for my Jewish princess. Whither thou goest. Perhaps he would take her to the famous Catalan restaurant on Rue des Grands Augustins. He had heard about their good Spanish food, the flamenco guitar; it would be good to hear the click of heels, the castanets, the rich Andalusian rhythms, watch the black glances of the women dancing . . .

Leaving earlier than usual from her class, Ruth made a decision she was never to regret, an act of revenge and self-indulgence, an act Adrian could not have suspected.

From the telephone directory she secured the address of the artist and photographer, Man Ray. She had attended, a week earlier, a Man Ray exhibition, a gala opening where the art critics and Parisian notables and eccentrics had gathered. She recalled her meeting with the artist, in the crowded, hot and noisy gallery. A mere handshake, but there was warmth in his eyes, she remembered.

Gertrude Stein's brother was on the premises, posturing. There were the *haute couture* women, one of them underdressed to the point of being naked to her coccyx. Another was entirely in transparent black chiffon, sitting on a gilt chair, leaning forward, her nipples glowing like small headlights.

And now, today, bursting with fury, an uncontrollable anger at her husband and his infidelity, she wrote a cheque for five hundred dollars – her first financial splurge as a bride – and took herself to Man Ray's Rue Feron studio, unannounced. She smiled at his alleged boast that he was the last of the red hot Dadas . . .

He met her at the door of his studio, greeting her, a

virtual stranger, with warmth. She suddenly realised that he was shorter than she, and stocky. His eyes were coal black. He invited her in, offered and poured her a drink at once, began to ask questions, chiefly about her background. His accent, surprisingly, reminded her of Chicago. It was both warm and brusque, tough-guyish. His eyes were grazing over her body, face, hair, back to her eyes. He was explaining himself as a painter-turned-photographer and as she listened to him, watched his bright jet eyes, she could not resist asking if he was from Chicago.

He laughed. 'Do I sound like one of Capone's boys, huh? No, I'm from Philadelphia – now you know the worst. Hah.'

His eyes, intensely alive and warm, were caressing her. She had dressed to assure his interest, and was heavily doused in an extravagant perfume. She wore no bra. She surveyed the studio, wondering whether his current mistress, Kiki, was on the premises.

My first visit to a real artist's studio, she thought, as she ran her eyes over the contents of the room. She had heard it called a 'palace of illusions', and she could see why. It was filled with his arcographs and rayographs, his solarised photos, numerous surrealistic objects and drawings and paintings. Alice in Dadaland, she thought. She found him charming, exuberant, an overgrown-boy character. He embodied for her, while an American, the romantic Parisian spirit; and everything about him and his studio spoke of Paris and the new art movement.

He handed her a drink and she blurted out, after taking a sip, 'I fell in love with your work, Mr Ray, and I would like you to take a photo portrait of me. I can pay you five hundred dollars. I know it isn't very proper, very business-like, but will you do it, please?' She paused, suddenly embarrassed.

She sipped her drink, aware that her hand was shaking, and he averted his eyes. He walked to the window of his studio, then turned towards one of the objects, a small noble figure on a pedestal. He seemed momentarily preoccupied; then he turned to study her.

'What sort of photo?, he asked.

'Nude – that is, to the waist,' she said, her heart racing.

'Isn't that pretty daring for a Midwestern American woman?'

'I suppose so.'

'Well, take off your blouse, please. We'll see.' He sounded like her family doctor *sans* stethoscope, and she began slowly to obey his instruction.

'I'd gladly pay more,' she said, 'and I'm sure it will be worth much more, but, well, I'm hoping you'll say yes. I would be honoured.'

She was now fumbling with the buttons on her light silk blouse; then removing it she discovered that her hands were trembling, and she was shocked to find that she had wet herself: her face turned beet red.

He continued to appear abstracted. Then he came closer, stared at her breasts.

'Charming. Charming titties,' he said. 'Beautifully erect.' He postured, finger alongside his nose, eyes narrowed, pretending deep study. He moved about as though attempting to find the best composition.

'But yes, I'll do it,' he said. 'But I must make it memorable. You have tender, beautiful breasts, but we will enhance them. Gild the lily, one might say. With art, capital A. Yes, I'll touch them up with a light coating – rose-water, attar of roses and baby oil. It will give them a sheen, interesting highlights. Dewy, moist breasts! Do you mind?'

'No, no, I don't mind. Please. Can you photograph me

at the piano? I'm a pianist – I may have mentioned.' She explained that she was studying in Paris.

'We'll take several shots, one sitting at the piano. First, let me arrange the breasts.' He chuckled to himself, repeating the word, 'arrange', giving her a sidelong grin. And he went to his palette table, removed a small bottle and poured a few drops from it into his palms. Then he rubbed his hands together as he approached her. His manner was that of a rogue about to commit a villainous act; a character out of Dickens. As he gently massaged her breasts they rose; and his ministrations brought a heightened pink colour to them, a gleaming hardness to the nipples. She lowered her eyes, finding herself becoming wet again between her thighs.

He said, 'Okay, now please go to the piano and take your normal position.' He watched her seat herself, then said, almost shouting, 'Now put your hands into a natural playing position, breasts erect. Erect! Good. Perfect. An exquisite moment.' He murmured something to himself, hoarsely, walking towards her.

He brushed and combed her hair with his fingers, adjusted the flow of her skirt, tilted her chin up a fraction, so that her face seemed thrust forward and upward, bringing her breasts into a similar forward thrust. He took a camel-hair brush and applied a delicate blue coating to her upper eyelids: then with a pencil he outlined her eyes heavily with kohl. There was, suddenly, a transformation; she had an aura of passion and intensity in her face and in her pose, a sensuality and a quality he had already suspected. His eyes glittered.

He turned on a low floor-lamp, adjusted it so that the light was projected from below. He removed the Kiki photograph from the piano top. He drew the window drapes, turned on a soft pink light.

'Play,' he commanded. 'Play something you love deeply,

something very special, so that it permeates the photograph.'

She thought for a moment, then began with Satie's *Gymnopédies,* allowing the melody literally to float above the slow simple chords in the accompaniment.

'My God, you know Satie's work?' he exclaimed. Then softly, he said, 'Erik was a dear friend, a near-genius. He influenced Debussy, you know. Do you know that he was about your age when he wrote the *Sarabandes*? He believed in the young . . . he would have approved of you.'

As she played her eyes focused on a photograph, Man Ray's famous *Violon d'Ingres* photo of Kiki, the notorious Parisian model and girl about town. There were other photos of her; also a copy of Kiki's *Memoirs*.

Man Ray's eyes, his playful teasing wit, his physical charm, his total persona had won Ruth over at once. To Ruth's youthful, Midwestern American eyes, he was a very appealing, sexually magnetic man.

Suddenly, standing behind his camera, he shouted, 'Hold it!'

One of her hands was suspended, raised about the keyboard. Her face was a poetic romanticised vision of youth yearning for passionate adventure. He took six photos in all.

He studied her, vulnerably exposed. She avoided his eyes, blushing furiously. 'Your breasts,' he was saying, 'they are like, well, like seeing the contents of the Gold Room of the Hermitage for the first time.' Pause. 'Simply dazzling.'

'Thank you,' she murmured. 'What an extraordinary compliment.'

'Come back in a week. I'll select the best one and it will be yours.'

Ruth said softly, 'May I ask that none be reproduced or

copied? I would be embarrassed if a copy became – became public. My husband would be furious.'

'I understand,' he said. 'We'll make one final print of the one you choose. I'll destroy the others, the plates. This transaction will be our little secret.'

He poured her another drink, then sat down beside her.

'Do you like this drink?' he asked.

'Yes, but what is it? I don't think I've had it before.'

'Ouzo, a Greek liqueur. Anise; a kind of cordial, like nectar.' He laughed.

Then he put his face close to hers and said, 'I have a modest suggestion to make. Will you remove the rest of your clothes? I'd like to photograph you, for my personal collection, from the rear. Standing. Full figure. Your face will not be revealed. And for that favour, or service, there will be no charge for your other photograph. You may tear up your generous cheque. You are too beautiful, too young, to be paying me. I make the duchesses and countesses pay. The Comtesse Greffuhle is one of them. And there is the Marquise Casati, with her three pairs of eyes. She pays!' He chuckled again. He exuded, suddenly, a mesmeric, feral power, a good male odour. She felt suddenly, marvellously, free. He took her head in his hands and kissed her on the mouth gently.

The next day Adrian decided to have a light early lunch alone. Ruth would not be returning from school until late afternoon. He chose the Brasserie Lipp, a few blocks from his hotel, and managed to get a seat on the ground floor because he was early. The Boulevard St Germain was not yet crowded. It would be relaxing, he felt, being alone for a few hours. He ordered the restaurant's speciality, *choucroute Alsaçienne* and lager, and discovered that his appetite was heightened the moment he smelled

the sauerkraut piled high on the frankfurters and ham. He sat back, contented, observant, at peace with himself.

He eavesdropped eagerly on the conversation of two young women, obviously British, certainly on the town. Their table almost adjoined his.

'Does he really have lots of money?' asked the one in the short red skirt and tight breast-bursting 'middy' blouse, a pert brunette, heavily freckled.

'Oodles and *oodles*,' replied her companion, a blonde, a giggly type who punctuated almost every sentence with a little burst of laughter.

'He looks like a sporting type, dontcha think?'

They continued their speculations and he tuned them out as he attacked his food.

A huge man, heavily paunched, with a bulldog's eyes and hypognathous jaw, sat down across from him, with a chic young woman, willowy and dressed entirely in black. He immediately ordered a bottle of champagne which arrived in a large silver ice-bucket. Much attention was suddenly given by the management to their table. Rich, or a political VIP, thought Adrian. But there was no way to overhear their conversation and he began to conjecture as to their professions and relationship. Obviously the man was at least twice her age; obviously he was excessively attentive. Adrian decided she was his mistress. He would write a short story about the two: she would be Odile, a would-be actress. The man, a Hungarian, was financing a motion picture and was assuring her that she would have a leading role. Or, perhaps she was a famous actress, merely unknown to Adrian. She would get the role; she would sleep with her benefactor three times, then would become unavailable to him, having fallen in love with another performer in the film, a younger woman. The irony of such a situation seemed to satisfy Adrian as he forked up his food.

He finished his meal, paid his bill and left, edging close to the table of the pair about whom he would write a story, hoping to overhear their voices, a bit of their conversation. As he passed their table they were both raising their glasses in a flamboyant toast. He decided they were a pair of bourgeois characters not suited to the rather banal storyline he had invented. Besides, Adrian was in no mood to write fiction; his involvement was with assassination – death. But, was this the day to devote to such a pursuit, with such a glorious sun, an air of happiness everywhere? He decided to find a good book-shop, choose a few books and take them to the hotel to await the return of Ruth. He had, he felt, overeaten and misjudged his capacity. He felt pressure at his waist, and he loosened his belt. Better to lie down instead. He walked back slowly to his hotel, picked up a copy of *Figaro* at the desk and rang for the lift. He would rest and scan the paper. But before the elevator arrived he felt an excruciating pain in his chest. He was frightened. He turned towards the desk attendant and asked him to fetch a doctor quickly. He sat down on a chair in the lobby as they began phoning for help.

Within half an hour, Adrian was in bed, having been administered medication. He had given the doctor the music school's name where they could reach Ruth. He was asleep before she arrived.

Suddenly he awoke. He smiled as he saw Ruth. 'I hope the doctor didn't scare you? I suddenly felt very lonely without you and I gave him your school's name to call. I hope you weren't frightened.'

'Rest,' she said. 'Don't worry about me. Do you feel better?'

'Yes,' he said. 'Too much kraut food. I'm okay, Ruth. Let me hold your hand, please.'

He looked into Ruth's eyes and knew that he would

always love her. But would she reciprocate, remain loyal to him, in view of his quixotic behaviour, his transgressions, his need for adventuring in the byways? What was her capacity to tolerate?

'I just had a sort of dream – I'm not sure it was a dream or a conversation or a subconscious or surreal monologue. I can't say which or what, but it made me feel that I know so little of myself. These dreams prove our bedevilment . . . '

She looked at him, her eyes liquid; close to tears. Such confusion . . .

'Don't bother your head with dream-meanings, Adrian. How do you feel? Is the chest pain gone?'

'Oh yes, I feel relaxed, no pain.'

He reached out for her hand and said, 'I want to tell you something I've just discovered about myself. I want to succeed in one thing more than anything else; I want to succeed in love. I want to succeed in our love the way a newborn child wants to breathe. Do you believe me?'

'I believe you, Adrian,' she said, bringing her lips down to his. 'Now try to get a little sleep.' She sensed that she would never manage to penetrate the depths of his mind, his needs, his secret life. There were, and always would be, unanswered questions. She would love to ask him what it was he wanted that he didn't have with her? He was obviously searching for an adventure, an experience. Sexual fantasy had something to do with it, she thought. But how to grapple with *that*? And then, there was the problem of his health, his heart . . .

From her memory bank came a phrase, from her beloved Proust and something about monogamy, his credo about marriage and love, what a man needed, should have, not one but a number of women. She remembered the deadly statement, 'If you live with a woman altogether you will soon cease to see any of the

things that made you love her.' Was this happening to Adrian, to their marriage? She could not, would not believe it, accept it. Besides, was Proust, a bisexual, capable of commitment to one woman, one person? And Adrian was most certainly a heterosexual, totally. Puzzles within puzzles . . .

Slumped over a small mountain of reference books at the Bibliothèque Nationale, Ruth was making a systematic exploration, not of music, but of the human heart. She was voyaging in dark waters, attempting to grasp its physiological complications and architecture. She read with care, making notes and small diagrams. This cosmos, constructed of muscle and blood, was for her an incarnate metaphor of life and death. The vocabulary of the heart's anatomy became for her almost Homeric in its words and phrases and images: '*When the ventricle is empty, the cusps fill with blood, and drop back to block the artery. When the ventricle is expelling blood, the emptied cusps are pushed into small dilations of the arterial wall, called sinuses of Valsalva.*'

Poetry! Terrifying words. And she read about oxygenated blood and the nature of oxygen hunger, and the experience of physical pain and collapse and despair. She knew, intuitively, that the sickness Adrian was experiencing was drawing him into a devouring and unfamiliar sea.

The protean aspects of Adrian's personality were, she feared, going to present problems for her, demanding a patience and forbearance she was not sure she was going to be able to maintain. Like tuberculars, who were, it was said, sexually hyperactive, she wondered whether a heart condition such as Adrian had, would also induce, perhaps psychologically, a sexual appetite beyond the so-called norm. Would it affect his social behaviour, his attitude towards her and their marriage? Would she become his

nurse or, as she once jokingly and alcoholically put it, his handmaiden?

Sickness aside, Adrian was a complex and decadent, and immensely lovable, young man. She would learn, she decided, all she could about his malady. And cope with it. The letter Dr Breakstone had sent to her in confidence outlined, in general terms and in modified and serviceable medical language, the nature of his disease. Between the lines he was also pleading for her help and understanding as Adrian's lover and nurse, wife and keeper.

Adrian's collapse in the lobby of the Pont Royal would, Ruth feared, be one of many such incidents. She would supervise his diet, his activities, his exercise and rest; and she would administer his medication. In return, he would demand in the gentlest of terms, an honesty, and the faithfulness, owing from a wife.

The ugly lipstick-soiled shorts which Adrian had discarded in his hotel laundry hamper flashed across her mind. She saw mentally, the stains, the proof of his infidelity, felt the sharp pain of anger. She decided to erase it from her mind. But could she?

That evening she decided to write Adrian's father a letter, giving him the details of the latest attack, based on what the hotel doctor had told her. She had not previously referred to his letter, nor the gift of a cheque accompanying it.

She put her reply into a carefully worded, non-alarmist letter. The responsibility was, at this moment, too great to carry alone. She would be accountable, providing she had the necessary support and advice, not to mention the facts. Dr Breakstone's letter had been candid, but slightly less than a total disclosure, and this, she made clear, she must have at once. Later she also wrote to her parents, asking her father for guidance. She reported that she and Adrian were happy and enjoying Paris, that she was

deeply in love, but she was now a woman burdened prematurely with a peculiar responsibility. Would this peculiar burden – the two words echoed in her mind – would it affect her life, her musical studies, her career?

She wondered whether she should share her secret life with the Merediths. She needed, longed for, a confidante. But was it wise to share so personal a problem? Would she care to be the recipient of such a disclosure if the situation were reversed? There was no answer for her, and the issue vanished from her mind for the present.

Chapter Ten

The fashionable, socially and professionally admired Dr Jeremiah Breakstone sat at his breakfast table, staring absent-mindedly at a letter before him. Stroking his beard he turned to his wife Sarah. She too seemed deeply concerned. She saw the delicate oily sheen that had appeared on his wide furrowed brow. Sarah knew the signs of inner agitation (he rarely showed emotion or stress) and kept her silence, waiting for him to speak. With his right hand he caressed the rim of the delicate Meissen cup before him. His beribboned pince-nez gleamed; his breathing was steady. He was sitting erect, his paunch carefully waistcoated. A lilac scent seemed to hover about him, a palpable mist, protecting him from the sweaty microbic world he inhabited.

As Jewish doctors went, he was a maverick; physically, a figure of personage out of a Chekhovian drama, exuding power and affluence, and authority.

An icy spring storm had hit the city that weekend and the gale-force winds could be heard howling around their corner apartment on the South Shore Drive near the Point. Fifty-mile-an-hour gusts, so his morning *Tribune* reported, were churning up the lake shore and sending waves crashing into the Drive itself.

Dr Breakstone's mind was elsewhere. The contents of the letter from Ruth forced all other matters to one side, including his morning schedule at the hospital. Adrian was uppermost in his thoughts and his heart. Sarah, to whom Jeremiah had read Ruth's letter, was far more agitated

than her husband, but she steeled herself to keep from weeping, studying his face, waiting for a sign, a word of comfort and hope. Was Adrian, in fact, dangerously sick? Was her husband telling her the truth when he said that while Adrian's heart condition was no light matter, he knew of many cases where such heart conditions endured, to ripe old ages? One of his women patients, in her late seventies, had had just such a condition all her life. With light exercise, modest activity, medication and a shot of good scotch three times a day she would outlive most of her contemporaries.

Sarah sat there immobile, watching him. His right hand fingered the cup handle, but he was not lifting it to his lips. If only the icy spring would turn and bring a little sun and warmth to one's bones . . . Sarah was eager to begin working on her terrace garden, her beloved roses and begonias. Soon, soon. Meanwhile, Adrian's heart condition: what did he – what did they – do to deserve such a fate?

Thank God the other boys were well. Sarah was too shrewd to offer any hint of criticism or recrimination. They had agreed between them that a two-year honeymoon- holiday in France would be a beneficial (and generous from their standpoint) programme for the young couple, giving Adrian a chance to enjoy life and to pursue his studies under the loving care of his beautiful young wife. She would be a good nurse and companion to him. It would be wonderful for his spirits, Sarah said. A small sense of guilt began to build within Sarah, however: did Ruth feel they had trapped her into a nurse-role where she had to dedicate herself to medical attendance on their ailing son? Sarah shook this thought off, angry with herself. What young girl wouldn't grab at the chance to be Adrian's wife, to marry into such a family? It was a love match, a good match; and Adrian's health would improve.

Jerry, her loving and distinguished doctor-husband, would know what to do.

And Jeremiah Breakstone was, indeed, cogitating on this very problem. He had a medical connection in Paris and would seek out the best cardiologist available to look after Adrian. That would be no problem. The psychological aspect was different however. And this he must resolve shortly. Adrian and Ruth needed moral support. He would dictate a letter to Ruth this very afternoon, after his hospital chores. It was vital that her spirits remain good, her confidence in her role as custodian of Adrian's welfare continue. He knew she was dependable. The threat she feared and expressed in her letter – the threat of disaster in their lives – must be laughed off, brushed away. She must be reassured that Adrian's condition was manageable and that he, Dr Breakstone, expert in such matters, expected Adrian to live long, at little sacrifice in or diminution of their enjoyment of life.

And now Breakstone had to meet with Judge Minelli. The judge was suffering from an enlargement of the prostate gland. The doctor was apprehensive, since he knew that Minelli would already have checked out medical books on the subject and was aware of the fact that if a prostatectomy was called for, then the dreaded cancer was possibly the causative element. He was too young: the enlargement of the prostate began, usually in the late forties, the fifties. Many men did not require prostate treatment until they were well along in years, in their sixties. And Minelli was still a relatively young man; hyperplasia of the glandular elements was definitely premature. Breakstone would, in any event, give him comfort, talk about hormonal matters and reassure him. But in his innermost heart, he wondered. With finger and instrument he had felt and measured the enlargement of the prostate; discussed Minelli's problems relating to

urinating with frequency and pain, given him dietary advice. He had also enquired, ever so discreetly, about his current sexual activity, and was not surprised to learn that he engaged in sex every day. Often twice daily.

Dr Breakstone turned to his wife who was watching him, wondering what conclusion he had reached with respect to their son. Judge Minelli's prostate condition was not only unknown to her, she wouldn't have cared less. Privately, she distrusted the man, suspected him of the worst, sometimes felt that he was a threat to her husband. Sarah, like Minelli's wife, was an innocent.

The doctor rose from the breakfast table, took his wife's hand in his, kissed her on the cheek and said, 'Sarah, I'm not worried about Adrian. Ruth will get a simple, affirmative letter from me, with the name of the best cardiologist in Paris. I'll reassure her. I think Adrian must be very careful of his eating habits. I'm so glad Ruth gave us the facts, very important, those details. Eating stacks of sauerkraut and pork would knock out any normal person. Can you imagine how much Bromo Seltzer I'd have to take after gorging myself on such a Brasserie Lipp meal? The sauerkraut gas! The pressure! Adrian simply must watch his diet, and Ruth will have to police it, for all of us. Don't worry, Sarah.' He paused, then added, 'I'm still glad we gave them this two-year holiday. It was no mistake. Believe me. All Adrian must realise is that moderation – moderation in *everything* – is called for.' He smiled and added, 'She's a very delectable sex object and I can imagine Adrian overdoing it. I'm going to put it as delicately as I can: sex, like all other gifts of Jehovah, must be savoured moderately, not gorged.'

Sarah smiled and said, 'Oh Jerry, you are the most mature, the most understanding man I know. How lucky we all are, Adrian especially, to have you looking after us.'

* * *

Several days later, over their fish and wine at a local bistro, Adrian was bringing up certain names given to him by friends back home, persons of likely interest to look up in Paris.

'Here's someone the Merediths thought we ought to meet,' said Adrian. 'He's an American visiting Paris at the moment, and his first book was just published. I got a copy this morning, at Sylvia Beach's bookshop; it's called *The Dream Life of Balso Snell*. I sampled a dozen pages of it and it's wild. The author's hero, Balso Snell, is exploring Homer's city of Troy. He finds the famous wooden horse we all know about, and decides to explore . . . He considers the several possibilities and finally chooses to enter the horse through the rear. His comment as he does so is "O Anus Mirabilis!" This guy will be heard from, I've no doubt. He's called Nathanial West.'

When they returned to their hotel room they were pleasantly surprised to find a large blue-and-white china pot with pink cyclamens in extravagant abundance. The card was from the Merediths, saying they missed the Breakstones.

'Why don't we ever think of doing something like this?' asked Adrian. 'What a kind, thoughtful and original idea. No purpose in the gift except to express friendship.'

'Let's send them something special,' said Ruth. 'A beautiful book.'

'Tomorrow we'll go to Sylvia Beach's and buy something new, or maybe *Ulysses*, and have it delivered by hand. What do you think?'

'I like that,' said Ruth. 'Even if they already have the book. Maybe we could get Joyce to inscribe it for them? Is he still alive?'

But the next day found their plans altered drastically. Adrian suffered another seizure at breakfast, with chest pains and a near-fainting spell. Ruth phoned the Pont

Royal house physician and secured, luckily, instant medical attention. An ambulance was commandeered and a vacant room was made available at the American Hospital. A three-day observation regimen was established and Adrian was given every known cardiology test. Ruth engineered a meeting with the hospital's head cardiologist and recited to him the case history. Adrian's father, she pointed out, was one of America's foremost surgeons and would be grateful for his personal dedication to Adrian's progress.

While Adrian had been through the rigours of hospitalisation before, as a young boy – a tonsillectomy and appendectomy – he had never been subjected to such a prolonged siege of tests, and nightmarish nights. As a boy and the son of a surgeon, he had come to know something of death and dying. But now, he suddenly became aware of the sounds of dying. At night, lying awake, he wondered about his own survival. He was near crazed as he listened to each sound from the various rooms on his floor. Echoes of death, fragments of death's history would reach his memory. He could hear the sounds of physical distress: coughing, vomiting, spitting, the wheezing and hacking of the aged. And then, his mind and attention were fixed – transfixed – one particular victim, a man seemingly strangulated with cough. Obviously the pain was extreme, accompanied by sighs between coughs, cries and moans. And then suddenly, he heard an anguished and terrifying sound, the voice of unendurable pain. Was he imagining all this? Was only Adrian hearing this dreadful death-drama taking place down the corridor of the hospital?

Once, long ago, Adrian remembered, at another time, as he inadvertently wandered into the maternity ward of his father's hospital, he had heard the outcry of a woman, a sound so heart-piercing, so terrible, the sound of a woman trapped with a child unwilling to vacate the womb,

trapped and tortured, that he vowed to himself – he was not yet ten years old – that he would never assume or endure the guilt, the responsibility of begetting a child if it caused such agony. The woman's shriek was vivid in his mind, now – so many years later.

The sounds of pain and dying were trivial compared to the fear engendered by the real pressure and pain within his chest. And he began to feel wistful about his magniloquent father, who could, somehow he knew, pull him through and out of this painful impasse; and he began to wish that his father were here, pince-nez and Vandyke notwithstanding. He muttered the words aloud, *Gloria Patri*, not realising that Ruth was sitting beside his bed. 'What was that you said, Adrian?' she asked.

He smiled and said, 'A bit of Latin, dear heart, glory be to the Father – Dr Breakstone, no less.' He relaxed for the first time.

In four days he was discharged from the hospital. It was almost like release from a prison. He was to exist on certain pills taken with iron regularly; his was to be a special chemical regimen which called for the daily intake of the now familiar tiny nitroglycerin tablets. The pills contained the same element that produced explosives; within its unassuming exterior was a flammable oil used for destruction and also, oddly, for lifesaving purposes. Ruth was to be custodian of the pills, and he was to swallow these alien elements for the simple purpose of staying alive.

Adrian realised that by simple neglect, by forgetting to take these pills, he would die; he could achieve total equanimity – or chaos. These minuscule tablets would help him to escape the assassin, or at least so the physician indicated. The assassin – his flawed heart – was his friend or foe, depending on the final solution Adrian would choose. Forty milligrammes per day of this alien matter

composed of carbon, hydrogen, oxygen and nitrogen – the triester of glycerin and nitric acid, endowed with explosive violence and energy – was, it was alleged, beneficial in coronary artery spasms, in man and in dogs. Nobel, the great Peace Prize Patron, found it attractive, as did the scientists and writers who were annually tapped by the Royal Committee in Stockholm, for recognition in their fields. Alfred Nobel, who invented and gave the name to dynamite, was a pacifist, Adrian recalled.

Adrian found it ironic that a Nobel Prize had been awarded that year to Pirandello, a writer singularly endowed with grim humour.

'I asked the doctor about sex,' Adrian said to Ruth, when they had returned and settled down in their hotel room.

'I hope you intend following his instructions,' she said. 'You are to avoid strain, high emotion, excess of all kinds.' She pointed at his heart with a stern but loving expression on her face.

'There's an old vaudeville joke,' said Adrian, 'that ends with the line,"but what a way to go".'

'No one's ready to go yet,' she replied.

Adrian began undressing, removing his shirt, shoes, trousers. 'Let's interosculate,' he said.

'What in heaven's name is that?' she asked. 'Sounds medical.'

'Interpenetration.'

'How does it work?'

'I'll show you.'

And he did.

The news of Huey Long's assassination reached Adrian and Ruth via the Paris *Herald Tribune* the next morning. Dr Carl A. Weiss was the murderer; but there would be no trial: Long's bodyguards had killed Weiss instantly.

The irony of Long's death was not lost on the world since he had that very year published a book entitled *My First Years in the White House*.

Adrian's moratorium on the theme of assassination ended at this point and he found himself reimmersed in the subject.

So 'the Kingfish' was dead. He had promised to make 'every man a king'. And now, the remains of this demonic politician were about to start mouldering in his grave. The bombastic southerner had reached his inevitable and ignominious end. Adrian spent the morning fruitlessly seeking out information about Dr Weiss, the assassin.

Adrian was busy adding commentary to his World Assassination Chart. He looked over at Ruth. 'There will be many more murders in the next half-century, among politicians and kings, more than among common hoods. The drive for power and the competition for public office, the temptations and luxuries, the privileges of high office, will force ego-driven men to commit every manner of crime to make it. Winning, being number one at the top, having fame and power: this is a politician's sickness of the soul and brain, and assassination will become a highly profitable profession.'

'You can't possibly be right about all politicians,' said Ruth. 'There are many decent, strong, idealistic men and women who want to serve in public office on different levels, because they are people of good will.' She looked at her wristwatch and said, 'And now I must run; I'll be late for class. I'm playing Ravel and Mozart – a mini-concert, really – and I don't mind admitting I'm damned nervous. I've lost six pounds, practising, in one week. If approved, I'll be performing in public soon, at the college's annual public concert.'

'I know you'll be brilliant,' said Adrian. 'Wish I could be there to hear you, see you – but I think I'd make you

nervous.' Then he added, 'I'm seeing Marcel for lunch, back early afternoon. Good luck, dear.'

'Please, Adrian, no high emotional arguments. Be sure to take your medication; and a light salad is all you should eat. Please.'

'I'll be at a greasy spoon called Le Baobab,' he said. 'It's on the Rue de l'Université. Okay?'

He spent the next hour working at his writing table, sorting out some recent notes. He had turned necrologist and the news of the day relating to Long's death had him humming. Why was there so little information about Weiss?

The phone rang; it was the young Marxist, Marcel. Would Adrian mind if they changed their luncheon place to Procope on Rue de l'Ancienne-Comédie? Marcel said they would sit at the table once occupied by Voltaire, and later, by Verlaine. Who could resist that?

Adrian left a note for Ruth giving her the restaurant's name, saying he would return by three o'clock at the latest. He signed it in block print, VOLF-GANK AMADAOOS MOTSART.

At the Procope Adrian found himself a few minutes early. He ordered a drink and proceeded to study the place. He knew that he would in due course use it as a conversational footnote. He would 'table drop'; he would tell of sitting where Verlaine and Rimbaud had sat. There were no cafés at home where such associations could be evoked. Although he had once occupied a table at the Chez Paree where Al Capone had taken his dinner.

Marcel arrived and they got into a lively conversation at once. Adrian brought him up-to-date on his personal, medical situation. By coincidence, Marcel knew a good deal about angina pectoris and rheumatic heart; he expressed doubt that Adrian was a serious case because of his youth; and also, because he did not live in a 'pressure environment'.

The conversation rambled, and Adrian wondered when Marcel would open up his big guns. Then he finally brought up the subject: there was to be a meeting that very evening where a prominent young novelist (American) was to speak. Adrian balked.

'I'm not really interested in revolutionary talk,' he said. 'I'm not convinced that my personal need for freedom of action, my intellectual free-wheeling, would be condoned by your formalists. I'm a maverick, a common or garden variety decadent American intellectual who is involved in other matters. For example, my basic interest is in personal freedom. I want to set myself free. This isn't possible, nor consistent, with your Party goals and strictures. I couldn't be a Party worker, ever. You and I are in disagreement on many issues, though not everything, of course. I'm sure we both agree that religion is causing more destruction than anything you can name, including plague, drought and earthquake.'

Adrian paused, sipped his drink, smiled. Then he added, 'Consider angina pectoris: I'd have cardiac trouble for certain if I joined up with your Party. That would be the result of my getting into Party activity. I can't participate, I must remain free, uncommitted. You probably find that a cop-out. Reneging.'

Marcel's face darkened. He lifted his glass, studied Adrian over its edge. 'No, but you are a familiar type,' he said. 'I understand you. I even pity you.'

'Why pity me?'

'You pretend to be a liberal, a radical, but you won't lift a finger. It's unthinkable for you to make your feelings public. You wouldn't dream of proselytising. The revolution is, for you, and your kind, table-talk. Parlour radical, that's what you are, and countless other American intellectuals. Very deceptive, I'd say.'

'Deceptive? Why? I promised you nothing,' said

Adrian, 'so I'm not deceiving anyone.' He studied Marcel for a moment, then added, 'But I'm committed to truth, not causes. I'm of little use to organised ideology or organised movements.'

'What you say makes no sense,' said Marcel.

'Personal integrity,' proclaimed Adrian. 'That's an element of my credo. But my notion of integrity may not be yours, or your Party's.'

'You are a dreamer, and you need a transfusion, a transfusion of reality,' Marcel said, smiling.

'The left-wing intellectual world isn't my world,' said Adrian, softly.

'What do you know about Marxism, or Communism?' asked Marcel. 'I'd guess that you are badly in need of some orientation.'

'I know enough to back away from it,' Adrian responded, laughing. 'I know that Communism and dictatorship are one – they go hand in hand. I find dictatorship loathsome. Persecution, torture, dictatorship: these are among the obvious tools of Communism. And power! Ugh. The kind of power the Communist leaders employ: it's a power that doesn't hesitate to torture and destroy and humiliate and diminish anyone who is found in disagreement. What the Communist is doing bears no relation to the Utopia I have in mind. Any system or nation that will suppress speech, the press, the poets and artists, that I can't tolerate. There's no laughter in Communism, no joy.'

Walking home from the restaurant, Adrian paid little heed to the street signs and finally found himself lost. As he stood at a street corner hoping for a taxi, he was startled by a touch on his arm, almost a soft caress. A young woman, about twenty years old, with a sweet ovoid face, was smiling at him shyly. He took her for a Korean.

She spoke in French and proposed that Adrian might enjoy her company. His anger with Marcel soon turned to

sexual hunger and a longing for adventure, and he smiled, took her arm and asked her to lead the way.

She said her name was Maya. He was curious. More girl than woman, she aroused him by her apparent innocence though obviously she was an experienced whore. She told him her home was Rangoon, that she had studied French and English, but because of her father's death, she had left school. She had come to Paris less than four months ago, and found it to her liking. It was obvious that her young, sensual body would make her fortune. Adrian was enchanted with her, ready for her, but as they walked to her hotel room he wondered about his capacity.

Maya lived in a third-floor walk-up, and her living quarters consisted of a small bedroom and a corner lavatory concealed by a screen. The room was dark, decorated with fake jade- and silver-coloured objects, with a thin blue carpet underfoot. The room was heavy with incense and Adrian felt the need for air. He also needed to lie down almost at once.

'Do you mind talking a bit, first?' he asked, and she smiled, starting to undress. Her skin was olive and smooth and young. As she undressed she mentioned her fee, and he counted out the francs and laid them on the bed beside him. He added that she might be obliged to do all the lovemaking and he explained about his heart.

She undressed him, caressed his chest, his genitals and anus. Then she kissed him and he found himself tonguing her lips, her inner mouth, and pressing his fingers into her crevices savagely. Suddenly, he climaxed gasping, realising that it was all over too quickly. She was already applying a small towel to his groin. Then she was getting dressed. It was a new experience for him, climaxing without penetration. Maya returned from the lavatory with another small towel that was strongly scented and ran it gently over his body. She realised that he was not strong

enough to leave at once, so she sat, smiling, waiting. Finally he rose, dressed, caressed her bottom and left, embarrassed. There was no goodbye between them, no kiss.

At a *pharmacie* in St-Germain-des-Prés he bought a bottle of Listerine. He walked back to his hotel, unwrapped his purchase, prepared a warm-water solution, then carefully gargled. The words, trench mouth, crossed his mind. His medical sophistication and instinct told him that the throat was as likely a carrier of ugly gonococcal spirochaetes as the vagina. He was also mindful of the fact that Listerine was no preventative against VD.

He sat back in the green velvet armchair near the window and stared out at the rooftops of Paris. What was happening to him? This was his second betrayal of his bride since their arrival in Paris. The English girl in the clown-white make-up and platinum blonde hair; and now the gentle Burmese whore. Was his life in Paris to be a series of such sexual forays? Was this need for new sexual partners a kind of death wish? A kind of search for sexual self-immolation: the praying mantis syndrome? He knew, feared that all this would be replayed in his subconscious, recurring in the white nights ahead, in his dreams. And then, he thought fleetingly of Janice Gambelli and how she had resolved her unfortunate problem.

He went to the bathroom, gargled again, ran a tub and soaked for half an hour. Then he took a nitro tablet, felt it dissolve instantaneously, relaxed, went to bed for a nap. For once he had a dreamless sleep.

As he awakened, he felt Ruth's presence. He opened his eyes slowly, stared into her eyes. She was sitting at his bedside, hands folded in her lap, watching him.

'Hello, gorgeous,' he said.

'You looked like a sleeping angel,' she said. 'I couldn't help watching you, your breathing seemed so serene. Did

you have a good luncheon, a good visit with Marcel?' She ran her fingers through his hair, arranging his damp curls.

'I walked out on Marcel in disgust. The man's Marxism finally got to me; he's so committed to proselytism, not friendship. I couldn't take it and I simply wasn't interested in involvement with his brand of baloney-politics. He ruined lunch for me. He enjoys laying his shit on one.'

'What else did you do?" she asked.

'Nothing.' The lie came easily. 'Walked home, took a nap.'

'Anything wrong with your throat?' she asked. 'I see you bought a bottle of Listerine.'

'Oh that, yes; I felt a rawness in my throat, may have a cold coming on; so I did some gargling. Listerine sometimes helps.' He avoided her eyes as he spoke. 'How did your performance go?' he asked.

'I found your note,' she said, smiling, 'with Mozart's autograph. The concerto was fantastic, and I have a surprise for you, for us. I've won the first prize. I'm scheduled to play in the fall programme, in Paris. And then, guess what else? I go to London, Vienna, Salzburg, Berlin: four concerts under the school's auspices. All expenses paid plus an honorarium.'

'Marvellous,' he said, hugging her to him. 'You're going to make it! You're on your way, then.'

'It means a lot more work,' she said. 'I've got three other compositions to tackle: Rachmaninov's Second, Ravel's complete *Miroirs* and Schubert's Opus 90, the first set of Impromptus. And what's most interesting, I was approached by a concert manager who thinks he can book me, including, guess where? Carnegie! And Chicago and Houston!'

'I married a star,' said Adrian. 'Brava!'

'I'm expected to give the manager an answer next week, he wants me to sign a contract. How do you like that?'

He embraced her again. 'We've got to celebrate. Tonight. Let's ask the Merediths to join us. Something gala.'

The Merediths were obviously well-known to the Maxim's management, and they were given the centre table facing the main room. The food, wine and conversation were good and lively; Ruth's spirits were high; it all added up to their best Paris evening thus far. Ruth felt some embarrassment about the excessive cost of the dinner, and the matter of reciprocity, but she held her council, not wishing to appear provincial. She wondered what her parents would have done in her position.

Maxim's clientele consisted mainly of very young women escorted by elderly men, or vice versa, and tourists bubbling over with exuberance and touristic cheer. The *fin de siècle* blended with the decadent English, the expatriates and the several Orientals. Elegance, somehow, was lacking. Everything seemed studied, for show. There were buckets of wine everywhere. Ruth and Jill were receiving gallant and fastidious attention from the maître d'hôtel. Ruth could barely contain her elation, especially after her second glass of wine.

She had been working feverishly, relentlessly, perfecting her style, sweating over difficult passages, listening to teachers, records; practising and polishing her very demanding showpiece works. Now she was being rewarded. The dinner-party gave her precisely the sense of release and relief she needed. Simply, she toasted the Merediths for their friendship, and Adrian for his support.

As she sat there surveying the fashionable women in their chic gowns and expensive jewellery, breathing the perfume and rich kitchen odours, she felt a new joy. She had a good marriage, despite the medical problems, despite Adrian's dilettantism and flirtatious disposition.

He provided her with the background, the essence of romanticism and the sophisticated Continental atmosphere she had read and dreamed about. He was so handsome. Perfection was not to be expected from Adrian, nor constancy; but love (in his fashion), adventure, surprises – yes. She would adjust and cope and work hard to become a success: and she would enjoy the rewards, privately and publicly. She was already disposed, though not consciously, to seek out secret pleasures, develop a secret life, in order to survive. There was an attractive young Russian pianist at the *Conservatoire* who seemed taken with her . . . But first she would become a professional, an international concert pianist! And it was happening more rapidly than she had expected.

Ruth scooped up the last spoonful of her *fraise* soufflé and sighed.

'This dessert,' she said, 'is comparable to one of Ravel's *Miroirs* – poetic and indescribable.'

Later, when they settled down in the Merediths' living-room, Ruth was urged to perform. She went to the Bechstein. 'I'll play the fifth segment of the Ravel, the *Alborada del Gracioso*. It's really beautiful. I may have trouble with the fortissimo passages. I ate too much dinner,' she said, rolling her eyes ceilingwards. 'But, we'll see. Remember, I'm still perfecting it.'

She proceeded to play with a limpid, lovely, sure-handed quality. They were enchanted.

'My dear,' said Jock, 'you're already an accomplished concert pianist. An artist!' He threw her a kiss. 'Such grace, such authority. Ravel would have been damned pleased with your performance. You'll be interested to know that he sat at that very piano, on that very stool, and played for us one night a few years ago. A marvellous performer. But now, one more nightcap.'

He began removing the cork from the champagne bottle while Jill produced tulip-shaped crystal goblets – no Lily cups for this occasion.

'Ruth, your music reminds me of a legend about this champagne. You know about the old Benedictine monk who said about his Dom Perignon, "I'm drinking stars." Well, that's how I felt about that Ravel and your performance. Like sparkling stars.' Jock held the glass high and one could see the bubbles. They joined him in toasting Ruth.

Then the conversation turned to Adrian.

'Do you get pleasure from talking politics, Marxism, with Marcel?' asked Jock.

'Not quite,' said Adrian, laughing. 'But comes the time when candour is called for. I finally let Marcel have it. It's the only policy when confronted with a bull-headed or bullying intellectual. I can't stand proselytising, and he was coming at me full force today. I think our so-called friendship is ended.'

'Then I'll change the subject,' said Jock. 'How are you progressing with your treatise?'

'Oh Christ,' said Adrian, 'sometimes I think it's all just a crock. But lately I feel that it's like trying to swim the ocean with an arm behind my back. The subject is spread out like a stupendous seascape reaching back to prehistoric times, to the slime-time. I may be at the midpoint of the project, but I think I'd prefer not discussing it tonight if you don't mind. It could be boring as hell, and it is, frankly, getting too much for me.'

Adrian had had three glasses of champagne and had been sipping brandy before leaving Maxim's, giving Ruth some reason for concern. She studied his face, his abnormally bright eyes and flushed cheeks. He was, she realised, becoming garrulous, and a bit pompous.

'Getting back to Marcel,' said Adrian, 'I probably upset

him, but I've come to some new conclusions of late. One is that lying is the simple cause of our universal problems.' He paused for reaction. 'And that's about as revolutionary an idea as I've ever proposed.'

'Come now,' said Jock. 'Total candour is unthinkable. It would destroy all society. Businessmen would go bankrupt if they stopped lying or misrepresenting; marriages would collapse if husband and wife spoke with total frankness. What about secret liaisons? Mistresses, lovers? Friendships would cease; and certainly there would be an end to all political relations.'

Jill raised her hand as though begging for attention. They turned towards her, questioningly. 'It would be interesting to experiment with some impromptu candour,' she said. 'Are you and Ruth up to it, right now? And you, Jock? A sort of party game.'

'I try to avoid pain whenever possible,' Ruth said. 'Total candour could be painful. But, if you're in that mood, I'm curious to see where it leads.' She shrugged her shoulders and looked at Adrian.

'May I go first in this fascinating experiment?' asked Adrian.

'I can tell in advance, Adrian, it's going to hurt,' said Ruth.

'Well, let's see,' he said, taking a sip from his glass. 'Okay. Will it distress you, Ruth, if I admit right off, that while I love you, I find other women desirable?'

Jill groaned audibly.

'How desirable?' asked Ruth, eyebrows raised.

'Well, *temporarily* irresistible – for purposes of casual fucking.'

'Now that's certainly total candour,' said Ruth, cheeks flushing. 'You really do put everything simply and bluntly, right out on the table, Adrian. Yes, I think that honesty is a healthy ingredient in marriage.' Then she added, 'But

on such a basis, the whole concept of marriage turns into an arrangement of selfish convenience and inclination.'

'Arrangement?' he asked.

'Yes. Marriage shifts into something other than a pure and true friendship. Arrangement is the troublesome word. Frankly, the word arrangement is one I don't like; it sounds like a deal. But there it is. We tell each other the truth. We do what we feel is necessary. We try to retain our dignity, our decorum, etcetera. But it isn't what *this* new bride imagines it ought to be.' She paused, then said, sadly, 'It's throwing a monkey-wrench into something delicate and beautiful and fragile. It's a corrupting thing. To sum up, Adrian's code is to live by the dictates of his penis.'

She studied him calmly, and the Merediths studied her. She was unsmiling, grim now. 'We're still on the candour kick, right?'

'I guess so,' he said.

'Okay. Candour, here we come. If you embarrass me, Adrian, publicly or even privately, just once, I'll leave you. And Adrian, there will be no tearful farewell. It will be *la comedia è finita.* No discussion. Fair enough? Candour enough?'

Adrian looked shocked. 'But I love you. We love each other. What about that?'

She stiffened. 'Then don't fuck around,' she said angrily, and rose to her feet. She stood there for a moment, then said 'Excuse me,' and swept from the room. They heard the bathroom door slam. Jill followed her and then returned a few moments later, saying 'She'll be okay.'

Adrian looked at the Merediths. 'Ruth seems to be pissed off. I think I haven't matured, quite. Not yet, eh?' He paused for a moment, then added, 'Perhaps I am a shit, but surely not irredeemable.'

Jock turned to him. 'Then you have been fucking around, as Ruth put it?'

'How would she know?' Adrian asked. 'Assuming I have.'

'Jock, Adrian,' Jill interrupted. 'Women have ways of knowing things. If you, Adrian dear, have been having affairs in Paris, you haven't been discreet, or careful. Nor intelligent.'

'Perhaps I have a problem,' said Adrian. 'I feel gluttonous. I meet up with an attractive woman, someone who makes it clear she's receptive. What do I do?'

'Behave responsibly,' said Jill, unsmiling. 'What would you expect or advise Ruth to do if some attractive male propositioned her?'

'I can't say. I can't answer that. It's an abstract question. I'd hate to see Ruth fucking around.'

'Okay,' said Jill, 'you've answered the basic question. And if you'll pardon my saying so, and we are playing candour, you are a chauvinist. Which really means you're a prick.'

Adrian laughed uneasily. 'Am I really?' He sank back into his chair, looking deflated.

'Of course.' Jill turned to Jock. 'Tell him, Jock. Someone has got to advise this handsome boy about life and human relationships. Somebody has to instruct him in the simple business of getting along. He wants to stroke every female ass he sees. Women, especially wives, don't go for that, Adrian, they don't tolerate that kind of behaviour. If Jock began to make a play for every young woman coming into our orbit, I'd protest. Jock and I have an understanding. We value what we have together, more than an occasional genital one-night stand.'

'Exactly,' said Jock. 'You've got to appreciate what you've got.' Then he said, looking at Jill, 'I think Adrian is the prototype of the kid locked in the candy store. He's

surrounded by temptations. Also, he's attractive, and women, lonely, unfulfilled women, are drawn to him. Paris is full of them, including young, hot and eager girls from the States. They're in heat. And the whores.' He studied Adrian for a moment. 'And what about your heart condition, Adrian? Since this is candour-time? Isn't that a factor in your overall behaviour?'

At that moment Ruth returned to the room.

'I've been a jerk,' Adrian said to the room at large. He rose slowly, swaying slightly. 'It's been another great evening. And maybe the making or unmaking of Adrian Breakstone. Shall see. And thanks for a wonderful dinner. Apologies are due, Ruth. I hereby humble myself, Ruth.'

He turned to the Merediths. 'It was to be Ruth's evening and I pissed on her parade. I've got some work ahead of me. I owe you an evening, Ruth. As for the candour game, we'll finish that another night. Okay?'

'I think,' said Jill, 'we should *terminate* the candour game as of tonight.'

The next morning, in the early dawn, at five o'clock precisely, Adrian was awakened suddenly: a particular train of thought had been threading through his subconscious, and the climax of the mental procession awakened him, startled him, so that he pulled his body back and upward, his head against the bed's brass headboard, in order that he might focus his whole conscious attention on the revelation.

For revelation it was. Or cliché? He wondered. Namely, that violence was a universal, *natural*, ongoing process; that murder, rape, acts of passion, betrayal, torture, harassment physical and psychological, they were all part of Nature's law: natural law. Eat or Be Eaten.

Law and order, morality, decency, courtesy, compassion, charitable acts: they were all parlour games, tea-

party games. *Kinderspiel*. There was, he realised, such a thing as the Criminal Spirit. Be there first with the bullet, the dagger. Demand and conquer. All of society had an underbelly of criminal activity, and this was true of all countries in all periods of history. How simple it all was. The Church was aware of it and it stayed in business by waging permanent war against evil; or, as many insisted, the Devil. The Devil was waiting at every turn. In many guises. How true, how true. And just as the little fish was to be swallowed by the bigger fish, the Devil was certain to prevail and conquer.

What did the murder of a Tony Hacha or a Huey Long – or even an Abraham Lincoln – matter when one considered the stream of history? The need to kill, to devour, to destroy was a natural instinct. Some would argue that it was an acquired characteristic, others inherited. What matter? Countless millions had died unnatural deaths for the benefit of the living. Fish eating fish. Of course! A natural law! What was Adrian bothering about with his charts and notes and minute observations on justice, motivation, on the life and death of an insect named Ganzara?

He rose quietly from his bed, put on his robe and slippers, and sat down at the windows, facing the grey dawn. The sun was not quite visible yet. The sky was grainy. He leaned his head on the windowsill and thought: Put all of this nonsense out of your mind, pack up your old journals, notes, papers and books relating to the great cliché, man's inhumanity to man, and pursue some other field of study; chess, mathematics, poetry. But first, enjoy life.

As he returned to bed he saw Ruth opening her eyes.

'Anything wrong?' she asked. 'Are you all right?'

A loving wife, concerned with his well-being. He kissed her cheek, lay down beside her and took her hand.

'I'm really at peace. Let's sleep another hour.'

Chapter Eleven

Dr Breakstone found himself awake earlier than usual. The small baroque bedside-table clock said fifteen minutes past five. His reflexes being what they were, he remembered at once that his morning schedule at the hospital called for an appearance at eight; he could in fact sleep for at least another hour. He stretched, yawned, and arched his back so that his head pressed against the blue moire silk headboard and his toes extended out and beyond the edge of his blanket. It felt good to stretch and he strained at it. Stretching, lengthening the body, was an element in his 'stay-well-through-physical-consciousness' campaign which he preached but seldom practised. ('Stretching the body makes the body smile all over,' he would say.)

Yes, he would walk to the hospital this morning, a half-hour stroll – and then – and then, at noon, he would disappear for two hours.

He lay back, deep into his pillow, and thought of the beautiful, sultry Kama. He thought next of Amanda Billingsworth, the meat packer's daughter-in-law, and her operation. His fee, he decided, would be fifteen hundred dollars and five hundred of that he would squeeze into Kama's warm palm. Five crisp one-hundred-dollar bills for two hours with Kama. That would demonstrate his affection! And ensure her devotion. He would stop at his bank at midday for cash to deal with his meeting with her; c.o.d. he chuckled: cunt on delivery.

Kama had many things in common with Dr Breakstone.

They had similar feelings about Paris, for example. One of Kama's favourite places in the world, she said, was the Musée de Jeu de Paume, and her favourite picture was Manet's *Déjeuner sur l'Herbe*. 'I would have liked being the model in that picture,' she had said, 'or,' she would add, 'his *Olympia*.' And Dr Breakstone would confess that his most favourite of all places was Fauchon in Paris – for caviar and *pâté en croûte*. They both agreed on the appeal of Edith Piaf's 'La Vie en Rose'.

But he kept to himself the intense excitement he derived from the sweet smell of musk that arose from her body. He longed for her fragrant embrace . . .

Dr Breakstone slept alone, in his own bedroom. When they had moved from the West Side, years ago, he and Sarah, his wife, decided that a busy doctor's life required special dispensations. His irregular hours, the frequent crises, midnight phone conferences, intrusions of every possible sort: yes, he needed a separate bedroom – for Sarah's sake. There were of course his surprise visits to her bed as the mood dictated.

He lay there visualising the operating-room, his colleagues, his staff. He stroked his belly, realising that he would have to do something radical about his paunch. He rolled over and out of bed; stretched his arms upward, walked slowly on his toes to the bathroom. Removing his pyjamas he studied his naked body gravely. Yes, one day soon, wine and rich foods must go. He was about to step on the bathroom scales when he decided it would only torment and depress him.

He leaned over the deep, six-foot-long bathtub and turned on the taps. He also unscrewed the cap of a bottle of his favourite cologne, a lilac-scented concoction imported from Germany. He poured two ounces of the liquid into the tub, then proceeded to shave. His Vandyke beard called for some minor trimming; and shaving, a euphem-

ism as he termed it, occupied barely a minute of his time. Next he brushed his teeth, studied with shock a slight indication of growing space – air! – between two centre-front teeth. He half-rotated his body a dozen times, hands on hips; then he jumped from one foot to the other, delicately on his toes. Finally he stepped into the tub.

He sank back in the lukewarm water and then turned on the hot tap with his toe. He was soon soaking blissfully in ths steamy aromatic tub. The soap he used was also lilac-scented and he lathered his body, thinking again of Kama. He inhaled the lilac steam with pleasure.

She loved to run her tongue down his chest and belly, exclaiming and moaning over the delicious lilac taste of his body. His groin was a titbit she usually reserved for the 'coda', as she called it. 'You are simply delicious,' she would say, speaking into his navel, 'and ahm mighty ravenous.'

Breakstone's weight was near the two-hundred-and-fifty-pound mark; he would not permit it as a subject for discussion, especially with Sarah. When he advised a patient to diet and lose weight – 'for health rather than cosmetic reasons' – he would smile and add, pontifically, and as though reading the patient's mind, 'Do as I say, not as I do.'

His thoughts returned to Amanda Billingsworth. He exercised his fingers vigorously in the hot water as he thought of the removal of her uterus. It would require two hours of his time. He had already explained the procedure to her, and why it was prudent to have the operation performed at this time. He would require fifteen minutes with her later, for comforting, after she came out of the anaesthesia, and another five minutes with her husband. The nervous and imperious wasp, the very rich Walter Billingsworth would want the doctor's assurance that all

was well. After which, he would need another half-hour with his hospital staff, checking out calls, paperwork. And yes, Jake Ricci, the linen-king, who supplied most of the leading restaurants and hotels in the city with napkins, tablecloths, towels and sheets, would need five minutes of his solicitous attention. At seventy, Ricci's aggravated emphysema would surely finish him off within a few weeks. He had to comfort the man, somehow. He allowed his mind to toy with the thought that Ricci's final bill would come to about eight thousand dollars . . .

Towelling himself vigorously, a giant bearded cherub, he walked back to his bedroom to dress. He glanced at a book on the bedside table; he had almost forgotten to put it away. It was a small, slim volume with the piquant title of *The Lustful Turk*. The authorship was attributed to 'An Arcadian', and the date on the title-page was 1828. It was illustrated with a dozen explicitly erotic engravings, and bound in gilt-tooled maroon calf, with a gold crescent on the front centre cover.

Breakstone would admit to a few of his intimate friends that the only way to relax after a long hard day was with either a warm female body or an erotic novel. 'An hour or two with Eros is better than an apple a day,' he would proclaim, chuckling. He had bought the book from his favourite bookseller, Ben Adamson, a few days earlier. He kept his 'library' of erotica in an iron safe in his home office adjoining his bedroom. He placed the *Turk* gently on one of the shelves, then twirled the knob, locking it securely. He sighed as he thought of the surprise the safe's contents would provide his heirs. His son Adrian would of course be delighted.

He yawned. Dressed, freshly bathed and combed, and beard neatly trimmed, he entered the dining-room where he found his breakfast awaiting him. The morning paper had not yet arrived. He usually breakfasted alone, prefer-

ring his own thoughts and privacy. Life began for him at this table each day.

He swallowed the final half-inch of coffee, then rose, pulling from out of a slender vase a small pink rosebud which he inserted in his jacket lapel.

Yes, he would walk slowly to the hospital and surprise the staff. He wasn't due there for at least an hour. He rang for the elevator, entered it and looked with satisfaction at his appearance in the large, gilt-framed mirror. A fine figure of a man! Yes, he thought, the cliché applied to him. Anyone could see he had vigour, authority, grace.

The doorman greeted him with warmth and announced that it was a fine day for a walk. The lake across the drive seemed placid; the sun was moving up and beginning to spread its warmth over and through the familiar morning haze. Dr Breakstone took a deep breath and stepped on to the sidewalk. As he did so he heard the roar of an engine followed by the sound of backfire; then came another backfire, though he already knew it was a gunshot, for he had been struck twice. He was being gunned down.

He reached for his chest, feeling a terrible pain, then sank to his knees where he began to gasp, then sway like a felled bull. Then he crumpled, lying face down on the cement walk. As he lay there, through his mind flashed the image of Mayor Hacha dying in Miami. Then nothing. The rosebud from his lapel had fallen from his coat and lay a few inches from his half-concealed face; thick red blood spurted from his body.

The doorman had seen the car roar off; he had glimpsed two men, Negroes, one with a shotgun, in the front seat. Both wore large, very dark sunglasses. But he blocked the entire scene from his mind – the men, the gun. . .

He would later tell the police he had been in the men's room briefly and had not seen Dr Breakstone leave. He

had no testimony to offer except that the doctor was a fine man and that the shooting was a terrible thing indeed.

The murder of Dr Breakstone was a front-page story in all the city's newspapers; the radio broadcasters had a field day with it. Speculation on the possible motive covered a wide spectrum but there was no single conjecture that made sense, no theory that could be based on evidence, circumstantial or nonexistent. Well-known figures, including the Big Fellow, were interviewed. He said the doctor was a friend, that he would pay $10,000.00 cash for the apprehension of the killer; the death of Dr Breakstone was, he said, a severe loss to the community – and to him personally.

Johnny Torino called Sarah offering help. He would make a few enquiries but he knew nothing about the killing. 'It could be very personal,' said Torino. 'Something very private, if you know what I mean. Why would anyone want to kill the Doc? He will be missed by many people.' He added after a pause, 'Be calm.'

A rumour spread quickly, that one of the Gennas, the hot-headed one, had tried to blackmail the doctor, failed in the attempt, shot him and then fled to Marsala, Italy. It turned out to be a false, planted story, quite baseless. The Genna in question had been visiting a relative in Detroit at the time of the shooting. 'Who would want to rub out the Doc?'

There was a jigsaw puzzle here. There were odours, rumours. The possibility of a mystery woman came up frequently. The doctor had been seen in the Shoreham recently, with a beautiful dark woman, possibly an actress or night-club entertainer. She seemed to be crying. So the story ran. But if Dr Breakstone had a mistress, it was his own well-kept secret. Judge Minelli knew nothing about it. Minelli had, in fact, called a 'council meeting' to see what could be learned. He seemed deeply disturbed over

the shooting. He pronounced the murder a personal disaster. In a newspaper interview he said Dr Breakstone was one of his dearest friends, that it was time to stop the crime wave. But there was no crime wave at present; only the cold-blooded shooting of the one man, Dr Breakstone.

The members of his family had no clue, no guess as to who might want to kill this distinguished, kindly, law-abiding citizen, 'this paragon'.

The obituaries were full of praise. Those who knew him, as patient or socially, all said, one thing was certain: Dr Breakstone never went back on his word. He delivered what he promised. He was always available, made charity house calls; his hospital facilities and his private clinic were at his patients' disposal any hour of the day or night. What a loss his death was going to prove.

The police talked of the bullets, one in the heart, one in the brain. Great marksmanship.

Motivation? Drugs were mentioned from time to time; Dr Breakstone allegedly was the hot centre of a heroin system and double-crossed a big source, refusing to pay for a half-million-dollar delivery from Mexico.

'False!' cried Torino. 'Not the Doc. Never.'

An abortion that failed? The Big Fellow's favourite girl got knocked up and the Doc bungled the job?

'Bullshit,' said Torino. 'I know all about that. The Doc fixed her up and we sent her to Kansas City. She's there now; we phoned her and she's okay. I talked with her myself, so stop the bullshit about Big Sophie.'

One Syndicate mobster, the dreaded North Side arsonist and drug dealer, Salvatore Polizzi, was suspected of having an altercation with the Doc, but it turned out that he was vacationing in Sicily when the shooting took place. He cabled the family with 'deep sadness and regrets' from Corleone two days after the shooting. The wire was turned over to the police but it was not made public.

Dr Breakstone's assistant-secretary went through the doctor's personal diaries and professional calendars and they were studied for that particular day, the day of the shooting. Who would know where he would be at a given hour? Where he was going was indicated briefly: the specific operation (Amanda Billingsworth's) was on the calendar; nothing else. He often took an early morning walk and it would hardly be noted in his schedule. He had one social engagement for that evening, a play-opening; nothing earlier. No one could have known of his decision to take a walk at that particular hour. Obviously, someone was parked nearby and waiting, possibly for hours.

In the end, it would be left to Adrian, on his return from Paris, to deduce, in an abstract sense, the identity of the murderer.

Book Four

Chapter Twelve

It was decided that Adrian would return to America alone. With her impending concert and intensive working schedule it would have been an unnecessary sacrifice for Ruth. Adrian had insisted that he could make the voyage alone, and that all details of his father's funeral – he'd be too late to attend the services – would be handled by his family.

A week later, he was home with his mother, occupying his old bedroom. He found Sarah in emotional tatters. No one seemed able to console her. 'Why did God visit such a punishment on such a good man, the doctor with the golden hands?' She proceeded to devour Adrian, first with kisses, then with tears and emotional demands. Tears and more tears.

Adrian held a council of war with his brothers. They discussed the wild rumours that were circulating about their father. A mysterious figure had appeared, heavily veiled, at the funeral. No one knew her identity, nor did she speak to anyone. She had arrived in a private limousine, attended, at the graveside, and left alone. The entire sequence was reminiscent of some famous movie scene – a strange woman coming with flowers and departing silently. The obligatory mystery woman. There had been a large turnout, perhaps two hundred at the cemetery, and the immediate family was concerned, embarrassed. Poor Mama.

Adrian could only utter the cliché he remembered from one of the Sherlock Holmes stories: *cherchez la femme*.

And it was this that prompted him to pursue a certain peculiar bypath, that helped eventually to disclose the murderer's identity.

Old-fashioned, insulated and unsophisticated (but hardly stupid), Sarah had her own private views on the killing of her husband. In the deepest recesses of her heart she knew that her husband's very secret life and secret thoughts, which she could not share, were less than pure. No man is shot down on the street by a hit-and-run killer unless he is in deep trouble. Jeremiah Breakstone was killed for a reason. She dared not explore the reason, dared not conjecture, refused to discuss, publicly, any aspect of the case. A dreadful mistake had occurred. The gangsters shot the wrong man. That was her glib answer and it gave her, outwardly, some satisfaction. Her grief, her anger, her loss were commingled with a woman's innate logic: her man had been playing around on the shady side of life. She sat and wept. She still loved and admired him deeply. All men were flawed, weak, but some rose above these weaknesses.

Adrian had discussed his father's financial affairs with his brothers and as far as they could determine, after several conferences with his accountant and lawyer, there was a substantial estate; all of it left to Sarah. About a million dollars in cash, stocks, bonds and real estate. What his accountant pointed out as perplexing, however, were certain cash withdrawals from Dr Breakstone's banking account, sums of two thousand five hundred and five thousand dollars, drawn with a puzzling regularity over a period of years. The doctor usually left pencilled notes of explanation for the accountant on unfamiliar matters, but in this case there were none. The sums over one ten-month period totalled thirty-five thousand dollars. The brothers agreed that this matter should not be

mentioned to their mother, but, in due course, it should be brought to the private attention of the police commissioner.

The Will surprised them since they had expectation of inheritances. They had been left out totally; nor was there any consideration for charity, friends, relatives, servants. It was an embarrassing blow, and even Sarah was saddened by her husband's thoughtlessness.

Adrian sat at his desk, pondering the possibilities and the moves. Like acid turning the blue litmus of his emotions to red, the idea of his father's murder was eating into his brain. The murder was not another mindless act – not in Adrian's judgment. It had been carefully programmed, he was certain. The deadly drama had been planned and prepared with pinpoint timing; there had to be a purpose in it.

He rose from his desk, began pacing the room, then laughed. The word, pussy, crossed his brain. Thinking the thinkable: pussy! What else? 'Like son like father,' he said aloud. There had to be a woman in the piece. One of his father's friends was the late assassinated Tony Hacha. Another intimate friend was Judge Angelo Minelli. Now, *there* was a man to see. For some reason the Hacha name triggered the Minelli name; this man was more than his father's friend, he was a mover in his father's life.

Adrian secured Minelli's phone number from his father's file and phoned him, arranging for a luncheon meeting.

Adrian knew many things about his father; one was his interest in women, a carefully guarded secret. In public the famous doctor would display gallantry – the kiss on a woman's hand, the extravagant compliment – all intended to prove that his interest in women was a public, a social and open matter; that the real man was devoted to his wife alone. He could flirt with women, tease and compliment

or shock them in public; harmless, his friends would call such behaviour. But Adrian knew otherwise. His father was a hot-blooded, sexually driven man, the friend and confidante of Syndicate leaders, whoremasters. He was locked into the criminal world even though no member of it. Between his father and Judge Minelli there was a special kind of bond, a covenant, perhaps; a private as well as public or social relationship. Adrian was not entirely clear about it.

He noted with acute interest the resonant *molto* voltage of Minelli's trained voice on the phone, his immediate acceptance of the luncheon invitation. His voice conveyed the 'any son of Dr Breakstone is a friend of mine' tone; he was unctuous and eager to prove friendship and concern. Adrian could trust him, would find him someone to count upon. He listened to the oily voice and wondered.

They met at the all-Jewish club on North Dearborn Street, a club to which his father had belonged for many years. Adrian was utilising his father's membership, preferring the club to a public restaurant. It was soon obvious that the judge was making a great exception, on a Saturday: taking time out in the name of brotherhood, Adrian said to himself.

Apparently Judge Minelli had been a club guest of his father's on many occasions, since he was recognised and greeted formally by name, not only by several members, but by the maître d'hôtel. Adrian wondered whether a judge was always called *your honour* in public places.

They glanced at the menu, and the judge decided quickly, ordering chicken in aspic and a glass of Alsace Riesling. Adrian ordered a chef's salad and milk.

Minelli began at once. 'Your father was an old, valued friend, as you know; he had greatness.' He paused and looked at Adrian to appraise the effect of this dramatic encomium. The word, *greatness*, rang like a bell. 'He was

a big man in his world, a great healer. Only a lunatic could have killed him. No sane man would want Dr Breakstone dead. Insanity.'

Adrian nodded, waited. Minelli picked up his glass, studied the sun's refraction in the polished cut glass, sipped the pale liquid slowly. His swarthy, close-shaven olive skin and gleaming black hair, his well-waxed moustache and glossy manicured fingernails were not, somehow, characteristic of a judge. Vestiges of Minelli's formative years, his pimping years, showed through the grooming and elegant English tailoring. Minelli's lips were blood-red and full. 'The crimson lips of a Sicilian Dracula' crossed Adrian's mind and he smiled. Minelli, he knew, was not a man to tangle with, a barracuda of a man; lucid, legal and lethal.

Minelli continued, 'May your father's soul rest in peace.' These were no idle words and Adrian looked up. Minelli was said to be a religious man. His *requiescat in pace* for Adrian's father was murmured quickly, and rang true; it was not uttered simply as a comforting phrase for the living, the dead man's son.

Adrian decided to come right to the point.

'I hope you won't mind my telling you what's on my mind, why I decided to disturb you. My purpose is obvious: I wonder if you can help me find the murderer.' He stopped, sat staring at Minelli, focusing his eyes on the bridge of the man's large nose. This man, thought Adrian, is very young, under forty, certainly, a clever negotiator, and a judge with a reputation for a mercurial, quick mind. He detected the slightest twitch at the corner of his mouth, the barest spasmodic movement of his moustache. The eyes remained steady, would have seemed deadly except that he was trying to display compassion.

'Adrian,' he began, 'how can I help find the murderer? If I thought I could, and you know that I have resources at

my disposal, don't you think I would have done so right away?' He looked at Adrian with a slightly surprised expression. 'Remember, he was my friend. I would be glad to put the murderer behind bars, or in the electric chair. Gladly!'

'I hear so much talk about a woman in my father's background,' said Adrian. 'Is there such a person, and if so, is there any connection between her and his murder? What do you think, privately? Off the record, of course.' He blushed at the trite assurance.

'A woman in his life?' said Minelli. He assumed a virtuous, judicial posture. 'Let me put it this way: if you had a light, flirtatious arrangement with a woman – nothing serious or permanent – would you call that "a woman in the background"? No. Now, there is a woman – and remember, your father had dozens of women admirers, none serious – but this particular one had no serious bearing on his life, and certainly not on his tragedy. I happen to know the woman you're referring to. I won't say that she's the acme of respectability. She isn't. But she isn't a whore, and she was taken with your father; and she gave him much pleasure. It has nothing to do with you or your mother or your family. The woman is mourning your father just as you or your mother or your family – and I – are mourning his passing.'

Adrian was nonplussed. Minelli's expressionless face, his reassurance puzzled him. How to proceed further? He knew that he was moving into deeper waters, fast approaching the heart of the matter. Then he blurted out, 'Could you introduce me to her?' He was almost pleading.

Minelli averted his eyes, picked up his glass and saw it was empty. Adrian immediately signalled for the waiter and ordered another glass of wine. Minelli sat stiffly, staring over Adrian's head. Then he said, 'I know what's going through your mind, Adrian. You would like to find

the murderer of your father. Well, so would a lot of people, including the police. They are doing their best, but no luck so far, no success.'

'I'm not so much interested in killing the murderer of my father,' said Adrian. 'Murder per se seems to me pointless. Intrinsically it solves nothing. That, by the way, is the thesis of the book I'm working on. I'm interested in knowing who did it, and why. What was the reason for my father's murder? That's my question. What *did he do*? A son must know this. What did my father do to deserve being gunned down on the sidewalk in broad daylight? He wasn't a bootlegger, a gangster, a thief. He was a healer.' His voice rose as he spoke, and he felt beads of sweat on his upper lip. He took a sip from his glass.

'Well,' said Minelli. 'I personally find the motive of secondary interest. I might just want to punish a man because he spoke harshly, insultingly to me, or combed his hair in an offensive fashion, or spat on the sidewalk. So what? But I might put a bullet through his or her head if I knew for certain who killed my good friend, *if* I knew positively who the guilty person was. Yes, I could become an executioner, and I should not like to be quoted on this, considering my profession. I believe in an eye for an eye, the Hammurabi code.' He smiled and picked up his glass. Then he continued, since Adrian said nothing, 'Too many criminals have motives. Most are related to passion or greed, or vengeance. Perhaps somebody had a powerful need for revenge. I don't know. Certainly your father wasn't shot for greed. He wasn't robbed. And I don't think he was being blackmailed. If he was, he never mentioned it to me or to any of his friends. And why should he, of all people, be a blackmail victim? Because he was a successful doctor?'

Neither spoke and Adrian waited. He would pursue

the basics of the matter, ruthlessly. He took a deep breath. 'The woman you referred to: was she married?'

Minelli paused before answering. 'Do you think that is germane, Adrian? If so, the answer is yes, she's married, but her husband is not capable of murder, or anything else. For one thing, he's a sick and disabled man; for another, he couldn't possibly know about your father and this particular relationship. I can't answer any more questions about this matter, Adrian. But believe me, you are on the wrong track.'

Then he attempted to change the subject. 'I hope you and your bride are enjoying Paris. I hear she is a very talented pianist; is she studying there? I may be coming over in a few months. I'll phone you if you give me your address. I'd like to show you and your wife my Paris – I've got a few favourite spots.'

'Thanks. Yes. Ruth is studying there. She's preparing for a concert tour. I've been working on a book.'

'Ah, on murder, I think you said.'

'Yes. Assassination in particular. It all stemmed from the killing of Mayor Hacha. I was in Miami and witnessed the shooting. I've made a study of certain cold-blooded killings, mostly by hired hands, throughout history. But the subject is becoming less interesting to me.'

'Why is that? Surely it's a likely subject for an imaginative writer.'

'I've begun to realise that morality, like virginity, is as obsolete as the dinosaur. Genuine Christians are extinct too. Killing and crime in general – and surely you must know this – are on the increase. I feel like the storybook Dutch boy with his finger in the dyke.'

'Well, in writing such a book you aren't exactly trying to initiate a reform, are you? I'm assuming yours is a socio-historical study . . . '

'Yes and no. I had a theory about assassins – but it's

unimportant, perhaps banal. The subject is too big. Besides, who on earth really cares. Not even the Church, I dare say.'

Minelli's lips twitched perceptibly. He smiled. 'Perhaps you should return to your earlier interests: it was poetry, I believe?'

'No – I would prefer returning to chess or mathematics.'

'Well, I hope you make the right decision. And now, if you'll excuse me, I have an appointment in Wilmette. Please send my best wishes to your wife. If there's anything I can do for you, if there's anything I learn about your father's death, I'll be in touch with you. Consider me your friend, Adrian.'

'Thank you very much, Judge Minelli.' He signed the restaurant bill and they both rose and moved towards the elevator bank.

Minelli's car and driver were waiting for him at the kerb on Dearborn Street. As they shook hands, Adrian said, 'I'm sorry this proved to be a wild goose chase for me. I had somehow felt you would be able to answer the basic questions about my father's murder.'

'Why would you think that?' Minelli asked, getting into his car.

'I have reason to believe you know more about my father than anyone – including my mother. Perhaps I'm deceived. Perhaps you feel there is more here than I should be told.'

Adrian saw Minelli's eyes widen, his lips tighten.

'Are you implying that I haven't told you the truth?'

'Withheld the truth – that would be closer to what I'm thinking.'

Minelli was settled back in his car, but the door was still open. He leaned forward, turned to face Adrian and said, 'I've learned to keep my counsel in important matters; I am considered a trusted friend.'

'Why aren't you giving me the information I'm looking for, why aren't you behaving like a friend?' Adrian realised that he was pushing hard and that Minelli was not a man to push. But the moment for answers seemed at hand and he was breathing hard, building an anger he could not stay.

Minelli touched his chauffeur's shoulder and said, 'Please get me a cigar at the club's counter.' The chauffeur left and Minelli turned on Adrian and said, unsmiling, containing an obvious fury, 'Do you remember a girl named Janice Gambelli?'

Adrian, taken aback by this tangent, paused, then said, 'Yes, I knew her briefly; what about her?'

'Well, Adrian, since you question my integrity, let me tell you about Miss Gambelli. She became pregnant; she went to your father for an abortion since you refused to see her. Unlucky girl, she was late, too far gone, and she died in your father's private surgery. Her brother was making loud threatening comments and your father decided it would be wise if his son went to Paris, at once. He arranged for your trip, and he also paid off the brother. It was and still is a private matter.' He turned his face from Adrian and said, 'Please let this be our last meeting – consider me nonexistent.'

Adrian felt death in his heart, a need to cry out. Instead he said, 'No, no, no. You are a lying, dirty prick. It's a lie!'

At that instant the chauffeur returned, entered the car and Minelli slammed his door and ordered the driver to proceed. As Adrian stood at the kerb he thought: will I be strong enough to block out this disclosure? He watched the car disappear at the corner of Dearborn and Wabash and he said, aloud, 'None of this happened, none of this is true. You lying prick, you.'

But he knew that Minelli was not lying. The girl – a

young Italian from the ghetto area of the West Side – had crossed his path at the beach one afternoon, and Adrian, exercising his charm, seduced her. He still remembered her young and yielding body in the back of his car. He did not see her again, but learned that she had become pregnant. He had hung up on her when she phoned, hoped the incident would pass, dissolve from his memory. How the circumstances, and his ignominious behaviour came to Minelli's attention, he could well imagine. Adrian had managed to file and forget, although now, Janice's large eyes came to him, the seductive body. Christ, what else was there to remember? His father and Minelli had arranged everything . . . and an angry brother was paid off. One brief fucking encounter . . .

He stopped, suddenly realising that Janice's brother could have murdered his father: the abortion . . . the death. His father's urgency in getting him off to Paris . . . It was all terribly clear.

But no, he would not accept Minelli's implication. There had to be others, or one other explanation.

He walked slowly down the street. A light rain began to fall and he pulled up his coat collar, quickened his gait. He would visit his favourite book dealer, Ben Adamson. As he walked, his mind was plagued with Minelli's angry disclosure – an incident he had managed until now to erase almost completely. Janice Gambelli: Adrian had blanked out the entire matter, and he marvelled that he could. But now, it would haunt him . . . this sweet-sour incident in his life. He would drive it from his mind – he must.

Adrian forced himself to concentrate on other aspects of his father's life and death. As he walked, his mind was assaulted by a crossfire of possibilities and contradictions. He focused on the notion that Minelli might be involved personally, deeply, in the death of his father. He had

sensed guilt and wariness in the man across the luncheon table that noon. That was Minelli's style. The man had privileged knowledge. Obviously his father had told Minelli about his plans for Adrian – getting him out of the country quickly, paying off the brother – the matter a simple financial one. So close a confidante of the doctor's would be privy to the matter of who killed Dr Breakstone – and why . . .

Yes, there was something fishy about Minelli and his evasiveness. Adrian's instincts prodded him; a woman had certainly killed his father, and Minelli knew everything about it. Was probably involved. Yes, this was the area to pursue. And how deeply mired was his father in other such intrigues?

He pondered on his father's great act of generosity, paying off the girl's brother, sending Adrian out of the country and out of possible harm's way – and all this without a hint or word to Adrian. What sort of man was his father, Jeremiah Breakstone?

Other avenues came to mind, and as he walked in the rain he thought of the Syndicate and the underworld friends of his father, some of whom might profit from his murder. But that was unlikely. The murder had to be an act of passion, revenge, a personal matter. To order the killing of such a prestigious figure, the inducement would necessarily be extravagant. Only a woman spurned, deeply humiliated, only a powerful woman of volcanic anger could have instigated the act. Or was it – Adrian squirmed at the recurring thought – the act of Janice Gambelli's brother? Adrian's confidence, in the end, in his logical processes, gave him assurance that he could uncover the villain in short order. He would reconstruct the crime. He began muttering *Cherchez la femme*. His personal guilt and involvement were unthinkable.

* * *

Ben Adamson was an old friend of Adrian's. He was a short, stocky, jocular and gifted man, with wiry red curly hair, rimless half-glasses, a protruding stomach. His shop, slightly off the beaten path, to avoid the high rents, was reasonably accessible. A real bibliophile would find it readily. It was a small shop, the classic Dickensian establishment with mullioned windows, behind which could be found British and French imports, examples of early and modern printing, an illuminated leaf or two from ancient liturgical volumes, leather bindings, colour-plate books, collector's items, not forgetting a few current bestsellers.

Inside the shop there were books piled on the floor, in corners, and on counters. Adamson loved to watch the browsers struggling with the stacks of books, the expressions on their faces as they came up with their discoveries, their 'finds'. The skilled browsers called them 'sleepers'.

Not generally known was the fact that Adamson was a leading local distributor of pornography. Exotica, he called it. Adrian had discovered the shop several years earlier and patronised it with a quiet passion. His charge account was a substantial one, his reading taste, omnivorous. By accident, he learned that his father was also a client, and was, in fact, a serious collector, and presumably a reader, of erotica. Dr Breakstone was discreet, Adrian knew, in his collecting activities and kept his books locked in a large iron safe in his home office. When Adamson learned who Adrian was – in relation to Dr Breakstone – he was unable to keep to himself his father's porno-bibliophilic secret. They had shared a few good laughs together over Adrian's father's interests.

Now Adamson greeted Adrian with a special warmth and solicitude, expressing his sympathy. 'Everyone,' he said, 'knows of the tragedy, Adrian, and for myself, I'm personally distressed; he was a fine man. What a loss. He was in his prime.'

Adrian thanked him. 'I have a very special favour to ask, and I know I can count on your discretion.'

'You may consider it so,' said Ben. 'What can I do for you?' He was assuming that Adrian was concerned with the disposition of his father's erotic books. What, after all, would happen when the executors opened the man's safe and found his scandalous library?

But he was surprised when Adrian asked, 'Ben, did my father ever come to your shop with a woman?'

'I can't recall that he did. Frankly, I doubt it.'

Adrian studied the bookseller's face. Ben returned the stare, waiting.

'Did you ever make delivery of a book or books to any woman *for* my father? An erotic book, that is?'

Now Adamson paused, averting his eyes. 'A few times. I'll have to check.'

Adrian now felt his heart pounding. 'Can you give me the name and address of the person you delivered any package or packages to? You must know, Ben, that it's more than a casual interest I have.'

'Yes, I know. I'm not sure that I can. You know how informally I run this place. Let me take a look. Your father's charge account, like yours, did not include actual titles of books in the case of erotic purchases. I sometimes delivered books to his office with disguised titles. I think I delivered a few packages for him a few months ago, to someone . . . let me check the charge ledger.'

He bent down, pulled out an oblong record book from beneath the counter, and turned the pages. He stopped and studied a page.

'Here it is. The most recent one. Two books delivered by hand to Mrs Jackson, 1120 Lovecraft Avenue, second floor.'

'Any titles indicated?' asked Adrian.

'Yes, *A Tale of Two Cities*, *Jane Eyre*. A two-volume item – with Von Bayros illustrations!'

'Where the devil is Lovecraft Avenue?' asked Adrian. Suddenly he felt butterflies in his stomach. 'May I sit down?' he asked, 'and can you get me some water, please?' He was almost certain he would black out; his head felt strangely light, his body weak, his energy depleted.

Ben took one worried look at Adrian's face, pulled out a chair and placed it behind him. Then he went to the rear of the shop and brought a glass of water. Adrian took two pills from a small gold pillbox he carried, and swallowed them.

'A touch of angina,' he said, placing the palm of his hand on his chest. 'I'll be okay, Ben.' To himself he said, I must not lose consciousness. I must hold out.

'Where did you say Lovecraft Avenue is?' asked Adrian. 'I never heard of it. I know the name of course, H. P. Lovecraft, the author of fantasy stories.'

Adrian felt the weakness returning and sipped the water; then bent his head low, between his knees, holding his breath for a long count.

'Are you sure you'll be all right?' Ben asked.

'Yes. Please, where is Lovecraft Avenue?'

'A half-mile from here, south. It's in a large apartment building. Flat 10-A. And by the way, she's black. A beauty.'

Ben looked away, busied himself with some mail.

The fact of her colour registered, and Adrian smiled weakly. 'Any other details? Such as, does she have a first name?'

'Yes. Would you believe it? It's Kama, as in *Kama Sutra*. I know you won't believe it but that's her first name. She may have acquired it somewhere along the road.'

'Her married name is Jackson? Kama Jackson? What is she like?'

'The two times I delivered books to her she opened the door herself and received the packages. I could smell an Oriental incense in the hall leading to her apartment; I could also smell her powerful aphrodisiacal perfume, and when I left, the scent lingered. I remember all that. And oh yes, she's tall, about your height.'

'And she's never been to this shop?'

'Not to my knowledge.'

Adrian stood up, paced the shop's length, then he shook the bookseller's hand. 'I'm indebted to you, Ben.'

He located Mrs Jackson's Lovecraft address easily. It was a longish walk from Adamson's shop, in a quiet, residential neighbourhood next to the so-called Black Belt of the city. It was a tree-lined street, quiet, with brownstone houses and a few recently erected high-rise buildings; the area was called Ridgewood. A few cars were parked along the kerbs.

He found the name on the lobby bellboard, and rang. A woman's voice responded promptly; a soft, low-toned voice. When he announced his name, there was a pause, and he thought he heard a gasp. He must have imagined it. Then she said, 'I can't invite you up, but if you'll come back in ten minutes I'll meet you in the lobby.'

'I'll be waiting; thank you,' he said.

Kama Sutra Jackson. The name on the bell said simply Jackson.

Adrian left the lobby and strolled leisurely around the block, studying the buildings and the few shops; there was a pharmacy at one corner and nearby was a coffee shop.

When he returned to the Jackson building he saw a woman standing alone, near the kerb, with a small black French poodle. She was a tall, slender Negro. Her large eyes and bobbed shining black hair might be called her

principal features except that there was a sensual quality to her body that also arrested one's immediate attention. The breasts were alive and high, the waist narrow, the hips and buttocks richly endowed. The ankles were delicate and she wore a simple terracotta skirt and a black silk blouse. The shoes were turquoise.

Adrian approached her and said, 'Mrs Jackson?'

'Yep,' she said. 'Shall we walk? Perhaps we can have a cup of coffee in the shop around the corner.'

'Fine,' said Adrian, and they began to walk. The drizzle had stopped; the air was fresh and the scent of flowers was strong, originating in the flower boxes on several street-level windowsills. A pretty scene, he thought: white man, pretty black lady, flowers, trees, dog. And a dead man on their minds.

'How did you locate me?' she asked, smiling.

He turned to look at her closely, at her perfect teeth and wide eyes. My father must have been mad about her, he thought. Her lips were red though unpainted, slightly parted; the teeth glistening; mouth inviting. Her fingers were long, the nails gleaming and polished; mother-of-pearl pink. Her nose was narrow, short, slightly upturned. Pert, one might call it. Who and what was she? He would soon learn. She radiated an aroma, a perfume that Adrian could only describe as sexual.

'I'd like to start at the beginning,' said Adrian.

'Why not?' she smiled. 'Less confusion, right?'

He opened the door of the coffee shop, spotted a corner booth in the rear; the waitress pointed to the booth and they occupied it. The poodle was placed on the bench beside her.

'How far ago is the beginning?' she asked.

'I was in Paris on my honeymoon. I got the news of my father's death – of my father's murder – and I returned as fast as I could. No one I've spoken to had much informa-

tion to offer. Naturally, I'm puzzled since I knew of no one who would want to kill my father. He was a fine doctor, not a quack. He had many friends, not to mention grateful patients. No enemies as far as I can tell. Do you know of any enemies he might have had?' He added, 'He was killed like a hoodlum.'

He turned to face her fully, eyes peering directly into hers.

'How could I possibly know?' she said.

The waitress approached and they ordered coffees.

'Is there any information you can give me about him that I ought to have? As his son, I'm more than casually interested, you know.'

'What sort of information do you think I have?'

'Well, any clue to motive? Why would anyone want to kill him? That's my first question. And who might be interested in his death?'

'I repeat, what do you think I have by way of information. Why me?'

'You were a close friend of his, I'm told.'

'Yes, that's what I'm asking *you*. Who told you about me, about my friendship with your father? And surely, he had many friends. Have you interviewed all of them?' She looked hard at him, then added, 'His female patients, for example.'

'No, I haven't. I wouldn't know where to begin.'

'So you began with me, huh?'

'Right. I began with you. Actually that isn't true. I saw a few other friends of his. One mentioned you and I'm not allowed to say who. Please, let's not make an issue of it. I promise you, the informant is irrelevant.'

'Irrelevant, huh?' She sipped her coffee then continued, 'Not good enough. I never met any of your father's friends. Our relationship was extremely quiet and private. We Afro-Americans don't mix socially with prominent

white doctors. Although I was born here, our culture seems, according to many, still pretty much alien. You, for example, are also of another, an alien culture, but you are able to mix freely with most of the members of the so-called Caucasian or white race. You're free to move among Negroes. I think, Mr Breakstone, the operative words are *free to move*. Anyway, I'm mystified. Because, sonny, your daddy and I were lovers but we never were seen in public together, and I doubt that he mentioned my name to any of his friends or relatives.' She added in a lowered tone: 'Your father and I both loved Paris and the south of France, but he wouldn't dream of taking me there.'

Adrian studied his fingers for a moment. 'I was hoping we would not have to get into that kind of thing,' he said. 'As far as I'm concerned, you and I are of the same race: only our skins are different colours. I'd like to leave it at that. If I, as a Jew, have to shoot it out some day, in the end, you and I'll be doing it together. From the same front porch, so to speak. I'm a Jew and I'm in your boat. I am not a racist. Race talk is bullshit talk. Forgive my bluntness. That's how I feel.'

'Pretty speech, and I appreciate the sentiment. Nevertheless, I'm black and you're not. I have no illusions. I'm also an object of interest to certain white men. Your father was especially friendly. We had a good, private relationship. Let's say he appreciated my virtues. Is that what you wanted to know? About our relationship?'

'I want to know anything you can tell me that will help me find the killer of my father,' Adrian said.

'That's the police's job, isn't it?' she said, sipping her coffee. 'Let them use their talents and muscle. I can't and won't get involved in police work. I gave your father what he wanted. I knew him for about a year. We got along fine. Somebody wanted him dead. I didn't.'

'That's a pretty casual way of putting it,' said Adrian.

'Casual, did you say? I'm not the widow, man. I'm not a beneficiary. I never attended any theatre or dinner with him, never took any vacations with him, trips to fancy islands in the West Indies, nor to the French Riviera or Paris as I mentioned, nor to Rio, nor London. No sir. We would meet in a hired room or motel; we made love. He always said he liked dark meat, not too well done, and I really gave him his money's worth. Your father wasn't a romantic but his language – he must have read a lot of dirty books for it was pretty interesting; and I must say he was a mighty passionate man. Couldn't get enough of me. Am I shocking you?' She paused, and asked the passing waitress for another cup of coffee.

'No, you're not shocking me. I'm getting an education. A friend of my father's – perhaps you know Judge Minelli? – said my father had greatness. Nice word. Ernest Hemingway uses it in connection with bullfighters. I guess my father had greatness as a bullfighter, a torero. Matador of the motel mattress. Hah! I'm being cynical. Perhaps I'm envious of my father, making love to a beautiful woman like you. I envy him, Mrs Jackson. Or may I call you Kama?'

She laughed. 'Kama was your father's idea of a proper name for me. I liked it. He insisted that I use it. You know its origin, of course?'

'Yes, I do,' said Adrian. 'Tell me more, please.'

'What more to tell? I knew your father for over a year as I said. He paid me quite well. I was usually available since my husband is not ambulatory. I've worked at odd jobs. Teacher, companion to lonely men and women. Yes, women. And I like good clothes, good food, money, jewellery. I'm really a very simple, average person. If you can afford it, I'll make love with you. You

may fuck me, if that kind of language suits you. I'm professional, available, and as you may suspect, well-recommended.'

Adrian was visibly startled. He paused, swallowed, carefully choosing the words to cope with her bluntness.

'Please tell me about your husband. I presume you live together.'

'Sure. We live together. Hiram Jackson is his name. He was injured. A bullet struck the base of his spine and he's paralysed from the waist down. He spends most of his life in a wheelchair or in bed.'

'What was his profession or business?' asked Adrian. 'It's not my right to ask, but I'm naturally curious.'

'He's a musician; played sax. He was very good. Did some recording, too. And he's a handsome man. But not much as a man now, not to a woman, you understand. And it isn't easy for Hiram, seeing his wife making it with other men, for money. Especially white men.'

'I understand,' said Adrian. 'Did your relationship with my father disturb him more than the norm?'

'That's what they call a real leading question, sonny. But I'll answer it, although I don't know what you mean by norm. He's bitter, morose. Won't see his old friends, won't play his sax, won't take a job. He lives on hate. He reads a lot. So, as I said, I'm available, but I'm not your hooker, your ten tricks a day girl, you understand. I have standards; I want to enjoy my work. And I want to be well paid. And I don't fool around with freaks or slimy pricks – if you'll pardon my French. I don't like men who think of women as sex machines.'

Adrian seemed lost in thought, then asked, 'What do you consider proper pay for your work, if we can call it work?'

'Are you asking this question in terms of yourself or as an academic question?'

'What would I, Adrian Breakstone, have to pay you for, say, an hour of your time? In bed, that is?'

His gaze moved from her eyes to her lips. He watched her voluptuous red mushroom-textured lips move, and each word spoken seemed to take on a sexuality, a sexual quality that was not associated with normal speech. She said, 'I would want five hundred dollars for a weekend's fun; a hundred dollars for one night. And if a fur wrap came along with the fee, it would make me especially happy. And, as the girl said, "for that I could make a perfect fool of myself."'

'And how does your husband feel about all this?'

'As I said, he is a bitter, angry man. He is difficult, insulting; but I must take care of him. His accident was, in a sense, my fault. He got that bullet in the spine in a little shoot-out one night when he caught me down on my knees doing a number. The other man was faster than Hiram. I don't think he meant to damage him so seriously, but that's how it happened. To make a long story, I get paid well and Hiram gets most of it. You could call him my pimp except he doesn't solicit trade for me. He detests my work, the men. Me, too, I guess.'

'Do you think he'd see me, talk to me?' asked Adrian.

She looked hard, unsmiling. 'That's a pretty dumb question. He'd clam up. You wouldn't get a word out of him. He'd hate you on sight. Especially if he knew you were Breakstone's son. Good God, man, you're not very bright.'

'I guess you're right. But I'm puzzled by a few things. He must have hated my father very much . . . '

'Before you go any further,' she said, 'there'll be no more talk about your father, or his death. I know nothing about the killing. I have no idea who did it or why. My husband certainly had nothing to do with it. No motive.'

'Hate is a pretty good motive,' said Adrian.

'Sometimes, but Hiram hated all the men I slept with. And they're all still alive – last time I looked.'

'Were any of them Jewish and prominent and financially well-off, pillars of society?'

'None that I recall, but so what? Hiram couldn't have differentiated. They were all *johns*, paying the rent, fucking his wife. One was as good or bad as another.'

'How did you get to meet my father?' Adrian asked, his voice choked and dry.

'Minelli.'

'Does he introduce you to many men?'

'Your questions are getting offensive. Minelli is an old friend, a valuable and powerful friend. The less said about him and me, the better. Got it?'

'Got it,' said Adrian.

She turned on her smile; her teeth glistened. She put her hand on his. He found her fingers soft; the nails, he observed, were pink and opalescent, the skin delicately veined with a palpable, sexual pulsebeat. The hand stroked him twice. She said, smiling, 'I could take you and eat you and suck you too, like a sour and sweet kumquat. You're pretty and nice.'

She dropped her hand below the table, leaned slightly against him. He felt her fingers at his fly. He leaned back, rose from his seat, trembling; throat dry, chest aching, heart beating furiously.

'I've got an appointment and I must go,' he said. He pulled some bills from his pocket, dropped one on the table, said, 'Thanks for your time. Excuse me for rushing off.'

And he was gone. The coffee shop was almost empty now.

She sat there stony-faced. She reached over for her poodle, lifted it to her lap, caressed it.

'The poor, sad, motherfucker,' she said softly into the dog's ear.

Adrian was having a meeting with a red-faced bald-headed bull of a man with a huge red moustache. They were in a walnut-panelled office, located at the top of a building adjoining the City Hall. The man was the police commissioner. The subject under discussion: a Negro, non-ambulatory male, in a wheelchair, married to an attractive black woman of easy virtue.

'Yes, thanks to you, we've checked out Jackson's bank account. And yes, there have been some abnormal deposits. But he claims the money is legitimate and he doesn't feel required or obliged by law to explain the source of his income.

'We can't charge him, and we can't move him. We can't prove a goddamned thing. And frankly, I don't see why a man would shoot his wife's lover if he did indeed provide large sums of cash via his wife's sexual services. What would he gain by having your father killed? It would automatically cut off the source of income. Since the man was paralysed from the waist down, he couldn't possibly claim invasion of his conjugal rights. Now could he, Adrian? And Adrian, this conversation is private, it is not being recorded and is strictly between us. I know how painful the subject must be to you, but you brought it up, you brought it to me personally. Judge Minelli is a friend of ours. He thinks we should drop the whole thing. Right? I discussed it with the District Attorney and he agrees that we would be wasting time and the taxpayer's money. And we might also be the cause of family embarrassment by pushing this thing. Your mother; your brother . . . he's a prominent rabbi, I understand . . .'

Adrian sat silently, staring at the man.

The commissioner paused, pulled a crumpled sheet of paper out of his desk and thrust it towards Adrian.

'I got this so-called letter this morning; it's signed *A Friend*. It relates to your father's murder. Here, read it.'

Adrian looked at the commissioner in astonishment.

The letter, composed of cut-out letters from a newspaper, and pasted up like a ransom note, read as follows:

> DOC BREAKSTON LIKE BLACK PUSSY BLACK
> PUSSY HAVE HUSBAND WHO DON'T LIKE
> WITEY BLACK HUSBAND MEAN MAN WITH
> MAFIA FRIENDS WITEY NOT RICH ENUF TO
> MESS WITH BLACK PUSSY BANG A FRIEND

Adrian looked at the commissioner.

'A shorthand document that wraps up the life and death of the great lover, Dr Breakstone,' said the commissioner. 'Reads like something out of the comics: three-panel strip.'

Adrian felt his heart go thumping. His temples throbbed with pressure, and he put his fingers to them, as if to check the compression. Suddenly he leaned forward and shouted, 'Mr Commissioner, that's no way to talk about my father. He was gunned down on your city street, by a thug. I don't see anything comic strip about that. That letter should be enough to justify arrest. Even if it won't electrocute Jackson, it will help nail him down.'

'Okay,' said the commissioner. He was livid but still in control.

'You make that nut letter sound like my father's obituary,' said Adrian, almost shouting again. He took a deep breath. 'He was a fine man, a fine doctor; he was charitable, a servant of the community. I want the assassin caught. You can squeeze a confession out of Jackson, and if it's inhuman to interrogate a man in a wheelchair, then let's be inhuman. Torture him. So what else is new?'

The commissioner stood up slowly, studying Adrian. Then he put out his hand to him, said, 'You'll be hearing from me.'

Adrian was dismissed. He knew he had blown the meeting. But somehow, he did not regret going so far. Okay, so he was an hysteric. But who wouldn't be?

The commissioner left the room and Adrian found himself alone. He rose and walked slowly out of the office and out of the building.

Two days later the newspapers and radio reported the arrest and confession of a South Side cripple, a Negro jazz musician. It seemed he had hired a hood to drive him and had shot down Dr Breakstone for personal reasons not disclosed. The driver of the car was not named, nor was he located.

Adrian and his brothers gathered for a meeting. They met in Ralph's study and agreed in solemn conclave that their mother should go south, to Florida, to the Roney Plaza, for a rest. Her two daughters-in-law should accompany her. Sarah, surprisingly, consented to the plan. The three women left the city, checked into the Miami Beach hotel, began a quiet recuperative programme.

The large cash expenditures disclosed by the cheques cashed by Dr Breakstone, continued to puzzle the sons. The brothers expressed concern for Adrian's future and finances, but came up with no proposals. Adrian did not refer to his visit to Kama Jackson, nor did he hint at an expensive woman in the background.

A few days later, after the police had arrested Jackson, Adrian paid her a visit. This time, on hearing his voice on the lobby speaker, she said, 'Come up.'

Adrian heard the poodle bark as he rang her door-chimes. She opened the door, nodded, gestured for him to enter. He found the foyer and living-room spare: a

polished parquet floor with a small bright Persian rug in the centre, several chairs and a sofa. No lamps were visible. She led him to the sofa, a large zebra skin covered affair which faced a small framed photo of Marcus Garvey in colour (and resplendent uniform) on the opposite wall.

She smiled as she observed him studying the photograph. 'You'll note it's inscribed to my husband; a funny man, Garvey.'

'Were they acquainted? Or friends?' asked Adrian.

'Hiram is sympathetic to Garvey's views; more so since he began to be bitter about all whites. He insisted on having the photo up there, to remind himself and his friends of the enemy: whitey. He thinks Garvey's views will win out in the end. No, they were not friends.'

'Was that a real preoccupation? Whitey and enmity: After he was shot?'

'Definitely. And of course the fault was largely mine. I'm open-minded about all races and colours, and when I occasionally showed some interest in, or partiality towards, a white man, Hiram could get mean.'

'The meanness extended to all of your personal friends?'

'More or less. I suppose you're referring to your father?'

Adrian took several seconds to reply. 'Yes,' he said.

'Come with me,' said Kama. He rose and followed her to the bedroom.

'I want to show you something. It will explain several things.'

The bedroom had three doors, one of which was partially open and revealed a bathroom. The other, obviously a cupboard door, was closed. As Adrian stood at the bedroom entrance he watched her move towards the cupboard. She opened the door, stood aside, and said, 'Take a look.'

He came forward, stared at the contents. There were four fur coats hanging on the metal rod; one was a lush,

floor-length black mink; one was a long white fox coat. There was also a lynx and a beaver coat.

'Those fur coats are a few of the gifts Dr Breakstone gave me, out of friendship. Hiram, my husband, blew his stack every time I came home with one of these friendship gifts. Somehow, cash didn't bother him. I'm showing these to you in case you're interested in knowing how much your father esteemed me, and why his bank account may reflect large withdrawals. He also gave me some pearls and a great emerald ring. I adore all sorts of green objects, and I'm not referring to grass.'

She gave him an amused look. Adrian stared, said nothing.

'Let's go back into the living-room,' she said. 'A drink?'

'Thanks. A scotch. With ice, please.'

'Sure thing,' she said, moving by him, brushing his body lightly with hers.

The musk scent of the room and the woman were familiar to Adrian, but not identifiable by name. The dress Kama wore, a knee-length pale blue silk dress, sleeveless and breast-revealing, affected Adrian perceptibly and she smiled as she handed him his drink.

'Sit here,' she said, patting the space beside her on the sofa.

He sat beside her, sipped his scotch.

'You've got some heavy thoughts on that pretty mind of yours, I know,' she said. 'Why not spill 'em, and be friendly?'

'Your husband is in serious trouble,' he said. 'You know that, of course. Do you think the police are barking up the wrong tree?'

'You must think very little of me and my intelligence,' she said. 'I wouldn't discuss that subject with my own mother, let alone with you.'

'You're right,' said Adrian. 'I'd be stupid to ask any

questions about your husband. At any rate, I had a need to see you, as you know. I came back from Paris to see what I could do about my father's death. There's almost nothing I can do. Nature, and the police, will take charge, and whatever happens, so be it. I've a few personal problems to resolve. Nothing to do with you . . . ' His voice tapered off and she turned to study his drained, almost defeated expression.

'What is your profession? What do you plan to do?' she asked. 'If I may be personal.'

'I have no profession, no definite plans. I'm on a honeymoon in Paris. I've got to start doing something tangible about supporting myself and my wife. My father's death cuts me off entirely. My mother inherits everything and I think she will hang on to every dollar so long as she lives. In a way, I can't blame her. Why should she support me? I should be working.'

'You do have a problem. So your father wasn't as generous as I thought he could be. Never thought his son would have to worry about bread.'

'I shouldn't be discussing this with you. You couldn't care less; and you've got a problem too. Your husband.'

'No problem,' she said. 'I'm a fatalist. Those fur coats you saw in the bedroom, they'll keep me warm. The man who owns this building has a sweet tooth, and he thinks I'm sweet. So who's got a problem?' She stood up. 'We both have things to do, places to go. Best of luck to both of us.'

Adrian held out his hand. She took it, smiled. 'See you around.'

He paused at the door. 'A favour, please. May I have your phone number. I hate to come here as a surprise visitor, unannounced, calling from the lobby . . . '

She pointed to the phone. 'Help yourself. Copy it off the disc.'

He copied the number into his notebook and left.

Chapter Thirteen

Paris

Dearest Adrian:

The Merediths went off to Spain for two weeks and invited me to occupy their apartment. Who could resist, considering that their piano is God-sent. (I love their *le style camp* bedroom too.) Am working harder than ever in my life, sometimes six, seven, eight steady hours daily. Am making headway. The Bechstein is a dream instrument and makes the Rachmaninov a bit easier for me. I'll be here until the twentieth so you know where to reach me. Glad to be out of the hotel for a while; there's s-p-a-c-e here!

As for you: I hope you're getting a decent amount of rest, and are watching your diet and medication. I'd love to hear from you on anything relating to you, the whole situation, plans for returning to Paris (me), etc. Tried to reach you by phone without success.

Not much to report. Am keyed up about the concert and the tour prospects. Have discussed it a few times and it appears to be for real. No fantasy. A contract awaits my signature and before signing it I'd like you to see it. Jock read it before he went to Spain and thought it was okay. If the public likes me, I may be able to support you – almost – in the style to which you want to be accustomed . . .

Wish I could be with you, my dear, but you don't need me there, and I know you'll be back soon. I hope very soon. Don't strain.

I work and sleep, and take an occasional walk. Have seen no one, except a friend at tea one afternoon. (She let me read part of one of the manuscript volumes of her Diary. Wow!) The piano has me imprisoned, and I can't wait for you to come back and release me for a bit.

Love, Ruth

Dear Ruth:

Happy about your respite from the cramped hotel. The gift of the Merediths' digs for two weeks is terrific, lovely. They are such good friends. Enjoy it all, even if it means working your fingers to the bone on that Bechstein. As for me, here: the police have arrested a black ex-musician, a wheelchair cripple who is a strong suspect. I'll fill you in on the details when I see you; it's too bizarre to believe. The killer, if he is indeed the man, had a very odd motive. He hated white men and my father in particular, and you might never guess why. Well, my love, daddy doctor was having an affair with his wife. Other details later. Meanwhile, not a word of this to anyone, please. Very important!

My mother has been ushered off to Florida for a rest and change of scene. She's in a state of confusion, desolation, shock, loneliness. But her financial position is ideal: she is the *sole* beneficiary of my father's total estate! Not a sou for any of the children, no charitable gifts. Mama gets it all. Which means, dear one, I and my brothers must wait for Mama's demise before we inherit. The real estate, bonds, stocks, art, antiques, cash, all go to Mama. If you think this is strange, then hear this: aside from the funds Papa gave us for our two years in Paris, we have no other visible means of support. (I'm not

thinking of the cash gift to you from your parents. That's yours.) So, while there's a lot of time to do some intensive thinking and inventory-taking, and we can certainly enjoy ourselves in Paris for at least another eighteen months, I'm going to try and seek out a means of earning a living. Does this diminish my filial affection? Guess!

As it turns out, in the not distant future, you may well be the breadwinner in this family. For which I'm happy for you as well as for us. But I must, sooner than later, hustle up a job, a decision about the future. I've been thinking about teaching, but I don't think I can take that, not in more than mini-doses. Writing is my first inclination but there's no pot of gold at the end of that rainbow, not for the stuff I want to write. Death and violence: well, I'm beginning to see that it's more suited to fiction and films, but not in the form I've had in mind. My plan for a book on assassination is in abeyance; I keep thinking of the audience: a few hundred or few thousand people throughout the world who really care. Most people, subconsciously, relate to evil, crime, pain, torture, even burning at the stake! Can you see the big publishers in New York or Paris bidding for the rights to my study?

Now sit tight, my pretty. There are depths in me about which you know nothing. And I'm not referring to the so-called depths of depravity . . . I have a mathematical bent or talent (everyone says I have talent). I'm going to work out a financial programme that will produce wealth for us. To put it bluntly, I'm going to put my mind, my logical mathematical talent, to work on the simple problem of making money.

Making money without working at a nine-to-five

job: that's my goal. I don't think I could endure working for an organisation, a corporation, a team (I loathe the word: teamwork); I'm an individualist and not stupid. Are you following me thus far, my dearest?

My plan is to concentrate on a method, a scheme, a programme or plan that will produce a million or so dollars for me – us – without having to conform to the industrial or business rules of our society. There are so many idiots about, idiots who own great yachts and estates, and none seems to have the mind or talent that I possess. I'll resolve this problem by hard thinking, utilising my native talents, my imagination. It can be done, I know. When I return to Paris, I want to discuss our problem with Jock. He neither toils nor spins, and is rich; I should like to learn a few secrets possessed by the rich. Of course having a wealthy parent helps. It isn't as *complicado* as you might imagine. And I'm not jesting.

To put it in simple terms I'm determined to become rich and autonomous; independent but involved in only those pursuits that interest me, that give me pleasure. And I'll not become a ward of the state, a parasite, a kept husband. A nine-to-five slave, a corporate cipher.

I'll be leaving for Paris in a week or so, providing nothing unforeseen prevents it. I don't intend staying here for the trial of the accused murderer. I'm not needed in any capacity. I think this man – his name is Hiram Jackson – is guilty. But that's neither here nor there. I want to be with you. I miss you and your sweet face, and your body. I want to see and hear you at the piano. I hope, in my absence, you haven't found another lover; that

would distress me. I also hope the above doesn't convince you I'm a lunatic.

Yrs
Adrian

Adrian checked his notebook, located Kama's phone number, and called her. She answered on the third ring. The voice was soft, provocatively erotic. Precisely as his fantasy would have it.

'Is my voice familiar?' he asked.

'You are coy, Mr Breakstone,' she said. 'I have twenty-twenty hearing. And all my other faculties are functioning equally well.'

'Reassuring and gratifying,' said Adrian.

'To what do I owe the pleasure of this call?'

'To enquire if you are free to see me today.'

'For what purpose?'

'I would enjoy your company and I'm prepared to compensate you in American currency, as you once explained it. Are you interested?'

'Can you be more specific?'

'How much can you give me in time for one hundred dollars?'

He heard her laughter. 'For sentimental reasons and others too difficult to describe, I can give you most of the afternoon, if you get here by noon, latest. Let's say, for one hundred dollars you may have lunch and potluck dinner of sorts, with me at Chez Kama. I'll cook up a nice soul-food lunch. Does that suit your convenience and needs?'

'To perfection. I'll be there in half an hour.'

'*Ciao*,' she said.

His father's dark meat. How depraved am I? But go. Go, he said softly to himself. Go. Go!

An answer rose from the depths of his subconscious: you are without morals, scruples, character. But alive!

He laid out the cash expenses for his foray. As he prepared for his visit he thought, this day and night will provide a memory that will sustain me in my twilight days and nights. I'll extract a poem from this day and night; and he thought, too, in her black and pink cunt I'll find the means to destroy that cocksucker father who was once a friend, a king, a confidant; a pal. We trusted each other, but now I'm deserted, repudiated. He stopped, thinking. There's the opening of my poem . . . and for the closing I'll write something affirmative and the icy rain will cease to fall in my heart, dear Kama. He paused and wrote the lines in his notebook. And then, there came to him a recollection of himself as a small boy, peering through the crack in a door, staring at a half-naked woman on a table being aborted, and his father calmly explaining the meaning of it all, explaining his love and palship . . .

A fucking poet with a hard-on for a beautiful dark whore, he thought; and my beautiful Ruth, my bride, is labouring in Paris with Rachmaninov. And Ravel, and Mozart and Satie . . . and I, a prick wagging a man . . .

The taxi reached the Lovecraft address. He paid the driver, entered the lobby and rang Kama's bell. She pressed the buzzer immediately, and he was on his way up to her apartment.

She met him at the door, *sans* French poodle, dressed in a white silk kaftan. Her coffee-coloured cheeks were touched with pale rouge, her lips were vermilion and shining. Previously he had noted the absence of lipstick. He saw a tray of food on the coffee table and several glasses and bottles. There were also, he saw as he entered, handmade cigarettes in an open yellow glazed ceramic box; obviously joints such as he and his friends at the university had been smoking a year ago.

She poured him a scotch and he sat down. A record

player was filling the air, softly, with the plaintive Billie Holiday voice.

'Do you know that voice, that sweet, melancholy voice?' Kama asked him as he seated himself beside her on the zebra-covered sofa.

'Yes, and that's Krupa at the drums . . . and Benny Goodman, right?'

He sipped his drink and added, 'Did you know her real name is Eleanora?'

'Welcome to the club,' she said. 'Now let's chat.' Her eyes were glittering.

An awkward pause. Adrian seemed to be sorting out his thoughts. finally he blurted out, 'I'm so glad you were able to see me. Could I – may I ask you a few questions?'

'Such as?'

'Well, have you seen your husband?'

'No.'

'Do you hold out hope for his release?'

'No. None.'

'Then you think he's guilty of the murder?'

'Not at all. I think he's crazy and that he'll be put away as insane. They wouldn't electrocute a cripple in any event.'

'What will you do?'

'Go away. Disappear. South of France, Paris, Martinique, Majorca, Argentina. I'll find my way, a new life and a better climate. Who knows, there will be exciting surprises and encounters. Maybe a nice old man will establish me in a villa in Nice. I'll arouse his sleeping cock. I have dreams. I have my body. I have youth. Women are luckier than they imagine. The trouble with most women is lack of imagination. They think it's wrong or bad to be a whore. There are clever whores and stupid whores. I'll never lack for food or comfort. I know what a man wants and I'm prepared to give it to him. There's only one pitfall: losing control. Drugs. That's the enemy.'

'I'd like to ask you . . . ' She stopped him, her forefinger raised, in the middle of his sentence. 'Please, no more of this. You and I have a business arrangement, if you'll kindly remember. I want to shake the mess out of my mind; my husband was no husband for years. I'm not guiltless, but he gave me misery, lonely nights, pressures and, I don't mind telling you, cause for fear of my life. I don't think he's redeemable and if they decide to convict him and put him away in the loony bin, that's about it. I simply have no tears left. Okay. End of subject.'

'And my father?'

'Ah, your father. Well, Adrian, I loved your father, believe it or not. He had style and balls. But he was a flawed man. I won't try to analyse him, that's your problem. You're his son. Christ!' She paused, then asked, 'And so, how about a drink?'

'I'm still working on my scotch, thanks.'

Adrian reached into his inside jacket pocket. 'Before I forget, I have something for you.'

He pulled out an envelope and placed it on the coffee table.

'Doesn't one usually put that on the mantelpiece?' she asked, smiling. 'Except, we have no mantelpiece here.'

'Now, you're embarrassing me,' said Adrian. 'I'm inept. I've never done this before. Consider me a kind of virgin.'

She laughed, ripped her finger through the sealed flap and removed Adrian's money. Two fifty-dollar bills.

'How neat, how nice. Thank you. And now, no more commerce, just a nice social day. And as I said, a fresh drink?'

'Okay, another scotch please.'

As she poured the drinks, giving him a double, she said, 'A friend of mine stopped in to visit. She's in the kitchen, fixing us some food. Her name is Louise Fletcher, an

Australian lady here on a holiday, an employee of a film company. I met her a few years ago; you'll like her, I'm sure.'

Adrian looked crestfallen. He took a long stiff drink from his glass.

'Don't look so dejected,' she said. 'She's not staying. Not for long. But she's very special.'

Louise was a very well-structured young woman, with long straight golden hair, a radiant smile, and plump breasts almost bursting out of her pink sheath of a dress. The combination of hair and dress produced a startling vision, and Adrian found himself gaping with pleasure and surprise.

'Adrian, meet Louise,' said Kama as the woman entered the room. 'Louise must leave us shortly, she has a date, but I'm glad you two can meet. She's a world traveller, may be in Paris next month. Right, Louise?'

'Yes, in two weeks. I usually stay at the George Cinq. In case you're free for a drink . . .'

'I'll be nearby, at the Pont Royal, in about ten days,' said Adrian. 'But it isn't a permanent address; we're looking for something larger, for a longer stay.'

Louise put down a tray. 'Soul food,' she said. 'Tripe, fit for the gods.'

Adrian beamed. He raised his eyes, smiled, breathed exaggeratedly 'You call it soul food. My mother, who makes tripe four times a year, calls it *vampim*, a Russian word, I think. Since you cooked it, I must ask you how come an Australian beauty knows how to cook tripe?'

'My birthplace is Brisbane,' she said, 'but I've been everywhere. Including Harlem where I once worked on a film. And thanks for calling me an Australian beauty. That's real nice.'

He surprised them – and himself – by saying, 'Louise, why must you leave us? Why not call and break your date?'

'Why?' she asked, smiling, slipping a forkful of tripe into her mouth, her lips moving slowly, sensuously as she chewed. Blonde and white, she had the attributes of a sensual black woman.

'I like you. Kama and I have a date. But in your case, three is not a crowd. Three could be cosy.'

'Thanks for the compliment. Do you want to play? Do you want to watch? Fool around? What?'

'Everything,' said Adrian.

'Well,' said Kama, 'you own my company for the afternoon and evening. My friend here must run along soon. What's your pleasure?'

'I'll leave the initiative to you. And to you, Louise.'

'Good,' said Kama. 'Before you go, Louise, I wish you would let Adrian know how you feel about him. He likes music, food, books – and also, I think, fucking.'

Louise sat down next to Adrian, and Kama got off the sofa, sat on the floor, legs folded, watching.

Louise ran her fingers up along Adrian's leg, watching his face. The tips of her fingers played along his thigh: sensual scales, piano fingers, tactile music, and his heart began the fearful and familiar pounding, leading him on, he knew, over a sheer cliff . . .

'I'm drunk,' he said. 'What was in that scotch?'

'Nothing but scotch,' said Kama, 'and you had a little soul food.'

'Well, I'm drunk; also, I think I'm horny.'

'Watch,' said Kama.

Louise, now also on the floor, made a gliding movement of her body, almost snake-fashion, and approached Kama, head on. She ran her hands up Kama's skirt, followed with her head, disappearing beneath her skirt.

'Adrian,' asked Kama, 'are you watching?' She was now lying back spread-eagled, accepting Louise's ministrations.

'Yes, I'm watching,' said Adrian. 'Is this the floor show? Do I become involved, part of the act? I want to be part of the act. May I?'

'Feel free,' said Kama. 'Do what comes naturally. You're the guest of the establishment.'

Adrian got down on the floor, unzipped his fly, produced his now enflamed cock, and proceeded to prod Louise's ass with it. Her panties were still on but Adrian was determined to proceed, somehow. His hands were clawing at her pink, silk-covered pudendum visible from the rear.

'Don't,' said Louise from the depths of Kama's skirt. 'That hurts.'

Adrian drew back. Puzzled, watching Louise wallowing in the recesses of Kama's groin, he studied her silken legs, ass and thighs writhing. He could imagine the salivic rapture of mouth and tongue on and in the slippery orifice; the noisy sucking at the labial area. He was beside himself. His father's death, his personal problems, Ruth in Paris, pounding away at the Bechstein: it was all a distant montage, a surreal and alien and bizarre image. Touched with a mad intensity, he knew he could not presently be the mourning son; he was possessed by a blind lechery here, within the home of his father's murderer, and with the murderer's wife.

The day ended in exhaustion; Adrian could not recall when he fell asleep. When he awakened around five o'clock, he found himself in the middle of a large bed: Kama's. The words that came to his mind were 'used up'. His shoes, trousers, shorts were off; his necktie loosened, a towel across his middle. He lay there, reconstructing the events of the day. Louise, the Australian bombshell of flesh and bisexuality, the blonde marvel, was gone presumably. He recalled her lovemaking with Kama, and then with him.

With a rush, he recalled Kama's extraordinary lovemak-

ing with him. She had begun with a slow tongue massage, as she called it, then she bestrode him, rode him with a frenzy and thoroughness that left him depleted; he recalled her tongue deep in his throat; he recalled saying before passing out, 'I think I'm dead.' All of this he now pieced together, and marvelled that he could remember it.

His throat was parched, his chest and larynx aflame. He got up, found his jacket and removed two pills from the pocket – his little white nitro tablets. On his way to the bathroom, for water, he saw Kama asleep on the sofa, naked, breasts and crotch exposed and glowing in the twilight of the room. He stood there for a moment, transfixed. Then shakily, in need of medication, he moved on and found the bathroom.

When he returned he saw her standing near the bed. She was smiling, posturing demurely, one knee dipped before the other. He slapped her bottom, entered the bedroom and collapsed on the bed, groaning.

'Enough activity?' she asked. 'Would you like something to drink, to eat? Anything?'

'Come and lie down beside me,' he said.

She approached the bed, sat down and studied his face, his body, his flaccid penis. Her fingers strayed across his chest and groin. She smiled.

Lying there, staring at the ceiling, Adrian thought of Hiram Jackson, the tragic, forgotten man.

'What is he like? Care to tell me something about your husband, Kama? I can't help thinking about him.'

'How to tell you?' she began, speaking slowly. 'I fell for him the first time I saw and heard him play in a South Side club. He had a nice slow easy style. He could gig with some of the best and he recorded a dozen records, mostly with the Serenaders: maybe you heard of them? Tenor sax was his thing. He played with Hampton and Pollock and the Black and Tan Orchestra and some others. He was a

quiet man, hardly drank, didn't smoke or use stuff; serious about his work. Did you ever hear "My Mammy's Blues" or "Fight that Thing"? He recorded them. Kinda hard to find them now. We have them in our collection. He had talent. I liked his intensity: kinda tough guy. He got involved in black politics and talked about the Back to Africa Movement. Intellectually he was above the average. As far as I know he never got into trouble with white chicks although they seemed to go for him. He often talked about moving to New Orleans but I never encouraged it. Although I was tempted during certain lean times. He was not the Big Lover and maybe, just a little, I began to disappoint him in my demands. I did some hat-checking, cigarette-peddling in tough periods. He's older than I am, but not much. I guess you could sum him up as serious and a solid jazz man. After his accident, he began to read a lot, and collected so-called racial records and accompanied them on his sax. Once in a while he'd have a pal in, but not often. It was pretty depressing to be with him for very long.' She paused, stared at Adrian, then added, 'But now he's a sullen, mean man. I sometimes think he'd like to kill me. Probably blames everything on me.'

'Weren't there good times too?' asked Adrian.

'Sure, sure, when he was working and the music-making part was good and the friends we had were all on top of the world with big bands. But a girl gets bored and itchy. Lots of distractions. You know. What more can I tell you? The good trickled out, the best is behind us. Today, I'm looking out for number one. And fun.'

'And what about his future? Assuming there is one?'

'I dunno. I'm no longer anybody's keeper, except my own.'

'Thanks for filling me in, Kama.'

She turned and looked into his eyes, smiled.

'I'll make us some coffee. Okay?'

'No,' Adrian said. 'I've got to go. A date with my brothers.'

'Oh, I thought we were going to have dinner.'

'A raincheck, please,' Adrian said. 'I just remembered that I have to have dinner with the brethren; family business.'

'So be it,' she said. She went to the living-room and placed two records on the player. Billie Holiday again. The sweet sadness of her voice carried into the bedroom. Suddenly, a sense of pressure in the chest made him pause, listen. And he looked at Kama and said, 'Kama, I must leave. Thank you.'

She laughed. 'Tomorrow, or the day after, you'll have another hard-on and you'll be thinking of me, and Louise. Boys of your age get the hots every hour on the hour . . .'

'Could be,' said Adrian. 'But I may have harder problems – no pun – to resolve.'

'Well, keep in touch,' she said. 'I may be leaving this burg as soon as the police and the state decide what they want to do about the alleged murderer, Mr Hiram Jackson.'

'Do you have any place specifically in mind, when you leave?' asked Adrian.

'None. But it will be faraway, faraway. I'll fly faraway like a bird. Me and my fur coats and memories. Maybe your Paris. Who knows?'

Chapter Fourteen

The meeting with his brothers gave Adrian little comfort. They were fat cats, comfortable. His brother, Harvey, the rabbi, was delivering a sermon: 'we must keep the family name above suspicion, untarnished.' He valued his position and social status and expressed his concern with teeth-clenched passion.

Adrian spoke briefly, pointed out that the alleged murderer was probably insane. A wheelchair killer was an exotic news item, an interesting new criminal concept, and would earn him more than normal newspaper space. But, as far as the family was concerned, there should be no scandal. The motivation would probably remain buried with the killer.

'Let's not succumb to hysterical confusion. Sobriety!' concluded Harvey.

And then, the issue with which Adrian was most concerned, arose: his personal future.

'What are your plans, Adrian?'

'I haven't had a chance to think about the future.' Then he added, 'A job; teaching perhaps; I have enough money to hold me over a year. And then – I simply don't know. Ruth will probably be earning a little money as a concert pianist.'

'Concert pianist?' said Harvey. 'That could take years before real money comes in. Pianists are like painters and writers: sometimes it takes half a lifetime before one begins to make a living. Nothing personal in that remark, Adrian. Facts of life, you know.'

'I suppose what you have in mind for me is a job, and the sooner the better,' said Adrian, directing his eyes ceilingwards.

'Well, you know the terms of Papa's Will. As long as Mama lives, and she may live to one hundred and twenty,' said Harvey, 'there will be no money for us; possibly some small handouts at best. So – Adrian should start thinking about a job.' His voice was oozing sincerity.

'What sort of a job?' asked Ralph, looking at Adrian.

'Nature has bestowed certain gifts upon me,' said Adrian, arching one eyebrow, 'but none seems to relate to the matter of making a living. I'd be a dreadful office manager, for instance. Nor could I design machinery or sell used cars. Weaving and spinning, carpentry, making men's pants, none of these occupations would suit me. I could write a book on several interesting subjects. I could translate from the French, which would give me some pleasure, but very little money. So what do you suggest?'

He sat back, studying his brothers as they in their turn sat, examining him as though he were on a witness-stand.

'I'm not an effete, nor a cripple, and I'm a realist,' continued Adrian. 'But I don't intend spending the rest of my life trying to earn a living doing something I don't enjoy. I do have one asset that is worth more than any talent, and that is a mind, an imagination if you will. I have some ideas that could be harnessed and turned into money: big money. In fact, I've been giving a lot of thought to an idea. Something that came to me in Paris – while looking at art prints and posters. When it's firmed up I'd like to discuss it with you. It calls for financial support; so be forewarned.'

'Naturally, any idea you have,' said Ralph, 'needing our support, will get our best consideration, although in terms of money we may be limited. You know very well where we stand financially. We work for a living, Adrian.'

'Yes, I know. I'm not asking, or going to ask, for a handout, so stop worrying.'

'By the way,' said Ralph, 'Uncle Sylvester needs some help in his factory; in the accounting division. Would that interest you, Adrian?'

'Uncle Sylvester is a crustacean; to put it bluntly, a *putz*,' said Adrian. 'I don't mean to put him down totally, but I doubt whether I'd be able to work for him. Possibly he might work for *me*! But I thought he was on shaky ground, near bankruptcy.'

'That's not very respectful of you,' said Ralph. 'You may be right about his being on shaky ground, but he's been that way for over ten years. He seems to hang on; meets his payroll. And he gets a new car every two years, takes expensive vacations. I've even heard he has a hot little tootsie somewhere in Michigan that calls for sudden mysterious business trips every week or two.'

Adrian listened, seemingly in deep concentration; and he was indeed giving profound consideration, suddenly, to Uncle Sylvester as a possibility for his future. He regretted his smartass remark about his uncle possibly working for him; some perverse devil prompted it, of course. He had no specific reason to speak disrespectfully of his ageing uncle.

Uncle Sylvester owned a small factory that produced arty-crafty objects, cheap copies of small pieces of furniture such as coffee tables and end tables, imitation antique-framed mirrors and other objects that could be called marginal borax in the furniture business.

'Look, dear brothers,' said Adrian, 'we all know what a *grobber* our uncle is, and the crap he produces, but he has managed to stay in business as you say, for God knows how many years. If he needs help in his accounting department, let's find out. What I don't know I can learn in a few weeks. I can take a crash course in accounting, for

heaven's sake. I've had top grades in calculus, I'll remind you. Papa called me the family maths genius. Remember?'

'Are you sure you want to make a decision now?' asked Ralph. 'You have lots of time left from the two-year honeymoon Papa gave you. Enjoy it. Besides, Ruth may have other ideas; you said she was preparing for a concert, and possibly a tour. You could wait. Her plans shouldn't be treated lightly.'

'I'm not being cavalier,' said Adrian. 'I'm trying to be a realist.' He paused. 'I could go to Paris, think a little, then return with Ruth. As a matter of fact, I'd like to do just that.'

Harvey smiled. 'No one doubted that for a moment,' said Harvey, giving Adrian his most authoritative smile. The smile irked Adrian and he thought, how pleasurable it would be to come up with a brilliant business idea, a stroke of financial wizardry, and show the family what he really had inside his skull. He'd make them all dance and applaud. Business, making money, was a dull game and he'd show them how to put fire under it. He could, he would do it. Some of the dullest and dumbest men he knew had made fortunes from infantile wits. Adrian simply had the intelligence and imagination to excel and he would demonstrate it before long. He would concentrate, just as he did at a chess game, or while working out a mathematical problem.

Shortly after, Adrian left. As he settled back in the taxi heading for home, the idea struck him.

He sat there, silently, staring at the back of the driver's neck, turning Uncle Sylvester's name over in his mind. The idea grew rapidly, expanding until it almost overwhelmed him.

In the taxi he evolved a plan, or at least the kernel of a plan, based on his subconscious thoughts relating to art

and prints. There were numerous unanswered questions, but he was convinced that he had struck on an idea that would make him a millionaire, an instant rich man, without benefit of a job or time clocks. He thought, either I'm a madman or a genius. The scheme was so simple and also, both a cultural enterprise and legitimate. Most millionaires, he thought, use foul means to gain their fortunes. If the plan works, he said to himself, and he found himself actually whispering aloud, it would be a straight, clean business proposition that would net him hundreds of thousands. Perhaps a million dollars. His brain began to whirl, his heart leaped and he was eager to get home, to his desk, and begin working out with pencil and paper the scheme that was unfolding in his brain: low-priced colour prints in frames, for the masses!

This day, he thought, promised to be one of the most fruitful and pleasurable in all his life.

The following day Adrian lunched with his Uncle Sylvester, his father's only brother. They exchanged mutual expressions of grief and loss, and when the amenities were over, Adrian realised that his father's death had not really had the impact on his brother he had expected. The fact of murder impressed him. Otherwise, it was business as usual.

They ordered their food and Adrian then broke through the small-talk.

'Well, how is your business, Uncle Sylvester?' he asked. 'Is it on the upswing? Are the profits holding up? Are you manufacturing anything exciting?'

'I'm not happy with my office,' Sylvester replied. 'The system is antiquated. We need some modernisation; the records are lousy and my book-keeper is getting senile.'

Sylvester studied Adrian for a moment. How to convey to his nephew the *Weltschmerz* in his heart? His melan-

choly? He'd love to shed the entire burden of his factory, run off with his young mistress to some fantasy island somewhere in the Caribbean, maybe Cuba, and enjoy his remaining years. He was bored with business and its demands on him; he was tired of the constant uncertainty, the tightrope walk, the ever present prospect of bankruptcy.

'To be frank with you, Adrian – you're my nephew and I can trust you with confidences – my business is an up and down thing. I'm not properly financed, never have been. I have good seasons and bad, and when the bad times come round, it's murder. I've gotta keep on my toes. And when the accounting department doesn't support me, it's especially hard. Collections are poor and I need somebody to crack the whip. Somebody who really cares about the business, cares about my interests.'

He looked at Adrian, put down his spoon slowly and said, 'Adrian, I know you're a bright student, a literary boy; bookish. I like you, trust you. You could be useful to me and my company. And you could profit too, make a career for yourself.'

Adrian sat respectfully attentive, slowly eating, listening to the message between the words. His uncle needed him, needed help. Needed someone he could trust. And his sad eyes, suddenly showing a vulnerability, moved him.

'What would you do, Uncle Sylvester, if someone put some cash into your business? Do you have ideas for expansion, new products, new areas to work in?'

'Yes, lots of ideas. I could use a few hundred thousand dollars. A cash tranfusion, that's what I need.'

Adrian paused for a moment. Then he said, 'I'd like to go back to your office after lunch and look around. May I? I'm interested in my future now that Papa is gone and I must think of my own welfare. Must support myself. I may have a few ideas.'

'Good, good, Adrian. We'll go back to the plant and you can look around, ask questions. I need fresh blood, new ideas, a spiritual uplift. From who else than my intellectual nephew?' He grinned broadly.

They finished their chicken salads and drank up their coffee.

Sylvester's Buick was outside and they drove about a mile from Fritzel's restaurant to the factory, an old two-storey building on the West Side, in a dreary industrial area where the air was heavy with cement dust and foul with the odour of a gasworks.

'Uncle Sylvester, what do you think of the man they arrested as Papa's murderer? Do you think he's guilty?'

'Frankly, Adrian, I hate to talk about the whole thing, especially to you. Your father and I were not too close, but I know some things about him, things that one doesn't talk to his son about.'

'You mean women, Uncle Sylvester?'

Sylvester turned and looked at Adrian, surprised. 'What do you know about your father and women?'

'I wasn't born yesterday.'

'Well, then, you understand – and this is confidential – there was a woman in your father's life, not a white woman, either, and it is rumoured – an ugly rumour, Adrian – that her husband found out about the affair. I don't want to be quoted; maybe the whole thing's pure fantasy, made-up gossip. But one hears things. Very confidentially, I even saw the two of them together, in a South Side Negro night-club. Now my lips are sealed and I'm sorry I told you that much. I'm real sorry, Adrian. I shouldn't be talking this way.'

'Why not, Uncle Sylvester? We are men of the world, members of the adult society. We know what moves men and women. I know about sex and infidelity and temptation and sexual appetites and affection, and everything

that makes men do what they do . . . like animals, at times . . .' Then he added, with a harsh note in his voice, 'And I know what shits men can be; beasts, betrayers, sadists . . .'

'Okay, Adrian, so your father played around a little. He was a big man in his field, there were many demands on his time and energy. He needed some relaxation, the company of a young, sexy woman. Your mother is a wonderful woman, but let's face it, she did not keep up with him. He needed a taste of life, and he took when he needed. I'm no judge; I'm human, I'm weak, I do what I must do. Maybe you've heard stories about me, too. Your father and I, maybe we inherited the same inner drive. But enough of this. I hope they hang the son of a bitch who shot Jerry, but I also hope the scandal doesn't blacken our name. We have a fine name in this community. You know that.' Echoes of his pious brother . . .

Sylvester looked grim. They had reached the factory and the parking-lot attendant took the car. They moved towards the factory door.

The building was badly in need of paint; it lacked any hint of prosperity. It was a sad, scaly, unhappy-looking building. And Adrian thought, this could be my big chance. I must play my cards right. Think!

'Why don't more women shoot their lovers?' Adrian asked.

Adrian and Kama were having their farewell visit. He was leaving the following day for New York and Paris. She was standing by, waiting for the trial of her husband. Adrian refused to remain, to witness what he felt would be a charade, the disposal of the pitiful 'wheelchair murderer' who, in a sense, was opting for self-immolation.

'I agree wholly with that notion,' she said. 'Men are not to be trusted, none of them. Most men lead secret lives.

They have secret appetites and fantasies. They are always looking over the fence at the next plot of grass, believing it to be greener.'

'You're a wise woman, Kama. I could learn much from you. The truth is, I don't understand women at all. Really, I don't. And in saying that, admitting that, I also acknowledge achieving a new, higher rung of maturity. Right? But as for leading secret lives, almost every human being does. Every man, every woman, has another side, a dark side.'

'Adrian, you don't understand women, as you say, but actually, you know them well enough to know that you will never understand them. A woman can love you totally, from head to toe, she will follow you into fire if required to do so. She will want to possess you, enslave you, own you. She will want to put your cock and balls in a cage and keep the key in her cunt. But once owning you, she will keep her eye on the passing parade. She will not give up her fantasies, her secret life . . . Women are sentimental. Fantasists, too. And answer this question: what woman wouldn't want to be fucked by Clark Gable? Any happily married woman, so-called, would grab the chance and not consider that she had cheated on her husband. And wouldn't most men want to take that platinum-blonde cunt, Jean Harlow, to bed? Of course they would. And what does Harlow have that I don't have? Frankly, and being quite objective, I think I can deliver more sexual pleasure than a Harlow. I'm professional. She may think she is, but I'll bet you she's a lousy lay.' She paused, laughing. 'I'm really nuts,' and she reached for his crotch. 'One final roll in the hay before you sail the ocean blue, sailor boy.'

Chapter Fifteen

Adrian was back in Paris, hurting with desire for Ruth. The porters, the train, the taxi, the Pont Royal elevator: everything was achieved in slow-motion.

She met him at the door, at nine in the morning, scrubbed, scented, wearing his favourite pale-pink negligée. He felt a weakness from desire for her, love for her. Her large dark eyes were never more luminous, her lips never more eager for his kisses. He understood the impulse to rape . . .

They embraced, they kissed, he held her back to study her face, the fine marble sheen of her brow, the sweet chin, the trusting eyes, the warm lips.

'I'm taking you to lunch,' he said. 'We'll catch up on all the news. But first, tell me, how goes the music? Are you working hard? Too hard? Are you happy with your progress? Are the prospects for the concert tour solid?' And then he added, 'And do you love me still?'

'Yes, yes, yes,' she said, laughing. 'I'm working hard; the loan of the Merediths' apartment was a godsend. I practised morning, noon and night; and I think I lost ten pounds in your absence; can't you tell?'

He studied her figure, her slender waist, her sensuous hips; he walked around and examined her cello-shaped torso, gently gliding his hands over it in circular fashion; he turned her around and kissed her thrusting breasts through the soft flowing material of her negligée.

'I have one brief comment: you're mouthwatering.' And he seized her, drew her towards the bed and he was

making ardent love within seconds. He entered her body with a rapid manoeuvre and a sigh, and lay upon her breasts, kissing and sucking her lips, chin and throat, gasping for air.

'This is where I want to die,' he whispered. 'On this sweet field of battle.' His ejaculation was instantaneous.

His lips were still at her throat and she said, softly, 'Like Dracula, you're queer for the neck.'

'Like King Kong,' he replied, 'and I intend to eat you, but wait a few moments until I recover.'

'Oh please eat me,' she said. 'I've been dreaming of it ever since you left. Eat me, lover, eat me.'

Later, lying back and resting, Adrian told Ruth something of his trips, though nothing about Kama. He said he wanted to see Jock: a business discussion. He explained about his father's Will and his need to work, and about his Uncle Sylvester and the possibility of joining his staff.

'But can't you study instead, get your degree, become a teacher?' she said. 'Aren't teaching, writing, translating what matter most to you? Surely, working in a factory isn't for you.'

As Ruth spoke, Adrian realised she was both saddened by the prospect and disappointed in him. She had expected his sights to be higher.

'You have a lot of time to consider your future,' she said, stroking his shoulder. 'I want this to be a wonderful year for us, enjoying France and some of Europe; let's not sacrifice what we have by worrying about the future. We're both young enough to wait a while, aren't we?'

'Yes and no,' said Adrian. 'A man who marries undertakes a responsibility towards a future. Sounds stuffy? Don't worry; for the present, we're going to make the most of the gift my father gave us, namely Paris. We'll carry Paris back home when we leave. But there's no reason why I can't confer with Jock about a business idea I

have. It just might work, and if it does, I could become a millionaire quickly.'

'Come, Adrian, what a silly thing to say. Nobody becomes an instant millionaire any more. Unless he strikes oil. Only the millionaires become richer. And the oil sheiks.'

'We shall see what we shall see. I was given a mind,' said Adrian, 'an imagination that can be put to work. Money is a child's game, despite all the abracadabra and economic bullshit and Wall Street journalism. The business experts who write for the newspapers are paupers. Did you know that? They tell you how to invest, but they can't afford to get their suits pressed! Making money is a simple problem to be worked out. I have a mathematical mind. Wait and see, my pet. You'll be astonished at the man you married. I'm unlike anyone you ever met. Unlike my brothers, unlike my Uncle Sylvester. Wait. There's a wonderful surprise in store for you. Just have confidence in Adrian Breakstone, boy millionaire to be.'

'Well, if you're going to be that rich, let's get dressed, go out and spend some of your loot on a fabulous meal,' she said. 'I feel like oysters. How about it, sport? With champagne?'

'Now I know I've got to make that million!'

'If you want to combine business with pleasure why not ask the Merediths to join us, for a celebration and business talk?'

The Merediths were free and most willing to join them. Adrian felt that the forces of nature were coming to his aid. As they took the long walk to the restaurant he gave Ruth details of the plan. She listened intently and looked at him admiringly.

'I had no idea you were such a business whiz,' she said. 'It makes a lot of sense; there's a gamble in it, of course, but essentially it's sound. Of course you've got a lot of

groundwork ahead of you. But I feel you can handle it, providing you don't overtax yourself, physically.'

As he outlined it – the matters of securing rights to great art reproductions, printing facilities, framing the pictures and selling them on a mass scale – it was exciting to Ruth. He explained that the range of pictures would run from Old Masters to the best of the twentieth century, as well as a few gallery posters. The pictures were to be reproduced so that they could be framed and housed in hotel rooms, the average apartment, schools and elsewhere. To get the price down to a manageable level they would be obliged to work out a deal with Uncle Sylvester. He could produce the package. Adrian could sell them to the chain-stores and mail-order houses throughout America. He believed that he could sell several million low-priced prints, decently framed, and that a marketing programme could be worked out. He would contact the major buyers himself. But first, printers, art publishers and artists' agents had to be approached. Also the key museums. Culture for the masses: but positively no kitsch!

The more he talked, the greater was his enthusiasm, and Adrian stopped at one point, grabbed Ruth and hugged her, whirling her around on the sidewalk. Her full support was what he wanted, needed. That she was able to grasp the concept and the potential, delighted him. That she was surprised and pleased to discover this unperceived business acumen in her husband elated him.

'You thought I was a dilettante dreamer, a clunkhead,' he said. 'Actually, I've got a bear by the tail; I'm out to make a killing. I want to prove that making money is child's play. It can and will be fun. I think I can achieve what I'm after within two years or so. And then I'll get out of business and devote my time and energies to making love to my beautiful wife, and studying philosophy,

mathematics.' Then he added, teeth clenching, 'So much for Papa's estate. I'll make my own estate!'

The Merediths were surprised to find Adrian in such a euphoric state. When he proceeded to spell out the details of his business plan, over dessert, Jock was all attention. Ruth and Jill remained silent.

When Adrian finished it was Jock who took over. 'I'd like to get into that venture with you, Adrian. I think you're on to something interesting. And for once, it's related to a cultural rather than a grubby toilet-seat proposition. I don't mind admitting that I'm approached pretty often with partnership and sponsorship deals, all of which I find both suspicious and boring. Your idea pleases me; it's something that really can merit support. Good art at low prices in the American home. I don't think it can miss. The big Van Gogh show at the Institute in Chicago, with hundreds of thousands of visitors lined up for blocks, proved something. You're definitely on the right track, Adrian.'

'I forgot to mention one thing,' said Adrian. 'I'd write to the key museums of the world and ask each of them to name the half-dozen most popular pictures in their collections; I'd want to know which postcards were their bestsellers. I know that in the Chicago Art Institute, the biggest-selling postcard by far is Grant Wood's *American Gothic*. I think I could sell hundred of thousands in frames.'

'Okay,' said Jock. 'You need co-operation from certain artists, agents, museums and galleries, for reproduction rights. You need a good printer who can reproduce the pictures decently and cheaply. I think that there are at least three such printers in Paris. As for the framing and selling, I see no problem. From what you mentioned of your uncle's factory, and the baubles, tables, mirrors he

produces, he could handle this programme. Someone must contact both the museums and printers, but also the chain-store buyers. Who can do that?'

Adrian looked at Jock, shaking his head slowly. 'You underestimate me. I can sell anyone on the various elements of this project I've just sold you, my friend. The museums will get a small royalty; the printers will get a big printing contract; my uncle's factory can and must make the frames and mats, and package the prints, according to my instructions. Some advertising in the trade and association publications as well as co-op ads with the stores in the public press will get our framed prints acceptance. I want to sell about three or four million framed prints, about twenty-four subjects in all, and net well over a million dollars. That's my personal goal. If you, Jock, want to finance the programme, you can work out the arithmetic and assure yourself a good, fat profit. Perhaps I could go to an American bank and get financial support. But I think you might enjoy getting a piece of the action. It would give me satisfaction, frankly, to include you in the scheme.'

Adrian paused, as though for breath. 'If you see any flaw in my programme, please speak frankly. I can be logical, practical. I'm a realist, despite my lack of sophistication in business. I've never had a job. I've never been on a company's board. I never met a payroll. I don't want any part of the American business organisational system. Whatever I decide to do, it will be done as an individualist, on a short-term basis. I value my freedom, my autonomy. And when I make the money I'll quit. I set a dollar limitation on my ambitions. And I don't mean that I see retirement as a goal. I see freedom of action, the freedom to study, write, travel, enjoy life, as the goal.'

Ruth, Jill and Jock looked at Adrian in silence. Then Ruth bent over to him and kissed his brow. 'I never

suspected my romantic lover was such a hard-headed businessman. I think he has a marvellous idea, and I support him all the way.'

She turned to Jock and Jill, adding, 'I think you should think about the scheme, and let us know in a day or two. If you decide against it we'll still love you. You're our friends.'

Finally they were ready to leave. Adrian and Ruth parted from the Merediths, deciding to take a slow walk back to the hotel, 'to air our heads'. The Paris sky was a vibrant cobalt, the air clear, the great buildings majestically, dramatically illuminated.

'I'll miss all of this,' Adrian said, 'if and when I get to work. You know, I think I was hooked on the art idea, subconsciously, when we visited our first exhibition in Paris, at the Galérie Michèle I think it was, and bought some posters of the show. Thousands of tourists bring back posters. Students have them in their rooms, their dorms. Tourists respond to art, bring back those crappy kitschy prints on sale along the Seine and in the souvenir shops, those pathetic etchings of landscapes and windmills and castles. But a well-printed Van Gogh print, for instance, tastefully framed and available for, say, five or six dollars: who could resist that? Think of the schools as a market; and there's the gift market. I'll bet we could sell a million copies of the *Sunflowers* print alone. One of the great Rembrandt self-portraits, the one in the Frick, for example, would be popular. And what about that marvellous *Turkish Seraglio Bath* group of nudes by Ingres?'

He paused. His excitement, obviously, was not to be contained. Ruth took his arm. 'Enough business talk for tonight, Adrian. I think we need one more bottle of wine, and there's a good Burgundy back at the hotel crying to be opened.'

* * *

Adrian took no barbiturate that night. He felt he was exhausted and would sleep well, contented with his new ideas, his planning. But a strange dream came to him and he awoke remembering all its details. The dream was brief and clear.

A faceless man approached him and said, 'My name is Gregor. My profession is morality.'

'What sort of bullshit profession is *that*?' asked Adrian. 'Are you a doctor of divinity, a shaman, a rabbi? I don't know of such a profession, nor any activity dealing with morality. And, in any event, what do you want with me and what have I to do with your profession?'

The man's face was indistinct, hidden, as though he deliberately remained in shadow, as though, on a stage, his face alone, among all the players, would be without light.

'Your recent sexual conduct makes it unlikely that you can succeed in any honourable enterprise. Also, you shit in the grass. I saw your faeces in the grass and you know that is both illegal and also reprehensible. You lead a secret life.'

'Everyone leads a secret life,' Adrian shouted. 'And what do you mean by honourable enterprise? It's all a lie.' Adrian added, 'How awful of you to lie like that. And what do you mean about sexual conduct?'

'You philander. And you are doomed to dilettantism. Why don't you sell your wife's body? You could find many buyers. Or give her to Hiram Jackson as a gift, a toy. Put a pink nightie on Ruth and give her to Jackson. He would love to play with her, love her, eat her. She's edible, you know.'

'What has my wife got to do with you or Jackson? Who are you and what do you want from me? I think you're obscene and a thief.'

The man laughed. 'I am a professor of morality. I'm

engaged in beautiful and moral activities. Hiram Jackson would enjoy Ruth's body. Poor man. Take Ruth away from the piano, the concert halls, the classrooms. Dress her prettily and let me have her.'

'I can't,' Adrian shouted. 'I can't. I can't.' And as he uttered the last word he opened his eyes and saw Ruth above him, shaking his shoulders.

'Adrian, what do you mean, you can't? You were shouting in your sleep. Were you having a nightmare?'

'A man named Gregor was molesting me,' said Adrian. 'Do we know someone by that name? It sounds familiar. Or is it a character in some book I've read?'

'I don't know such a name; no. Please, try to sleep. Let me give you a sleeping pill.' Then she added, 'You've got too much on your mind.'

Yes, thought Adrian, my subconscious is hyperactive. He took two Seconals and soon fell into a dreamless sleep.

During the following week Adrian and Jock made appointments with publishers of art books from whom they obtained information about colour printers and poster lithographers. They also secured the names of the foremost colour printers in Milan and Verona. They then visited the Louvre and learned that rights to certain master works were obtainable, including kodachromes. An intensive, active week resulted in useful leads, and at the weekend, they decided to go to Milan and Verona.

Within two weeks they had the information they needed: costs, samples and delivery assurances. They met several leading art agents who controlled reproduction rights to certain living master painters and made tentative arrangements that would, granted all details falling into line, lead to firm contracts.

The matter of getting material for the mock-ups arose: the samples to be framed and submitted to the potential

customers. But first came the question of the frames, production facilities and costs. And finally, the financial support that would enable Adrian to get the wheels of his enterprise turning.

Through an important business scouting connection in New York, Jock was sent the names of the appropriate persons or buyers at the leading chain- and department stores as well as the mail-order catalogue firms throughout America.

It was almost time for Adrian to return to America and confront his uncle, Sylvester, with the plan for Operation Master Prints. He arranged for a commercial artist to lay out an elaborate broadside announcing the advent of the 'World's Most Beloved Artworks that Everyone Can Afford to Own'. The broadside included two actual colour prints ('substantially reduced in size') and a drawing indicating what the prints would look like in the frames.

The advertising copy was resplendent, in the best art-hype tradition of mail-order advertising. Adrian and Jock had laboured over the copy until it was letter-perfect, understated but convincing. They had the type chosen and arranged, the brochures proofed and printed, and then two dozen, each with two-colour plates tipped into position, were produced. They were almost ready for action: the testing of the market. Of course, they needed a realistic bottom-line estimate from the manufacturing end, the actual costs of frames, labour, printing, packing. It was decided to omit glass because of packing costs and breakage. A shellac coating, substituting for the glass, would give the prints the high-gloss effect desired.

Adrian showed Ruth one of the completed sales-kits. She went through the material, read the copy carefully, then proclaimed it all terrific.

Jill Meredith, and of course Ruth, remained behind in

Paris when Jock and Adrian sailed for America. They cabled Uncle Sylvester in advance, arranging for a meeting.

Jock's attorney prepared a tentative proposal, with Adrian's approval, offering formally to buy fifty-one per cent of Uncle Sylvester's business. Jock would reorganise the company, set up a board, and Adrian would be given a contract as general manager and executive vice-president. Jock would sign all contracts. His salary would be modest but he would be guaranteed twenty-five per cent of the gross profits, off the top. Uncle Sylvester was to receive $100,000.00 in cash for his share.

Jock and Adrian held a trump card up their sleeves. In the event that serious resistance would be put up they would start their own company and hire away the factory's key personnel at higher salaries. Jock was almost certain that a small factory could be located that could be tooled up and restructured to serve their picture-framing needs. The operation was comparatively simple.

The three men met for dinner at Uncle Sylvester's club, where his late brother had been a member and where Adrian had recently lunched with Judge Minelli. Jock came right to the point as the first drinks were produced.

Sipping his scotch on the rocks, Uncle Sylvester studied the two men, surprised, and curious, and cautious. His eyes were now screwed up, his lip twitching. He knew something of Jock's background and his personal holdings. He knew that Jock was not a fly-by-night even though his style was just short of a playboy's. Uncle Sylvester was curious, too, about Adrian's position in the proposal, and he waited patiently for further disclosures. They came quickly.

As he listened to Jock's presentation, and learned of their plans for the production of popular-priced colour prints in frames, his interest heightened although he

maintained his composure. When the whole proposition had been spelled out, he excused himself for a visit to the men's room. (His bladder was bursting.) He must collect his thoughts.

Jock asked, 'How did I do, Adrian?'

'Perfection. I'd say you made it irresistible. We'll find out in a few minutes, after Uncle Sylvester digests your speech. Five will get me ten that he's bought the deal.'

When he returned from the men's room, Uncle Sylvester began in an autobiographical fashion, slowly approaching the issue. He wanted Jock to realise how many years of his life he had invested in his business, how long he had struggled to maintain his company while severely underfinanced most of the time. He wanted to impress them with his business acumen, and more important he seemed to think, how tough a fighter he was in the clinches. It was the classic rugged businessman's speech.

'I met my payroll every week, and I can tell you it was often by a miracle. I walked a tightrope many a week, but I never let my workers down. Not once. I borrowed money at high interest, and managed to make it work.'

He paused and lit a cigar. Slowly he exhaled a large cloud of smoke.

'For over twenty years – twenty years,' he repeated, eyes narrowed, 'I've kept my factory going. Not bad for a one-man operator and a handful of workers. Not bad. But I had the support of good people. I could go to a customer and get cash in advance or on delivery, even from the big chain buyers. They co-operated; they financed me often.'

He paused and studied the two men.

'What can I tell you, Jock? Adrian? Your proposition is interesting, the picture-framing print programme sounds good. Sure, my factory is ready-made for such an operation. I can handle it all, from soup to nuts. No sweat. Sure I could use the money. But I want to sleep on it. I'm not

sure I'm ready to give up control of my business. You can understand that, can't you Jock?' He smiled wryly. 'Control is a sweet thing to have. Giving it up is not easy. Right?'

'Certainly I can understand,' said Jock, smiling. 'But, aside from being a good proposition for you, it would be good for your nephew. He is ready for a start in the business world, and he thought up this project. He's got imagination. And what's more important, he's ready to go to work and sell it across the country. How many youngsters do you know, cultivated, educated young men, who would want to take on such a big selling job? It's a tough hustle; those chain-store buyers aren't pushovers. It's going to take a lot of skill. This is a luxury item, not a commodity like, say, a toilet seat or a coffee table.'

While it was generally known that Jock Meredith's father had been something of a financial buccaneer in the Midwest, his son was of an entirely different temperament. Despite his alleged interest in wine, women and song, his business instincts were sound. There were financial fiascos in moneyed families, but not so in Jock Meredith's case. He loved the pleasures of life, but he was mindful of the value of money. He once confessed to Adrian, almost apologetically, that he never spent more than his income; that his capital was intact and that he frequently found his fortune augmented by stock splits, compounded dividends and increased interest. He confessed that champagne and caviar were commonplace items in his personal 'grocery expenditures' but he always checked out the invoices himself and did not hesitate to raise holy hell and damnation with his suppliers if he found an error or a petty larceny overcharge in his bills.

In the matter of Sylvester Breakstone's factory and Adrian's business proposal, Jock had discussed all of it in minute detail with his attorney and also with his banker.

They both gave him affirmative support and advice; in each case, they considered his involvement a good one. In fact, the attorney expressed the wish to invest personally. He saw no flaw in the plan, although he admitted that every business scheme had its dark side, the unforeseeable flaw or weakness that made the so-called foolproof deal a risk. A forgotten competitor, for instance. In Adrian's proposal they felt there was a sixty-five/thirty-five chance of succeeding, a better than gambler's chance. It was on this basis that Jock went along with Adrian. And it was not so much his wish to make money, but his boredom and need for action that persuaded him to become involved.

The 'cherry on top', as he put it, was the fact that they were dealing in a cultural 'situation', that they were promoting art, bringing good art to the masses. There would not be a single bad picture in their catalogue, nothing schlocky, kitschy or in bad taste. Each picture would be a popular masterpiece, a world treasure, exciting, enduring.

Jock looked long and hard at Uncle Sylvester.

'We'd like an answer soon,' he said. 'Can you give it to us tomorrow?'

'That's pretty fast, I'd say,' said Uncle Sylvester. 'Why such a hurry?'

'That's part of the deal. An immediate answer. Yes or no. Tomorrow.'

Since his mother was in Florida, Adrian found himself alone in her house. He was in his own room again, at his rosewood desk, again gazing out at the lake, ruminating, weighing his future, pondering his choice of a business career. Today the lake depressed him. He turned over in his mind some of the details of his plans and wondered at the wisdom of his choice. He knew that his energy was limited and that his strength would be drained before he

was finished with his difficult and complicated task. At least a full year would be required. Would his uncle accept the deal? What would Ruth do about her career? Once the print deal was concluded, a decision had to be reached about Ruth; in fact, the marriage would be inextricably involved in his business plans. Perhaps she could remain in Paris and he would visit her, or vice versa, every few months. An expensive and time-consuming procedure. Presumably, she could resume her musical studies in America, and plan her concert tour from her home base rather than from Paris. Tomorrow, when Uncle Sylvester made his decision, he would think out the personal and logistical aspects of the problem.

Adrian sat back. His eyes were drawn towards a bowl of varicoloured anemone. He thought of them as 'passion flowers' because of their vivid colours and their 'ecstasising' behaviour. He saw something of himself in them, his ready tendency towards passionate expression, rapture. He studied them, sensing subconsciously, with foreboding, a tremor that was heightening in his chest. He must not, ever, overlook his pills.

After taking his medication he decided to have a nap. He fell into a deep sleep and awakened in his darkened room. For a moment he was disoriented. Then he looked at his watch and decided he would see his brother, Ralph, possibly for dinner and a discussion of the business programme. He had not mentioned the plan to any member of his family and suddenly realised that he would be chastised and judged severely if he kept so important a matter to himself. He was in no mood for scoldings or lectures.

He telephoned Ralph, found that he was home and invited himself to dinner.

Before leaving for his brother's house, a matter of a dozen blocks' walk, he consulted his pocket notebook and made another phone call.

Kama answered and expressed surprise at his call.

'Rather late hour to be calling,' she said. 'Where've you been?'

'Apologies. Just returned from Paris for a week or so. Thought I'd find out how you were. Radiant, I hope.'

'Peaches and cream,' she said. 'Everything's mighty serene. Hope you recovered from our last séance?'

Adrian laughed. 'Séance, eh?' Then he added, 'When does the trial begin? Or isn't that definite yet?'

'The trial,' she repeated, parrot-fashion. 'Oh yes, that. Still indefinite. May not take place for a month or two. No one seems to know. Seems there's a lot of meeting, checking out witnesses, stuff like that. I'm not consulted much. Not after two long sessions. Rough sessions, I can tell you. Now they leave me alone. And I'm waiting.'

'Can we get together tonight?'

'Tonight?' she asked, surprised. 'What's up?'

'Just like to see you. How about eleven o'clock? I have a dinner date, family stuff. Can you be free at eleven?'

'Eleven's okay. You be here at eleven?'

Adrian hesitated. 'How would you like to come here?'

'Where's here?'

'My mother's house. She's away. Florida. I'm here alone.'

'You're a mighty funny man. In your house? Where your late father resided? Correct?'

'Yes. I could pick you up and take you back. Or you might like to spend the night here . . .'

'You know, I don't even know where you live. Your father never told me.'

Adrian told her the address and she said, 'Ooh la la.' Then she added, 'How about the doorman? Do you get many lady visitors of my complexion at that address? Even when they come back from Miami Beach they don't have quite my colouring. Soth Shaw Drive,' she deliber-

ately taffied out the words in deep down black southern style. 'Well, well.'

'Any guest of mine is welcome in this house,' said Adrian. 'I'll pick you up at eleven. Okay?'

'I'll be ready and waiting. Do I bring a toothbrush?'

'If you wish.'

'Done.'

Adrian's brothers, Harvey and Ralph, were at Ralph's house. Their wives, Marlene and Tania, were still in Florida with Mama. It was their bi-monthly dinner gathering, with or without wives, a custom Harvey had proposed early in their marriages, a kind of gathering of the clan for solidarity and fellowship, alternating visits between their homes. The brothers greeted Adrian warmly, full of questions, curious about Ruth, eager for news of his plans, on the alert for some sort of announcement. The brothers had discussed the possibility of Adrian's needing and wanting a loan. *Sans* wives, it was a meeting rich in brotherly *gemütlichkeit*. The Breakstone Musketeers.

Adrian seemed relaxed, spoke of Ruth's pianistic progress, her concert plans, with enthusiasm; his love of Paris. And then he moved into the subject of Uncle Sylvester. When he had finished outlining his business proposal, the brothers expressed astonishment at Adrian's imaginative and enterprising scheme, the speed with which he'd gone to work.

'You're not asking for our assistance, Adrian, financial or otherwise?' said Ralph. 'You're acting! Great.'

Obviously he would be interested in their views, Adrian said; their reaction to the plan. Also, their personal assessment of Uncle Sylvester's possible decision.

The brothers agreed that the deal was good for all concerned. A break for Uncle Sylvester. Since Adrian was gambling no personal funds, and Uncle Sylvester was to

come out of it with a fat up-front cheque, and since the business appeared to be in a rut, in fact, creaky and mouldering, the risk was entirely Jock Meredith's and his banking supporter. Or was it to be only Jock's money that was at stake? The risk of loss was not Adrian's, and certainly not Uncle Sylvester's. The possibility of striking it rich, fairly quickly, pleased the brothers. Amen, brother, amen.

'Adrian,' said Harvey, raising his wineglass in a toast, 'to you and your business success. It's good to know that you have solid business acumen as well as literary talents. The youngest businessman in town. For myself, I hope Uncle Sylvester agrees to the proposition. From where I sit, it's almost foolproof.'

'Amen,' said Ralph, again. 'And if we can be of any help, don't fail to call on us.' Adrian smiled, knowing that by 'help' Ralph did not mean financial. Spiritual, brotherly: yes.

The conversation turned to other matters, the preparation for the trial of the alleged killer of their father, the black musician, Hiram Jackson. There appeared to be no news, no further disclosures. No motives, no scandalous revelations. That he would be seeing, fucking, Jackson's wife in about an hour, gave Adrian cause for a cat-that-swallowed-the-canary smile. The brothers were puzzled.

'Adrian, do you know something we don't know? About Papa, I mean,' asked Ralph.

'I'm sure Adrian would share with us any of his confidential information about Father's death,' said Harvey. 'The rumours about a woman have died down, thank heavens. The assassin is a madman, no doubt about it.'

But he obviously paid someone, hired a driver to take him in a limousine, to shoot down Papa,' said Adrian. 'The man is a cripple, paralysed from the waist down.'

'You'd be surprised how well such cripples can manage

cars,' said Ralph. 'Autos are specially built for non-ambulatory men, ex-soldiers wounded for life.'

'Be that as it may,' said Adrian, 'we know nothing. I tried to get some information from Judge Minelli – I suspect he knows something – and got nothing. Zero.'

'We talked to him, too,' said Harvey. 'He may know something but he's a close-mouthed man. Tough and uncommunicative.'

'The DA is also closed up like a clam,' said Ralph. 'We know Papa had underworld friends, clients among Torino's Syndicate. But certainly, he wasn't involved in anything criminal; it was simply part of his medical practice, and a lucrative practice it was . . .

'Well, this man in custody: I'm sure he'll plead insanity. He's not screaming innocence; he's not talking. One thing that we heard: he said to one of the policemen who was giving him a hard time, "I'm not a hood, I'm not an assassin." There's no taping of that statement, but that was reported. What do you make of that? And, oh yes, he also allegedly said to a reporter that it was a "matter of honour". It was not confirmed.'

'Fascinating,' said Adrian.

It was about ten-thirty when Adrian left his brothers (Harvey was staying over with Ralph). Adrian said he'd walk home. But about two blocks away from Ralph's house he hailed a cab and had himself driven to Lovecraft Street and as he arrived at Kama's building he spied her at the corner, with her poodle.

'Hi,' she said. 'Thought I'd take Colette along; she'd miss me if I didn't come back tonight.' She laughed. 'Tonight. Yeah. Tonight is almost gone. You don't mind my bringing Colette, do you? Gotta take care of my pal.'

'No. I didn't know that was her name; didn't know it was a her, in fact. Now that I know, can I ask a question?'

'Sure ask away.'

'About Colette; can she write?'

Kama said, 'That's a howl. Well, no, she can't write, but she sure knows her French.' This brought another laugh from Kama.

Adrian looked into her eyes, closely. Her laughter was high, pure *high*; she was energised, he could see. Coke high.

'She knows her French. Well, touché,' said Adrian, leading Kama towards a taxi.

'I took you at your word,' she said. 'One toothbrush, and oh yes, Chanel Number Five.' And she laughed the high laugh again.

'You're in great spirits,' said Adrian.

'Never better.'

'Great.'

Pause. Then she said, 'How was Paree, and how long you staying?'

'Paris was fine. Good as ever. Am going back, leaving in a few days, I think. Not sure yet.'

'You're not waiting for the trial?'

'No.'

She was wearing a rust-coloured suede dress and turquoise beads. At one side of her skirt a slit ran straight up to her hip-bone, and beneath it was sheer iridescent pink and milk chocolate skin.

Adrian ran his finger glissando-fashion up along the exposed skin.

'Nothing nearly as nice in all of Paris,' he said.

'That's a fine compliment, boy,' she said. Another loud guffaw.

Then she said, 'Not even your wife?'

He made no reply and the taxi pulled up to the kerb before the building.

The uniformed security man nodded, 'Good evening, Mr Breakstone,' and they passed into the elevator.

'Comfortable?' he asked her when they were in the sitting room.

'I will be when you get me a drink.'

'In half a minute. I think there's champagne on ice.'

'Ooh la la,' she said.

'You speak French,' he said, laughing. 'You and Colette.'

'Us both. *Mais oui.*'

He took her by the elbow and led her quickly into his room.

He looked into her eyes. They were black, yellow and red eyes, eyes from a half-forgotten dream.

'What a sweet room,' Kama said, running her fingers across the top of his rosewood desk, parting the curtains for a view of the lake. Her eyes moved lazily over the room, the French furniture. Then she jumped on his bed, lay spread-eagled on the king-size four-poster and said, 'Boy, will you kindly draw my bawth.'

'I'll draw you a bath, Kama, but if you call me boy once more I'll do something to you that you won't like at all.'

'You'll spank me, I know. I apologise. Nothing personal, sweet.'

He smiled, walked into the bathroom and she heard the heavy gush of water released and running in the tub.

'Want some cologne in that water?' he asked.

'Take my Chanel Number Five out of my bag, please, and splash a little in the tub. That'll do it nicely.'

He opened her handbag, removed a flask and as he was closing the bag noticed a small, black revolver. He whistled.

'What's that all about? The whistle?' she asked.

'Couldn't help noticing the artillery, your pocket tommy-gun.'

'A girl's gotta have some protection in this jungle. I've

got a permit for it, by the way, in case you're real interested.'

'I thought Colette was your bodyguard.' Kama's poodle was cuddling up with her on the bed.

'Funny man. Colette is my scout, my social advance girl, not bodyguard. She wouldn't bite the meanest rapist or holdup man.'

'Why the gun?'

'Gotta protect my virtue.' And she showed a dazzling set of teeth as she laughed towards the ceiling.

He shook some of the cologne into the tub and returned, sitting at the edge of the bed.

'Want to massage my feet?' she asked.

'Mmm,' he replied.

He took her right foot into his hands and began to massage the instep. The arch showed a pink groove, probably from a tight strap. He rubbed it softly, then took her other foot in his hands and gave it his attention. He sat up suddenly, and began removing her clothes. She wore nothing under her dress. In a flash she was out of the bed, racing towards the bathroom. She tested the water's temperature. As she bent over the tub he received a full wide view of her tantalising rump and pudendum, but before he had time to reach and caress her, she was in the water. He stood above her shimmering golden-coffee and pink body, the silken black hairy growth at her crotch, her round firm breasts seemingly afloat on the water's surface.

He began to undress. His pillbox fell out of his pocket, reminding him that it was medication-time. He swallowed two of the tiny white pills. Naked now, he sat on the tub's edge, facing her, his feet snuggled and wriggling beneath her buttocks in the water, erection at full mast. She sat up in the tub, bent over to stroke and kiss his knees, his thighs. Then she moistened her forefinger with her tongue, stroked his penis with it. 'Sizzling!' she exclaimed,

laughing. She bent forward and full-mouthed, began to moan. Colette was heard barking in the bedroom, and was ignored.

The running water and the intense mutual preoccupation of the lovers prevented them from hearing the buzzer from the lobby. When they heard the shriek at the bathroom door, the word, '*Gottinyoo*!' Adrian knew in a flash that his mother was home: unexpectedly, unaccountably home. He knew in a split second that nothing he could ever say or do could erase what his mother had seen, could erase the shock of surprise and outrage Sarah felt as she witnessed Kama and her son in the most intimate of imaginable human actions.

Kama slipped back into the tub, horizontally; Adrian rose, put a towel around his waist and said, 'Please, Mother, close the door.'

Sarah uttered one Yiddish word which Adrian could not identify, for she had already backed away; and when Adrian followed her he found her collapsed in a full, dead faint on the floor. He rushed back to the bathroom, found some spirits of ammonia in the cabinet and applied the reviving liquid to her nostrils. He held her head, rocking her gently on his knee, his heart pounding, his thoughts racing, searching for the words he would need when she was restored to consciousness. A momentary wave of dizziness engulfed him but he managed to pull out of it quickly.

When she awakened, he found he was relieved of the responsibility to explain, to speak. 'Don't talk, don't excuse. No explanations, please, Adrian. No words. I feel sick. And so ashamed.'

He tried to look into her eyes but his focus wavered. She removed herself from his embrace, stood up slowly.

'I came home suddenly. I was fed up, bored with Miami Beach, with my two daughters-in-law. I didn't know you

were home. How come you're not in Paris?' And then Sarah's eyes shifted towards the bathroom. 'Get that nigger hoor out of *my* house. I'm going to my room; when I come out in five minutes I want her out of my house. Out!' Her eyes widened. 'My God, how could you do this to me, Adrian? In my own house. Did the security man in the lobby see her with you? Are you crazy? Like your father, already . . . Get her out!' she screamed, and Adrian feared that she would faint again.

Kama emerged from the bathroom. Colette capered softly behind her, whimpering and dancing. She knew something was amiss.

'Dogs always know when there's trouble,' said Kama, dressing. 'So, the shit hit the fan, huh?' she said softly.

She was touching up her face. In less than five minutes she was dressed and leaving.

'I'm so sorry, Adrian. I need some cab fare. I'll talk to you tomorrow. Call me. Good luck, friend. That mother of yours will cut off your balls. Be careful. Like I said, I'm real sorry, but I fear that you're in for some problems. Make the best of it. Repeat, don't let that mother do a castration number on you. Lover.' She took the money from Adrian and slipped out of the house.

Adrian stood at the door, his mind blank, his heart beating furiously. He must lie down at once. He made it to his bed, feeling faint, his stomach turned to jelly. He curled up, and waited for the dizziness to pass.

Chapter Sixteen

Officer Greenbaum was talking with the police commissioner in his office. The PC was having his mid-morning coffee at his desk; a large, glazed Danish pastry lay half-eaten on the blotter.

'The simple facts, sir, are that there's a lot of hot and unsolicited support coming from the black musicians. I've talked to at least a dozen guys, some of them name band leaders, and they all say that the shooting of Dr Breakstone was justified; a case of morality or something. How do you like that! That his wife was making it with prominent white men, and especially heavy with Breakstone . . . There are too many witnesses now, and everyone seems to feel Breakstone had it coming. Jackson's going to make headlines when he starts naming names, especially the Doc's. There's a Free Jackson demonstration being planned; they're asking for a parade permit.' He paused, scratching his head. 'The Doc, it seems, gave her expensive presents, fur coats and stuff, even took her to some of the South side clubs . . .'

The PC took a large bite of his Danish and growled, 'I know all about that, Officer Greenbaum. What I want is evidence that Jackson has a record of violence, that he's a potential killer.'

'Well, the sympathy for Jackson comes from way back, when he was in that shoot-out after he caught his wife blowing a white judge. And I think you know who that was, sir.'

'Let's not go into that, for God's sake. That's ancient history.'

'Yes, but that particular incident put Jackson in a wheelchair, out of commission. That's when he began building up a case against whitey.'

The commissioner was now sipping his coffee, picking up sugar crumbs with his finger.

'He's in a tough spot. If he's smart, he'll . . . he'll blow his brains out.' He stared over the cop's head. 'I think that's enough for today. Thanks, and keep your eyes and ears open, and not a word about this little conference. Right?'

'Right, sir,' said Officer Greenbaum.

When the newsmen were called in to hear the police commissioner's report on the suicide of the pathological black killer, Hiram Jackson, the vocal response and general cynicism were not surprising. It was all most embarrassing to the police department, to the citizenry.

The Negro press headlined the story in outrage. 'An offence to decency and credibility.'

'Now we've heard and seen everything,' said the *Tribune*, editorialising on the 'new low in the city's crime level'.

Officer Greenbaum held his tongue; expressed no surprise. After all, poor bastard, Jackson was a psycho (a popular word among the cops) and what could he do? And the brand-new Chevrolet coupé which he found parked in front of his house (and an envelope with the keys to the ignition in his mailbox together with an unsigned Happy Valentine's Day note) gave him an excuse for a three-day fishing holiday. He drove to Michigan for some relaxation, and unavailability.

Adrian's mother came into his room that morning, placed

the paper on his bed and pointed to the front page. Horror was in her eyes. Her face was tear-stained, haggard; there were heavy black rings under her eyes. She left without a word.

Adrian reread the story of Hiram Jackson's alleged suicide. A call came to him shortly after breakfast. An anonymous call. It was not a pleasant message: he was warned to stay away from Hiram Jackson's widow, to keep his mouth shut about the case. Or else.

He phoned Kama but the line was busy. He tried every five minutes, and finally, after an hour, he got her.

'Yes, I read the papers. Let's not talk now. I'm leaving town. After I have the body cremated. I really want to get lost, deep down lost. Sub-let my apartment. Maybe I'll go to Paris. Can't say where yet. What's your Paris address?'

Adrian, surprised at her question, gave her the name of his hotel, suggested that she also try him at the American Express in Paris. He would be back in ten days or so. The phone clicked. Hers was a zombie voice, panic-striken, not the buoyant Kama he knew. She was scared.

He called Ralph, discovered he was ahead of him. He had read the papers and had spoken to a newspaperman. He had refused to give any opinions, merely regrets that a trial had been prevented, to clear his father's position. There was high emotion in his voice. Yes, Ralph's wife had come back yesterday, with his mother, unexpectedly.

He phoned Uncle Sylvester. Yes, he had read the papers. Highly suspicious, wasn't it? But he sounded relaxed, and it was Adrian's guess that they had a deal. Sylvester suggested a meeting at his office at two-thirty, and Adrian phoned Jock and arranged for them to lunch together beforehand.

The assassin self-assassinated? Corruption and immor-

ality. Mercifully, the state was spared a costly trial. Names would not be named. How could Jackson commit suicide? Where did he get the gun? In his prison cell?

The implications of the suicide story were obvious. A front-page editorial spoke of the need for a new police commissioner, for a city-wide reform; the callousness of the police. A cold-blooded killing was now being called a suicide. The reporter tried to estimate how many fake suicides had been claimed in the city during the past five years. What kind of prisons and security did they have, anyway? The payoff system at work again. The press had a headline holiday: circulations would double that week.

Judge Minelli's name was mentioned by no one, Adrian noted. A neat bullet-hole in the base of the left ear of a spade sax-player, and life could be beautiful. The taxpayers had saved a half million dollars in court costs.

Chapter Seventeen

Adrian met Jock for lunch at Riccardo's and they discussed strategy and the best psychological approach. Uncle Sylvester must not feel that his business or authority were being taken away from him. He must have at least a five-year employment contract; but a limitation on expenses had to be imposed. His personal life style was his affair, but out of his own pocket. This must be handled delicately.

Jock planned to bring his personal accountant in for a careful study of the books, debts and overheads especially. The equipment, the lathes and the quality of the machinery, and the efficiency of the various departments, all had to be examined with care. They would need a meeting with the key personnel, to assure them of their continuing jobs, providing there would be a heightened co-operation all around.

Adrian began to see an entirely new personality emerging from Jock: he was able to handle this enterprise, Adrian felt sure. As for himself, he knew that he could perform in all the other areas. And Uncle Sylvester must be made to feel that he was a needed, an important member of the team. Indeed, despite certain reservations they had about Sylvester, they knew that at least in the early, transitional period, he could be useful. If not, they'd order him out, and send him his cheques by mail. But he had to be given the respect due the founder, and his title must be not less than executive vice-president. Jock was to become chairman of the board, and Adrian, president and art director.

The atmosphere at Sylvester's factory was charged with the tensions and the electricity of rumour and curiosity. Somehow, the key personnel were aware that something serious was about to take place in the managerial hierarchy. Up until the present moment, there was one head, one boss. Uncle Sylvester was Mr Autonomy; not a single light bulb, no roll of toilet paper, could be bought without his personal approval. Nor could any person be hired or fired without his full knowledge. A serious, radical transmutation was about to occur. It was in the air. They could see it in Sylvester Breakstone's face, in his walk, in his tone as he marched up and down the aisles of his factory, looking by turn happy and stern.

When Adrian and Jock arrived, he ordered them into his office at once. It was an old-fashioned room, with worn leather chairs and a threadbare carpet. His large, oak desk was piled with papers, photographs, a massive copper ashtray, the usual battery of executive 'tools' and the customary executive onyx pen-stand.

He waved them to seats. 'Gentlemen, let's not stand on ceremony. Let's begin by repeating the precise terms you have in mind. Mr Meredith, would you like to begin?' And he sat back in his padded chair, clipped the end of his cigar and went through the ritual of lighting and puffing, with a heavy air of solemnity.

And thus began the meeting. When it was concluded, the basis for an agreement had been reached. Within a week, assuming everything was found to be in order in the office files and factory, contracts would be drawn up and signed, money paid over, and a new phase of operation would commence. The 'dawn of a new artistic and prosperous era would begin', as Sylvester put it.

Adrian would make a fresh survey of the plant – one day would suffice – and would return to Paris. Jock would stay on and work out the details with lawyers and the key

personnel. If new employees were to be hired, he would oversee the hiring. No disagreement, not a single critical or harsh word was uttered. Immense respect was paid to Uncle Sylvester, a matter of deep concern to Adrian and Jock.

Later that day, Adrian telephoned Ruth's parents and gave them news of Ruth, of her health and progress as a musician. They expressed their sorrow at the loss of his father and hoped he would come to see them, but he told them he had to return to Europe at once, that big business was afoot.

'My son,' said Harry, 'if a little cash can be of help to you, let me know; remember, you and Ruth are all we have and we want to share what we have with you.'

Touched, at a loss for words, Adrian thanked him, assured him that they needed no help and would remember his kindness.

'I'd like your opinion of that so-called suicide of the alleged murderer of your father, Adrian; do you believe the story in the papers?'

'No, I don't, Harry, but does it matter? The politicians and criminals have a way of resolving problems, assuming he didn't commit suicide. The fact is, my father is dead. If Jackson was the murderer, it doesn't matter to me whether he died by his own hand or was assassinated. The authorities know how to wrap things up neatly, or rather, how to sweep problems under the carpet. I guess they're the ultimate realists.'

'Yes,' said Davidson, 'the police have a way . . .'

'I'm glad,' said Adrian, 'that the case is finished, wrapped up. And I hope never to see another word about it in the papers. The trick is, living with the facts as I know and feel them; and also, Harry, living with a lot of troublesome doubts and questions. I guess time takes care of such things.'

Adrian mentioned briefly the art-print enterprise which he was preparing to enter and was heartened by Harry's instant enthusiastic response.

The conversation tapered off and Adrian said farewell, replaced the phone. Ruth's father was a man to count on. Uncomplicated; a music lover; a family man, as the phrase went. The salt of the earth. No hells or Himalayas of neurasthenia for the Davidsons. Harry in particular. He had his anchor, Mozart, and his family. But could one be sure? Was Harry Davidson, pharmacist, as wholesome and kind and non-neurotic as he appeared? Normal, devoid of the familiar Jewish diseases? Or merely mad for Mozart? Should he be given the benefit of the doubt? No, said Adrian. Somewhere, some time in the amniotic depths of Harry Davidson's Semitic origins was transmitted a passion for music, in the genes and chromosomes and other sub-microscopic elements bearing our characteristics and appetites. Somewhere was transmitted the tendency towards madness and joy, the ineffable.

And what of Kama, guilt-ridden but carefree? Surely hers was the greatest guilt burden of all. Hiram Jackson's pain and murder – could she contain such a burden, remain free of guilt? And what would father-in-law Davidson think of Adrian, the young bridegroom and philanderer, dallying in the dark side or possibly the lunatic side, while his loving daughter laboured in a Parisian *école*?

Adrian allowed his thoughts to return to his voyage and future, the very real work ahead of him: Adrian Breakstone, business executive, entrepreneur. Fortune-seeker, bringer of culture to the masses. The fulfilment of dreams of instant success: this was to be his goal and preoccupation. His sensitivity and awareness would be focused on his new business; he would show the world

that an aesthete could master the art of money-making with one arm tied behind his back!

But it was not easy to push aside certain feelings about Kama as he thought of seeing Ruth in Paris. And perhaps Kama . . . How much longer could he deceive his wife? Would he continue to succumb to every attractive inviting female, every alluring, enticing cunt he encountered? Was he, in fact, a junior-grade satyriac? Was his lust and lechery going to turn him into one of those pitiful and disgusting characters no one invited to their homes, a molester of wives and young girls?

The young Jewish intellectual in pursuit of black ass, Nigra nookie. His excitement at simply seeing her naked could induce ejaculation. Could such a man give a woman pleasure, satisfaction? Well, hardly. Had he inherited this exotic taste from his father? Was it in the bloodstream? Were there many black women in his father's life? He was inclined to believe so. The words from the poet's ballad came to him: 'I loved my daddy. But what did daddy do? Found himself a brownskin chicken.' He found himself humming, improvising the music.

He left his desk, went to the bathroom, listened to his heartbeat, took his pills, studied the fatigued puffy eyes that stared back at him in the mirror. As he entered the steamy bath he suddenly thought of the aromatic, finely-veined melon breasts of Kama, afloat, and his mother's shock at catching her darling son *in flagrante delicto*. He loved the phrase. Caught in the act of being sucked off by a beautiful woman in a perfumed bathtub; *fragrant delectable*.

He finished quickly with his bath, towelled, dressed and packed his bag. Since he was not in good standing with his mother, he hesitated, wondered how she would receive him. He went to her bedroom and poked his head into the dark room. My God, he thought, staring at his mother, a

Rembrandt woman in tragic chiaroscuro; her eyes glowing in the gloom.

'Mama, I'm going back to Paris,' he announced gently. 'Goodbye. I'm sorry I offended you. Be well.'

The face in the dark travelled with him.

Chapter Eighteen

When, after another boringly long voyage, he met Ruth and saw her face, Adrian knew that more disturbing news awaited him. He could feel the coil-spring tension in her body when he embraced her, saw it in her eyes; they were not the smiling eyes he loved.

After greeting him and asking about his health, about his adherence to his pill-taking regimen, she said, 'I have some awful news for you Adrian,' and she handed him the cable which had come the previous day. He assumed it related to his business discussions but saw instantly that it was from his brother, Harvey. It advised him in one laconic sentence that his mother had died the previous day of heart failure.

The extraordinary coincidence of receiving two death notices in Paris, making him an orphan within a month, left him numbed. He stared at Ruth, then back to the cable. He was suddenly alerted to another element related to Sarah's death. It was in some very real, indisputable and determinable way due to him. He sensed instantly that he would need to endure an awesome burden of guilt; that he would need expiation.

It would be impossible to make amends, but it would be torture not to share his culpability with someone: his brother, his wife, a rabbi. His mother's heart failure was the end result of her grief, her disappointment in her son, her shock at his outrageous act of infidelity, his gross behaviour in her own home. Adrian knew that what she

had glimpsed in the bathroom on her return from Florida was more than she could endure. Her refusal to speak to him thereafter, her mournful, bloodshot, tragic eyes indicated the extent of his evil deed. In Sarah's eyes, her best-beloved, her favourite son, had betrayed, besmirched her. Broken her heart.

Adrian mused over the fact that his simple act of entertaining a young woman, under admittedly odd circumstances, could stab, murder his mother, bring on her death. For, to the best of his knowledge, she had been in reasonably good health. But he had to know, and at once. He must telephone Harvey and determine what, if anything, he knew; whether Sarah had mentioned anything about Adrian and Kama. He turned to Ruth.

'Did you talk to my brothers?'

'Yes,' she said. 'It was heart failure, as it says in the cable.'

'Did they say anything else?'

'No history. It was the first attack she ever had.'

'Any medical explanation? What did the doctors say?'

'Shock, sudden shock and pain caused it,' said Ruth, averting her eyes. He noted, fascinated, that the conformation of her face seemed altered in some way. It had a tightened look.

'But what?' asked Adrian, his voice pleading for the accusation, the truth . . .

Finally Ruth said, 'Do you want me to be frank with you, Adrian, do you want the truth?'

'Of course. I don't know what this is all about. What did Harvey say? What did anyone tell you?'

He stood up, went to the sideboard and poured himself some scotch. He drank half, went to the bathroom for water and returned, sitting down on the edge of the bed, staring at Ruth.

'Okay, I want to hear everything. But for God's sake,

let's not make a Greek tragedy, a Euripidean production out of my mother's death. She had a heart attack.'

Ruth's eyes seemed hooded. She was unsmiling.

'I can put it simply, Adrian. Your brothers think that *you* killed your mother.'

Adrian heard himself shrieking. His heart was racing.

'What did you say? What insane thing did you say? Am I hearing correctly? Is there some conspiracy to drive me crazy?'

'Harvey tells an extraordinary story. Your mother returned from Florida, unannounced. She didn't know you were in the house. She found you in the bathtub with a woman . . .' She paused, rose and walked to the window. 'Your mother, it seems, gave your brother all the details. I gather she collapsed after she told Harvey what she saw. I gather it was more than your mother could endure from you, her favourite son. I'm not even sure that *I* can accept, or endure it.'

Her eyes were now tear-filled.

'Do you want me to go on? Harvey spared no details, and I guess your mother's threshold was reached and her heart stopped.'

'But what was said?'

Ruth studied him for a moment, then asked, '*Did* you have a woman in the house, in your mother's house? In the bathtub in your mother's house?'

Adrian stared at her, stunned. 'So. Yes. I did. What is this, a play called *Three Against Adrian*?'

Ruth took a deep breath, her eyes dilating. 'No. It might be called *Adrian versus Adrian*. There's something self-destructive about your behaviour, Adrian.'

'What else did you hear?'

'The woman, a Negro, I gather, was having sex with you in the bathtub. Is that true or false?'

'True,' he replied.

'Who was she?'

'You might call her a pick-up,' he replied.

'I don't believe that. Adrian, I don't believe you pick up coloured girls. I think you are a shit. Now tell me, who was she?'

'Does it really matter?'

'Yes, it matters. You brought her home, to your mother's house, through the lobby, flaunting her publicly, realising surely that someone would recognise you as a recently married young . . . oh shit, do we have to go on with this unspeakable thing? This discussion . . .? Your mother couldn't take it, and it killed her. Your friend, Oscar Wilde – you like to quote him – covers it nicely, except he didn't go quite as far as you did; his audacity and imagination didn't equal yours. You killed your mother, not with a word but with your arrogant prick!'

'Come off it, Ruth. You're preposterous, grotesque!' He was now shouting. He got up, walked to the window. Opened it wide, took a few breaths, returned to his seat. 'I need some fresh air. Want to take a walk and talk? To the Tuileries or whatever? I can't stand this room right now; I feel confined, choking. We can talk in the open air.'

'Okay, I'll get my jacket. But I'd rather go to the Deux Magots. I don't feel much like walking.'

They remained silent for several blocks; not until they were seated at the café and served their espressos did they resume their conversation. But the atmosphere was oppressing, Adrian thought: was this the beginning of the end for them? Death-watch time. It was like being part of a film being shot, but without benefit of script or direction.

Finally Adrian said, 'Look, Ruth. My personal world is getting hard to handle. Guilt. Anger. Confusion. I don't want to harm you, hurt you in any way. Or make you unhappy. I find it hard to explain the psychological forces that are driving me. When my father died, I discovered a

special, deep-seated need for some kind of catharsis. Call it that or purification or clarification or cleansing. In my own peculiar fashion I discovered that I could find the release I was looking for, if that's the word: *release*! Consider the factors in my case and you'll see why I could be verging on a classic schizophrenic situation. The signs are all there. And I do not, repeat, do not, plan or want to confer with a psychiatrist. I'm a rational intelligent person and I intend to work out whatever problems I have, by myself. Please listen carefully . . .'

Ruth had at times seemed inattentive, looking inward, with an impatient glance at him from time to time as he spoke.

'I'm listening,' she almost shouted. 'Carefully.' She sipped her coffee and added, 'No one's interrupting. You don't seem to be making sense. I've never listened so hard . . .'

Adrian went on, almost oblivious to Ruth.

'That black woman my mother saw in the bathtub. She was indeed performing fellatio on your husband: my mother saw enough, in one quick glance. That loving, Yiddish mama who saw her son, the paragon of intelligence and talent, saw him sitting there, getting sucked off – I'm sure she thought of you, Ruth, and what a tragedy had befallen her, and presumably you. I can't know everything that went on in her mind. Presumably, the colour of the woman's skin may have shaken her up, too. I can hear her telling my brothers what a *shreklich zach* it was, what a terrible thing had befallen her. But I must tell you something that my brothers aren't, no one, in fact, is, aware of: that black woman in the bathtub, she was – now, please listen carefully, Ruth – she was my late, dearly beloved papa's mistress.'

Ruth's head turned towards him and he thought he could hear the neck-bones snap. Her eyes were fierce and

her body stiffened as though she were suddenly out of control.

'What craziness is this? I feel mixed up with some kind of insane Jewish-American Karamazov family. Really, Adrian, you must be joking.'

'No, I'm not joking. Nor could I invent such a joke. And you can see why I'm having some trouble with my equilibrium. Which reminds me, I've got to take a pill.'

He felt a palpitation for a fleeting instant and he thought he saw Ruth bathed in a pink mist. Was it a trick of the afternoon light?

He removed a white tablet from his pillbox and placed it under his tongue.

'No, I'm not joking,' he said. 'But Ruth, my beloved bride, it's all true. And I was compelled, by some inscrutable, unfathomable power, to do what I did. I sought out the mistress of my father – the wife, by the way, of the man who probably killed my father – and I fucked her, and in fact, established a kind of relationship with her, as witness my bringing her home, to my mother's home. Was I searching, as I said, for a catharsis? Answers to some questions relating to my father? And while on that subject, my father was a preposterous turd. He appeared to be generous to us, giving us the two years in Paris, etcetera. But he did leave me out of his Will, as you know. And, oh yes, now that Mama is dead, and I haven't shed a tear for her demise as yet, I'm sure that my two brothers and I, the next-of-kin, will inherit everything. Think of that! I haven't given that any thought yet, but now that I do, I'm sure she had no time to draw up a Will. What she would have inherited must go to her next-of-kin, her three sons. Ruth, think of that, if you will.'

'You are not only a disgusting person, but I think there's a moral deficiency in your make-up. It's pathological!'

'Having said that, dear Ruth, would you please tell me one thing, one thing that matters more to me than anything in the world?'

'What *thing* is that,' she said, heavily emphasizing 'thing'.

'Do you still love me?'

She turned her head away from him, burst into tears and shouted, 'You son of a bitch I think I still love you. I must be sick.'

As they walked back to the hotel, Ruth turned to Adrian and asked, 'Exactly how was she anyway?'

'How was who?'

'Your black inamorata, the Afro Queen of Sheba, the lady in the bathtub. Was she good, your chocolate sweet potato?'

'Her name is Kama. How was she? Not bad.'

'Come on, now, Adrian. Not bad. Really! She must have something very special. Something I don't have. What, for example? Lots of interesting muscular action, new positions?' She arabesqued with her fingers, her hands . . .

'Well, the usual positions . . . I wish you'd drop it, Ruth.'

'No! There must be something more, something special about her, something really compelling to get you to do what you did. Élan? Black verve?'

'Look, Ruth. Black is exotic. I know this sounds racist, but her skin has a scented quality. It gives off a definite scent, cinnamon family, cloves, perhaps. The blacks deny the notion, but my nose tells me there's a very special quality . . . I think odour is an important factor in sex, natural body-odour, I mean.'

'You sound like a dog, if a dog could talk. What else? There must be more than odour. Women use perfumes,

you know, with clove and cinnamon odours . . . They say that sexual connoisseurs have a special taste for dark meat. Is the dark meat it? What exactly is it like?'

'I wish you wouldn't go on about this.'

'Why not? I'm interested in your secret life, your dark side.'

He remained silent.

'Perhaps it was simple experimentation. Your enquiring mind?' Then she burst out, 'Your father liked to experiment too, didn't he? Papa and son, both with a predilection for black pussy. Maybe I'd enjoy some black cock . . . I wonder.'

'You're getting offensive; I'd prefer dropping the subject.'

'I just might decide to take a Negro lover. There must be something exciting that I'm missing. Is that offensive?'

'Now you're being facetious, as well as offensive.'

'As a matter of fact, I'm not facetious. Nor offensive. And if I do run into a black man who appeals to me, I may just proposition him. Can you tell me why not?'

'I won't tolerate it.'

'You what? This is Paris, my dear husband. I'm a liberated woman. I might go further, and add: I'm a wife betrayed.'

'You heard me clearly; I will not tolerate it.'

'That makes the prospect even more exciting. Perhaps a Moroccan, or a Hindu. It would be interesting to sample various shades of cock, don't you think? Maybe a Chinese or Japanese, too.'

'Your sense of humour is degenerating and I don't appreciate it.'

Ruth walked in silence for a minute then asked, 'Do you plan to see this woman – what did you say her name was? – black woman, again?'

Adrian was silent. Then he burst out, 'Kama is her name. No, never again.'

'I don't believe you,' she said. 'And I know you've had other affairs; so your concern about marital fidelity on my part is grotesque.'

'I don't know what you're talking about. What affairs?'

'Well, Adrian, next time you have a woman go down on you, ask her to remove her lipstick first, or else remove your shorts. I saw red lipstick on a pair of your shorts, in the laundry hamper. If you can explain that away, then you are a nimble liar. Do I make myself clear?'

Adrian was stunned. 'I can't try to explain how red lipstick got on my shorts,' he said. 'And by the way, do you inspect my underwear as a regular duty, as part of your marital obligation?'

'Not really, but to coin a phrase, murder will out.' Ruth switched subjects suddenly. 'Do you plan to return to the States in the near future? And you haven't said anything about Jock and Uncle Sylvester and the business proposal, the art prints. What happened?'

'I wanted to tell you all about that but, as you well realize, we were sidetracked. The deal seems to be shaping up. In fact, I think it's on. Uncle Sylvester and Jock are working out the contract details. He does all the signing. He accepted in principle; in fact, I think he considered the whole project heaven-sent. Especially the up-front cheque he will get, the $100,000, and Jock gets majority control.'

'So if all goes according to your understanding, Jock will be in control of the business?'

'You could say so. I'm included in the basic agreement, you know, on a five-year contract giving me twenty-five per cent of the gross profits on all sales of framed prints. And if I leave the firm before the five-year contract expires I continue to collect my percentage of the profits.'

Adrian paused, waiting for her reaction.

'How do the cost figures look? And in what shape is the factory? I remember some talk about its being a rundown plant.'

'Some new equipment will be needed, but nothing serious. The basic machinery is there, and the staff looks pretty good. I'm planning to go to Milan and Verona the moment I hear from Jock that the contracts are signed.'

'Do you think Jock will have any problems about money?' she asked.

'No. I went with him to his banker; also met his lawyer. Jock is solid. Also, surprisingly sophisticated in business matters. He brought up several dozen interesting points with Uncle Sylvester, business points that really count. Jock obviously has had training or schooling in business. He's a cautious one. And that's what pleases me. He's not a talker; he comes right to the point, zeros in on the essential issue. He thinks we will each come out of this with a net million within fifteen months. Of course, the main burden is on me: the selling of the deal to some fifteen big prospects I've got to see. But I'm not worried. There are no flaws or serious bugs in the plan. We've gone over it every which way, and Uncle Sylvester came up with a few interesting and, I must say, valuable suggestions. Essentially, though, the baby is mine. Everyone recognises that I am the father of the programme. But I know that the chief burden is on me,' Adrian paused, his face hardening. 'I wish to Christ, Ruth, that none of the family stuff, none of the sex stuff had happened. I wish I didn't have a "round the clock" consciousness of my heart problem. I know I'm interfering with and affecting the work you're doing, your preparation for the concert, and the tour; it surely isn't helping you. I feel like a shit about that.'

'I'm a realist,' said Ruth. 'I've been working without

let-up. The concert takes place in ten days and I'm not worried, not any longer. I'm confident, in control of the Rachmaninov Concerto. As for the tour, press notices, assuming there are any, will help me get into the professional level. But I'm pretty sure that there'll be no problem. The head of the *École* told me in private that I'm their number-one candidate, their star. He used that word, star! They're giving me marvellous moral support, and I can use a lot of that right now.'

'And that gives me more pleasure,' said Adrian, 'than you may realise. I want to see you at the top; I'd like to see you do some recording. Imagine your father's pleasure getting a Mozart recording of yours. What a gift that would be for him, for all of us. I want to help in any way I can to further your career. Thus far I've given you problems.'

He paused, turned towards her and said, 'And Ruth, let's not quarrel. Try to understand me. I love you. I want to make love to you. I want you to love me. Let's go to bed.'

Ruth was silent for a moment. Then she said, 'Please, Adrian, not right away. Let's wait a little. By the way, let's call Jill and take her out to dinner. She's alone, and lonely. She knows you are back.'

'Whatever you say,' said Adrian. 'But you know that I love you, and nothing I do has anything to do with my love for you. Nothing.'

'And I love you. But, Adrian, you must stop making assaults on my nervous system, my piece of mind, my dignity and self-respect, if you'll permit those expressions. There's a *diablerie* in your behaviour, really, that I simply can't cope with, and if I may play psychiatrist for a moment, it's damned self-destructive. I'm not talking about sexual infidelity and such, although I'm not going to hold still for that any more. I'm concerned with our

marriage, your health, your future and mine. I'm determined to become a good pianist and a success on the concert stage. You've got to help me, support me. But if you keep up your catting around – fucking around, if you will – I'll not be able to stand up to my work. I'll wind up playing the piano in a nuthouse. It will become occupational therapy or something. Followed by catatonia, maybe. And then, there's promiscuity, a path I have not planned to follow . . .'

'Everything is going to change,' said Adrian. 'I promise. And I'm going to show you what a business whiz I can be. I'm going to make a fortune so that you'll never have to worry, nor I. And I'll behave. If that's the word. I've got research and study and writing to absorb me – you know my interests.'

Harvey, Ralph and their wives, and a crowd of relatives and friends met at the funeral parlour in Chicago's South Shore for the Sarah Breakstone services. Everyone remotely related to or familiar with Dr Breakstone's wife, including Uncle Sylvester and his family, and Adrian's *mechutonim*, the Davidsons, were present. And many newspaper readers who had followed the Breakstone murder case attended the mournful services. Harvey, officiating, spoke eloquently and excessively. His mother was a saint. 'And such a cook,' he added with a smile. Sarah would have been ecstatic, hearing her son, the rabbi, speak so movingly of her, and in three languages yet, which included a *zeeslech* Yiddish. Everyone agreed that his was a masterly eulogy; everyone nodded, sobbed at his theatrical summing up of her virtues and the blow of Fate that was again struck at a suffering family. Ah, Fate, and ah, that *malech hamoves* – the angel of death – moving in mysterious ways; and who could predict that or understand why so upright a person as his recently de-

ceased father, and so flawless a woman, his mother, should be removed from family and friends in their prime. There were few dry eyes in the chapel, and again, later, weeping was heard and seen at the graveside. So much tragedy, trauma, drama in one family.

Adrian's absence from the services was noted, and most carefully explained by the brothers. The irony of it all: the youngest son, missing the funeral of his mother (and missing his father's funeral, too!). This was on the minds of all. What a *shvarz yor* – a black year – it was for this sad young man, this 'highly educated' student with an ailing heart. The young *chossen's* absence was nevertheless too keenly felt not to be discussed as though, almost, perhaps, 'maybe it was deliberate?' (Wasn't Adrian an eccentric, an odd ball?) And then came the resonant voice of Harvey, awesome, in his most solemn manner, with ringing references to Job who too endured unspeakable suffering but never failed to love and believe in his God.

Sarah was portrayed finally, by her rabbi son, as a classic example of the grieving wife who, like the Hindu widow who commits self-immolation at the loss of her husband, found life unendurable. 'Her great good heart simply gave out from sense of loss.'

Sounds of weeping filled the air, rose and fell like a Greek chorus, supporting the rabbi's monologue. Altogether, a satisfying, lachrymose and effective funeral service. Especially gratifying was the 'full-house-standing-room-only' attendance, including some of the fanciest, most stylish socialites from the South Shore Drive.

Among the guests was Judge Angelo Minelli, who very pointedly asked about Adrian and frowned when told that he had just gone back to Paris and couldn't possibly return for the funeral. The judge apologised for his wife's absence. A mild illness prevented her attending.

'What a sad experience for such a young man, losing

father and mother within a month,' he said. The judge left in his limousine, and it was noted that he was alone and did not invite anyone to join him on his homeward drive.

The crowd began to disperse. The scent of rotting plants and flowers, the crunch of automobile tyres on the gravel road that wound in and about the cemetery, the leaden sky: it all accented, somehow, the prevalence of death.

Ruth's father was keenly aware of it all and he took his wife's arm and hurried her away from the gathering, frowning, making no particular farewell. And when they reached his parked car he made haste to depart, to rid himself of the odour and aura of the melancholy scene. There was, he felt, something evil and depraved in this place, a wickedness that was palpable. He could not understand it, but knew that there was more here than the simple matter of death by natural causes. There was, he felt, a mystery behind a mystery, more than a simple coincidence of Adrian's parents dying within so short a period. Somehow, somewhere, the tragedy lay within the mystery rather than in the dying. As he started his car's motor, he resolved to shake it all from his mind. He turned to his wife and said, 'So much for that; and what a terrible situation. I hope Ruth isn't affected.'

'Ruth is healthy,' she replied. 'The Breakstones – the more I see the less I know . . . it's all pretty gothic.'

'I hope,' said Harry Davidson, 'that nothing interferes with Ruth's musical career. I want to live to see and hear her play. That's all I want. The Breakstones must not, cannot, dare not, interfere with that. You agree?'

'Agreed, my dear. And she will. With God's help. You'll see, she will.'

'As they say,' said Harry. 'Next year in Carnegie Hall. That's our second Jerusalem.'

'Amen,' she said.

* * *

The word finally came to Paris from Jock: the contract was approved and signed. His lawyer, the famous Louis Korwin, had vetted it. Uncle Sylvester had accepted the $100,000.00 cheque, and also graciously yielded to secondary position in the company, the firm he had founded over twenty years earlier. Adrian was advised to proceed.

Ruth, Adrian and Jill celebrated on the evening they received the news from Jock. Adrian left for Verona the next morning. He told no one but Ruth that he would make a side trip to Calabria, once his work was completed in Verona. But after a three-day stay in Calabria he returned to Paris. He was disenchanted with his findings and less than enchanted with southern Italy. His failure to see or hear anything of interest or value in Calabria also gave him a sense of embarrassment. He must erase Ganzara from his mind, for the present and near future.

Chapter Nineteen

On his return to America, Adrian spent a few days in New York, meeting with chain-store executives. Then he got a train to Detroit for a day's session with a mail-order firm. From there he went back to Chicago for conferences with his sales and promotion staff, and Uncle Sylvester. In his absence, a young go-getter named Allan Molloy was hired. He was a mail-order specialist who had managed to line up in short order two major catalogue gift houses; they were, he declared, wildly enthusiastic about the framed prints. A sample order for a minimum of fifteen thousand framed prints comprised the test order. Everyone was overjoyed.

'We're going to celebrate your getting a foot in the door,' said Adrian to Allan. He felt it incumbent upon himself to show his appreciation of Molloy's triumph. Congratulating him, Adrian said, 'Let's have a blowout dinner to celebrate. It's on the house. Name your restaurant.'

Uncle Sylvester was unable to join them, so Adrian was host. Adrian expected Allan to name one of the leading hotel dining-rooms, or one of the standard steak houses.

'How about the Chez Paree?' Molloy asked. 'We're both on the loose. My wife's in Milwaukee this weekend, visiting her mother.'

'As you say,' said Adrian. He had Sylvester's secretary phone the night-club for reservations.

Molloy was in his mid-thirties, with a shock of thick black hair and a jolly but pugnacious face. He had a stock of jokes and a fair knowledge of the world of sports. Books and

the arts were not his domain. But he was not unamusing and Adrian felt relaxed with him, pleased to be in the company of a lively 'contributing member' of the team.

Molloy's jokes turned more and more towards the sexual, and during their dinner Adrian waited with mounting curiosity to see what Molloy would propose next.

Adrian paid the cheque when it arrived, then said, 'Now Allan, what's your pleasure?'

Allan's was the cliché reply, though nevertheless a surprise: 'We usually say "fuckin" when that question is asked,' said Molloy. He ended with a whoop of laughter and Adrian joined in, a company man all the way.

'Seriously,' said Adrian, 'while this is my home town, hired tail is out of my line. I'm an amateur and I'm afraid my experience has been mainly with charitable amateurs. Even my first encounter with a woman, a professional, was paid for by – well, you won't believe it – my father. A delayed post *bar mitzvah* present. That's quite a while back as you can imagine. But I still remember the place. It was run by a blonde named, I think, Viola. The late Mayor Hacha had something to do with the place, and my father was the Mayor's doctor and friend. They probably hatched up the date together. Come to think of it, I wonder why I never went back. It was a great experience, Viola's.'

Molloy looked at him with astonishment. 'You've got a surprise in store for you; that's where I was going to suggest we go tonight. Viola's. I've been there a few times. Viola herself is really the madam now, and she's got a great little stable: young, peppy, some real dolls.'

'Is it still on Division Street? asked Adrian.

'Exactly. But I think Viola's improved the atmosphere since you were there. She handles only a limited and exclusive clientele.'

'Well, let's go,' said Adrian, getting up from the table. 'This could be an interesting experience.'

They taxied to Division Street, got out of the cab and walked a block. They found themselves at the door of an ordinary red-brick apartment building on a tree-lined residential block.

'This doesn't look familiar,' said Adrian. 'Viola must have moved since I was there centuries ago.'

'It sure doesn't look like a whorehouse,' said Molloy. 'It would fool anybody.'

He rang the buzzer, announced his name over the speaker and the lobby door opened. They walked up a flight of stairs and found themselves facing an ordinary apartment door. A maid opened it at once. Behind her stood a muscular, middle-aged man in a tuxedo. He nodded and smiled when he saw Molloy, greeting them both with a modulated, 'Welcome, gentlemen.'

The living room was a gaudy scene with red lamps establishing a theatrical and erotic mood; it stopped them momentarily. The maid took their hats and coats and led them into the annexe where a piano and well-stocked bar were conspicuously visible, and two very young women, a blonde and a brunette. Adrian guessed them to be in their late teens or early twenties. The sheer scantiness of their dress indicated that action would not be too long in coming.

Adrian and Alan introduced themselves, giving their first names only, and Adrian said, 'How about a drink?'

They found themselves served at once: tulip-shaped glasses bubbling with champagne. And then two more women entered the room: an auburn-haired woman and a very young Chinese woman who could not have been more than eighteen.

'Now it's getting interesting,' said Adrian to Molloy. 'Why don't we each take two?'

'Can you handle two?' asked Molloy, pretending surprise at so bold an idea.

'Nothing ventured, nothing gained,' said Adrian.

'Wanna flip a coin?' asked the blonde.

'Good idea,' said Adrian.

Molloy tossed a coin, calling heads. It proved tails. Adrian grinned, put his arms around the blonde and the brunette and said to Molloy, 'See you around, chum,' and they moved off.

The tuxedoed attendant approached Adrian, saying *sotto voce*, 'Do you want to talk business with me, sir?'

'Why not?' said Adrian. 'Is Viola around? I'll settle for the whole bill including all extras and a couple bottles of champagne. But I'd like to pay my respects to Madam.'

'On the double,' said Mr Tuxedo.

'Hold it,' said Adrian. 'What do we owe you?'

'Two hundred and fifty will cover everything, the works. Unless you want to stay over, in which case it would be double.'

'No, just for this evening,' said Adrian and he peeled five fifty-dollar bills from his wallet. Then he added another fifty as a tip.

'Wait here, please,' said Mr Tuxedo, 'I'll see if Madam is free.'

They sat down, Adrian and his two companions; and wine was served them at once. Then Viola appeared through the red beaded curtains.

Viola had a bright smile, well-rouged lips, glistening blonde hair. The décolletage of her ankle-length pink chiffon dress dramatically displayed large rounded breasts, powdered and white; and the rouged nipples burned through the chiffon.

'We've met before, I think,' she said as she shook Adrian's hand. 'Can you refresh my memory?'

'Perhaps. I was slightly past my thirteenth birthday. My father arranged for my initiation. His name was Dr Jeremiah Breakstone.'

Viola looked startled. 'Let me think,' she said. 'May I offer my condolences? I knew your father, a great doctor, a fine man. A friend of my closest friend, also gone, Tony Hacha. So you're Breakstone's son?'

'Yes,' said Adrian, studying her troubled face.

'Looking at you, so young, so handsome, I can't help thinking – so much history has passed for me. Your father was a very good friend of mine and his death, as well as Hacha's, was personal. Please excuse me. Enjoy yourself.'

Viola turned and walked back through the beaded curtains.

Adrian stood, watching her leave. With a rush he realised who and what she represented. She had given him his first sexual experience, but what was she to his father? And to Hacha? A boy of thirteen walking into the naked blonde woman's room and being devoured, sexually traumatised – it came back to him with a vividness that he was almost unable to assimilate.

Adrian felt a tug at his arm. He turned to the brunette and said, 'Lead the way. I'm all yours.'

They proceeded to a large room with an elaborate, king-sized bed in its centre. A mirrored ceiling; heavy brocade drapes; the obligatory nude painting (a faithful copy of one of Bouguereau's glossy paintings, *The Triumph of Venus*) dominating one wall. This was a room for one purpose only.

Adrian stroked each of his women's bottoms and said, 'You're in charge.' Then he removed his jacket, and lay back on the bed.

They proceeded to busy themselves over him, undressing him slowly, with provocative strokings and kissing, nibbling his ears, tits brushing against his face.

'How about a shower?' asked the brunette, 'and we'll join you?'

'Inspired idea,' he said. 'But hey, I didn't get your names.'

'Linda, that's me,' said the blonde, 'and Annette, that's her.'

'Okay, Annette, Linda, lead me to your bath.'

Adrian's erection and ejaculation occurred almost at once upon entering the shower with the two naked beauties. Their bodies and caresses, their expert fingering of his genitals and buttocks, were galvanic stimulants and he wondered fleetingly if he could perform again, within the hour. They escorted him back towards the bed, towelling him, drying and caressing: like a prince, he thought. A melancholy gripped him as he lay spread-eagled on the great bed, watching himself in the ceiling mirror. The diminished lust following his ejaculation embarrassed him. He watched the two women in attendance, somewhat like ballet dancers, playful, graceful. His body, he felt, was badly in need of some sun; he saw himself as a corpse, with the white pallor of death.

Then the blonde was suddenly upon him, kissing his nipples, his navel. Her lips were soon upon his cock, drawing slowly at the head of the limp instrument.

The other woman, Annette, was probing, massaging, groping with her fingers and then her tongue, from the rear. Adrian began to feel a throbbing, a heightening tumescence. As he lay there, conscious of the expert manipulations of the two whores, he reached out, caressing each, one on the buttocks, the other on the head. The blonde, Linda, had let her hair down and it was now spread over his middle as she worked away at him with her lips and tongue, and gently, too, with her teeth.

Adrian now felt a slow, luxuriating, mounting sense of exquisite pleasure that grew, strangely, slowly, into pain. And then across his brain flashed someone's words – a poet's? – 'the terrible energy of the dead' – and the words

– oh Christ, whose were they? – coincided with an excruciating explosive stab in his chest, and another – a thrust of hot pain up his left arm, a searing wave of pain. Then he uttered a frightened cry, a choking childlike final cry.

Adrian's *cum* spurted and creamed the lips of the blonde; and the brunette withdrew her hand with a start; stared, mouth open, eyes wide, in fear and in wonder. She saw the rolled-up eyeballs. It was her first view of death.

Annette pressed the house buzzer for help. The man in the tuxedo appeared at once, sized up the situation, removed his coat and began pumping Adrian's chest, sucking and breathing into his mouth; pressing and shaking, too. But soon he saw the futility of his efforts. The poor young slob was dead.

At that moment, Viola appeared. She studied Adrian's face silently, then took the women and the house man aside. A quick conference was held and a decision reached.

They searched his pockets and found his wallet that told them where he lived in Paris, in Chicago, and then the attendant went to fetch Molloy. He arrived shaken, studied his employer's body as the blood drained from his face. Together they dressed Adrian.

At one point Molloy felt faint, thought he would expire. He had had too much to drink, he explained. The interruption was traumatic for him. He was shaken, disoriented, frightened. He sat down, head in hands, speechless. Viola gave him a small glass of brandy and he sat staring at his erstwhile companion, trying slowly to comprehend the magnitude of the problem facing him.

They carried Adrian down the stairs. Molloy was to drive Adrian to a hospital by taxi. Their story: he had had too much to drink; forgot to take his pills (they found his gold pillbox and Viola recognised the little white pills for

what they were); had a seizure. Molloy handed the attendant some bills; the girls sat at the far side of the room, silent, watching.

The next morning, Uncle Sylvester and Adrian's brothers were called by Molloy, advising them of the death of Adrian. He disclosed the full facts of the matter, deciding shrewdly that otherwise he would eventually be caught up in a lie. It was agreed that the matter would be handled with delicacy and the utmost discretion. Ralph would make the telephone call to Ruth in Paris. Molloy, parenthetically, let it be known that he was an innocent accomplice: Adrian, he said, lowering his voice, 'wanted to get his ashes hauled.'

The bottle of nitroglycerine tablets they found in Adrian's pocket puzzled Molloy; he had no knowledge of Adrian's heart problem. In any event the little bottle would have been meaningless to him. Presumably Adrian had forgotten his dosage before making it with Viola's girls – Viola's best – in the late Tony Hacha's Division Street bordella. And Viola, returning to the privacy of her office, removed her shoes, poured herself a small whisky and pondered on the fact that she was becoming a repository of human history and despair, almost more than she cared to bear. For the first time in years she wept, as she thought of the handsome young man's face and body, and of two other men in her life, the young man's father and Tony Hacha, her one-time pimp and closest friend.

The two young whores stood in a corner of the room, numbed and staring; two unwitting accomplices who helped Adrian to his peace while performing an ancient ritual.

Viola reached for a handkerchief, wiped her eyes and picked up the phone. As she heard the voice at the other end she said, 'Angelo, this is Viola. Can I see you? Just for old times' sake? Something awful has just happened.'

Book Five

Chapter Twenty

Chicago, 1979

Ruth Breakstone was reading in bed when the phone rang precisely at noon. She waited, eyes to the ceiling, counting: one, two, three, four, five, six, seven seconds . . . *Where in Christ's hell is Susan*? 'Damn that phone!'

The modulated but insistent ringing was interrupting a familiar ritual, the re-reading of one of her favourite novels.

Ruth resented anything that interefered with her habitual revisits to her favourite author, Proust. On this particular morning, having enjoyed her first Jack Daniels screwdriver of the day, she was savouring the grace of its effects: the peace, the animal wellbeing, the quiet wallow; the bodily and intellectual delight provided her by life.

The passage in Proust's volume (*La Prisonnière*, one of the thirteen in *À la Recherche du Temps Perdu* series) that had held her transfixed at the moment when the phone rang, was the extraordinary description of Albertine in bed, asleep, her vulva 'closed at the junction of her thighs by two valves of a curve as hushed, as reposeful, as cloistral, as that of the horizon after the sun had set'. The rare perception of this particular writer moved Ruth deeply. Of all the books in the world this was her favourite as was its milieu.

She lay back, staring at the ceiling. She stretched. She waited, staring, then glancing at the door.

Where the goddamned hell was Susan? Her maid-cum-

all-utility person, not forgetting cook, confidante and companion.

Waiting, she shifted her buttocks.

The ringing resumed.

'The phone, Susan, pick it up!' she shouted.

Pause. Silence except for the ringing.

A Schubert quartet was coming to her softly, throbbingly, on tape from her stereo. The D Minor, for inexplicable reasons, matched her mood when reading Proust.

Ruth had beside her a silver tray on which stood an empty white china coffee pot and cup; likewise a small glass in which a quarter of orange juice and bourbon remained.

A slender pink Chinese cracked bud vase held a small yellow rose; it was barely opened. One dainty leaf was attached to its fragile stem, proclaiming its green, delicately-veined existence. The innocence and sweetness of the rose were not lost on Ruth.

The previous evening she had given one of her best recent concerts, an all-Mozart programme, at Orchestra Hall which was her Midwestern equivalent of the Eastern Holy of Holies, Carnegie Hall. Her first public appearance anywhere, at the piano, had been there. It was in her early teens, she used to say, with Frederick Stock conducting. What was the work she had performed? All she remembered with clarity was the chill in her bones at the time, and the row of seats occupied by the members of her family. And, somewhere in that hall, purely by cosmic coincidence, had been the unknown young man, Adrian, whom she would eventually marry.

Lying on the floor in its usual disorder was the *Chicago Tribune*. In its Arts section was a review of her performance, with a two-column photo displaying her with her now familiar mane of white hair. The bold Caslon banner

proclaimed RUTH BREAKSTONE PIANO BRILLIANT. The critic described her playing as 'more individualistic with the passage of years', praising her for her 'assertive reading and power', etc. She was bored with the clichés, the reviewer's jargon-shit; happy, nevertheless, for the attention and generous space; in particular, for the 'standing room only' attendance and the fifty extra paid admissions who were given chairs on the stage. What she relished most, however, was the flattering comparison to Magda Tagliaferro, who played, according to the critic, 'like one possessed'.

She arose, walked to the windows and drew the curtains apart. She returned to her bed to enjoy the sight, the sun pouring into the room, bathing the pale pink and blue carpet a golden misty grey-yellow Monet pond colour. The white and gold furniture made one think of Baked Alaska. An immense crystal vase filled with white heavily-scented peonies, lush and opulently ripe, stood on the floor near the window.

On the wall panel, over the pale lime-and-veined marble mantelpiece, facing Ruth's bed squarely, hung a Man Ray lithograph: his famous elongated red lips afloat betwixt clouds in a blue sky, bringing to her mind Albertine's vulva . . . The lithograph was boldly inscribed 'To Ruth' in pencil by the artist in its lower left margin.

Lying in the immense bed beneath a Chinese cobalt blue silk cover, her snowy white hair stark against her fresh Rio tan, Ruth was a vision of sybarite euphoria. In her mid-sixties, she was a continuing mystery to most of her friends, and the press, and to her public in particular. She would disappear for months, then reappear phoenix-like for what seemed to be a visit rather than a return to her home. She would see a few select friends, perform in public and privately, then she would be gone,

off to Europe, Morocco, elsewhere. Venice, Florence, Barcelona and Tangier were favourites. Likewise Rio, where she had friends. In each of four cities there was a pied-a-terre. She boasted that she rarely bothered with hotels, that hideaways of her own existed all over the world, addresses known only to her lawyer, banker and manager.

'My lovers will know where to find me if they are sufficiently ardent,' she would say; and no one was to know whether she was boasting or jesting.

The phone rang again, and she found it, finally, impossible to deny. It was a transatlantic operator.

'Allo, allo,' the voice from Paris said. 'I have a call for Mrs Ruth Breakstone, from Mr Mordecai Ericson.' The surname was carefully spelled out by the operator in a clear, heavily accented voice.

With a flush of pleasure, she said, 'This *is* Ruth Breakstone,' and she recognised the unmistakably harsh, arrogant and still youthful voice which she had not heard in perhaps fifteen years.

'Good God, Mordecai,' she said, 'how long, how many years since I last heard from you?'

'Who counts?' he said. 'But I'm alive and that's what matters. At least it does to my millions of readers.'

Conceited as always, she thought, but consistently engaging. 'It's wonderful to locate you. How lucky. You sound younger than ever. You have a young girl's voice, by God.'

'You didn't call me from Paris to soft-soap me,' she said. 'Flattery doesn't become you, Mordecai. I'm definitely not younger; my mirror reminds me of this fact daily. What about you? Do you have all your teeth, your hair?' (Vanity would fetch him, she knew.)

'My teeth? Hah, the better to eat you with. As for my hair, I stopped caring about that years ago.' Then he

added, 'Only the scales continue to defeat me. Two hundred pounds five this morning.'

'It's the good life, Mordecai, pasta and pastry: our enemies and our beloved. What have you been doing other than eating, and writing those erotic novels which I adore?'

There was a pause. 'Other than writing? Hah. Well, I'm still fucking,' he said.

She heard his quick laugh, recalled him totally now; wondered if he was in fact toothless, bald, fat. Had he aged? Would she recognise him? She had seen photos of him on the jackets of his books, in magazine articles. But everyone knew how vain authors (and pianists!) were, how they used only those photographs taken in the pink bloom of youth.

'Ruth dear,' his voice suddenly lowered. 'I have a great favour to ask. I want to see you, to take you to dinner and have a long visit with you. Say, a two-day visit? Are you free this coming weekend? I can leave Paris tonight. What I want from you' – he continued nonstop in the same lowered voice – 'yes, it's a big favour, is something relating to Adrian. Do you mind discussing Adrian?' He rushed on. 'I hope you don't mind my bluntness. Why play games, for God's sake?'

There was a pause. Would she really mind, she wondered, discussing her late – very late – husband, dead so many years? What on earth was Mordecai up to? she wondered. Using Adrian as a character in one of his tough, fast, sexy, *roman à clef* stories? What on earth for? Adrian was no celebrity, no power figure.

But she replied, 'No, I don't mind discussing Adrian, although I haven't spoken about him to anyone, really, in a very long time. My dear, for you I don't mind, you may be sure. I don't play games either. I think I can give you some interesting details . . . Are you really writing Adrian into a novel?' Her voice took on a tone of concern.

'Not writing him in,' Mordecai was saying, 'but I want to use some echoes, some of his aura. I remember him so vividly, in Chicago, Miami and especially in Paris. But I want a better fix on him. It's a thirties novel, set in the Midwest, with emphasis on Mayor Hacha and his assassination; the politics, crime, prostitution, the syndicates, the stuff Adrian was so emotional about, always making notes, you'll recall. We had some good discussions, Adrian and I, about that judge, Angelo Minelli, and Adrian's father, the doctor . . . Adrian keeps coming to mind over and over again. I need him, Ruth.'

'I know what you mean, Mordecai,' she said. 'Adrian resurfaces for me constantly. I keep crossing old paths, the paths we both walked together, people we knew. Just the other day someone was quoted as saying about Chopin, "He was always dying, dying all the time", and it was true of Adrian.'

'I must make a note of that,' said Mordecai. 'Very good. That quotation about Chopin – it says it all.'

Ruth said, 'He thrived on the masochist within me. Yet, he was so dear. But also hateful. In the end *sui generis* is my bottom-line judgment despite the scar tissue I can show. In a way, I'm glad you want to bring him back, and I hope you'll do it without offending . . . you do know that he gave me some hours of torment, but also pleasure that I'll never forget.'

'I'll handle it with love and understanding, I swear,' said Mordecai. 'There were remarkable aspects of his personality and mind, and I'm so glad you'll co-operate, fill me in.' There was a pause, then he said, 'I saw your photo and the review of your last Paris concert in the *Herald Trib*. My God, Ruth, you looked like Liszt in that photo.'

'How awful,' she said. 'Well, maybe the hair, but Mordecai, Liszt had at least a dozen warts on his face, and all those lovers, one of them a real crazy. Now come!'

'Apologies. Of course the physical resemblance ends with the hair. As for the piano technique: I recall a critic in the Paris *Trib* calling you a quote, bravura pianist with a colossal technique, unquote.'

Ruth brushed aside the compliment. 'Why didn't you come to see me, Mordecai? I'd have loved seeing you after the concert.'

'I was in Majorca, doll. I saw the *Tribune* article there. But I most certainly would have seen you, heard you, if I'd been in Paris at the time. I understand you're firmly established among the female piano immortals.'

'And that's a chauvinist remark! Not quite. There are quite a few women on the de luxe piano circuit. Good ones. But thanks. And please, no more Liszt comparisons. I must talk to my hairdresser . . .' He heard her laugh, and knew that all was good between them.

'Then we have a date,' he said. 'I'll phone you when I arrive. I'll probably stay at the Ambassador East. I've got a friend there, back of the desk. I can't wait to see you; maybe you'll give with a bit of Mozart or Bach for me, eh? Privately, Ruth? *Eine Kleine Nachtmusik*?'

'Gladly,' she said. 'But we have a lot of catching up to do.'

She did not bid him goodbye, but, as was her habit, merely hung up. She adjusted her pillow, sat back, allowed her memories to take over. She recalled Adrian's slender waist, his decadent good looks. He could have been a young Oscar Wilde; he had the style. And every man with the problem of thinning hair must have hated Adrian's lush curls. Women were smitten with his hair and his features, aside from his personality. She saw his type in some of the early Italian paintings; part spoiled dandy, part authoritarian and aristocrat, part imp. She saw how he enjoyed outraging people. With Adrian it seemed a daily necessity, and he had performed with such recklessness.

Ruth reached for the crystal decanter on the floor, removed the stopper and poured the golden liquid into her orange-juice glass. A *warm* Jack Daniels Screwdriver! Never. She buzzed for Susan, for ice. And where the hell was the girl? She called out, 'Susan!'

As she laid aside her book she had an irresistible need to examine herself retrospectively, turn back the calendar. No more Proust now. She pulled open a drawer in her bedside table and drew from it a framed photograph. She studied it in its *art nouveau* silver frame, then stood it upright on the table, facing her. She gazed at it, nodding.

'Such boobs,' she said aloud.

It was the Man Ray photo of herself, naked to the waist, with shining oiled breasts. Her eye make-up was heavy, theatrical. The picture was taken when she was in her early twenties. A stunt, taken in Paris, she now recalled so clearly: the day, the bright Paris morning, a young bride, when she went in a burst of fury and jealousy to Man Ray's studio on the Rue Ferón.

Ruth Breakstone had never shown Adrian the photograph. Nor anyone else. It remained secret. As was her affair with Man Ray.

Years later when her companion-maid, Susan, first saw it, she smiled. Her comment was 'Ooh la la.' Susan, an attractive young Englishwoman, less than half Ruth's age, was privy to all of Ruth's activities, her secret life. Devoted, she was both servant and friend, and understood Ruth's needs and moods. While she would take some licence on occasion, her deportment was always beyond reproach in public. Ruth would have been devastated if Susan were to leave her.

Usually, the Man Ray photo was kept in a drawer, in a suitcase or trunk when she travelled. Ruth would never confess to anyone how much in love she was with the girl in that photo. (How narcissistic could one get?) But now,

she decided that when Mordecai came to visit her, she'd allow him to see the photo, with the exquisite young breasts, and that look of high elation. She was Mona Lisa and the Primavera, a Raphael Madonna, too: formerly Ruth Davidson, the pharmacist's daughter.

She could not help speculating on Mordecai's reaction, and on her motivation. The world-famous novelist would surely respond. The photograph, presented at, say, a Man Ray retrospective, could create an international sensation, certainly in the music world; the photo-magazines would adore it, not to mention her business manager. Maury would drool at the prospects. Yes, she would do it.

She continued to stare at her photograph. Then she began to weep. She sobbed. Not for the illicit love affair, not for her lost youth, the breasts, Adrian. No, her tears were for the realisation that despite fame and fortune she had not made the most of her youth, her life. Misspent youth? No! Unspent youth. Man Ray had immortalised her breasts but now, in her final years, how she regretted the unnumbered opportunities spurned out of cowardice; mourned the gifts not taken from admirers, the moments denied for loving, for which she had now only remorse and pain, a deep sense of loss; remorse for the grey days of her life.

Susan finally arrived, face pale and drawn, bringing a crystal bucket of miniature ice cubes. Ruth dropped three cubes into her glass, poured more bourbon over the ice, then turned to examine Susan's face.

'Where were you, Susan, for God's sake? The phone rang and rang. Luckily, it was Mordecai Ericson. By the way, we're having him as a dinner guest this weekend. Yes, Mordecai Ericson. No less! He was calling from Paris. He was the call you didn't pick up.'

'I'm sorry, I had to go to the drugstore,' Susan said. 'I

was indisposed. My period – a rough one this time. A gusher.'

'I'm so sorry, Susan. Take care. My evening with Mordecai will be a very long, very special one. Those two old cardboard boxes containing Adrian's papers and journals. I'll want them for Mordecai; he's writing about Adrian.'

The Schubert tape had run its course on the stereo.

'A novel about Adrian?' asked Susan, eyes widening. 'I liked Ericson's last book, the one about the Rita Hayworth type. Will you be in it too? An Ericson character?'

'I really don't know. It might be fun. Or embarrassing. But he's interested in Adrian, mainly, and matters related to the research Adrian did on Mayor Hacha and the assassination, etcetera. I promised him co-operation.'

Susan continued to stand there, thinking, waiting, then frowning.

'Adrian,' she said, almost to herself. Shadows under her eyes.

Ruth studied her, thinking, a dependable girl, trustworthy; totally devoted.

'There's a review in the *Tribune*. Please clip it,' said Ruth. 'I'm going to watch TV for a bit, and then a shower and to work. My lower back needs a little working over, dear.'

Susan picked up the papers and left. Ruth waited a moment then reached for and pressed the 'Space Command' remote control instrument for the TV news programme; watched, half-listened as she sipped her drink.

A series of commercials came on, interrupting the news. An oversized blonde, extravagantly overdressed, appeared between two large, gleaming and expensive automobiles. She was hawking the cars in a voice that might have served for the announcement of the Second

Coming. Ruth pressed the *off* button on the control instrument, turned over and buried her head in the pillow. She would remain in bed for another half-hour, after which some push-ups, a back massage, a quick shower and her daily three-hour session at the piano. Discipline was her religion. 'Play until you drop,' she would tell students. 'And then, shoulders back and continue to practise.'

Today, she was ravenous for another encounter with Albeniz's 'Iberia'. She would engage in what she called an *explication de texte*; in two weeks or so she would master and possess it in its entirety, note by note, phrase by phrase. The work would become a part of her tendons, bloodstream, her fingers and nervous system. Each note and phrase would be hers.

Ruth had come to love Spanish music in recent years, and her concert programmes often included one of the Spanish masters. She now performed with regularity in Barcelona and Madrid. What appealed to her about Albeniz was the fact that he had made his debut as a pianist at the age of four. Ruth would sigh and confess, to interviewers, that she made her debut rather late in life, in her early teens. In Orchestra Hall. The complete 'Iberia', a formidable work, would be her challenge. She was eager for it in every sense.

She rolled over, turned the TV on once more, listened and watched, and learned about local murders, fires, political manoeuvring in the upcoming elections; a labour union official assassinated; a young student pushed off a subway station platform and decapitated; the routine stories of the day in a big city. She allowed her mind to wander. Mordecai's coming visit. She thought also of what she would and would not disclose to him. She pressed the TV gizmo and the screen was blank. She returned to her past.

There were byways, exotic adventures, romantic excursions and interludes in her early life, many that would intrigue Mordecai. The friendships, difficulties in their first year in Paris. The parties; quarrels and mishaps. Adrian's strayings, her widowhood and finally, her early success as a pianist, her concerts, her first triumphs.

But what would her husband, Adrian, have felt about being *used* as a fictional character by the notorious novelist, Mordecai Ericson? How deeply did Mordecai intend probing? Ah, Mordecai; sensualist, voyeur, sexist, no respecter of privacy. For that matter, what did he already know about Ruth and Adrian that would prompt him to explore their private lives? Surely their pals, the Merediths, had provided him with some morsels, privileged information? Tidbits that would get Mordecai salivating? Surely there was more than Adrian's ideas, his concerns with political violence, commercial sex, and assassination. Mordecai was probably already fortified with the meat and bones and was simply searching for verification, the widow's point of view; and the trimmings. The giblets.

Ruth tried to recall conversations with Mordecai in the old days in Paris and a few brief encounters years ago in Chicago. What had she told him in those days of anguish? About Adrian's amatory adventures, his fucking around? His dazzling business venture, his sudden death, her early concerts? She thought of Adrian's father, remembered his strange behaviour when she first met him, his personal probings. Her mind returned to the Paris of their early days: the artists, musicians, eccentrics they had met. She thought of Jock and Jill. Alas, Jock was gone too. The women, somehow, seemed to be the survivors . . .

Returning to Mordecai, she wondered how much he knew about Adrian's affair with the Negro woman, Kama, whose husband took his melodramatic revenge. She

thought of Adrian and Kama in the bathtub with Mama at the door . . . She decided to bypass this, all of this, if she could possibly do so. She wondered how much she should reveal of the Merediths and their entourage. And what of herself?

Could Mordecai, skilful, inventive, demonic though he was, manage this circus like a ringmaster, capture the immense cast? And of course, today, hopscotching the years gone, she wondered why bother at all? All that expenditure of digging, disclosing, when it was really her present life, her music, her piano, that mattered, proved to be her enduring, faithful lover. Only the keyboard mattered, where the darkness would lift and where her fingers, caressing the responsive keys, would bring her peace. Those lovely white, seven-octaved ivory keys arrayed before her, always waiting.

Ericson as a novelist had developed a multi-million dollar knack, a razor-sharp eye and sure hand with respect to market. He knew intuitively what the reader and filmviewer wanted; and he provided, year after year, acceptable story-fare expertly and diligently. He had become immensely successful: five of his novels were already on film. His stories were usually based on recognisable people: celebrities in business and finance, titans of politics and world affairs, not forgetting the international jet-set studs and rogues, the beauties and sex kittens. If he was interested in Adrian, he would necessarily want to include Ruth since she was now an international figure. Though not in the notorious sense. She had a style of her own, a warm yet stately manner in public; she was low-profiled and avoided the clamour and tensions often associated with personalities such as, say, Callas; nor were Horowitz or Rubinstein her models for deportment. But she did often attract off-the-music-page notice. Bright-eyed, svelte of figure, an aura of quality was about her.

Often seen in the company of younger men, it was inevitable that she would attract the press and, of course, the envy of younger women. She had managed, somehow, to avoid underground notoriety. Her position as a gifted pianist, a virtuoso, was indisputable. She secured near-maximum fees for performances; and her recordings produced a substantial part of her income. She had learned early that good recording contracts were essential and her manager saw to her welfare in this area brilliantly.

As for being suitable material for a novelist, the imagination of the novelist would supply the answer. There were areas and byways in her personal history that would serve well in fiction. Her young, six-foot Moroccan servant-cum-lover for instance. In her early sixties, she still harboured a continuing sex hunger, and she had even contributed anonymously to the Hite report on 'sex in the sunset years', attesting to the fact that the sexual drive could be maintained 'until death do us part'. And how she adored that incredible body and blue-black cock! Would anyone, would Mordecai Ericson, suspect that? Or would he imagine certain other aspects of her private life and appetites? She knew much about his talents for research – and his tenacity was frightening. He would have made a star investigative reporter. Well, she had no responsiblity to any person in this wide world except to her audiences and her adoring business manager. Some lusty gossip and conjecture might be fun. As Maury Bloom would say, 'If it makes the papers it will sell tickets.'

She rose from her bed, performed her mandatory push-ups, entered her bathroom. She found Susan standing there, and quickly she entered the shower stall with Susan behind her.

She pondered briefly on Mordecai's potential as a lover. Fat, probably heavier than ever, he might not be the avid

lover of his reputation. Susan soaped her back, kneaded her hips and shoulders, and followed her out of the shower towelling her mistress vigorously, after which Ruth splashed cologne over her shoulders and thighs, then entered the living-room in a thin white dressing-gown. There stood her beloved grand piano, the Bechstein, waiting.

Albeniz, here I come to do battle, she said to herself, smiling, jaws set. Not battle, really, but to make love to his beautiful music.

Ruth would be at the piano almost three hours today. And she would conquer 'Iberia'. For ten days she had been giving it her best. She shouted towards the kitchen to Susan – asking her to put on a recording of 'Iberia' on the stereo. For comparison; study. Ruth remembered hearing Rubinstein play sections at the Suite in Madrid; the audience had gone bananas over his performance. She thought, I'll show that old fart – and those Andalusians too – how it should be played. When I finish, they'll crawl – they'll think I'm Spanish born. Nobility! She would listen to his recording. Tomorrow and tomorrow she would play the entire suite.

The languorous 'Almeria' was coming to her from the stereo, and she accompanied it. She saw herself, seated, with a mantilla over her hair and shoulders, lights on her face and hands, and thousands of the Spanish eyes were aglitter. Her entrance, her performance would be, in itself, a great pasodoble event! Ruth Breakstone, the West Side druggist's little girl . . . she did have a Catalan face, the eyes and skin, by God – and the nose.

Ruth had read some of Mordecai's interviews: she was an avid reader of magazines and newspapers. She thought now of Mordecai and some of his observations, his shock tactics, his so-called views, very few of which she accepted

as genuine. She felt an eagerness to see him, to hear and feel some of his wickedness, his blunt truths. He always spoke in extremes, realising he was playing games, testing for responses, always for eventual use in his novels. He was always working. She would find him stimulating so long as he chose not to be serious. No music talk, thank heavens.

Yes, she would tell him much about Adrian and their life; and it had to be disclosed. Why not? Time was fleeting. Should she burn Adrian's letters and journals instead? Who else would give a fuck? And what about her rapid loss of innocence under Adrian's amoral attrition? Was he too not an assassin? Killing her dream of romance and trust? Luckily, she had had her music to sustain her, to keep her from being ground down and blown away. His letters and papers would not be destroyed. Not yet. She would not become one of those censorious wives of history, like Lady Burton . . .

She would tell him everything about Adrian, the dear monster. And Mordecai could make it more than entertainment. If Adrian had lived into the seventies, what would he have thought, what would he have made, of the Kennedy murders, the King and Mountbatten assassinations? The others throughout the world? The daily slaughter?

Mordecai's next call came on Friday, at noon.

'Just checked in,' he announced. 'How are you, love? You're still prepared to see me, I hope?'

'Of course,' she said. 'Welcome, double welcome. Hope your flight was comfortable.'

'Concorde is really the only way to fly,' he said, 'if you can overlook those seats – they're built for undernourished assless nuns, or under-aged virgins. Breakfast in Paris, lunch in the Ambassador East. Not bad. And now, I want to see your beautiful face, and where would you like to have dinner? You name it. I'm rusty, really, out of touch with this town.'

'Oh Mordecai,' she said, 'I hope you don't mind, but I've planned for us to have dinner right here, in my apartment. Can you stand it? You've never been here, I don't believe. I'll have your favourite roast beef, rare. Seven-thirty, okay?'

'I'd planned for an orgy outside, in some posh place,' he said, putting a mournful note into his voice; but secretly he was delighted. They could really talk up a full-length book in her rooms; hair down, jacket and tie off, and shoes too.

'I'll be there, seven-thirty, hungry and ravenous, for you. And in advance, my love, thanks for the hospitality; I'm really looking forward to tonight, seeing you, being with you.'

She said, 'See you. It's the sixteenth floor; just announce yourself and breeze up. I'll have a dry Gibson waiting for you.'

She hung up.

At seven-thirty sharp he arrived: peonies and a magnum of Taittinger under his arm. And a large parcel, beribboned, which, when unwrapped, proved to be a king-size bottle of *Bal à Versailles*.

Mordecai was, as ever, plump, tanned, moon-faced and in his usual understated dress, in the fashion of Brooks Brothers: white shirt and black tie, black Gucci loafers and a black suit.

He was quite bald. His eyes were bright, his lips thin but smiling, his waist, at least two inches wider than when she last saw him. But altogether appealing. She thought quickly, if he should diet, he would lose much of his present appeal . . . I must tell him.

She kissed him on the lips and said, 'Do you mind if I say, simply, wow? With that perfume, no man will be safe from me. The stuff is positively wicked, you know. You really do remember, Mordecai!'

He smiled. 'Of course I remember. You look edible, Ruth, as always.'

The frosty Gibsons were ready, in snifter glasses, on a low movable bar, and they toasted each other.

They stood at the french windows, studying each other, smiling, speechless, hating to break the spell. Then Mordecai glanced out, down at the boulevard, then back to her. 'This beautiful room,' he said, 'is far more handsome than any restaurant I know in this town. It's almost worthy of you.'

'You are gallant, Mordecai, but please, please, cut out the shit.'

'Every word is sincere,' he said.

'This apartment,' said Ruth. 'I bought it a year after Adrian died. I love it; it accommodates all my needs, and my piano in particular. It houses the largest collection of Mozart recordings in the world, I think. I'm located marvellously: ten minutes from Orchestra Hall, half an hour from the airport. I bought the apartment after I began collecting that wonderful loot, Adrian's fantastic business deal. You know about that, I think.'

'I'm not clear about that,' he said, 'but you'll refresh my memory later, I hope. I'm like your narrator in Proust; in search of lost time . . . the privileged moments. I'm out to reconstruct a small but special segment of history, and you can help me more than anyone I know. As for Adrian's loot, didn't that come, in part, from a killing he made in the art-print market?'

'Yes,' she said. 'We have much ground to cover. But first, I must know all about you. Your beautiful ballerina wife. You're world-famous . . . I've got most of your books, probably all of them; some are here, some in Paris and Tangier. Some I've re-read. You're going to have to inscribe them for me, you know.'

'A pleasure,' he said. 'But it's you who are world-

famous. And I have all your recordings, I think, including the shellacs and all the Angels. I'm told, and it's believable of course, that you're one of the three greatest living pianists, and you've outdistanced all the Mozartians, including Alicia de Larrocha. Am I correct, or are you going to go modest on me?'

'No, I won't be modest. No concert pianist is. The critics, and especially the paid attendance, say it for me. But I've enlarged my repertoire. I play a wide range of music today. I'm doing an all-Albeniz programme next week. Will you be here? I'll have tickets for you, Mordecai.'

'Of course I'll be here. Great. I'll stay.' He studied her, smiling. 'So, you read all my stuff. Anyone else, besides Proust?'

'So you remembered . . . As a matter of fact I read everything; music aside, without books I'd perish. Confidentially, they're almost as good as sex. Romance, adventure, science fiction, poetry, plays, pornography: I read everything. I even read some of the heavy intellectuals and one novelist who writes about goats and computers copulating. Fancy that, Mordecai! But I promise not to annoy you with literary questions,' she went on. 'I want to know more about you and your private life. Is there one? I gather you bought a house in Rio. I was there last month for a few concerts. I gave the Cariocas a taste of USA music and they responded with gusto to Aaron Copeland's Piano Sonata. I got a great review, and it's really a marvellous piece that few people know about. Too bad I didn't meet up with you. I didn't know, at the time, that you were there . . . What's it like, your Rio house?'

'Sort of Taj Mahalish . . . Not Brazilian at all . . . a chateau in white marble, with a Moorish barbican . . . an indoor pool . . . you know, nice.'

'One day I'll drop by; I love Rio and have many friends there. And before I forget, how long do you plan to stay in town?'

'Well, I want a few days at the public library and City Hall. Then I'll tour the town, the slums and garbage, the new skyscrapers. I've got to re-examine some areas that I deal with in my novel. The old Metropole Hotel for instance: does it exist today? You wouldn't know. Capone held some of his board meetings there. It's the thirties I'm interested in, the whole Tony Hacha era. And the killings. They call them contracts today. Hacha may very well be my central character. Haven't decided yet. And there's Judge Angelo Minelli. You knew him of course. I know that Adrian knew him; he once told me a weird story about the guy. Powerful, twisted. A perfumed, pomaded monument of evil, right out of central casting . . . Is he alive?'

Ruth smiled and asked, 'What do you expect to get out of these researches?'

'There's a minor epic buried here,' he said.

'Tell me about your wife. How is Nadia? Last time I saw her in Paris, a century ago at least, she did a charming belly dance for us at the Merediths'. Remember?'

'Yes, I remember it. She was trying to put down an Egyptian cunt who was upstaging the women at the party. Remember? And, since Nadia carries her finger cymbals with her, she did a creditable job, don't you think?'

'She did indeed.'

'I must tell you something,' said Mordecai, changing the subject. 'And I hope you won't be annoyed. In that attaché case I brought, I've got a tape recorder.'

'Oh God, no,' she said. 'Must you, Mordecai?'

'If you say no, it's no. But it will be one hell of a big help if I could have it running while we talk. I swear to you, if there's anything you don't want used, simply add the

words "off the record" and it will be done. But get it all on tape, please. I'll follow your orders scrupulously. Fair enough?'

She studied him for a moment. 'It may inhibit me, Mordecai. I can get careless with language, just as you can, and I'd not want to be quoted verbatim. In any event, it's my understanding that this is a novel, fiction all the way. Right? No similarity of names, etcetera. Correct?'

'On my honour; as a friend,' he replied.

'We can keep it on during dinner if you wish,' she said. 'And later, I'll lend you something: Adrian's papers, letters, notes and journals. I've kept them all these years. There's a fascinating volume of diary stuff that will curl your hair. Am I a friend?'

'An angel, Florence Nightingale, Anne Sullivan, a saint; the woman I love more than anyone in this world.' He came over to her and embraced her, kissing her reverently. 'I'm a lucky guy,' he murmured.

'I've kept every letter Adrian wrote me,' she added, 'from the very first one shortly after we met. You'll find his personality there, loud and clear, as they say, sometimes loving, sometimes offensive. In each of them he reveals himself, his passions, his fantasies. Some of his wild dreams, too. Also his views on death and assassination. The killing of Tony Hacha seemed to have set him off: he discussed it in his first letters to me. You were there in Miami, did it affect you too?' She paused. 'Hacha had an extraordinary interest for him, his easy accommodation of whorehouse enterprises and civic efforts fascinated him.'

'Tony Hacha had me hooked, too. His career, his genius for political power, and that machine he built. How an ignorant bohunk, an uneducated immigrant boy who began as a pimp, can make it in America through sheer energy, ambition, bullheadedness . . . well, maybe I could

be talking about myself, or any number of American success stories, couldn't I? But this guy had genius in his genes. He made millions out of whorehouses and real estate. Never once in trouble with the law, except when he was young and beat up girls when he got drunk. He was a bull of a man, socially a slob and yet he understood the value of culture. And Judge Minelli: he is something to consider. A sinister, almost Florentine character. He had a little empire of his own, not to mention a shady background, a thing for young girls, a permanent hard-on, and the classic sodomist killer instinct.'

'He's dead, you know,' she said. 'I know how he died, too. Adrian goes into his background at great length in his journals: you'll find it hot sordid stuff, also gruesome. Some of it you won't believe. He's right out of the Medicis.'

She paused, then changed the subject. 'I'll surprise you when I say that I no longer suffer over some of Adrian's outrageous acts. You see, I know that he loved me. But he couldn't help himself. He couldn't resist throwing eggs into electric fans. But it was much more: the need to experience all of life, because he suspected his time was limited. The exotic, especially, appealed to him, made him take risks. He was on a collision course from the day he could walk. Adrian almost, but not quite, forced me to leave him. I never did actually leave him, except once, briefly . . . I'll tell you about that later; as a novelist you'll relish the incident even if you won't believe it; perhaps most of your readers wouldn't.'

At which point Susan entered and announced dinner.

As they rose, Ruth glanced at the window facing the lake. A blazing sunset was turning everything to gold. The lake was ashimmer, almost blinding.

'Come here, quick,' she said. 'We've got a Turner sunset to celebrate our reunion.'

They stared at the sky and water, studying the wild red and gold, the sinking ball of fire. Venice in Chicago!

The giant, pale yellow-green stalks of asparagus were perfect in texture and taste, and of the right temperature. She heard Mordecai murmur, 'Three stars, lady,' as he placed the tip of one of the fat buttered shoots in his mouth, performing a sword-swallowing act. The roast beef was also exactly to his taste, as were the tiny Irish potatoes in their skins, dripping butter, and the endive salad with the giant Greek olives and tissue-thin slices of onions; and then, finally, the chocolate mousse over which Mordecai couldn't stop exclaiming. Ruth's wines were good California vintage and the French champagne Mordecai had provided finally had the two diners groaning, slouching deep in their chairs. But they talked throughout the meal and Ruth, in turn, cleverly she thought, elicited information about Mordecai that he surely had not intended to provide.

'My next book,' he said finally, 'will have a serious theme: crime without punishment. The idea's been with me for years. Adrian talked to me about it at length, long ago, in Paris.

'More and more, murder for hire is commonplace. Excessive power produces a madness which produces the lust to kill. Power is an abstract thing and can be purely intellectual. Anyway, that's basically my subject. Adrian's subject. I'm also intrigued by the widespread use of torture – we haven't got far from the medieval methods . . . have we? Religious fanatics as well as political tyrants use it. So what else is new?'

Mordecai lit a small cigar. 'Let me take up where Adrian left off. Of course Adrian was becoming overwhelmed far beyond all reason. He was going through a lot – more than anyone realised. He must have had a

secret life neither you nor his family or friends could imagine. His appetites and impulses took hold of him and forced him to act. I simply see a damned interesting theme and story in it – and I mean Adrian – giving me a chance to utilise my peculiar talents. Adrian had much more on his mind than anyone might suspect. His interest in Hacha indicates something worth pursuing.'

He paused, studying his cigar. 'My hope,' he continued, 'is that Adrian had a lot of material I can use. The notebooks, journals and clippings, his letters to you, there's an immense archive I'd like to tackle. And I have a hunch that Adrian's work will save me a lot of digging. And' – he rose and walked towards the window – 'I'd like to use some of Adrian as a character. I don't think of him as Jack the Ripper, for heaven's sakes, but there's more to him than met your eye as well as the world's.'

Ruth sipped from her glass, studied him for a moment, then said, 'Let me tell you something, Mordecai. The stuff Adrian left me as part of his legacy may surprise you. His estate was a pretty hefty one, but these papers, while of no value to a banker, are in a sense, priceless. Even though some of them are clearly ranting and near the lunacy edge, with overtones of fiction. Poetic, too. He was a poet. I haven't read it all frankly, but you'll find it irresistible material.'

She started to laugh. 'It may even shock you, Mordecai. I'm thinking of some of his personal extravaganzas. In the end, however, the most dramatic thing of all, he couldn't record. It was not possible to relate since it dealt with his death.'

Ruth paused, awaiting his response. But his was a poker face.

Ruth said: 'His death by sexual self-immolation may be old hat to you. I suppose, in the end, we all learn that there's really nothing new. But I must say that some of

Adrian's letters are startling – they made me realise how real and personal and alive a letter can be. Adrian's, in many cases, forgetting his pedantic nonsense and the excessive literary allusions, etcetera – are alive, and give us the essential boy and man.'

Mordecai studied Ruth silently for a moment; she watched him with a strange premonition – that he would do or say something disturbing. As she was about to speak he said, 'Ruth, did you know a girl named Janice Gambelli?'

She pondered the question, then said, 'No, I don't think I ever heard of her, knew her. What about her – who was, is she? Should I have known her?'

'Not necessarily. But Adrian knew her. She died in a cloud of mystery. Adrian was somehow involved . . .'

'How do you know about this person, Mordecai? If she was in Adrian's life I would surely have known her.'

'Not necessarily, Ruth. Remember, I'm an ex-newspaper reporter. I pick up oddments, human oddments. Anyway, I was curious about this young woman and I'll probably do a little research on her before I leave town.'

Ruth repeated the name, Janice Gambelli, softly, then shook her head. 'One of Adrian's little secrets perhaps.'

Ruth rose from the table, ringing for Susan. 'We'll be in the study,' she said. 'Hold all calls.' She turned to Mordecai. 'And now to work, Mr Novelist. But first, I want to show you something in the bedroom – and not what you think.'

'Aren't you going to play something for me, first?' he asked, his head tilted as though begging.

'Yes, but on stereo. I'll let you hear some of my recent Bach recordings, okay? Besides, I've had too much wine. Bach calls for a clear head.'

'Okay for now, then,' he replied.

They entered her bedroom and he spotted, instantly,

the framed photo on the end table beside her bed. He walked to it, magnetised, and picked it up, examining it closely.

'I'll be damned,' he said. 'A Man Ray photo of Ruth Breakstone. Right? I'd like a copy of this for my study.'

Ruth laughed. 'Over my dead body. Literally, Mordecai. But I'll tell my trustees to give it to you after my cremation. Not before.'

'I'd adore having it,' he said. Then he added, 'God, what tits.'

'Why thank you, sir. How gallant of you,' she said, laughing. 'But yes, not bad, if I may say so.'

'Really, Ruth, it's stunning. I had no idea. I thought I had seen most of Man Ray's stuff. I have his catalogue. What did Adrian think of it?'

'He never saw it. No one, except Susan. We all have something private in our lives I suppose: this is it, for me. Oh, there are a few other secrets in my life.'

'How did you manage to keep *this* a secret?'

'It was my private act of vengeance, of sorts, against Adrian.' She laughed. 'Call it the bride's revenge.'

'It's not only the breasts, but the hair, the way it falls, the way it is combed. There's nothing so beautiful as a woman's hair when it's right.' He paused. 'Revenge, huh?'

'Yes, sort of.' Then she said, 'Man Ray combed my hair for that shot, he did it with his fingers. He also applied the oil to my breasts with his own hands,' she added softly.

He continued to stare at it. 'What a guy. I wish I had something like this from one of my early periods,' he said wistfully. 'It speaks well for you, your personal qualities, your courage, Ruth. Now I know why you're a great musician, and a great woman.' Then he added, smiling, 'I wish I had had the foresight to do something like that at that age. I have no memorabilia of my youth, no early photos of myself. Nothing.'

He paused and looked searchingly at Ruth, as though to determine her reaction. 'Oh fuck it,' he said. 'I'm getting sentimental. Your fault. That photo of yours. It's a knockout. I'd give anything for it, but I don't want to inherit it from your trustees. You'll outlive me anyway. But thanks, Ruth, for letting me see it. Christ, Ruth, it makes me feel copulative!'

He peered into her eyes for her reaction.

Ruth laughed. 'Something to consider, isn't it?' she said. 'I wanted you to see that photograph of me taken by Man Ray. It was taken on my honeymoon, in Paris, at a period when I was very angry with Adrian. He had done something naughty: fucked an English whore living in Paris at the time, came home with lipstick on his shorts. On our honeymoon, mind you. I loved the guy. Maybe he did it to relieve some of the tension of his marriage. I can't recall what I decided at the time. I was sick in love with him; he could do no wrong, but I was in a rage. The photo. I don't think any copies exist except perhaps in Man Ray's files. Never trust a photographer, I always say. One day I suppose it will pop up in a retrospective show of his. All I know is, I was in a white-hot fury. It was a turning-point in my life, in my not so sentimental education. I was a serious music student,' she went on, her voice quickening. 'When we lived in Paris, you remember, I was determined to be a concert pianist and worked like a demon, and I practised until my fingers and rump ached. At the same time I was a wide-eyed bride, fresh but not especially innocent, but fairly vulnerable. I was devoted, monogamously oriented. He, on the other hand, had had some interesting experiences, and even if some of his adventures were pure fantasy, he had a strong erotic predisposition or appetite, shall we say. However, he confessed to me that his best sex was while masturbating. What a charming thing to tell one's bride, eh?'

'He must have been a barrel of laughs,' said Mordecai. 'I'm all ears, Ruth. Keep talking.'

'Apropos of nothing, except our past, but remembering Man Ray, did you ever meet Kiki?' Ruth asked. 'Man Ray's mistress?'

'No, but I saw her once in a Montparnasse nightclub, drunk as a coot and dancing solo in the aisles, until she had to be literally carried off.'

'Well, I met her once. Never in his studio. I attended an exhibition of Kiki's work. She had a small but interesting talent, and especially with collages, sort of primitive but charming. I had, some time ago, the gallery catalogue, written by the poet Robert Desnos, but it seems to have disappeared. I think Kiki could have made a real career for herself, but her character didn't allow for the discipline.'

'Did you buy any of her work?'

'Unfortunately, not. But I remember that most of her pictures were sold on the first day.'

They moved into the study. He saw a wall of shelves, most of them housing a collection of records; thousands of them.

'My God, all Mozart?' he shouted.

'Mostly Mozart,' she said. 'I mentioned them to you. They are chiefly from my father's collection. But I've added about half: new recordings. I now have two gods. Bach is the other one.'

She pointed to a sofa for Mordecai to sit down, then buzzed for Susan. When she appeared, she asked her to bring 'the boxes', which turned out to be cartons containing several large legal-sized manila expanding envelopes, each carefully bound with violet silk ribbons.

Ruth began removing the envelopes from the cartons and handed them to Mordecai: one was marked LETTERS; another JOURNAL; the third was marked ASSASSINATION/

GANZARA, etc. Another was labelled HACHA AND WHORES. Another said NOTES. Each of the labels was on white paper with large letters in violet ink.

As Mordecai handled the folders he asked, 'Am I allowed to borrow these? What are the ground rules, Ruth? This looks like precious cargo to me.'

'Precious it certainly is, to me. You'll be startled at some of the contents of these folders. Adrian did a lot of reading, research, and writing. He read very widely and in many strange areas. For example, I remember he was preoccupied with Bertolt Brecht's play, *Saint Joan of the Stockyards*.' Ruth paused as if to collect her thoughts. 'Am I boring you?'

'No, no, Ruth. You're wonderful. I wish you'd keep talking. I want this kind of free-wheeling information, your life with Adrian, the hills and valleys of your relationship. That must have been something.'

'Well, yes. Surprises without end. Some of them wouldn't be believed in your novels, and you aren't an amateur in elasticising certain aspects of life.'

'For example?'

'The kind of incidents one finds in certain fiction, the stuff one wants to believe but isn't sure about . . .'

'You mean, like fucking chickens, sleeping with your brother, that sort of thing? Or is it a lower lever of trash you're referring to? I have some suspicions about Adrian's games.'

'His papers and letters,' she said. 'They'll speak eloquently for Adrian. And I'm not being cynical, now.' She paused. She seemed to be weighing a move in a chess game. Then she said, 'My brief marriage convinced me that marriage is less than an ideal state. I learned what alley cats men can be, and that infidelity is universal and if a woman can't accept polygamy as a natural element in her life then she shouldn't marry. Does this strike you as

naïve? Put me down as opposed to marriage. I've been asked why I didn't remarry, and the answer shocked my friends and interviewers: I can't stand a husband who fucks around.'

She added, 'Adrian couldn't resist an interesting or provocative female. As a wife, there's no way I could live with it. Today, in my alleged maturity, I could make accommodations, I think. Secret lives are accommodatable . . .'

Mordecai nodded, made no comment, then continued with his preoccupation. 'Before getting into Adrian's letters and papers, I have a hunch about him; that the dreamy-eyed, curly-haired Adonis had a lot of violence bottled up beneath that poetic, cynical, cultivated façade. Despite his heart condition, I'll bet he could have handled a wild boar barehanded, if the occasion arose. His interest in Ganzara and Hacha and the criminal underbelly of our city, the political machine and the Syndicate, had him bedazzled. Sex wasn't his only catnip. He could have worked well in that world. He could have succeeded anywhere. He proved it, I guess, when he decided to take a shot at commerce. Didn't he?'

At this point, Ruth knew that Mordecai was on to something; that he was more than met the eye. Also, something told her that he had a hard-on for her. It would be interesting. At his age, could he manage it . . .? He appeared so intent.

He pulled out and leafed through one of the scrapbooks, stopped and smiled. 'Ah, this should interest *you*,' he said. 'A quotation from the poet, Tristan Klingsor, and his book, *Scheherazade*. Adrian notes that Ravel set it to music. He read aloud, "Where assassins smile to see the executioner cut off an innocent head with his oriental sword . . ."'

'It's the piece called Asia. I know it well,' Ruth said.

'I'm not going to look at any more of this now, but I'd like it packed and sent air freight to Paris – and please let me make all the arrangements.'

At three that morning Mordecai decided, at Ruth's suggestion, to stay over for the balance of the night.

He left Ruth's apartment before she awoke. His hired driver would meet him at the *Daily News* which would be his first stop. He had a need to check out the Breakstone files; there were elements to the story he required. Consciously or otherwise, Ruth had failed to allude to Kama Jackson in her discussions. He had heard about the woman, but knew almost nothing about her or her role in the lives of Adrian and his father. And Mordecai had forgotten to ask Ruth about the so-called mystery woman.

At the *News* morgue, he came upon a lead that made him lick his authorial chops. An intuitive researcher in arcane areas, he knew that he had to follow up the gossip column reference to 'the woman' who was referred to as an exotic lady related by marriage to the Negro murder-suspect and jazz musician who had killed himself, allegedly. In the crumbling yellowed pages of the paper there was this bit of gold dust – a specific reference to Dr Breakstone, a brief column item, one sentence – that made him sit up. His investigative antennae vibrated.

Finding Kama, 'the woman', was a much easier task than he had anticipated. Luckily, she was indeed alive, and living in Chicago. She had not departed for Paris or parts unknown. Few changes had taken place in her life. One significant change was her marriage to an optometrist named Alexander Wisdom, who, by coincidence, owned the apartment building in which Kama had been living. He was successful, one of the few Negro practitioners of the profession in the city. He was a man of substance, social standing, and had long professed a sweet tooth for Kama. The other change was her doing: Colette had been

replaced by an Australian blue-black terrier named Papageno.

Checking the City Hall records Mordecai found the essential information, and he moved quickly, aggressively. He telephoned her, introduced himself and luckily, she knew his name and had indeed read some of his novels. She would meet him, that very noon, at a neighbourhood coffee shop.

Broad-hipped and full-bosomed, she was still chic, Mordecai thought, attributing her chic not to her red sarong-style dress, not to her lavender shoes, her coal-black and shining straight bob, her small gold looped earrings and the pink-tinted, oversized gold-framed glasses, but rather to the manner in which she moved, held her head, smiled, used her eyes. Chic and worldly wise. A handsome chick if on the over-the-hill side . . . Except his father would have called her *zaftik*.

'Nice to meet one of my favourite authors,' she said on greeting him inside the coffee shop where he had been seated already and waiting.

'Nice to meet a real live fan,' he said, grinning. 'Which of my books did you like best?' he asked, studying her eyes through the pink glasses.

She laughed, opened her purse and pulled out a paperback reprint of one of his earliest novels, *Give Love a Chance*. 'This is my favourite. Would you mind autographing a paperback copy, Mr Ericson? I've read it twice, as you can tell by its condition. I just love this one.'

'Glad to inscribe it for you, but first, should we order some food?'

'Just coffee and a bit of pastry,' she said. 'Too early for lunch.'

They ordered and he signed the book, including in the inscription his favourite line: 'With love and tender feel-

ings', which delighted her, for she broke into a laugh and said, 'Why thank you, sir. Thank you.'

When their food came she said, 'I'd like to come right to the point. And I'm sure, Mr Ericson, you would too.'

'Please call me Mordecai, or Morty as some friends do,' he said. 'As for coming to the point, I'm sure you suspect the worst: I'm writing a novel about Chicago, about violence and passion. Before I go on, do you have any objections to discussing an ancient subject, namely, Dr Breakstone?'

Kama raised her forkful of pastry to her lips and as she began to chew she studied Mordecai's face. Her own was expressionless.

'Is the book you're writing in *story* form, fiction?'

'Naturally, I've never written anything but fiction. But all fiction, as you surely know, is based on one's experience and observation, and one's imagination. No actual names are ever used, of course. And when I do use a situation out of real life I always alter the background and the time. No one has ever sued or tried to sue me for fictional representation. For instance, if I were to use you as a character in a novel, you would never, really never, recognise yourself.'

'I don't know whether to take that as a compliment or a put-down,' Kama said, smiling.

'Neither,' he said. 'A writer creates out of all sorts of materials, including sand and fibres and dreams and stones and stray elements. For example, if you and I were to make love, and I were disposed to use the experience in a story, you wouldn't recognise me, nor yourself, for that matter. The essence of the experience is what I'd try to capture.'

'Fantastic,' she said, laughing. 'Now I know how your books are written. But frankly, could you disguise all of the true aspects of the situation? Would I, assuming I was

a character in that scene, be able to tell for sure that you were writing about me?'

'Perhaps you would,' said Mordecai, 'but I don't think anyone else would.' He paused. 'You are an intelligent, responsive woman; you would identify with the scene we're discussing, but you could never go to court and sue me for describing our lovemaking. Because it could be someone else.'

'Is that due to your legal sense, your caution, your fear of litigation, or simply that the actual is not good enough, that the imagination must be operating?'

'You're marvellous,' said Mordecai. 'You've put it succinctly, better than any literary critic or novelist could. You're a woman of the world.'

'Yeah,' she said, 'a woman of the world, that's me. I've seen a lot of the world and I'm one of the lucky ones. I've had some fun and kept my sanity. And some of my figure.' She laughed. 'But you wanted to see me about something special, didn't you?'

'Yes,' said Mordecai. 'The book I'm writing is pure fiction and romance and action. I heard about Dr Breakstone and somehow it seemed to me that there was something inherent in his murder that would work well into the story I have in mind. Dr Breakstone. You knew him, I gather.'

'You gather correctly. I also knew his son, Adrian. A pretty boy, very bright, tense, with a heart problem, I remember.'

'Exactly,' said Mordecai. 'Adrian is a fairly prominent character in the story I'm planning. A romantic, sexually driven young man with an appetite larger than his capacity, if you get my meaning.'

'I get your meaning. I knew Adrian briefly. We had a few visits, just a few, mind you, and I knew he was on some kind of collision course. He was involved in some

complicated business deal. And – forgive my language – pussy was his undoing.'

'There's a title for my book!' Mordecai exclaimed. Then he turned a serious face to Kama, searched out her eyes, and said, 'Would you care to tell me about Adrian's sex drive? And for that matter, his father's? And I hope I'm not becoming too intrusive. There's no tape recorder here. Whatever you tell me you can deny. Or, for that matter, I may not use. But frankly, I'm fascinated by your sexual hold on father and son. Do you mind?'

'Man, you're moving in fast, and getting mighty personal. You're lucky that you're one of my favourite writers. You know that, don't you? Your questions are getting pretty sticky.'

'Kama, I once was a newspaper reporter – the *Daily News* – and you know what reporters are like. I never got over the brash and crude methods reporters use. Nothing personal. It's all in the interest of what's being written. We call it copy. And I know you're a lot more than copy. You strike me as a live, healthy, happy woman. You may even resent everything I'm saying or leading up to. I hope you realise that it's all impersonal, a novelist at work. That's what it's all about. I'm being selfish. I'd even offer to pay you but I wouldn't want to insult you.' He paused, sipped his coffee. Then he added, 'Authors are takers. They'll take from their own wives, mothers, friends, mistresses, in order to write a book. Parasites. Except, we do entertain you. You admitted that. We hold up a mirror of sorts and show you some aspects of life. A lot of people, women in particular, like to imagine themselves as being in that mirror. You know what I'm saying?'

She studied his face, picked at her pastry. Then she said, 'What do you really want to know?'

He replied simply, earnestly; and for the next hour she

narrated her experiences with Dr Jeremiah Breakstone and his son, Adrian, and the aftermath.

She admitted never having met Adrian's wife, but often having wondered about the 'poor Jewish princess' in Paris. Suddenly she stopped, and said, 'I think that's all I want to say about the whole mess. I'm a happily married woman, I lead a good quiet life. I have a few friends in from time to time. My husband's business keeps him occupied *very much*. You understand. Now then, would you like to come back to my apartment for a brandy? The afternoons are lonely. You would be most welcome, Mordecaï.'

He did not show his surprise, nor did he hesitate to accept her invitation. They returned to her apartment where he remained for almost an hour. Kama was the first woman he had made love to in recent years who was in his own age-bracket. 'I fucked an old woman today,' he said to himself, 'a woman about my age . . .' He would assuredly use the episode in a novel, soon.

Paris

Dear Ruth:

Forgive the delay in writing. Intrusions and the usual pile-up. Great flight: caviar all the way. The booze on these Concordes gets you there fast, too. From now on, for at least two weeks, it's OM, and buttermilk in my isolation booth; work/diet/silence on the Rue de Grenelle. And a little quiet fucking.

You looked radiant, in every way. You're a glowing example, Ruth, of 'life begins after forty'.

Oh yes, I was able to see a lot of the city before I returned; one day's prowling on the West Side, the two-family-house bohunk streets (now entirely black) where Mayor Hacha lived as a lad. Cheerless as a Dublin slum. I also got to go to and through the

South Side. I've now got plenty of raw material to work with. Lots of discipline to exercise. In the past month I put on eight pounds. I've got to go on a starvation kick. For the next two weeks I'll be beating up my IBM, with the help of buttermilk and some of that good stuff. Hope to get down to 200 pounds!

Adrian's papers arrived safely and are in my office vault. In due course you'll get them all back, intact. Some of the holographic stuff I may have typed up – under the most secure auspices. *Grazie*!

and love, Mordecai

PS Oh yes, almost forgot: I met a lady named Kama, and got some filler material for the book; some of it pretty sizzly.

PPS I find a notation about a taxi-dance girl in Adrian's files. Can you fill me in on this? Something out of the blue . . .

Tangier

Shalom, Mordecai:

Happy to hear from you. Enjoying my quiet and quasi-sybaritic life in my Arab hideaway. Playing five hours each day nevertheless. A bit tired. It was an exhausting long season, though rewarding. Age may be creeping up . . . must resume my daily exercises. My aching back. I'll show you how it's done if you want to reduce that paunch of yours. Nothing personal, my friend. Been reading the reviews of my past session. Very nice all in all; not to mention the loot. But now, rest and pleasure.

Pleasuring myself, that's the day's programme. What I have here in Tangier is refuge. Enjoying my arranged comforts, simple luxuries, and my latest acquisitions.

What is it like, this hideaway? The kasbah and I

live cheek by jowl, and I'm protected by a flower- and vine-covered eight-foot-high wall, with an ancient ivy-covered gate. A desiccated old man guards it for me. The air has an odour of mint, and the sky which I see through various filigreed windows, is the purest picture-postcard blue; and when someone asks, 'Who lives in that charming little house in the garden behind that high wall?' the answer is, 'An American broad (ageing) who's always pounding out her heart and hands on a piano . . .' But, as I was saying, since you did ask about my house and life here there's lots of 'good stuff' as you call it; and I think you would enjoy the kef atmosphere (or effluvium) that prevails; and lots of stereo tapes; beautiful fruit to look at and eat; roast lamb most delicate, a few friends (writers, too), soft days, larger-than-life roses in and around the garden inner wall. I can see you utilising my sitting-room for one of your scenes: very *seraglio*!

I really don't mind answering most of your questions. Don't bother about sharing royalties, please. I'd rather you kept me out of it entirely; my tax burdens are not minor. And I have no 'favourite charities', just a few indulgences and a few friends. The indigent never leave empty-handed.

Now to your question about *that* dance-hall girl. Yes. it's true. She was a dark Gypsy type, a bit unwashed, dirty-looking, in her early twenties, I'd say. Maybe nineteen. Younger than I, certainly. Probably Algerian, maybe part Italian. Sexy, yes; a touch of Sophia Loren around the eyes. I know, Mordecai: when a man looks at a certain type of female the word, cunt, comes to his mind. Instantly. This one certainly aroused such a thought. She wore no underwear and her body, including her pubis, showed clearly through her thin blue dress. It's all

still quite vivid in my mind (a woman's memory bank! and who could forget that particular 'happening'?!). I raged a bit when I found her in our hotel apartment, on my return from school one afternoon. Mind you, we were still on our honeymoon. It's unlikely one invents incidents like this, not in the Western world . . . anyway.

Adrian said he met her at a French dance-hall, sort of a dime-a-dance version. What brought him to such a place I did not attempt to explore. I remember studying her and wondering what he had in mind about her. She had very little English. She was a sexy slut and I could have murdered her without compunction. Adrian suggested a little ol' *ménage à trois* since she had no home. A common arrangement, he said. And he added I might like to *try* her too. I said thanks a lot, no, not even if she took a few baths. I eschewed that scene! (If you don't believe all of this, I'll understand.)

I told Adrian I was leaving him for good and when he asked what and where, I said I was going to go out and find a dog and fuck it. (As you may gather, I was rapidly changing from the proper young Chicago druggist's daughter under Adrian's tutelage.) I took a hotel room for a few days and then I phoned him. I had a few visits with a young female novelist. He was in a frenzy; said the girl was gone and for me to return. I returned. Why do women succumb, accept such bullshit treatment?

Shortly thereafter, I met, and took for revenge, a secret lover, a young Indian from Madras, who taught me many interesting things . . . but that was a long time ago. Make what you will of it on your IBM typewriter; it'll make it throb.

Love,

Ruth

PS Did I mention a guest room here? It's yours if you should decide to escape 'from it all' and care to visit me . . .
PPS At the risk of shocking you I must put down what I think about Adrian in the 'bottom-line' sense. Like his father, he was sexually curious, adventuresome, insatiable. Sex was on his mind most of the time. Adrian's behaviour was part of what I called the Breakstone Syndrome, or Condition. It confirmed what I was beginning to learn, that all men lead secret lives, fantasy lives but not the kind women lead . . .

April, Tangier

Dear Mordecai:

I feel like recording a few random thoughts. Frankly, I think it is my memories that give me the greatest zest, give the most meaning to the present. Specific virtuoso performances. (A gold medal in Moscow, another in Italy.) I've had adventures and pleasures and triumphs: halls ringing with applause and bravas. Conquering a particularly difficult piece of music and performing it to some special critic's or musician's delight: that gives meaning, somehow, to these old bones and arteries. While most of the music reviewers' platitudes are tiresome, there are half a dozen musicologists whose words are like caviar to my ego's palate. I love to take risks and expose myself to these responsive few.

I think I'll go to my piano now and limber up on a few Scarlatti sonatas. Meanwhile, come to Tangier and I'll share some of my indecent memories and exposures (on the piano keys) with you.

One hour has passed. Now back to you, my friend: in a recent letter with numbered questions, you asked me if, in my present frame of mind, I had problems or fears, fear of anything. Interestingly, I don't fear death or the ravages

of old age. I can manage to handle imminent death: one learns about such matters in Tangier. When you come here and listen to some *Jilala* music, you will know what I'm saying.

What I fear, dear friend, is loss of memory, the inability to recall a musical phrase when performing publicly. The day I find I have a real memory lapse while playing, I'll check out and go to a nunnery.

By the way, a not too distant neighbour in these parts is Paul Butler: composer, writer, man of wisdom, a gentle man; and his house guest is Jimmy Baldwin. They stopped in the other night and we had an improvised concert: *le style hot*. First time in years, real boogie-woogie, too.

Tell me when you're coming.

Love,

Ruth

Paris

Dear Ruth:

Murder Takes a Holiday. Ergo, am comin' around the mountain, in about a week. Okay? Maybe I'll stay. Can't wait to see you. Alas, the arthritis is setting in, but not where it matters.

M.

Chapter Twenty-one

(Cable to Ruth one week later)

ARRIVING TANGIER THIS SATURDAY RESERVED
SUITE MUNIRIYA NO REFLECTION ON YOUR
HOSPITALITY HOPE TO SEE YOU NOONISH
LOVE

MORDECAI

Susan immediately telephoned the manager of the Muniriya, the one de luxe hotel in town, confirming Mordecai's reservation. He had requested it through a travel agent: 'best accommodation available'. Which meant a two-bedroom apartment overlooking the sea, plus a private bath and seviceable plumbing, Allah willing.

Ruth ordered a gift of fruit and flowers for his room on arrival. She also began making preparations and phone calls for an authentic gala Moroccan welcome. Luckily, there were several interesting celebrity tourists in town.

Susan, Ruth, and Ruth's favourite, six-foot-four Ahmed, servant and friend, began planning the entertainment and provisions. A dozen more potted plants were ordered for the lawn and house, to supplement the scrubbier ones: giant-size blue and pink hydrangeas, two of which would be stationed at the gate's entrance.

The following Saturday, shortly after noon, Mordecai was heard knocking at the outer gate, pounding the great brass knocker. (The antique knocker Ruth had found in Portobello Road; it comprised a pair of brass breasts with half-inch thick nipples of brass, with a buxom dimpled

brass face in-between. 'Knockers, doubling in brass,' Ruth would say.)

Ahmed hurried to the gate, opened the large, creaky door and greeted Mordecai at once. An old man who sat in front of the gate, immobile, a venerable guardian of sorts, was accepting coins from Mordecai, bowing his thanks with head to the dust.

The house, its garden path banked with numerous pots of flowers, violets, roses and dramatic varicoloured amaryllis, stopped Mordecai momentarily. He looked bedazzled as though stepping into a magical world after having just escaped the clutch of swarming beggars and noisy children, not forgetting the unpaved and deeply rutted road, the poverty, squalor and dust. It was a floral heaven he beheld now, an intoxication zone, and he realised at once its enchantment and tranquillity. He stood motionless at the entrance to the path leading to the house, and his arms were outstretched. 'Ah,' was all he was able to say as he surveyed the house, the flowers, plants and trees, and Ruth, who was fast approaching him.

'*Shalom* and welcome and hi you all,' said Ruth, embracing him.

He surveyed her, stood back, then said, 'Here I am, a fat man in Eden. Somebody said Tangier is part slum, part heaven, and I'd say right now that I'm in the heaven part.'

Then he added, 'Just look at those violets,' pointing to a long curving row of about a hundred potted African violets of various colours, lining the path leading to the house.

He greeted Susan as an old friend, and was interested to see that she was not now dressed as a maid or servant. Her white silk slacks and pink blouse exhibited a figure he had barely suspected; an eyeful, he noted. A dish.

Ruth introduced him to Ahmed with particular care.

Ahmed bowed from the waist, a sweep of the arm indicating a royal welcome, and his prayerful hands were elegantly placed together to underscore his Moslem negritude. Ahmed was young, broad of shoulder, slender of waist, dressed in an embroidered snow-white *djellaba* which contrasted strikingly with his slender dark hands and face. His eyes were large and bright, his smile warm, the teeth pure ivory and impossibly perfect. Mordecai understood at once why Ruth was taken with him, had a special relationship with him. A ten-inch cock man. A well-hung man for all seasons, thought Mordecai . . . and young. He made Mordecai feel twenty pounds heavier than he was.

'We'll take a walk later to our favourite little beach, Merkala,' Ruth said. 'But first, a drink for Mordecai. Scotch perhaps?'

'Perfect, and on the rocks if available.'

'Ahmed, on the rocks,' said Ruth, and he was off with a smile.

'And lest I forget,' Mordecai said, 'your gifts: the baskets of fruit and flowers turned my dreary rooms into a garden. Many thanks.'

She took his arm, followed by Susan, and they moved towards the house. Ahmed was already on his way back with Mordecai's drink. They entered the living-room and Mordecai halted, stopped as though struck by a bolt of lightning.

The ground floor was divided into two large areas: one half was a living-room and the other half was obviously the music room, separated by a floor-to-ceiling double wall of plate glass, edged by a narrow mahogany scalloped moulding of Moroccan design: a great square glass cage. In the centre of the music room stood, startlingly, a great white gleaming Steinway grand piano on a large white rug. And on one wall Mordecai noted at once a Matisse and a

Bonnard, both with similar subjects: small nude odalisque figures in vivid reds, blues, greens and pinks.

Ruth explained that the dampness in Tangier made it impossible to accommodate a piano – the strings loosened constantly – so she had constructed an air-conditioned, dust-and-damp-proof glass room or cage for herself and the piano. The other walls were of raw burnt-sienna brick. Here she practised, played for her guests, and also made some recordings, with electronic equipment which also transmitted music to all parts of the house. From the piano, in a year-round temperature of 75°, she could observe her guests.

'Please sit down at the piano,' he begged Ruth. 'I want to remember you in this scene.'

She laughed and slid the glass door open. She seated herself on the white goatskin-covered bench and lowered her hands to the keyboard. She began to play slowly, leisurely, an adagio movement, an especially slow and haunting passage, and Mordecai suddenly realised he was listening to one of Erik Satie's compositions, and he remembered her photo and what she had told him of her early Paris days, when she had played Satie for Man Ray, sitting at his piano, being photographed.

Was she recalling now, as he was, that incomparable scene? Time and mood, were they recurring, as in a dream state? Was this a playback?

'*Madonna mia*!' he exclaimed as she continued playing, 'it was worth coming from Paris for this alone.'

She was still at the piano, lost in the musical poetry of Satie; and Mordecai applauded slowly, softly, and she smiled as she saw his hands approving, so lovingly.

Then she stopped playing, rose, returned to him. They walked through the house and she showed him the guest room, among others. She reminded him that it could have been available to him.

'I'm sorry you didn't take up my offer,' she said, 'but I know how precious privacy is, and at the Villa Muniriya you will have that, plus the best hotel service in Tangier. They have an excellent receptionist, in case you expect messages or want to make calls.'

'Thanks for understanding,' he said. 'It doesn't mean I won't be taking advantage of your hospitality, enjoying your house, and you.'

Ahmed approached and handed Ruth a drink on a small brass tray.

'My midday nourishment,' she said. 'Jack Daniels à-la-screwdriver. You'll think of me as an old souse,' she said, smiling, 'but with age comes wisdom, and I'm sure that Confucius or Mohammed or Frank Sinatra would agree that after one reaches one's maturity one should do what one damned well pleases. And this pleases me.' She laughed and took a sip from her glass. 'I can feel it right here,' she said, pointing to her navel.

Mordecai was dazzled by the house: loops of Berber amber and silver necklaces hung on walls and in corners; rugs, pillows, masks, skins and numerous exotic musical instruments were to be seen everywhere. There was also a surprising collection of narghiles in one corner of the room. And others about the entire house, too. Everywhere were small brass-topped tables, where guests could drink, eat, recline. And there were several huge sofas with velvet and silk tasselled and embroidered pillows from Fez and Marrakesh and from obscure little villages in the mountains.

Ahmed brought Mordecai another scotch, his second, and Mordecai declined it, shaking his head sadly. 'That one would do me in right now. But thanks.'

Susan was standing by, listening, observing. 'We have some plans for your entertainment and special pleasure,'

she said, smiling roguishly. 'And I hope you brought a good appetite with you.'

'Well,' said Mordecai, 'all of my appetites! But as for food – well, I'm a simple bred-in-Chicagoan, a pastrami man, and what does one do in Tangier about that?'

Susan smiled. 'Well, we have wonderful camel and antelope steaks that can be seasoned and made to look and taste like pastrami.'

Ruth laughed. 'This I'd like to see,' said Mordecai. 'On sober consideration, though, I'll pass; it's too late in life to make such a gastronomical leap.' Then he added, 'But you can count on me to accommodate a few nuts, raisins, a bit of bread, fruit and cheese . . . I'll get along.'

'We can do better than that,' said Ruth. 'I think you'll like our house speciality: crisp barbecued lamb. Right?'

'You've scored,' he said. 'Nice and crisp.'

'Nice and crisp.'

Later they strolled towards the beach. 'I hate to intrude with business,' Mordecai said, 'on this glorious, sunny day, on such a brief visit, but you understand that I'm here for some help. I'll come to the point, Ruth: I need some fill-in detail on Judge Minelli. Adrian's comments and notes on this character make me want to know more than I now do. For example, when did he die, or disappear or whatever? And what happened?'

Ruth was silent for a moment, then said, 'It's a bit complicated; some of what I'm going to tell you I learned third-hand. So make what you will of it; you're the novelist.'

'I'm listening,' said Mordecai, 'and damned intrigued.'

'Well, you know Minelli married Johnny Torino's only daughter. She was what some might uncharitably call an ugly duckling. I met her only once. She was indeed very plain, but she had decent features. She was certainly not

the kind of woman Minelli would have chosen as his bride, normally. You know the kind of man he was, and where his taste ran.'

'Yes,' said Mordecai, 'a pimp, a whoremaster, and sodomist among other things; his wife would have had, normally, to come from the loins of a Caligula. She'd have to be a fourteen-year-old whore, but beautiful, a show-piece.'

'Exactly. So how did their marriage work out?' Mordecai studied her face as they walked, waiting. 'It seemed to be a conventional marriage. I know they entertained modestly, and made the usual social appearances at those functions Minelli considered important. They visited the home of her parents twice monthly, for dinner. You must understand that Torino was both rich and powerful. That little, soft-spoken man could have been the dictator of a country. He had iron in his veins. Adrian's notes gave you his essential story. He retired, went to Italy; then he came back to America because he was bored. When he finally died – a natural death – Minelli's wife (nee Torino) inherited millions of dollars; and when her mother died she inherited again, large blocks of real estate.'

'Now,' said Mordecai, 'what happened to the Minelli marriage? Did her father's death turn the judge off? I'm sure his had been a frustrated unhappy life, playing nice husband to Torino's daughter. What happened? I can't seem to get a fix on his life. Nothing!'

Ruth smiled. 'I must confess, Mordecai, my interests broadened after Adrian's death. I made a few inquiries, learned a bit about the people in the "big picture" as they say, the people who were part of Adrian's obsession, namely Hacha. I got to learn a lot about this whore, Viola, now turned madam, and made it my business to meet and know her. What a marvellous discovery and friendship, of sorts, opened up. She almost persuaded me that being a

madam was the ideal profession; she is really something special.'

Mordecai laughed. 'Tell me more.'

'Well,' said Ruth, 'I finally got from Viola a good part of the Hacha story. She started him in the whorehouse profession, long before he became Mayor. You've read Adrian's stuff on that. I wanted to learn all about Adrian's death. Viola managed the house where Adrian spent his last night. She was Hacha's woman until he died. She saw and talked with him a few days before he died, in the Miami hospital.' She paused, laughing, and continued, 'I didn't mean to connect the two, Adrian and Hacha, but Viola was – strangely – in on both their deaths. Viola is now living in Tucson, Arizona, retired, operating a small, personal sort of house. She also went there for the climate, you know. Concentrates on sexagenarians. No pun intended.'

'I'd like her address,' Mordecai said. 'Meanwhile, let's get back to Minelli, Ruth.'

Ruth took his arm and said, 'Let's rest for a minute or two, there's a bench there, and we can watch the sea. It's so beautiful, don't you agree?'

They sat down, remained silent for a moment, then Ruth said, 'Okay. Minelli. That man, smart as he was, made a fatal mistake. He fired his servant, Jacob. He thought he ought to get a younger man for the job. Jacob had been with him for years, knew everything, probably too much, where too many bodies were buried, who paid Minelli – in cash, that is – and so forth.'

'A stupid thing to do, firing that man, a life-indentured slave.'

'Exactly. So it proved to be. Jacob needed vengeance; had a long chat with Minelli's wife. Told her about Cora, told her about Lou Prouty and other matters. Poor Mary Minelli. She discovered most of her husband's secrets. She

kept the disclosures to herself and then her parents died. Minelli no longer needed to defer to the Torinos. When he tried to make a massive anal entry, she became his enemy. She had no father, no mother to run to for help, advice. This all happened shortly after her mother's death. She had her father's instincts. She was a realist. And vindictive. And rich. She decided to extinguish her distinguished husband. She paid Jacob handsomely to do the job for her. Jacob drugged Minelli's nightcap of port wine – it's right out of Medici history. He put the judge to sleep, and then he rammed a Coca-Cola bottle up the judge's ass, smashing it with a hammer when it was all in; and the two departed. She went to Sicily. Jacob disappeared with a gift of cash from Mary. Minelli lived for a ghastly few days, but the internal bleeding did him in. He was inoperable. End of the Judge Angelo saga. And don't ask for any more details from me. The subject makes me sick, truly. But when and if you look up Viola in Tucson, you may get more anecdotes about Minelli. And you may be sure she was no admirer of his.' Ruth paused, then added, chuckling, 'I love that Viola; a real survivor.'

Mordecai was looking at the sky, the sea before him. 'I've got to sort some of this out, especially Viola. Where did she get all the information?'

'Ah, you don't know Viola. Of course. Her instincts for reality were frightening. She made enduring friends. She was, is, a mine of information.'

'Looks like I'll have to make that trip to Tucson,' said Mordecai.

'You could do worse,' said Ruth. 'A very wonderful woman.'

'So,' said Mordecai, 'you, too, Ruth, are one of the survivors, the last of the Mohicans.'

'Well, I did escape! I've got my health, most of it. And you're helping me wash the remnants out of my hair, my

system. Keep the notes, the journals, the letters that I gave you. Burn them when you're through.' She seemed almost angry now.

He waited. Then she added: 'You know nothing about me or my personal life after Adrian. How I studied almost a solid year with Nadia Boulanger, in both Paris at 36 Rue Ballu – the address is etched in my brain – and one summer at her Fontainebleau chateau. I had a year at the American Conservatory and a short but good period with Jean Françaix. You'll find all this background stuff in *Who's Who*, of course. But I want you to know that after Adrian and his incredible family, I shut out everything but my music. I slaved for almost ten years to get where I am. I've played everywhere . . .' A pained expression crossed her face.

Mordecai looked at her, surprise on his face. 'Did I say something to hurt you, Ruth? I certainly meant nothing of the kind.'

'No,' she said, 'but I suddenly came to realise how Adrian almost fucked up my life – up to a certain point, that is. Luckily, it didn't affect my music, my career. How lucky I was to have *that*.'

'Your father's genes and chromosomes, plus a lot of other wonderful elements, they helped you survive and achieve. You're extraordinarily lucky.'

'Luck is the word, but sweat too,' she said. 'I could have wound up in a loony bin.'

'Not you, Ruth.'

'Well, a loony bin with a piano.' She laughed, took his hand and said, 'Let's get back. We've got guests coming, you know, in your honour.'

Later, on returning home, they found guests already arriving, including the legendary Libby Berman. Mordecai was at once attentive to the sultry Libby. She was dressed in a black chiffon knee-length dress, and it was

not clear whether she was wearing a bra; a black chiffon bandeau served merely as a semi-transparent cover, a scrim, to both convey and conceal her breasts and glowing nipples, her smouldering beauty. The crimson aureolae seemed to burn like coals. She looked pleased and grateful for Mordecai's attention, and announced that she was a fan of his and in fact, was presently reading his current novel. Like so many beauties who were approaching the over-the-hill stage, Libby seemed happy to be remembered, but for her talents rather than for her complicated personal history; a history heavy in tragic events.

Mordecai thought how gladly he would fuck this extraordinary woman. He thought of her in terms of his passion, as a very young man, for Alla Nazimova. He had seen the Russian actress perform in *Hedda Gabler*, and remembered telling friends that he would give a year's salary if she would spend one night with him and allow him to eat her . . .

Music suddenly enlivened the room, Beatle music. And the new Lennon-Yoko Ono record stopped all conversation. Either Ahmed or Susan had put the record on for Libby's pleasure. For she smiled and said, 'Ah, John's new recording, with Yoko, a marvellous record.'

'So Lennon has come out of his five years' hibernation,' said Mordecai. 'Let's listen. I love that man.'

The record contained a moving version of the famous Eddie Cantor song, 'Making Whoopee', Yoko's version, a charming paraphrase. Mordecai was tempted to tell Libby that he remembered hearing her torch songs in Chicago. It was at Eddie's dark, cavernous club, a Near North Side café with a mirrored ceiling, and a floor inlaid with silver dollars. It was here that millionaire Chicago playboys tossed hundred-dollar bills at her feet as she sang her mournful ballads. And he remembered one particular night when an obese, greasy, loud drunk was heard to say,

'She's all cunt,' and he watched her walk slowly towards him and slap his face, then return and resume her song beside the piano amidst wild applause. But none of this he would presume to recall to Libby, a sultry and yet proper lady, come to pay her respects to a fêted novelist in Ruth Breakstone's home.

Susan came over and sat beside her, along with Mordecai. Libby asked for mint tea, although, Mordecai suspected, the request was a euphemism or code for something more potent, more exotic. As they sat there, Mordecai found himself studying Susan, and he tried to equate her with the young woman who had cooked and served him dinner in Chicago, in Ruth's South Shore Drive apartment. Now, here, in her Moroccan clothes and present ambience, he saw her in a new light, transformed; saw a sensuality and femininity that had eluded him in his first meeting. He even noted a dimple in her cheek, and a heightened colour. It was obvious that her role in Ruth's life was multifaceted, beyond that of a servant. Later, this was confirmed when guests began to arrive. He saw how gracefully she received friends and how she was given respectful and cordial greetings by all.

Paul Potter suddenly arrived. He brought with him two Arab musicians with instruments, Arabs who spoke no English but were all smiles and bows and eagerness as they were presented to Mordecai.

A young Algerian belly dancer appeared, and now she was dancing to some flute music performed by Potter's friends, and Paul accompanied them softly at the piano. He proved to be a skilful pianist. Despite his understated, subdued manner, he contributed considerable gaiety to the party because of his amiable personality, his conversational and anecdotal talent.

As the belly dancer cavorted in a slow, trance-like tempo, Mordecai rose and danced briefly with her,

disco-style. Surreptitiously (he thought) he slipped a hundred-dollar bill to her, together with his hotel card and room number.

Soon the party developed into a conversational free-for-all. When Tom Edwards the playwright arrived, he seemed shy, lonely, furtive. He was accompanied by a very young blond youth, a catamite, Mordecai assumed. Susan brought Edwards to Mordecai at once. The two men spoke briefly about film and book critics and reviewers and how they were all a dastardly breed, neurotic bastards, suited for concentration-camp ovens or worse. And next to reviewers came the publishers. Having covered the most obvious literary matters they turned to the problems of the middle-aged sphincter and the prostate gland, subjects of concern to Edwards and introduced by him. Then came the subject of drinking. Edwards, with an arm around his friend's shoulder, piously declared himself a teetotaller, as of that particular day. He asked for mint tea, and scotch for his young companion. He commented to Mordecai on Ahmed's handsome physique. 'Spectacular, wouldn't you say?' Then he added, following Ahmed hypnotically with his eyes, 'Just look at that small tight ass of his, will you? Now that really zaps me!'

'At the moment,' said Mordecai, 'there's another ass holding my attention; it belongs to Libby Berman.'

'She happens to be a dear old friend of mine,' said the playwright, unsmiling, his moustache seeming to bristle. The subject was dropped. Mordecai studied Libby and sensed that she had entered a sort of alpha state. Perhaps coke? *Quaalaudes*? That mint tea? She had a faraway look now. It had probably all been preceded by a good fuck, he mused. He decided to dismiss the subject; he recognised a conversational terminal point when it was reached.

Another musician arrived and Ruth greeted him with special warmth and a degree of solemnity, the fingers of

her hands in steeple formation. He was, Mordecai learned, a famous Moroccan folk musician, a specialist in *Jilala* music, so-called trance music, played on long, low- pitched transversal flutes and flat hand drums. When he finally sat down, his legs disappearing beneath his long jacket, he proceeded to drink tea. Then he deposited the glass on the floor, picked up his instrument and everyone stopped talking. The air thickened with kef and tobacco smoke. The lights were lowered and everywhere, pillows and couches were occupied with lounging, dreamlike figures. He played and Ruth again appeared at her piano and began to accompany the *Jilala* music softly, slowly. She played, it seemed, with just two fingers. The crystal notes fell slowly, punctuating the flute-player's theme, the rubato of his acceleration and hesitation. A trance-like atmosphere developed, a lulling ease. It was readily seen how this music could possess one, transform a roomful of people into a field of dreamers. Mordecai began to sense a powerful effect taking over. He looked at the guests. They were entranced. He studied Susan, dressed in a harem costume: reds and oranges and a gauzy scarf swirled about her like a cloud; she wore lush gold jewellery, and she was sitting back on a low-pillowed seat, drinking champagne. Her hair was down now, black and long, reaching her waist. Mordecai was suddenly moved. He had never attended a party quite so harmonious; and it was in his honour.

The Moroccan music stopped. Ruth remained at the piano. She began to play a Bach fugue; then halted abruptly, saying audibly, 'Oh shit.' And she approached the *Jilala* musician and urged him to continue with his playing, which he did.

The belly dancer resumed her dancing, without musical accompaniment but with finger cymbals. She seemed to have her eye on Mordecai and her dancing developed an intensity not visible heretofore. Her thighs and belly

rolled, rippled like water under the wind, magically; it was impossible to ignore her. Mordecai's face had a fixed stare. He was, however, staring at Susan.

Ruth sat down beside Mordecai. 'I must tell you something funny,' she said. 'The music you were listening to – it's used in certain religious rites. *Jilala* musical rites; and persons of Jewish faith or origin, African or other Jews, are strictly not welcome, not permitted to listen to it. It's *verboten*! So how many Jews are there in this house?'

Mordecai laughed. 'Hah, you and me, baby, the last of the Mohicans. Unless that belly-dancing cunt is Jewish.'

Ruth took Ahmed aside, Mordecai noted, and spoke with him briefly. Ahmed listened intently, nodded, smiled and left the room.

Through a haze Mordecai saw that the guests were leaving; most paid him personal respects and uttered all the platitudes due a guest of honour and a world-famous novelist. He glanced at his watch and saw that it was past midnight. He noted the belly dancer's glance towards him as she departed, alone; he thought how good it would be having her sitting on his face, swaying slowly . . .

When the last guest was gone, Susan suddenly appeared with two bottles of Dom Perignon, one in each hand. She stood in the centre of the room, grinning.

'I held these back for just us chickens,' she said. 'Want to open one?' she said, addressing Mordecai. 'Icy and ready.'

'If you can handle it, I can,' he said, and he took one bottle from her and proceeded to uncork it.

'A great night, a great party,' said Mordecai. 'One of the best ever. Your guests – well, it was a star-studded cast. That man, Edwards . . . a great playwright but socially puzzling. I think he's lonely when he isn't writing. His next autobiographical book should be entitled *My Typewriter, My Bride*.'

They laughed and he poured two glasses almost to their

rims, giving one to each of them. He sat down, sipped, and felt a carbonisation in his blood. Then suddenly he felt an exhaustion. A melancholy shadow crossed his face, a note of loneliness, disappointment. Ruth sat down beside him.

There had not been a fulfilling encounter for him; the evening had provided idle exchanges and interesting faces, but there was for him, despite the compliments paid by her guests, an empty feeling. In speaking of Edwards's loneliness, was he not speaking for himself? Was he not in the end, a solitary, the worker who stood apart and observed? He had often been called, crudely, a workaholic.

He pulled himself out of the reverie and said, with an intensity and earnestness that surprised himself, 'It was an absolutely marvellous party, marvellous.'

'I'm so glad,' said Ruth. 'I was afraid you would find some of the guests boring. Some of them are, let's face it, so narcissistic, self-consumed.'

'No, no,' he said. 'My types. I enjoyed them all and can't thank you enough.' He looked into Ruth's eyes, admiringly, aware of her charm, energy, durability. He thought of a few other grand-dame pianists and how dowdy they were, matronly and ageing in manner despite their stage gowns and hair and public adulation. Ruth had fire in her eyes; her lips were shaped for smiling and her figure, it was the body of a disciplined sensual woman who savoured life. She would never drag ass across a concert stage regardless of age; she knew how to walk, to dress, to move her elegant chassis: like a queen. He must tell her so!

'I won't forget this night,' he said. He put his hand on her knee.

He studied the two women, then said, 'I suppose you're both curious about my manuscript, and how I've handled

your persona, Ruth. Well, very soon I'll let you read a few sections of it, and I hope you'll find it – truthful, and publishable.' He laughed and added, 'You'll remember my mentioning a girl named Janice Gambelli; well, she's a member of the cast.'

'Yes, you did mention her name to me, Mordecai. I'm more than a little curious about her; did she have a role in our life – Adrian's and mine?'

'All I can say in answer at this moment is, definitely yes.' Then he continued: 'It's done, but needs some reorganising, restructuring, a few finishing touches. And yes, there's one scene that I'm counting on you to resolve for me . . .'

'What scene is that?' Ruth asked, watching him over the edge of her wineglass. His face was deadpan, emotionless.

Then he said, 'More details as to what really happened to Adrian in the end, for example. I think of it as the self-immolation scene.'

Ruth took a cigarette from the brass tray before her and lit it. She blew a cloud of yellow smoke towards the canopy-draped ceiling. Then she turned to Susan and said, 'Should I tell him, Susan, or show him instead?' Her voice was on a pianissimo level, but he heard her distinctly. He waited.

Susan leaned forward and asked, 'Have we aroused your interest sufficiently, Mordecai?'

'You've aroused my interest,' he heard himself saying. 'And by the way, do you have a snort of the really good stuff on the premises? It's late; I think I could make good use of it . . .'

Ruth turned to Susan. 'But of course. Susan, can you fetch some, dear?'

Susan left the room, returned instantly with a small silver receptacle, not much larger than a pillbox. She lowered herself to the floor, sat cross-legged before him and held it out to him in the palm of her hand.

He pulled out a miniature spoon hanging from a gold chain around his neck and dipped it into the box. The white powder was clearly visible, like a bit of snow or crushed aspirin highlighted by the sun. Each nostril received a serving, an inhalation of the powder. He placed the tiny box on the table before him, thrust his chin into the air and inhaled again, deeply, audibly. Then he rose from his seat.

'Okay, you cunts, tell me and show me,' and he began slowly to remove his tie and jacket. The women rose and each at his side escorted him to Ruth's bedroom. It was an all-white and windowless room, huge and bedraped in white satin. The bed was covered with a thick lambskin blanket hanging over and down to the floor, with vermilion and turquoise pillows piled in lavish confusion against the headboard. The scene was unique in one respect: there was a tall, broad-shouldered, mahogany-coloured man, totally naked, standing in one corner of the room. He was fondling a long string of large amber beads, Berber jewellery. His *djellaba* was neatly folded and lying on a small stool near the window. His incredible cock hung blue-black and idling; formidable.

Ruth had disappeared, and when she returned a few minutes later, she was wearing a blonde wig which altered her image. She began to remove her clothes, as did Susan whose full, erect breasts startled him.

Ruth said, 'Mordecai, when I go, as Adrian said to me several times, it will be not with a whimper but with a bang – a gang-bang.' She was stepping out of her panties as she spoke and Mordecai watched her spellbound.

'That sounds like a prelude to something interesting,' said Mordecai. 'Like an orgy, maybe?' he asked, smiling.

'Well, that's a bit old-fashioned,' she said. 'It's going to be a feminist happening, if that's the correct description. I don't like the word, feminist, but I'm essentially one. I

learned the art of taking over out of necessity. I've discovered that women, in many parts of the world – outside of Islam, that is – are leading, taking over, sometimes by indirection, but taking over . . .'

Mordecai replied, 'But what have you really learned, as a woman, forgetting the feminist part?'

'From my more than half-century of involvement as a woman,' said Ruth, 'I've learned that while many women are cunts (men taught me that), all men are assholes. I think that's really the essence of what I've learned about life. Most regrettable is the fact that most women don't know what it means to be a woman.'

Mordecai laughed. Ruth turned and looked at him, then said, 'Susan, please help Mordecai get undressed; unzip the man. Hurry dear.'

His obesity became evident – those fucking rolls of fat – as he became undressed. 'By the way,' he said, as Susan bent to find the zipper of his pants, 'when you read some of my manuscript, a certain almost completed section, you'll be surprised at a sequence in a seduction scene – the hot young lover discovers that he can't get it up.'

Ruth turned her head and said, 'But he does, eventually, doesn't he?'

'Oh yes, but with considerable assistance.'

'Isn't it usually like that, more or less?' asked Ruth, smiling. She was now spraying her naked thighs and breasts with a huge atomiser; the scent was *Bal à Versailles*. Her body, Mordecai noted, was that of a young woman, free of blemish, sag or wrinkle, firm and pink and marble-smooth. Miraculous, perfumed avoirdupois. She was, Mordecai realised, well-preserved, pink and plump – and desirable.

Susan, too, now stripped naked, pubis thrusting boldly forward, glowing like a succulent nymph in a Rubens

scene, struck Mordecai as an eager partner of Ruth's, about to seduce and devour. Her stance was somewhat like that of a gladiator's, or one of Gaston Lachaise's vital women.

Now, with Mordecai's nakedness, the scene was indeed beginning to resemble a painting by Rubens. Except that Mordecai, bearing no illusions, envisioned himself as a Pascin figure.

As for Ahmed: he was, thought Mordecai, a slightly elongated El Greco version of Michelangelo's David. But, in genital terms, David was outdistanced. And Ahmed's role was to be revealed soon enough . . .

The following night, muttering to himself the word, *ausgespielt*, he boarded his plane for Paris. He savoured a moment's breath of the tropical air, noting that the stars in the black sky were green, laser crystals of emerald . . .

Seated and belted, Mordecai tried to review and appraise his experience in Tangier. A closed book in his hand, his mind raced through various stages and encounters; but depleted and somewhat disoriented, he decided to relax and nap his way back to Paris. He swallowed two Seconals and shortly began to enjoy a somnolence to which his system had become accustomed over the years. But he was not asleep. In his swivel-chair a few feet from the cockpit, he found his mind wandering, returning to his work, the novel in final state of completion – the obsession of the past two years. His publisher was making repeated calls, sending cables, reminders: breathing hard.

It was almost two years since his previous publication and his public was waiting and salivating; at least, so said his editor. There was no contract, but a lot of panting . . .

He found his mind touching and fastening on the book's narrative arrangement, on structural problems and options; and he wondered suddenly, would it not be wise,

dramatic, good theatre, to open his story as of the present, this moment, now, in this very plane, with the author as the first-person narrator. Having experienced an unusually gala interlude, a priapic and cultural intermission, certainly worth preserving between the covers of a book, why not present it, titillatingly, as his opening. Would his editor and publisher care for such an opening? Ease of entry were the words that crossed his mind, and he smiled at the possibility and at the sexual connotation.

La Dolce Vita Moroccan-style. Yes, he would open his novel in Ruth's Tangier bedroom, and he would work backwards in his story, back to Chicago and tiny Tony Hacha standing bug-eyed before the whorehouse that would spell the beginning, the kick-off of his blazing career. Yes, he could structure the story backwards, like running a film in reverse. Half-asleep now, but obsessed with the narrative problems, the form, he smiled and thought, why not? It could work . . . It was a matter of shuffling paper, pages, sequences. I'll do it first-person, like Maugham, he thought.

He smiled at a small deception he had played on Ruth. He had, for some reason he chose not to explore, concealed from her the fact that he had already met and talked with Viola. Before leaving America he had tracked down Viola and secured from her some information and insights. He had gone out to see her, spent two days with her before returning to New York and Paris. In New York he had dictated almost fifty pages of the Viola material to his publisher's secretary, in one non-stop burst, and then taken a Concorde flight to Paris. What Viola had disclosed were close-ups of Hacha's death scene, material unfamiliar to Ruth. Viola had also enlightened him and entertained him far beyond his expectations. She had introduced him to some of the mores of Tucson, some of its so-called nightlife. He had chosen not to speak of it to

Ruth, but would surprise her when his book was published.

As the capsules began their soporific work, doubts set in: vacillation. Drowsily, he struggled for a decision. Would it all add up as a novel? He began to count his cast of characters, Hacha, Adrian, Viola, Ruth, Cora, Kama, Dr Breakstone, Minelli: players in a drama of death, assassination, violence and sex. But no, there were survivors, particularly women, who prevailed. Women were the survivors: Ruth, Viola, Kama, and yes, Jill Meredith. Would their story begin to equal, would it match the narcotic soaps, the morning-noon-night TV broadcasts offering up the wars, threats, guerrilla madness, the grim games of government heads, the deadly *Kinderspiel* in Washington? Power-and-Passion-spun plots, drama he couldn't possibly invent or equal.

Mordecai had not disclosed to Ruth one of the vital elements of the biographical mosaic he was making of Hacha. In talking with Viola he found what he needed. He would withhold it from Ruth until she read the book. In the assemblage of materials for his spectrum-portrait of Boss Hacha, diffracted through the prism of Viola's memory, he had struck gold. Viola, a priceless source, proved to be his most valuable living witness to the rise and fall of Tony Hacha. Power, sex and booze motivated the man, and personal liberty. Graft and spoils were legitimate, part of his religion and philosophy. No pussyfooting in these areas for Hacha.

As for Viola, alive, amusing, boudoir-smart and still practising her trade on a private, limited, selective basis, he found her joyful in her willingness to give testimony. She was also, so she claimed, the last non-medical person to see Hacha alive.

She now practised what she called SCS (Senior Citizen Sex), ministering to elderly gentlemen-callers of a certain

vintage and pedigree: men who had lived well, men of achievement, men who wished to have their still-willing spirits ministered to, even though the flesh was somewhat weak. Among her clients were public figures, writers, artists and a few politicos.

Viola had seen Tony twice in the Miami hospital during his nineteen days' stay following the shooting. Two days before he died, she saw him briefly, she said. He had been in a long coma but awakened before he died. She spent an hour with him on the fourth of March, she said, and he spoke some harsh truths. He was not, never had been, he murmured through a now rasping voice-box, gung-ho for Roosevelt. He hated the man. He didn't give a good goddamn about the teachers' wages, either. He was always upstaged by them. He was angry that the world thought he was the bullet's intended victim whereas he was certain that the common people loved him. Why would anyone want to assassinate him? He was the common man's friend. Ask any saloon keeper, truck driver, union-dues payer. He didn't give a fuck for anyone in Washington . . . Chicago was his centre of the world.

Viola recalled Hacha's last agony, his suffering. Like Ganzara, he had suffered long with stomach pains, even before the shooting. Gastro-intestinal disorders, the doctors said. Then a heart attack occurred. But his will to live was immense. However, even with his herculean co-operation, the skilful surgeons, the endless transfusions, the oxygen tents, nothing could help him 'beat the rap' – his last words to Viola as he folded his veined and spotted hands over his bandaged chest, eyes closed, teeth suddenly clenched in pain.

She heard him mutter, 'Viola, listen, I gave the bastards something they'll never forget, a foolproof machine. It took piss and vinegar and balls. They'll remember me for the machine. You'll see . . .'

What interested Mordecai were Viola's comments on Hacha's sex drive. She claimed that he had maintained a steady sexual relationship with her 'all through the years, even after the grandchildren came'. Not less than twice a month he came to see her, professionally. On a few occasions she came to his office at the Hall. The old prestidigitator had bull's balls as well as the magic wand . . .

One reason she went to the hospital in Florida, she said, was in the hope that he would be well enough to accept her ministrations. When she first came to see him at the hospital she saw at once that his hours were numbered. She turned from him and walked down the hospital corridor weeping uncontrollably.

'Not when my mother died did I cry like that,' she said. 'What a man he was, from top to toe. I wonder if the world will remember him.'

Mordecai was devoting an entire chapter to the bedside tryst of Viola and Tony. He would immortalise the grand old fellatrice!

On the morning of March the sixth, Tony expired. Death from ulcerative colitis.

'A pretty good man,' said Clarence Darrow, ungenerously.

An ironic yet moving tribute to the man was the city's decision to change the street name, Twenty-Second Street, to Hacha Road. Frequenters of the Twenty-Second Street cribs, not to mention the street's pimps, were moved. And the newspapermen hoisted their beer-mugs at the ancient tavern, Schlogels, to Hacha's contribution to their era, to the stories and headlines he had provided them.

'A man with *cojones*,' Mordecai would say.

In the air, in an almost empty plane, aloft some thirty thousand feet in the blue Moroccan sky, in his half-dream

state, Mordecai saw Ganzara, heard him shouting the frenzied, final denunciations, curses, all with wide-eyed defiance. The gesticulating little man was being strapped into the electric chair in the Miami prison. Death in Miami. The scene, so many years old now, came back to him. He saw Ganzara's eyes, the short black thick greasy hair, the long head and square jaws: the face he remembered as the Miami police grappled with him, so many years ago. He had a photo of Ganzara in his wallet, taken in front of his prison cell, hand on hip, defiance in his stance and eye. Little man against the world . . . another world . . . and Mordecai remembered that Ganzara had shouted, 'There are too many people starving to death!' And why did he remember this now, when he was certain he had not reported this detail in his *Daily News* story? The world of Torino, Hacha, Capone – and Calabria. *Il cuolo aperto* – the obscenity came to his lips in a whisper. Unaccountably, swimming in his subconscious came the words of Solzhenitsyn's character, Nerahin – the book was lying in his lap – 'Stalin enjoyed killing.' The preoccupation of life is death he muttered to himself, then smiled at the notion, at his epigrammatic turn of mind.

Inexplicably, he heard strains of 'Eleanor Rigby' and 'Taxman'. He thought cosily of his silver Rolls, and of Joe, his Chicago-bred chauffeur. They would be awaiting him at Orly. He saw his beloved IBM typewriter, sitting majestically in the centre of his desk, awaiting his instructions. He pondered briefly, too, on the erotic *ringolevio* he had participated in at Ruth's house, not too many hours ago; he saw her glistening white thighs and Susan's jutting pubis, the bold breasts . . . How painfully drained were his loins . . . Such games, alas, were for the young.

Exhausted, he settled and sank more deeply into the arms of his cushioned seat, shifting his buttocks. He closed his eyes, clutched his book, saw a young man with

an electric guitar, in Edwardian clothes and a mop haircut. Then Mordecai was murmuring, 'What I'm doing is loving.' Suddenly he detected the pungent odour of his favourite perfume – and cigarette smoke that was definitely not tobacco. He opened his eyes narrowly and turned his head towards the other side of the narrow aisle. Sitting alone at the window was a young woman in tight blue jeans, with a wild haze of auburn hair, soft and inviting. She wore a short lynx jacket over her shoulders and large tinted glasses. Her low-cut blouse was of light pink suede. She wore no jewellery. She seemed absorbed in a copy of *Vogue*.

'Going to Paris?' he asked, eyes half-closed but staring at her. 'I mean, staying there?'

'Yes, Mr Ericson,' she replied.

'You know my name . . .'

'I've seen you on TV and in *Paris-Match*, and on the jackets of some of your novels which I've read.'

'Are you an American – you have no accent.'

'Manhattan-born, Cambridge-educated – England that is – and I travel a lot.'

Not fully awake, Mordecai nodded, thinking . . . this babe can't be over twenty-five years old. He studied her hips and thought, she has everything going for her. He could see a segment of her breast in the bra-less décolletage. Half-asleep but antennae buzzing he asked, 'Do you work?'

'But of course. I'm a free-lance journalist.'

'Oh,' said Mordecai. Then he added, 'I could use a part-time editorial research assistant this week. If you're interested give me a call. Leave your number at the Plaza-Athenée on Avenue Montaigne; they take messages . . .' He added, 'What's your name, dear?'

He closed his eyes. She faded out. Then he heard her say, 'Viola.'

'Viola?' He opened his eyes and turned to stare at her.

'How nice,' he added. Then he closed his eyes, sank back into his seat. Who would believe it! Viola.

He thought: I must call Beverly Hills when I get to Paris. Jerry must demand two million dollars for the world book rights and a million for film and TV rights. With a piece of the film's gross. He smiled. Let his agent sweat as he had been sweating over the novel for over two years. He'd send Ruth – that perdurable cunt, that marvel of a woman, the survivor – a white Porsche sports roadster as a gift. It was her book . . . *Ruth's Book*, he should call it.

Adrian, half man, half boy, dreamer, perceiving the world as a pair of legs and breasts . . . insolent, endearing, loved tossing eggs into electric fans. *Adrian's Book* . . . They had both lived their secret lives . . .

A deep-chested sigh was heard by the girl named Viola across the aisle as Mordecai entered a profound, embracing sleep.